Private First Class Melton of Alpha fire squad in the Second Infantry Company was a farm boy from Missouri, raised in strict adherence to his folks' religious philosophy. Sunday was church—maybe a game of baseball out on the back field, and Lord help the kid who swore! Old Mrs. Melton would have him out of the lineup and peeling potatoes in a split second.

Across the trace from Melton were members of the mortar squad from Shenyang's Fourteenth Army, also scanning the DMZ. The sun was setting and night patrols would soon begin, but no one expected anything more than a few catcalls and maybe a tracer or two.

"Melton!" A call came through the chilly darkness as Alpha squad edged down past a high rocky cleft closer to the wire. It was no surprise that they occasionally found out your name—it could have been provided by an intelligence agent who'd followed the disembarkation of the unit from the States, or maybe it had simply been picked up from one of the Chinese patrols overhearing conversation from their enemy twenty yards away.

"Melton! You miss your wife?" Because of the narrow defile the Alpha squad was almost against the wire.

"Your wife has boyfriend, Melton. You fight. She fuck."

By now the Alpha squad's point man was trying to suppress a laugh. "What's up?" another asked. "If it was your wife I'll bet you—"

"Melton ain't marri

D1011952

WW III: FORCE OF ARMS

Ian Slater

FAWCETT GOLD MEDAL • NEW YORK

A Fawcett Gold Medal Book
Published by Ballantine Books
Copyright © 1994 by Bunyip Enterprises, Inc.

Library of Congress Catalog Card Number: 93-90867

ISBN 0-449-14855-6

Manufactured in the United States of America

First Edition: April 1994

10 9 8 7 6 5 4 3

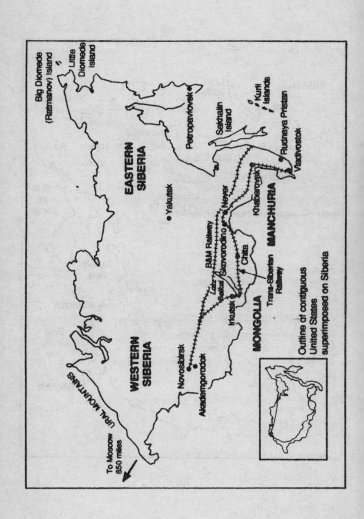

Big Diomede (Ratmanov) Island

Little Diomede Island

EASTERN SIBERIA

Petropavlovsk

Kuril Islands

Sakhalin Island

Rudnaya Pristan

Vladivostok

Yakutsk

Khabarovsk

MANCHURIA

Never

BAM Railway

Skovorodino

Tynda

Baikal

Chita

MONGOLIA

Irkutsk

Trans-Siberian Railway

WESTERN SIBERIA

Novosibirsk

Akademgorodok

URAL MOUNTAINS

To Moscow 850 miles

Outline of contiguous United States superimposed on Siberia

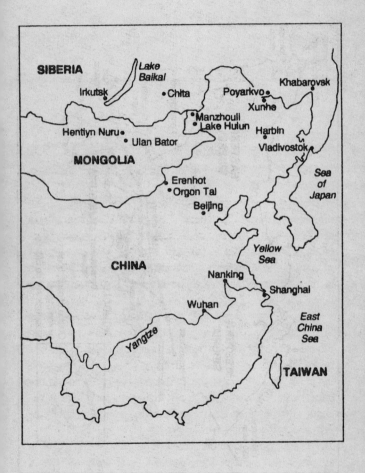

CHAPTER ONE

Spring

IT HAPPENED IN the last forty minutes before the latest cease-fire.

The Medevac choppers came in and found themselves almost immediately "bracketed" by heavy ChiCom 82mm and light 60mm mortar fire, a dozen U.S. Blackhawk helos either afire or unable to take off with the wounded—some of whom were ChiComs who had been gathered up and put in the wire litters that were carried both in and astride the helos.

One such wounded was Wan Zhang, a private from Shenyang's Sixteenth Army who had been hit by an unexploded American 60mm mortar round that passed into the man's body via his shoulder girdle, penetrating the pectoralis major and entering the axilla, the unexploded mortar bomb, seen clearly in the X ray, finally lodging subcutaneously down outside the rib cage in the patient's right side just above the crest of his right hip.

The only other case on record of an unexploded round in a soldier had occurred in Vietnam. Even without the X rays, the surgeon at the inflatable MUST—Medical Unit Self-contained Transportable—hospital behind the lines at

Orgon Tal could see the bomb's outline bulging in the patient's right side. They injected Zhang with morphine and left him on the stretcher well outside the MUST, lest the round go off and kill other patients as well as the ChiCom.

The operating table had to have sandbags all about it to a height of five feet in case something should go wrong and the mortar bomb explode.

"All right," said the chief surgeon, Colonel Walter Paine. "The operation on the prisoner is purely voluntary. I'll welcome any help I get, folks, but it's your call. Anyone want out?" One of the nurses looked at the other, but no one moved in the team of two doctors, two nurses, and the anesthetist.

"All right, let's do it," the colonel said. Despite the sandbags and the Kevlar vests and helmets they would be wearing, Paine said he would allow only one nurse near the sandbagged area at a time. Meanwhile, another blast wall was being erected between the operating room and the patient area of the MUST and around the anesthetist.

"Should let the mother die!" one of the patients opined, a sapper next to the operating room's wall.

"That'd make us just like the Communists," the Medevac corporal said. "Makes me damn proud to be American."

"Yeah," the sapper said, "well you aren't near the fuckin' wall!"

"I'll stay here then," said the corporal, who'd been passing through. "We can play a round of gin rummy."

"Please yourself."

Everyone except two men who'd been blinded in action saw the trolley slowly pass through the ward, the only noise the flapping of the inflatable hospital's sides like some huge kite in the threatening wind. Several men involuntarily held their breath as Wan Zhang passed them.

* * *

Fresh from the States, an eager young logistics captain was assigned to the Khabarovsk headquarters of General Douglas Freeman's Second Army, the spearhead of a U.N. task force sent to prevent any further annexation of territory in the Far East by either the newly declared Siberian Republic or China.

Freeman, his forces now on the northern plain 280 miles north of Beijing and the Great Wall, was absorbed in studying a relief map of China's northern and central provinces. Even so, he took time to acknowledge the major's salute with a friendly, "Welcome to Second Army."

"Thank you, sir. I—"

"What's the gauge of the Trans-Siberian?" Freeman asked without looking up from the relief map.

The captain was nonplussed—of all the questions—still, he kept his cool. "Fifteen twenty millimeters, sir."

"Chinese railways?" Freeman asked.

"Ah—the same, sir."

"Son," Freeman said, still immersed in studying the relief map, moving about the table, as intent on a possible artillery position as a pool player lining up his cue, "with that information you'd be responsible for the biggest logistical fuckup since Arnhem—where they dropped spare berets to the commandos instead of ammo. Take you days instead of hours to move a division. And what are you going to do with a sixty-ton Abrams M1? Carry it across from one rail to the next on your back? Chinese gauge is fourteen thirty-five millimeters. You'll be assigned patrol duty along the trace. Dismissed."

"Yes, sir." The captain saluted and walked out, his ego shattered. But soon—when he got to the trace, the DMZ between the People's Liberation Army and the U.S.—he was glad he'd been fired from the HQ logistics job. No way he wanted to work for a pickass like Freeman.

The incident, small enough in itself, was another example of Freeman's command of even the minutiae of logistics that added to his legend as America's foremost fighting general. But railway gauges weren't the only thing General Freeman was sure of. He believed, like the Taiwanese, that the truce agreed to by the diplomats of the U.N. and China would not hold and that there were many Chinas—none strong enough by itself to overcome the oppressive Beijing regime but all wanting more freedom—waiting.

General Douglas Freeman's Second Army stood on the northern plain beyond Beijing following a fierce tank battle with the Chinese People's Liberation Army from the Amur River south across the Gobi Desert. Sent to head the U.N.'s peacekeeping forces along the Amur River, the Americans, with some help from the British and underground fighters in the Siberian border area known as the JAO—Jewish Autonomous Oblast, or region—were now the only players in the Allied push south. Meanwhile, Admiral Kuang's Taiwanese invasion fleet lay poised a hundred miles across the Formosa Strait—eager to regain power in Beijing after all these years, should the opportunity present itself.

In the MUST operating room, surgeon Colonel Paine had called for forceps and gingerly begun to extract the 60mm mortar bomb from Wan Zhang, pulling it by its stabilizer fins, when it exploded, killing Paine with shrapnel that passed up under his chin, through the roof of his mouth, into his brain. One nurse was blinded in one eye, the anesthetist suffered multiple lacerations to the face, and the other doctor and nurse were badly burned about the head. The explosion, hitting the oxygen feed, immediately started a fire that was quickly extinguished, but not before it had rendered the MUST OR a burned-out shell. The story quickly passed down the line and was taken as a bad beginning to any kind of truce, the ChiComs quickly claiming that Wan Zhang had been tortured to death. With this in mind, it was clear to each and every ChiCom that it was better to die than fall prisoner to the Americans.

CHAPTER TWO

Bangor Base, Washington State

HALFWAY AROUND THE world, a combination Hunter-Killer/ICBM sub, a Sea Wolf II, the USS *Reagan*, was about to get under way. Some of the crew had been joking about making love—a dawn breaker—on the day they were to leave. Others said nothing about it, the tension of their impending good-byes having inhibited rather than released sexual passion. And the older members of the *Reagan*'s gold crew said little, for most of them were married and had children, and trying to make time for lovemaking on the day the Sea Wolf was about to slip out of Bangor was like trying to arrange a kid's birthday party. In the end, it defeated you, and so they hugged a lot, knowing they would have to wait until their six months of duty were complete and it was time for them to return to base and hand the *Reagan* over to the blue crew for the next six months.

The skipper, Commander Robert Brentwood, to all outward appearances was the cool, "let-go-aft" voice of reason as the sub slipped out toward Hood Canal and one of the degaussing stations that would wipe out its magnetic signature should enemy subs be lurking beyond the two-hundred-mile limit, trying to get a fix on the craft through comparing her signature to those in a threat library of "sound prints."

Officially the *Reagan* was not on patrol, but unofficially she was to make her way to the China station in the Gulf of Bo Hai because General Douglas "George C. Scott" Freeman did not believe the Chinese, who had agreed to a cease-fire, would keep their word. The only thing he was sure about was that the PLA's predominantly brown-water, or coastal, navy was going for blue or deep water capability, having bought another four CIS attack diesel submarines from the old Soviet Union's Baltic fleet.

A diesel sub could fire ship-to-ship missiles or ICBMs for that matter. Robert Brentwood, or "Bing" as he was called affectionately by his crew, had been one of those for whom the good-bye had to be a kiss on the cheek, his English wife, Rosemary, seven months pregnant, just recently moved from Holy Loch in Scotland to Bangor. The Holy Loch base had been closed down, a victim of congressional cutbacks, and so Rosemary now found herself in Bremerton, a U.S. naval town in northwestern Washington that served the Bangor base. Robert, age forty-three, was worried about the baby, and about Rosemary settling in at the American base, penetrating American English, and fitting in with the wives whose status was as carefully graded according to their husbands' rank as was the English class structure.

Rosemary too underwent the natural anxiety of being a new wife settling into a new country. There was another fear of which neither spoke: the exceptionally large REM dose of radiation that Robert and some of his crewmen had received in action earlier in the war when they had been victims of a leak in the "coffee grinder"—the reactor. Some had fared worse than others, a few having to have sick leave since, and it only added more anxiety to Rosemary, who was already worried enough about the baby due in the coming months. The sonograms of the baby, using the same technique as a sub does to detect the shape and position of another ship, did not reveal any obvious physical deformity, but there was always the risk of some other complication, which, as a new mother, she was naturally apprehensive about. Life, as Robert had pointed out, was full of hazard, especially with the possibility of another outbreak of hostilities with China, but they had decided on having at least two children. As he'd said good-bye to her he'd joked, "Remember now, you're an English teacher used to Shakespeare and standard BBC English, but you'll have to learn the lingo."

"Try me," she'd said.

"All right—you say 'boot,' we say—"

"Trunk," she answered.

"Okay, you say 'mudguard.' "

"You call it a fender."

"Very good," Robert said.

"Yes, but what about the supermarket?"

"Just look at the pictures," he responded.

She had smiled, slipping her arms into his. "I'll miss you."

"What—going shopping? Any of the other wives'll help you."

"It's not that," Rosemary answered. "I'll miss you wherever I am."

"Morning, sir." It was Rolston, the *Reagan*'s XO, snapping off a salute.

Robert let go of Rosemary's hand, returning the salute. It was a small thing, but his almost intuitive reaction reminded her about that part of his life he could never really share with her and that therefore separated them.

"I mean," she said again, "I'll miss you everywhere. Night and day."

It was unusual for Rosemary to be so insecure. In England, in her Shakespeare class, she ruled otherwise rowdy sixth formers with a firm hand and a resilience that had deserted her upon her arrival in the United States. Robert knew what it was like—that is, what was beneath it all. Earlier in the war, before he'd left Holy Loch on a six-month war patrol, he, like some other submarine captains, had been listed by the enemy for "special treatment"—for assassination. It was different now and more worrisome because the Gong An Bu, the secret arm of China's Public Security Bureau, had been after captains and their executive officers. Two XOs were already dead, found shot through the base of the skull—Chinese execution style. It was a calculated attack upon the morale of the submarine crews, many of whom were engaged in shepherding the vital convoy resupply to General Douglas Freeman's divisions in China. Of course they had the FBI and CIA investigating the assassinations, but as more than one godfather had reiterated, "The lesson of our age is that you can kill anyone." They had tried to get Robert on his and Rosemary's honeymoon in Scotland, but there the CID and MI5 had joined forces and turned the tables on the would-be assassins. Rosemary tried to change the subject. "Oh well, you might get to see your brother David over there. Say hello from me."

"Unlikely," Robert Brentwood said. "He's with Freeman's ground troops. Don't be afraid to use the gun," Robert told her.

"Afraid? I'm terrified."

"But I've shown you how to use it."

"Oh, is that supposed to reassure me?"

"Look, hon, the base security is tighter than a drum. Ditto the family housing. Anyone would have to be bonkers to try to break in."

"You don't think there aren't people who are bonkers?"

"C'mon, you know what I mean."

"I'm sorry, Robbie, I feel as heavy as a tank—I guess it's the 'prepartum' blues or something."

"Take a swig of that Scotch your father sent."

"Uh-uh," she said, adopting a schoolmarmish tone. "Not with the baby."

"Very well," he said as he might answer the officer of the deck. "Carry on."

"Bye, darling," she said, hugging him tightly. "Sorry I can't get any closer with Junior here."

"This suits me fine. Take care, sweetheart."

In the tradition of subs sailing from Bangor, the families of the crewmen piled into trucks and cars to race further along the sound where they would get one last glimpse of the men. Then the men disappeared, and duty took over in the litany of the dive.

"Officer of the Deck—last man down. Hatch secured."

Rolston took up his position as officer of the deck. "Last man down. Hatch secured, aye. Captain, the ship is rigged for dive. Current depth one three zero fathoms. Checks with the chart. Request permission to submerge the ship."

"Very well, Officer of the Deck," Brentwood said. "Submerge the ship."

"Submerge the ship, aye, sir." Rolston turned toward the diving console. "Diving Officer, submerge the ship."

"Submerge the ship, aye, sir. Dive. Two blasts on the dive alarm. Dive, dive." The sound of the alarm followed, loud enough for the crew in the combat control center to hear but not powerful enough to pass through the hull.

"All vents are shut," a seaman informed the OOD.

"Vents shut, aye." A seaman was reading off the depth. "Sixty-two ... sixty-four ..." A chief of the boat was watching the angle of the dive, its trim and speed. "Officer of the Deck, conditions normal on the dive."

"Very well, Diving Officer," Rolston confirmed, turning to Brentwood. "Captain, at one fifty feet, trim satisfactory."

"Very well," Brentwood answered. "Steer four hundred feet ahead standard."

Rolston turned to the helmsman. "Helm, all ahead standard. Diving Officer, make the depth four hundred feet."

"Four hundred feet, aye."

CHAPTER THREE

Khabarovsk

"WHY CAN'T WE stay here, Aussie?" Alexsandra sighed, reclining on the picnic blanket, looking over a long stretch of the Amur river, closing her brown eyes and stretching—albeit unknowingly—sensuously in the weak morning sun. "Why can't we stay here and make love forever?"

Aussie Lewis's eyes lingered on her white blouse. Just watching her breathing was a treat. "Because," he said, in the flat down-under tone of his, "you're a soft touch—always trying to do more than your share. If this truce doesn't last, you'll be at it again. Right?" Aussie propped himself up on his elbow, his blue eyes looking down at her. "Stone the crows, Sandy, you've done your bit—knocking out Chinese troop trains and all that. Washington's already given you a gong for duty beyond and above—you've done more than your bit."

"No," she said quietly, still not opening her eyes, "not as long as the Chinese threaten the JAO." The region lay in the disputed territory along the Siberian-Chinese border, the border being the Amur river to the Siberians and the Black Dragon to the Chinese. "If we don't fight," Alexsandra said, "we'll end up just like Tibet—another Chinese province. Anyway"—she turned on the picnic blanket, shutting her eyes—"who are you to talk? You and your SAS/Delta troopers." She was referring to the SAS/D troop—the British Special Air Service and American Delta force commandos that Freeman called on to plug any sudden gap in the line or to carry out deep missions behind the enemy lines—to fight if there was no truce, to collect intelligence if there was.

"Yeah, I'd go," conceded Aussie, who had rescued Alexsandra as one of many civilian hostages the Chinese had tied to the guns at the battle of Orgon Tal. To the astonishment of his colleagues in the SAS/Delta teams, Aussie Lewis had fallen head over heels for Alexsandra Malof—even to the point of having stopped swearing. His buddies—David Brentwood, officer in charge of his SAS/D troop; Salvini from Brooklyn; and Choir Williams, a Welshman—had wagered that the Australian couldn't last an entire week without a profanity. They still had two days to go.

"But—what I do," Aussie tried to explain to Alexsandra,

"is what I do. I mean, it's my job. Special Ops is my line of country. We're trained for it."

She smiled at him as she turned side-on to the weak sun that hung above the thick taiga, a great blanket of green that hugged the river and swept right down to its banks except for the little beach they had found.

"You can't tell me you do it for money. Because you're—" she began.

"Well—no," Aussie had to admit. "But what I mean is— well—" Uncharacteristically for him, he seemed at a loss for words.

"What you're saying," Alexsandra said softly, "is that I shouldn't go if there's trouble again—that you love me."

This was pretty rough talk for the Australian. Oh sure, he'd fallen in love, but he balked at her simple declaration. It wasn't macho to get all weepy and confessional.

"Yeah—I like you, Sandy."

"Only *like* me?" she retorted, holding back a smile, still looking at him warmly and mischievously, enjoying his discomfort.

"Yeah—well," he began, "you're a good bird."

"*Am* I?" An extraordinary thing was happening—the Australian was blushing.

Alexsandra threw her head back, smiling. She looked like the bird in *Casablanca*, Aussie thought. What was her name? Ingrid—Ingrid Bergman, that was it. "Yeah, well, I'm pretty keen on you, Sandy."

"Oh dear," she said. "This is very serious then, Aussie."

"Stone the crows!" he began. "What I meant to say was—" He stood up abruptly and started throwing rocks into the river. "I'm a bit keen on you," he said quickly, and immediately looked about in the forest, as if someone might have heard him. "That's what I mean about you and this sabotage business."

She got up and reached for his arm, and as he turned around to look at her she seemed to him even more beautiful than before, her dark hair lustrous in the spring sun. But he knew that along with her beauty was an iron determination that he wouldn't be able to stop her doing what she felt she had to do: fight the Chinese if they broke the truce. It would be an obligation for everyone in the JAO, and she knew that Aussie knew. They embraced, and Aussie whispered hoarsely, "God, I hope this truce holds."

"It will," she said, sounding utterly unconvincing. Already there were reports of "strain" all along the DMZ. The feeling was like watching a rope between two tug-of-war teams: The rope was still, but the force pulling it either way had not abated—the tension was in the very air you breathed.

At this point Aussie Lewis didn't quite realize the extent of Alexsandra's fame, for while she might still be domiciled in the U.S.-run Khabarovsk refugee camp, her deeds had spread throughout the dissident ranks of Gansu Province's Social Democrats and beyond Beijing to the Liberal Democratic party, the Free Labor Union, and the Chinese Progressive Alliance—all unofficially gathering under the banner of the goddess of democracy.

But she and Aussie Lewis were only two people among thousands, and no matter what her fame, events were swirling about them that would sweep them into different dangers whether they liked it or not. With over three million men in the People's Liberation Army and only 360,000 Allies, mostly American, the scope of the battles would be huge and confused if war broke out. Five thousand T-59 and T-72 tanks alone were already being marshaled by General Cheng on the basis of Lenin's military adage that "quantity has a quality all its own." The Americans had better tanks, and Cheng's strategy was simply to roll over the Americans with his four-to-one advantage. No matter how good an M1A1 tank might be, it had to kill three of his tanks out of every four just to stay even. The irony, however, was that it wouldn't be the sight of thousands of T-59s and T-72s being moved northward that would ignite the powder keg along the trace.

The two Gong An Bu—Public Security Bureau—men looked so much alike—short, stocky, and in poorly cut Western-style suits—that their prey—anyone suspected of being a member of the underground June Fourth Democracy Movement—called the men the "turtle twins." Being called a turtle was a great insult in China. One of the turtles told the boy to stand up against the cell wall, a dirty slab of cement defaced by dozens of pleas to, or denunciations of, the Party. The boy was seventeen years old and shivering, as much from his fear as from the cold.

"Hands behind your back!" the other security man commanded. The boy did as he was told and was shown the color photograph once more. It was a police photo of a dark-haired Caucasian woman in her thirties. Even the baggy prisoners' Mao suit couldn't hide a striking figure, and her brown eyes stared defiantly from the photograph.

"Well?" one of the twins said. "Where is she?"

The boy couldn't speak, his mouth dry with fear, and so he simply shook his head. The other man kicked him in the groin. The boy doubled up, collapsing in a heap on the slimy flagstone floor, cupping his genitals, writhing in agony and so nauseated he couldn't even utter a protest.

"Now," the other turtle said. "Where is she?"

The boy shook his head again. He had never seen Alexsandra Malof before this photo. All he knew about her was that after the successful U.S. Second Army attack against elements of General Cheng's long-range artillery during the great battle for Orgon Tal, the Malof woman had been rescued along with other hostages who had been tied to the wheels of the big guns. The boy knew that this Jewish guerrilla leader had played havoc with railway sabotage in the Manchurian fastness before her capture and subsequent rescue by the Americans. And the fact that she had been decorated by the Americans earlier in the war before the truce was making her a heroine throughout the democratic underground all across China, particularly among the minorities in Tibet, Xinjiang, Inner Mongolia and in most of the non-Han regions. If the beating told the boy nothing else it told him that if they were so worried about where she was, the truce might not last long—that a new PLA attack was imminent. He was only half right.

"Where is she?"

"Everywhere," the boy said. The Public Security man kicked him again but knew the boy was telling them an uncomfortable truth. She *was* everywhere—the mere mention of her name a rallying cry to any group of "hooligans" or other antisocial elements who wanted to overthrow the government. And there *were* reports of her being everywhere.

The boy had vomited on the floor. They forced him to eat it. "Now—where is she?"

"Everywhere."

They took him out and bludgeoned him to death on the rough flagstone courtyard. Normally they would have simply shot him in the base of the neck, but bullets cost seventeen cents American each, and for an army of three million the cost of ammunition was an item of budgetary concern.

Chairman Nie was coldly furious at the failure of the Public Security Bureau—the counterespionage group—to find her.

"Keep looking!" he told the PSB. "I want her—alive." He knew that to kill her would only make a martyr of her. Having her alive—in chains—would evoke the power of the state much more. She could be got rid of as soon as her capture and humiliation had served Nie's purpose of demoralizing the underground.

After he'd spoken with Alexsandra on the beach, there was a marked change in Aussie Lewis's mood. Known as one of the most proficient and profane fighters in the SAS/D team, he became unusually subdued. Salvini, Choir Williams, and David Brentwood, the younger brother of the USS *Reagan*'s skipper, all noticed that he was uncharacteristically censorious about others swearing—so much so that Brentwood, Williams, and Salvini speculated that wedding bells were in the offing.

"Come on, Aussie. You going to take the big jump—the great leap forward?"

Aussie was sitting on the floor, blindfolded, reassembling his P-90 submachine gun by feel alone, a practice all SAS/D team members had to be "time capable" of in utter darkness. He didn't answer them at first.

"Come on, Aussie. You dipping your wick?" Salvini asked.

"Don't be crude!" Aussie replied.

"It must be serious," Choir Williams joshed. "He hasn't sworn for a week."

"Uh-uh—two days to go," Salvini reminded them. "He won't last the distance."

"Ye of little faith," Aussie said, slapping the plastic see-through mag into the P-90. "You're about to be surprised."

"So," Salvini proffered, "you've already popped the question, eh?"

Aussie didn't answer. He needed more time and prayed

no one along the trace—Chinese or Ally—would pull the trigger before he had a chance to spend more time with Alexsandra.

PFC—Private First Class—Melton of Alpha fire squad in the second company of infantry from the Thirty-second Battalion hailed from the Midwest. Melton was a farming boy from Missouri and was raised in strict adherence to his folks' religious philosophy. Sunday was church—maybe a game of baseball out on the old rapeseed patch, and Lord help the kid who swore! Old Mrs. Melton would have him off the field and peeling potatoes before he could get back on the diamond.

Across the trace from Melton were members of the mortar squad from Shenyang's Fourteenth Army, also scanning the DMZ. The sun was setting and night patrols would soon begin, but no one expected anything more than a few catcalls and maybe a tracer or two if a patrol looked like it was growing too fond of any part of the DMZ—especially if someone was digging under the wire or using the light alloy minesweepers in hopes of plotting the best points for crossing. Neither side had had enough time, since the truce, to plant mines all along the trace, for it was a weaving, thousand-mile front that roughly followed the shape of a long check mark, the longer part of it going up and over the mountains beyond the north plain, the bottom of the check mark consisting of the American forces that had penetrated furthest south following the battle of Orgon Tal.

"Melton!" a call came through the chilly darkness as Alpha squad edged down past a high rocky cleft closer to the wire. It was no surprise that occasionally they found out your name—it could have been provided by a Chinese intelligence agent who'd followed the disembarkation of the unit from the States, or maybe it had simply been picked up from one of the Chinese patrols overhearing conversation or smelling aftershave from the Americans who in some places along the trace were only twenty yards away.

"Melton! You miss your wife?"

Because of the narrow defile the Alpha squad was almost against the wire.

"Your wife has boyfriend, Melton. You fight. She fuck."

By now the Alpha squad's point man was trying to suppress a laugh.

"What's up?" another asked. "If it was your wife I'll bet you—"

"Melton ain't married," the point man said.

So the Chinese had struck out—the Alpha squad hadn't fallen for the bait—but Melton didn't laugh. Melton wasn't amused at all. You're out on patrol, it's black as pitch and someone calls out your name. How'd they know his name? They just pick it up from listening across the trace? And if they hadn't, it meant Chinese intelligence had gotten hold of his name some other way. How? he asked the squad. Where? It made them all edgy.

"Just remember Freeman's orders," the squad leader said. "Anybody fires back for crap like that and they could start the whole fucking war again along the trace."

"Hey, Mel," the squad leader asked, "sure you didn't get hitched without tellin' us?"

"Don't worry," Melton said. "It ain't gonna be me."

"What do you mean, 'it ain't gonna be me'? You gonna spend your life jerkin' off?"

"I mean I'm not firing back because of that kind of crap." But Melton had been spooked. Now and then they could hear the unoiled, squeaking noise of tanks—T-59s and T-62s upgraded with appliqué armor that looked like big slabs of hinged concrete stuck on the tanks as they made their way along the trace, Cheng's units taking full advantage of the truce to bolster their positions all along the line.

CHAPTER FOUR

GENERAL CHENG WAS a soldier, not a sadist, and he viewed Chairman Nie's witch hunt for anyone who was either a member of, or merely suspected of being a fellow traveler in, the underground movement as an unhealthy obsession. Nie's constant charges of "antigovernment behavior and hooliganism" in General Cheng's view lowered morale among the civilian population as well as in the army—especially among the young. "We must be careful not to isolate them," he advised Nie.

"Isolate them? How?" Nie asked combatively.

"By pursuing everyone over sixteen with criminal charges. That's how. Before you know it you will have created more underground members than you've arrested."

Nie waved aside Cheng's concern contemptuously. "You fret too much, General. The state is more important than a few democracy mongers. You and I know that. Tiananmen taught them a lesson. It's time for another. Remember what Comrade Deng told us: 'Some people can only be educated by a bullet.' "

"Perhaps. But your Gong An Bu agents are making a meal of this, Comrade Chairman."

"General," Nie said, leaning uncharacteristically forward, so close that Cheng could smell the fish he'd had for lunch. "If we do not defeat the Americans, Beijing will fall, and if Beijing falls, you and I fall. This is not the time to waste indulging ourselves with bourgeois views of the young. They are like the young anywhere. They need to know the limits, and it's time to walk loudly with a big stick! Leave the internal security to me. You have enough on your plate with Freeman, so I hear."

"Don't worry yourself over that. I will take care of Freeman."

"Let us hope so, Comrade," Nie said, sitting back, looking around at the other members of the Politburo. "Or all our efforts will have been in vain."

After the meeting, as General Cheng rose to go, doing up his coat—while it was warm in the Great Hall of the People, he knew it would still be chilly outside—Nie sat back like a headmaster and asked him, "You will be making a preemptive strike, of course."

"Perhaps," Cheng answered with deliberate equivocation. In fact he had the area already determined through which his divisions would pour in a lightning pincer movement he had designed in order to trap the arrowhead of Freeman's forces. But to tell Nie the exact location could jeopardize the entire plan, for Nie would no doubt send his agents pouring in first to "cleanse" the area of fifth columnists and other politically unreliable elements. This would merely alert the Americans and their underground spies that that was the area most likely to be attacked. No, Cheng was determined not to reveal the location to anyone until he had informed his divisional commanders, and that would be only hours before the attack. He wanted absolute surprise.

Cheng would achieve his surprise, but not in the way he wanted. Nor would Freeman meet the attack in the way the U.S. general had planned—primarily with his armor, the will and determination of even the best generals often being thwarted by factors completely beyond their control.

General Cheng's chauffeur was standing idly by the black, shiny, Red Flag limousine, bobbing his head to a belting rendition of pop singer Cui Jian's song about the world changing too quickly. But the song's real message, like so many in modern China, was about China not changing fast enough. This way the song got past the grinning, blockheaded censors but carried its cry for more freedom to those of the younger generation. But if the censor had been slow at perceiving the satire, General Cheng, C in C of the PLA, was not.

"Turn that rubbish off!" he ordered as he approached the open rear door of the Red Flag limousine. The chauffeur quickly obeyed—he hadn't expected the Politburo's meeting to end so quickly. But Cheng had had little to say apart from his criticism of Nie, and putting forth his, Cheng's, prediction that the present truce between the People's Liberation Army and the U.N. force—in reality, Freeman's Second Army—would not hold. Sui, the Beijing garrison commander, had been visibly relieved, reiterating that the Politburo simply could not tolerate the fact that Freeman's army was only 280 miles northwest of Beijing. Sui had also wanted to know whether Cheng would launch a preemptive strike against Freeman's supply line— stretching all the way down from the Amur River to Orgon Tal—before the Americans made any move on the mountainous barrier of the Great Wall.

"Perhaps," Sui had proffered, "the Americans will launch a preemptive strike first?"

"No," Cheng had told him quite definitely. "It is the

weakness of the democratic state. It can only *react* to an attack. They have this worn-out, bourgeois belief that you must not start a war, that there is some moral imperative against it."

"And while they wait, we grow stronger," the Beijing commander had said hopefully.

"Yes," Cheng had agreed. "Our supply line is much shorter."

Out on the street, the people of Beijing were going about their work as if a war were the furthest thing from their minds, yet Cheng knew this was merely appearance and not the full reality, their true emotions hidden beneath impassive stares. One had to look for other signs, such as the song by Cui Jian and other ballads about a northern hero or heroine—ostensibly about a Chinese woman who had made a heroic stand against the invasions of Genghis Khan. Cheng knew very well that the song was really being sung about the Siberian, Alexsandra Malof, who had rallied Siberian and Chinese dissidents to harass the PLA's flanks in battles past. Still, Cheng was not as pessimistic as Nie, who thought that every youngster would automatically be turned against the older men in the Great Hall of the People. When it came to the fight, he was confident that nationalism would prove a much stronger magnet than the Communist party and what would carry the day in the Damaqun Shan—the wall-spined mountains to the north.

When General Cheng's black Red Flag limousine turned off from Beijing's Avenue of Eternal Peace toward Xinhuamen Gate, the two PLA soldiers on guard snapped to attention, their white gloves, dark green coats, fur hats, and glistening bayonets catching the pale spring light. A duty officer emerged from the guardhouse to check the credentials of General Cheng. Of course they knew it was him but in a country of over one billion people, many of them minorities, and dissastisfied minorities at that, and of students often flush with decadent liberal bourgeois attitudes, even in the Communist holy of holies, the Zhongnanhai, the compound housing the living quarters and many of the offices of the elite, nothing could be left to chance.

Often as he returned from important meetings, Cheng would deliberately pause once inside the compound to admire its tranquility and beauty, for here was another China. Dating back to the Qing Dynasty, it was here that the emperor would plow the first symbolic furrow of spring, where imperial banquets and the examinations for the highest credentials in martial arts were held.

Separated from the endless river of bicycle bells and civilians by high, thick walls, the gardens within the Zhongnanhai compound evoked calm after one's immersion in the daily struggle to govern a land whose people were as numerous as the sands of the Gobi Desert and who, though few foreigners ever realized it, were not nearly as cohesive and obedient to the precepts of Marxism and Leninism and the thoughts of Mao as they appeared. It took all of the party's strength and wisdom to hold them together.

But this day Cheng did not linger to sit by the Zhongnanhai's two lakes. He must ready the People's Liberation Army for what might well be the biggest war since Korea. Yet typically, not unlike Freeman in this respect, his attention to the minutiae of his profession—as in the way he studied the Americans for years, particularly their strategy—led him to pay attention to a request on his desk from the Thirty-first Army Group, headquartered in Xiamen.

The Thirty-first wanted to purchase fake aircraft silhouettes to fool U.S. satellite surveillance. Cheng scribbled a note that though such fakes could easily be purchased via the Hong Kong–based La Roche Industries, and were, he admitted, only a fraction of the cost of a real aircraft, cents compared with millions of dollars, it was nevertheless a waste of valuable resources. Instead he suggested requisitioning leftover blacktop paint from the Beijing main roads department and having students from the nearest technical institute, through "voluntary labor for the people," paint Shenyang F-12 and Soviet-made Fulcrum silhouettes on the tarmac in squadron formation. This fooled even the most sophisticated satellite cameras, and if the Xiamen commander was concerned about the infrared sensors on the American satellites, then Cheng advised placing thermos flasks at the tail ends of the silhouettes. This would give off enough heat for satellite infrared sensors to interpret the aircraft as "hot" rather than "cold"—conveying the impression to the Americans that all the aircraft were fully operational and, just as importantly, that fuel was apparently no problem for the PLA fighter aircraft—which it was. Then, after quickly denying the Thirty-first's request, he went, as was his habit during those times in his life when his responsibility weighed most heavily upon him, out of the southern entrance of the Zhongnanhai compound onto Changan Avenue.

Though not alone—the two public security men assigned to protect him only a few yards back—he made his way east, crossing Beichang Street, reaching the seven bridges that spanned the green-algae-covered moat before the Tiananmen Gate atop which Mao had proclaimed the People's Republic of China on October 1, 1949. Seeing the five entrances to the gate closed, Cheng paused, perplexed for a moment, until he remembered it was Monday. He took the absence of tourists as a good omen, as he, and shortly after, the two public security men, slipped through one of the side gates into the Forbidden City.

He understood, as did every member of the Party, that

the Forbidden City was but the remains of the most degenerate exploiters of the Chinese people, but, despite the fact that his commitment to Marxism-Leninism was as strong as ever, Cheng felt within the Forbidden City something he could not experience anywhere else. Standing silently before the five marble bridges that crossed the tartar-bow–shaped Golden Water Stream that led to the Gate of Supreme Harmony, the city's noise muffled by the great walls, he felt a serenity that transcended all thought, all cares—the kind of feeling his great-grandmother spoke about whenever she would return from the Christian temples with all their candles and their liberal bourgeois hogwash. It was the kind of calm he needed in order to consolidate his Tai—so that all his psychic and physical energy could be used to destroy his enemies.

CHAPTER FIVE

NEAR HUADE, 160 miles northwest of Beijing, on the road between Shangdu and Orgon Tal, the three-man Huade cell of the June Fourth Democracy Movement had made their decision. They would march the forty-three miles due west through the desert toward their truce line and blow the main line at a point twelve miles south of the Genghis Khan Wall, not the Great Wall, outside Tomortei and so wreck the line along which Cheng was rushing PLA divisions to Orgon Tal to bolster up Beijing's northwestern defense sector.

They took C4 plastique and an acid ampule charge initiator for a delayed explosion. By the time they reached the tracks the huge China sun had turned bloodred because of the dust coming down from the Gobi to the north where the Americans were on the edge of the northern plain. One of the three saboteurs molded the Play-Doh–like plastique into the concave groove of the rail and tapped a block of wood cut to fit after it to help direct the blast more toward the steel rail. Next he took an oil rag around his right hand, felt for the delay-pencil charge initiator, and broke its glass ampule at one end, releasing the acid that would eat away the anchor of the spring firing pin. When the acid had eaten through in about ten minutes, the firing pin would be released, slamming into the percussion cap and lighting the fuse.

By the time it would blow they would be well clear of the DMZ. At least that was the theory. They knew that whether the explosion blew out a section of track or not, their attack alone might presage a massive exchange between the U.S. Second Army and the PLA, and this was precisely their purpose.

In Huade, from whence they'd come, a "neighborhood watch" was in progress. Such watches were not just for thieves but for anyone who, in the opinion of the *jiedao zheanyuan*—"red grannies"—was not living up to the accords of Chairman Nie. Curfew was at nine o'clock, and by the time the three saboteurs headed back they had already been missed by the red grannies, the old women who proudly wore the bloodred party armbands and waved the party rule book—who knew everyone in the neighborhood, who was having a second child in violation of the party policy, who was having an affair with whom, and who was missing curfew. Public security was called when the three young men had not returned by the curfew. The three terrified families were questioned by the same interrogator, and none of their stories agreed. One family said their boy had taken ill while visiting an uncle in Shangdu. A second family pleaded that their son had gone for a walk and obviously forgotten the time. The third family, simply too tired to say anything specific, threw up their hands in desperation and said quite truthfully that they had no idea where their son was or what he was doing.

"He's a counterrevolutionary!" one of the old women charged, her bony finger shaking at the family in her excitement. "Always thumbing his nose at the authorities. He listens to Cui Jian," a second said, making disgusted noises with her tongue.

The Public Security man stationed two PLA soldiers with AK-47s with each of the three families and told them to cut the throat of anyone who gave the slightest warning to the boys upon the youngsters' return.

Rosemary was walking along the glittering aisles of the base PX, wonderstruck again at the sheer variety of goods. She started counting the different kinds of cereal but soon gave up. If submariners were the best-fed people in the navy, their families also had a cornucopia of goods to choose from.

For Rosemary, the two things the Americans got absolutely right were the supermarkets and the opulence of an American bar—not that she'd made a detailed study of the latter. What she didn't like, however, was after dark. Rationally she knew that it couldn't be as bad as the murder and mayhem depicted every night on television, but as she would soon discover, many other women, especially the

wives of COs and XOs, remained on guard. And the worst
of it was that they couldn't really talk about it. The navy
hadn't muzzled them, but like all good submariners—
except for that bastard Walker who had sold so many U.S.
secrets to the Soviets—the women were as silent about
navy matters as their men aboard the subs were. The navy,
the Tail Hook scandal of the nineties notwithstanding, took
pride in fixing their own problems within the family and in
any case had made the point that if the matter of "foreign
operatives," as they preferred to call the Chinese Gong An
Bu, were to hit any of the newspapers—particularly the La
Roche tabloids—the whole thing would be blown out of
proportion and only sow exactly the kind of panic the Chinese wanted to produce.

Besides, there was a reluctance on the part of the navy
sub wives to gab, because quite frankly they thought their
menfolk on the subs were a cut above regular fleet navy,
and they didn't want to seem to be like some Tail Hook
whiner. The best protection, they thought, was not to talk
about "foreign operatives," especially since now there was
a truce and things had quieted down over in China. Besides, if they felt they had to talk about it they could always
seek out the other wives and girlfriends—keep it in the
family.

Andrea Rolston, wife of Robert Brentwood's executive
officer, saw Rosemary wheeling her cart past the cold beer
fridges, the Englishwoman agog at the variety of malts and
lagers.

"Rosemary!"

Startled, Rosemary turned to see Andrea Rolston waving
at her from frozen meats like a long-lost friend, though
they'd met for the first time only three days before. She
liked the Americans' informality, their natural friendliness,
but with her background as a schoolteacher in Surrey she

found the Americans' gregariousness difficult to emulate—it was all a little overwhelming.

"Rosemary, you're just the one I was looking for!"

"Oh—"

"Yes. Now tell me, you got yourself a gun?"

Instinctively Rosemary wanted to say no, but the truth was Robert, albeit reluctantly, had left a .45 in the dresser drawer. He had taken her out to the small-arms range and had her fire it, but the noise even with the ear protectors and the shock of what she called the gun's "jump" alarmed her far more than the prospect of anyone breaking and entering.

"Good," Andrea Rolston said, "because you never know. And you remember, you just pick up the phone and give me a dingle. I'm right next door. If you don't have time, why, you just pop a couple right between the son of a bitch's eyes."

"Pop *who*?" Rosemary asked.

"What—oh, anybody tries a night creep on you—but wait till the SOB is inside. Then it's self-defense, pure and simple. I did it once!"

Rosemary's throat felt dry. "You did?"

"Bet your fanny I did. Some joker when we were stationed in Galveston. Course anywhere in Texas you can shoot 'em on the doorstep. That's enough cause. I love Texas."

"Yes," Rosemary said.

"Where'd you get that from?" Andrea said, pointing to a grapefruit in Rosemary's basket.

"Why—over here."

"Well you got the wrong bin, honey. It's softer than a baby's bottom—be half rotten. C'mon, let's take it back."

Rosemary followed, not knowing whether to laugh or not—to be touched or appalled by Andrea's ambush of her.

And so the teacher of Shakespeare walked along, deeply embarrassed as Andrea began dressing down the poor grapefruit man with such determination that Rosemary thought Andrea might shoot *him*.

"What'll she think?" Andrea said to the hapless manager. "She's a guest and all." And with that she delivered an enormously larger but firmer grapefruit than before.

"There you go, Rose. You don't mind if I call you Rose?"

"Ah, no. I—"

"America's the greatest place on earth, Rosie. No offense to your country but I mean that. But you have to look after yourself."

Until that moment, Rosemary had assumed she was able to look after herself quite well.

"Buyer beware," Andrea added. "You know they spray cucumber with that oil crap—makes 'em look fresher."

"No—no, I didn't."

"Well they do. Now don't you worry, Rose. I told your hubby I'd look after you."

"Thank you."

"Call me Dee. Everyone else does."

"Yes—thank you, Dee."

"You're welcome, Rose."

One of the Gong An Bu agents got out of his car that was hidden down one of the narrow *hutongs*, and walking quickly up the dark alley he went into one of the mud-cake houses and told the chief inspector that a message had just come through on the radio that there'd been an explosion on the Orgon Tal branch line.

It was enough to put the PLA in the sector on full alert. In response, Freeman immediately sent out an FAV—fast-attack vehicle—reconnaissance patrol as the sky was already clouding over, obscuring satellite intelligence. The explosion on the branch line and Cheng's reaction to it meant that for the first time in the three weeks they had known one another Aussie Lewis and Alexsandra Malof were separated.

CHAPTER SIX

"WHO COMPLAINED?" FREEMAN demanded without taking his eyes off the huge wall map of the three provinces of Hopei, Shantung, and Honan.

"I don't have her name yet, General," answered Colonel Norton, Freeman's longtime aide, and he was glad he didn't. If Freeman found out who the female was who had complained directly to the Pentagon, he'd go ballistic.

"If I've said it once," Freeman roared, "I've told those Washington fairies a thousand times, a tank is no place for a woman. Period! It's cramped, it's crowded—goddamn it, Dick!" he said, turning away from the map momentarily. "Why am I plagued by these skirts that are so hell-bent on getting their tits ripped off during the reload? Don't they understand? There are no seat belts inside, no restraints. Shell ejection can break an arm just like that!"

"All I know," Norton said quietly, "is that it's a perennial complaint against Second Army. And General, you are obliged by Congress to—"

"To hell with Congress. See any of those jokers in a tank? By God, remember Dukakis? And now they want me to put those delicate creatures inside an M1A1?" He suddenly sounded terribly old-fashioned. He was an anachronism in many ways—still stood up for a woman when she entered a room, opened doors for them, and was even known to give up his seat on the military buses on the way to postmaneuver conferences at Fort Irwin, for he made a point of traveling with his troops.

No wonder the callow young Turks thought of him as an early twentieth-century man.

"General," Norton advised him cautiously, "no matter what your personal feelings, the Pentagon has approved women for combat in all—"

Freeman turned angrily on his aide, then suddenly stopped his tirade, exhaling heavily, whacking a stripped stick of birch against his boot. The birch stick–cum–pointer–cum–swagger stick had traveled down with him from the northwestern part of Manchuria, where the deciduous oak forests, linden, and white pine ran right out to the edge of the northeasterly margin of the Gobi. "Well, Dick—you're right of course." *Whack!* "Appreciate your candor." *Whack!* "You're not here to pump sunshine up my ass but to tell me how it is." *Whack!* "So I suppose we're going to have to let some tail in to keep Washington off my tail."

"I think that's sensible, General."

"Yes, by God, I bet you do. You're with Congress on this, aren't you?"

"Well, sir, the navy already—"

"Yes, yes, I know. And you think I'm a stick in the mud."

"On strategy—no way, sir. But in this matter I think we're dragging our feet."

"*Are* we?" Freeman asked, looking at Dick Norton, who didn't blink.

"Yes, sir, we are."

"All right—all right—but not in my HQ company."

"I'm not suicidal, General."

"Huh," Freeman grunted affably, "guess not. Give them to Hersh—he's a ladies' man. He can tuck 'em in tight, but remember what I've said before. When nature calls and we're in the middle of a battle, they're going to have to pee and the rest of it in their helmets—same as everybody else. Period or no period—understand?"

"I'm sure they already know that, General."

"Knowing and experiencing, Dick, are two different things."

"They'll manage, sir."

"None of those damn sanitary pads, mind," Freeman said. "Take up too much space. Tampax or they don't go!"

"Yes, sir."

For a moment Freeman was silent, thinking of his wife— killed on his leave a few months before by a prowler who, as it turned out later, had been a Spetsnaz—a Special Forces—hit man when Siberia had been fighting Second Army. And now it was the Chinese he was up against. He turned his mind back to the pressing matter of tank transporters. Were there enough for the new up-gunned Abrams 12mm main battle tanks?

"All we need is ten days, General," Norton informed him, as if reading Freeman's mind. "By then our replacement armor'll all be down here at Orgon Tal and spread out east of us. SAS and Delta teams'll be rested by then, too."

"Well, the truce should last that long. What have we had in the way of border incidents—apart from this explosion the SAS team is investigating?"

"Intelligence reports it's tense—odd shot fired here and

there. Maybe Chinese killing takin." He meant the species of goat antelope that wandered the Manchurian slopes to the north. "But I still think the truce will hold for another few days."

There was another reason for what the boys had done near Tomortei. They wanted to disrupt Cheng's supply line all right, but they also wanted to send a clear signal to *all* dissident groups that the June Fourth Democracy Movement was alive, if not always well, and was ready to lead the way.

The FAV—fast-attack vehicle or "dune buggy"—with Aussie Lewis driving, David Brentwood on the .50 machine gun to his right, and Choir Williams mounting the TOW antitank launcher behind them on the elevated seat, had reported that the sabotage seemed to be nothing more than a single line break. It would take Cheng's forces a matter of hours to fix it, but then it would be open for rail traffic again. Freeman made calls up and down the line wanting SITREP, but except for the explosion on the Orgon Tal line, everything seemed quiet, the tension notwithstanding.

"Thank God for that," Freeman said, thwacking his right leg again with the birch stick before using it as a pointer on the map. "Because, Norton, if that fox Cheng hits us anytime before the ten days are up, we are up the proverbial creek without a paddle."

"Well, sir," Norton said hopefully, "the weather's closing in."

Freeman turned about. "Who told you that? Harvey Simmet?"

"No, CNN."

"Hmm—I ever tell you about that survey they did in England of all those weather wrap-ups on TV?"

"No, sir."

"Well they found out hardly anyone who listens to weather forecasts can remember anything that was said five minutes later. All those damn isobars, arrows, convection currents, jet streams flying about complicate it to hell. Best weather report came from a TV channel that had no graphics, no gimmicky electronics, just someone telling the audience that tomorrow it will be wet and windy."

"I guess you're right, General. I'm usually too busy watching the presenter."

"So am I," Freeman confided. *Thwack!* "Good-looking wenches on those newscasts."

"Yes, sir."

"Still," Freeman responded, his tone more businesslike now, "I'd like an accurate reading on the weather within the last half hour. Get Harvey up here right away, will you?" The general turned back to the map of the three provinces, one of which lay directly ahead of him, the other two on his flanks.

Norton glanced at his watch. Seventeen hundred hours. Well, it was just starting to get dark at mealtime. He didn't know how it happened, but usually whenever the general called for Harvey Simmet, the chief met officer of Second Army HQ was either about to eat or was asleep. Sleepy eyed, Simmet would trudge to the HQ tent usually wrapped up like an Indian during the winter of 1806.

Simmet wasn't in his tent, however, and had to be paged. He was just sitting down to his favorite meal, ham and mashed potatoes with raisin sauce, and he had his fork loaded.

"Old man wants to see you, Harvey."

Everyone in the officers' mess started laughing.

"Gotcha again, Harv! ... Atta boy, Harvey. ... Duty calls."

Harvey Simmet looked at the fork piled high with the succulent ham and potato dripping in the raisin sauce. ...

"No," he said emphatically, "I'm not going to rush it. Damn it—Cookie, can you keep this under the lamp?"

"Better than that, sir. Give you a fresh lot when you come back."

"You're a gentleman and a scholar, Cookie."

Norton slapped Harvey amicably on the shoulder. "I don't think the general'll keep you long." They left the mess tent.

"He's put a hex on me," Harvey said as they made their way up toward the headquarters hut. "Last time he sent someone for me I was on the can. You believe that?"

"Harvey, I believe you anytime. He wants to know if the weather's closing in."

"It is."

"Yeah, but you know!"

"Yes, I know, he wants it up to date every friggin' five minutes."

"Maybe, Harv, but remember Yakutsk."

"Yeah," Harvey said, glancing skyward at the velvet darkness of the Inner Mongolian sky. "I remember Yakutsk."

It was a town in the Yakutsk oblast, or region, northeast of Lake Baikal. The Siberians were chopping up Second Army's Ten Corps as they tried to withdraw across the frozen lake. Outnumbered and outgunned by more than three to one in main battle tanks, Freeman had given what to his men was the almost incredible order to withdraw, all the time asking Harvey Simmet by his side what the temperature was in the Yakutsk area—the coldest place in the Soviet Union, where the temperature often plummeted to more than minus seventy degrees centigrade. Simmet told him it was minus sixty and still dropping.

American tanks were ensconced in revetment areas, some dug in so deep in defilade position that only the edge of their cupolas and muzzle of their main gun showed as they waited for a point-blank exchange. Then they got another order from Freeman to retreat still further. A few tank commanders thought aloud that the old man's nerve had cracked. But when the temperature dropped to minus sixty-nine degrees, the general thanked Harvey and suddenly told the American tanks to charge. It would go down in military history as one of the most brilliant tactical moves ever made. From the mastery of the minutiae of war to the mastery of grand strategy, Freeman knew that Siberian T-72s and T-55s would now grind to a standstill. The inferior refined Siberian oil would begin settling out in the vicious cold, the waxes in the oil solidifying like chunks of cholesterol stuck in the bloodstream—hydraulics would overheat and the tanks would become immobile.

It had been called the Yakutsk turkey shoot, and Siberian tanks that one minute were a threat now were stuck, unable to move as the M1s, with the higher-quality American-refined oil, raced ahead through the deep snow, slewed and turned and took out the Siberian armor on the move. The snowy explosions, their bases black fountains of undersoil, rose high in the air as red-hot metal from the M1A1s tore into the T-72s and more than evened the score.

"Good of you to come, Harv," the general said, as if Harvey Simmet had any choice in the matter. "Harv, they tell me this weather's 'closing in,' moving in on our left flank from the Bo Hai Gulf. Now what specifically does that mean for Orgon Tal?"

It had been an hour since Harvey had monitored the in-

coming SATREP—satellite reports—and in two hours a lot
had happened: the wind picking up at the three-thousand-
foot level, cold air from the northeast hitting the hot Gobi
air, producing fog in northern Manchuria, and minor dust
storms from Ulan Bator in Mongolia down as far as Orgon
Tal 280 miles northwest of Beijing. Harvey made a call to
the met tent and got the latest isobar readouts and cloud
pattern through on the fax. It was not showing at the moment, but in his mind's eye the data told him that soon the
air pattern would go into an ominous circular spiral path,
heading in fast from the coast. But he saw it as good news
for Freeman. "Looks like a typhoon's forming, General—
over Bo Hai Gulf. Winds will increase from forty to sixty-
five—maybe seventy—miles per hour, and the cloud
density promises heavy rain that will probably peter out at
the edge of the Gobi here at Orgon Tal, most of the rain
falling on the mountain range northwest of Beijing."

"Bog his armor down, General," Norton said.

"And ours," Freeman commented.

"Yes, sir, but I mean—"

"Yes—" Freeman finished the sentence for him. "Lousy
weather for him to move in—to attack."

"Yes, sir."

"Thank you, Harv."

When Simmet got back to the mess there'd been a snafu.
Cookie had gone off for a few minutes to check the coffee
and someone had grabbed the last plate of ham and raisin
sauce.

"Ham's finished," Simmet was informed by a new
server.

"Jesus!" Harvey said. "I tell you he's got a hex on me."

"Sir, we've got an MRE." He meant one of the "meals
ready to eat" in a foil-wrapped dinner tray that could be

warmed by body heat and were unaffectionately known by the troops as "meals refused by everybody."

As Harvey Simmet stabbed his fork unenthusiastically at the chicken à la king and viewed the Tootsie Roll and crackers and gobs of mixed fruit and peanut butter, he cursed his luck. He had no way of knowing that in Beijing's Number Two jail there was an American, Smythe, a SEAL who had been captured during the raid on the Yangtze Bridge earlier in the war, who would have thought he'd died and gone to heaven, given the luxury of an MRE instead of the fetid rice and vermin he had to crunch up and use as protein in his cell. Who was it that said comparison is the source of all unhappiness? Smythe dreamed of MREs.

They had strung Smythe up by his thumbs so often that by now they were useless, forcing him to use his first and second fingers to shovel in the meager rice and cockroaches from the wooden bowl. Nie's interrogators for the Public Security Bureau wanted to know the location of all SEAL units. Smythe had told them he didn't know, which was true. But by now daily torture had become routine, his screams mixed with those of many others—nearly all of them classified as either dissidents or "hooligans" against the state, hooliganism being a meeting of three or more people.

"Where have you been?" the PSB asked the three boys from Huade who were all in their late teens and had seen their hopes of a new China disappear, blown away like the sand in the Gobi.

"Fighting the oppression of the state!" one dramatically said, causing an expulsion of breath from his mother, whose shame was as keen as her surprise.

"And you two?" the PSB asked the others.

"Fighting the oppression of the state!" they answered in unison, sounding rather silly, albeit serious.

"Parrots!" the PSB inspector declared. "Parroting your bourgeois bosses." Gun in hand, he demanded they tell him whom they took their orders from.

"From our heart," the oldest of them said.

"Your heart," the PSB sneered. "That's an unreliable authority, boy."

"From the goddess of democracy," the third boy said, adding, "Malof xiaojie"—Miss Malof. In fact she had given them no such order to sabotage—they had never even seen her—but mentioning her name he hoped would take the sneer off the PSB's face. It did. The inspector pistol-whipped the boy's face, instantly drawing blood, and he told the squad of eight soldiers inside the house to take them in hand.

The inspector was sure the three had never met or laid eyes on the criminal Malof woman, but he was just as certain, especially when he had sniffed a rotten-egg odor of sulfuric acid on one of the boys' sleeves, that they had blown up the track near Tomortei.

"You could have killed many soldiers," he told the boys. "Your brothers."

"They're not our brothers," the eldest of the three said. By now two truckloads of PLA had arrived, and the parents were beside themselves as the soldiers piled out of the trucks, beams of flashlights roiling with dust, and shouted commands coming through the darkness, which soon had the soldiers in a huge circle around the three boys and the PSB inspector. The inspector now held a bullhorn—the battery wasn't working, but he used it anyhow to bellow out to the soldiers. "Remember what the democracy hooligans of Tiananmen did to your comrades in arms!"

It was a powerful appeal, immediately visible in the way

the circle of troops seemed to constrict in a solid ring and grow smaller yet more menacing, as every soldier took a step forward against the saboteurs whose earlier defiance now paled in the spotlight formed by several beams. In Tiananmen, or rather throughout Beijing, the demonstrators once attacked by the soldiers had in turn attacked many of the soldiers, the most infamous incident being when one of the soldiers had been castrated and hung from a wire noose, his body nothing more than black cinder after it had burned in a torch of gasoline.

Now there were screams coming from the houses down the dark *hutongs*, punctuated by declarations of "It serves them right!" from the Granny Brigade, and on the inspector's orders the soldiers turned and fixed bayonets against any possible interference from the crowd.

It took at least twelve soldiers to hold down the three boys who were now screaming as each was castrated, the bloody lumps of testicles thrown into the dust like pieces of meat. Then they were left, hands tied behind them, all out of their minds with pain, bleeding profusely into the dust, the rough placards hung about their necks reading, "Long live the people, death to the fifth columnists!" The circle of bayonets remained until the last of the boys had made his final plea for forgiveness, screaming like a wild animal, and then died. One PSB inspector ordered the bodies thrown in the truck and taken to the sabotage site near Tomortei, where their mutilated bodies were to be tied to stakes.

When Chairman Nie was told, he promised himself that he personally would shoot the Malof woman after she had been publicly humiliated in Tiananmen. He had no doubt that they would catch her eventually, and as everyone knew, Nie had a patience that was impressive, even by Chinese standards. He had waited a long time to be chairman, and he could certainly wait a little longer to have the PSB hunt down the Malof woman. The best way of course would be to bait a trap she couldn't resist.

News of the capture of the three saboteurs and their fate traveled like wildfire down both sides of the DMZ and then on national Beijing radio, which also announced that China would insist upon maintaining her territorial integrity and would petition the United Nations to have the imperialist forces of the United States return the Jewish autonomous region to China where it belonged. It had been such border disputes that first caused the U.N. to send Freeman's Second Army and some British SAS troops to settle.

Nie's ambassador at the U.N. brazenly stated that regardless of the truce, the JAO was a separate issue and it must be ceded forthwith to Chinese control. It was an elaborate plan by Nie, for in fact he didn't care about the JAO—he even suspected that the Jews had proper claim, but if anything would flush the JAO goddess of the democracy movement out into the open where the PSB could get her, and at one stroke immobilize a leaderless Democracy Movement, this U.N. move might.

The truth was that Nie's plan—his baiting of the trap with the demand for Chinese sovereignty over the JAO— worked better than he'd had any right to expect, for PSB informants in the JAO reported that Alexsandra Malof was surfacing to go personally to the U.N. to plead the JAO case, envisioning the JAO area as a separate democratic state between Siberia and China. Nie ordered his PSB informants to watch all refugee camps from Orgon Tal to Khabarovsk.

That evening Aussie and Alexsandra were saying their good-byes before he headed south for Orgon Tal. Second Army had a plane ready for Alexsandra, believing that in the U.N. the beautiful and articulate Alexsandra arguing her case would win over many delegates.

"I'll not be too long away," she told Aussie.

"You be careful, luv," Aussie advised her. "Don't go strolling off by yourself."

She leaned over and straightened the collar of his SAS battlefield smock and kissed him. "I'll have U.N. body-guards," she said.

Aussie for once had nothing to say. Gently he pulled her toward him, and in their embrace he could feel the beating of her heart.

"No," Nie said, "not in the air. Our Shenyangs wouldn't get near them. The U.S. still has air supremacy, or had you forgotten that minor fact, Comrade?"

"No, sir," the chief of the PLA's air arm replied. "I haven't forgotten, but we wouldn't be using Shenyangs. We would send up our squadron of Soviet Fulcrums. They'd stand a good chance of getting through the American air cover."

"And," Nie said, "at what cost?" The air force chief began to say something, but Nie held up his hand, silencing him.

"I know what you're going to tell me. The Fulcrum is a match for the F-16 or whatever, but the squadron of Fulcrums in the Beijing grid are the only ones we have and none of them can be risked. Besides, the shooting down of an Air America plane would tear the truce apart. Particularly with a woman aboard it."

"The truce is very thin already," the air force general said. "These three hooligans you found sabotaged the Orgon Tal line. They were obviously sent by the Americans to provoke us."

Nie stared at the air force general as an irate headmaster

might upbraid one of his staff. "You can't seriously believe that, Comrade? That Freeman would precipitate an action before his armor is ready—before it comes down to him at Orgon Tal and points east along our Manchurian front."

But the air force general, though chagrined, retorted, "Perhaps not, Comrade Chairman, but what I am sure of is that no one could *ever* be sure of what Freeman will do. He's entirely unpredictable. If he hadn't tricked us before with his feints here and there and his main attack elsewhere he wouldn't be only two hundred and eighty miles from the capital."

"Oh, he's a fox," Nie said. "A fox, yes. I grant you that, Comrade, but he's not a fool. The Americans like all their matériel ready, tested, and accounted for, before they make a move. He won't move before his replacement tanks are here."

The air force general agreed but shrewdly riposted, "But if he has not got his tanks ready, we needn't worry about his moving against us."

Nie's face took on a splotchy effect, his temper infused by a recognition that the air force general had a point.

"I did not mean he will do nothing, Comrade, before the tanks are here. If you down one of his planes, however, he could very well unleash air strikes anywhere along the DMZ. Even over Beijing."

The air force general knew he was rapidly losing ground but fired one more salvo in the battle of egos.

"But Comrade Chairman, the weather system over the central northern provinces is thickening by the minute. Even with their SMART bombs and Stealth aircraft they could not operate during a typhoon. Their aim would—"

"Yes, yes," Nie concluded, as if he had already thought of it. "I know all that. But you still can't intercept her plane. You don't understand the political side of this, Comrade. Apart from you losing several Fulcrums in the attempt—planes which we can ill afford to lose—the mass media reporting a shooting down of Malof would enrage the Americans and British and worse, it would make her a martyr. I do not want martyrs. Martyrs are drawing power for any fool that's anywhere near the Democracy Movement. Her death in such a manner could galvanize the various undergrounds into a coherent force at precisely the wrong moment. I want her captured alive—humiliated—completely discredited by her providing us with a list of names of Democracy Movement members."

"Names which I venture you already have," the air force general proffered.

"Precisely. Then she will be seen as a traitor who broke."

"Then how do you propose to get her?"

Nie poured himself a glass of mineral water. His chiefs of staff were good at what they did, but sometimes he wondered if they knew anything else than what they were trained for.

"It's already been arranged," Nie said.

"In New York?" the general asked.

Nie did not answer.

Beneath the gold and blue dome of the Temple of Heaven, Cheng, commander in chief of the PLA, experienced what his Christian mother would have called a vision but what Cheng could only accept as a fortuitous thought spawned by a schooling in Communist theory—more specifically from his memory of Mao's rules of engagement. When the enemy advances, retreat; when the enemy retreats, attack. But break all these rules if the element of surprise presents itself to you in another form. The Temple of Heaven was now invaded by long, searching fingers of fog whose chill invigorated General Cheng. He had a plan inspired by the news from the coastal weather stations at Tianjin and Qinhuangdao on the gulf where it was muggy but strangely still, and where a spiral pattern was discerned by all the weather radars. Prediction, a *taifeng*—typhoon. Cheng knew that even in good weather over 70 percent of all the bombs dropped on Iraq by the U.S. Allied planes missed their target, and that was in good weather—the other bombs you saw on CNN having been carefully selected for the press.

Cheng walked quickly down from the Temple of Heaven along the raised walk, trying not to show his excitement, beads of perspiration forming on his forehead despite the spring chill. Once in the Red Flag limousine he ordered, *"Zhongnanhai,"* then lifted the cellular phone and just as quickly put it down. One of the "cultural attachés" at the foreign embassies could be using a scanner. He looked at his watch. It was 1600 hours. He would schedule the attack for 0500 in the predawn darkness so that by first light they would be on the American positions as the typhoon, having engulfed the coast, would then be in full fury over Orgon Tal.

There was a delicious symmetry to it for Cheng, something that appealed to his deep sense of the yin and the yang, of opposites and of balance. As Freeman, before the truce, had rolled south toward Orgon Tal with Manchuria on his left flank, his tanks drove through the protection of a desert storm coming out of the west from the Gobi, and now he, Cheng, would head northwest from Beijing toward Orgon Tal then northeast along the snaking Manchurian trace, his troops all the while under the protection of a typhoon. American infrared beams and laser beams, degraded by the bad weather, would be unusable in the screaming, rain-laden typhoon, the sky darkly leaden, rivers swollen, roads a quagmire where infantry could move but not tanks.

The PLA infantry divisions would swarm over the trace and, like a million insects upon a buffalo's hide, would kill it, rout the Americans. Cheng's divisions would then keep moving north, their arms reaching out like scythes in a pincer movement on Freeman's overextended supply line. Freeman would be cut off, an American island in the desert ready for annihilation.

If Rosemary Brentwood had thought the PX at the Bangor base was stocked full of anything you might need, her visit, with Andrea Rolston, to the Silverdale Mall revealed an even richer cornucopia of goods, and whether or not it was partially her pregnancy to blame, she felt quite overwhelmed. She had thought that the shops back in Oxshott in Surrey had enough variety to give you headaches of indecision, but in Silverdale there were even more choices to make. It made her uncomfortable—the noise, the lights, the Muzak, and the belting rock from a shoe store quickly put her nerves on edge, and she told Andrea to go ahead while she waited at the Bon Marché.

Andrea had been gone for about ten minutes when Rosemary, with the sixth sense developed as a teacher who, while facing a blackboard, generally knew exactly who was acting up and who was paying attention, glanced about. She couldn't see anyone looking at her but nevertheless felt it in her bones. Or was it the anxiety of pregnancy? Whatever the cause, it manifested itself in a definite suspicion that she was being watched. She felt a tap on the shoulder, jumped, and turned.

It was Andrea. "You okay, Rose?"

"What—er, yes. I just got a little start—that's all."

"*Start*—honey, you were taking off. Sooner you have that baby, kiddo, better off you'll be."

"You're right. I feel like a brontosaurus."

"Well come on back to the house and we'll put our feet up. What you need is a Manhattan with lots of ice."

"Sorry," Rosemary said. "No alcohol—the baby."

"Rosemary, you sure are the worrier."

"I know," Rosemary conceded. "I wasn't like this at home."

"This here's your home now, honey."

The shock of that revelation—that Andrea Rolston was right, that home would now be where the submariners lived—immediately made Rosemary despondent. She had known this was true ever since she'd married Robert, but the actuality of their move from Holy Loch in Scotland to Bangor in Washington State was now hitting her full force, and although she wanted to preserve the British stiff upper lip, she already missed Robert as if he had been gone a month, and despite Andrea's best efforts, felt terribly alone.

Still, Andrea's bonhomie was so persistent that it couldn't help but mitigate Rosemary's mood. And soon, Andrea told her as they drove home, it would be time to send the sub its "familygrams." These were messages of no more than thirty-six words in which a man's family had to condense all the important information on the home front. Rosemary tried composing one in her mind as Andrea talked on, but though she had taught the art of précis to a generation of English schoolboys, she now experienced difficulty in summarizing her thoughts—in large part because she felt so uncharacteristically lonely. But Robert wasn't to know this, and so she struggled with the familygram. "How about this for a familygram?" she asked Andrea. " 'All's well with Brentwood Junior. Made friends with Andrea Rolston. Feeling fine. Miss you. Rosemary.' "

"Hell, honey," Andrea said. "That's only—let's see, about—fifteen words."

"Well there's nothing much else to say," she said rather

lamely, and felt Andrea's hand on her shoulder, grateful for once for the spontaneity of affection that came so naturally to Americans and that to the English was so often off-putting to one brought up on a staid diet of English preserves and reserve. Then as spontaneously as Andrea had been with her—almost as in the spirit of quid pro quo—Rosemary asked if there was anything Andrea wanted to say to her husband. Rosemary could use the remaining number of her words on her familygram.

"Aren't you the sweetie?" Andrea said, and added to Rosemary's familygram, " 'Andrea's ready for meat. Can you bring home the bacon?' "

At first Rosemary thought Andrea was talking about some dietary problem, but when Andrea winked Rosemary's face turned beet red. "Andrea! Surely you can't send that!"

"Honey," Andrea said, bipping a passing motorist for coming too close on passing, "you should see some of the stuff those boys get. You know they pin the spiciest familygram up on the notice board."

"Oh—" Rosemary said. *"Oh!"*

"No, no," Andrea hastened to reassure her. "The guy who gets the familygrams pins them up with names clipped out after everyone's read theirs. That way you never know who sent what. Course," Andrea added with a gleam in her eye, "you can always guess."

Rosemary was appalled by the idea, by Andrea's infectious lighthearted view of life, and at the same time attracted to it. The executive officer's wife certainly wasn't going to die of ulcers. However, Rosemary, despite all of Andrea's gregarious banter, couldn't shake the feeling that she was being watched. But in the constant ebb and flow of traffic it was impossible to tell. She even watched those cars that passed them to see if they'd merely done it as a ruse only to drop back behind Andrea's car a few minutes later. Robert had done the same thing in Scotland earlier in the war when he suspected that enemy Special Forces troops from what was now the CIS had been following them from one bed-and-breakfast place to another. It gave her no comfort to realize that the CIS were no longer at odds with the West, for she knew through Robert that after the Sino-Soviet split had been mended by Gorbachev and others that Chinese methods were often extensions of lessons they'd been taught by the Soviets in the bad old days, just as the British Special Air Services and U.S. Delta Force had trained their allies. Besides, it was a more confusing world now with ever-shifting alliances and old scores to settle—and a much more dangerous one.

Andrea felt Rosemary's silence. It filled the car like a funereal dream. "Rosemary, honey, you have *got to relax* for your sake and the baby's. Lighten up. You should have bought that dress I showed you—the maroon. That'd look terrific on you."

"I'm afraid buying things—clothes—doesn't perk me up like I assume it does most women."

Now it was Andrea's turn to be appalled. "Rosemary, that's downright unhealthy. I can see I've got my work cut out with you."

"Oh please don't bother. I'm sorry I've been such a drag today. I just feel—"

"Blah!" Andrea said, tapping Rosemary's knee. "I know—believe me. Everyone expects you to be mad with joy over the coming event. Lordy, I felt like—what I mean is, everyone expects you to be on cloud nine. Wasn't with me."

"It wasn't?" Rosemary inquired, a sudden hope in her tone.

"No way. When I was due I was ready to go out and

play in traffic. Thought I was gonna die and the young Eddie with me. And then before I knew it they had me in an ambulance, sirens blaring so's to let everyone know I was about to drop one—Lord, I hate those sirens. Anyway, out popped Eddie. Ugliest thing you ever saw—all bumps and angles and face all flushed and bloody like one of those drunks on skid row. I was *not* a happy camper. Anyway, pretty soon I started feeling more myself again and now Eddie's my darlin'. Wouldn't trade him for anything."

"So you never had any postpartum blues?" Rosemary asked.

"Oh yes, ma'am. For about three months—sat in the living room in the dark."

"What did—I mean, if it isn't a rude question—what did your husband do?"

"Do? I think he did it by himself—a lot."

"Did—oh, *oh!*" Rosemary was beet red again. "I meant how did he take it?"

"Pretty good for the first two weeks, then he told me to get off my butt and stop embarrassing the hell out of him. Said it could ruin his promotion from XO to skipper—you know, nutty wife, undue strain on the family. So—" Andrea gave a truck coming too near a blast. "Those guys think they own the road."

"So you got over it?"

"I sure did. Course I did a lot of shopping. Got me out of the house." She winked at Rosemary. "He didn't like that much but what could he say?"

For the first time that morning, Rosemary visibly relaxed. She'd found a friend—rough at the edges but someone who, unlike many officers' wives, wasn't afraid to say she'd been afraid of having her first child. Someone she could talk to.

"Don't you fret, Rosie," Andrea said. "I'll stick by you."

"Oh, that is nice of you, Andrea. I confess to you I'm terrified of all the pushing and—is it, I mean is it as bad as it looks on all those documentaries?"

"Worse," said Andrea matter-of-factly. "Now get this. Eddie—Eddie Senior—took a video of it."

"Really?"

"Yes, really. What the hell for I'll never know—'less he was going to send it to 'America's Funniest Videos.' I was cussin' to beat the band. Then you know what?"

Rosemary really couldn't imagine. "What?"

"Eddie's mom—old battle-ax—saw it and said it was too bad Andrea couldn't keep control—'*control*'! She meant me cussing—old bitch."

When they got back to the house the sun was shining brilliantly and the water had the oily sheen of a calm. Rosemary tried to adopt its pacific mood, but at the gate the guards kept them a long time verifying ID—which was ridiculous, Andrea said, because they knew her by sight. She didn't say anything more to Rosemary, however, because she figured from the mood of the guards and their insisting that she open the trunk, something had happened while they were away. She quickly thwarted any fear Rosemary might have by commenting, "Well it's nice to know our boys are on the ball."

"Yes," Rosemary agreed. "It's reassuring."

"Uh-huh," Andrea said, watching the guard in the rearview mirror. "If he doesn't close that soon all my frozen stuff'll turn to mush."

They were going over it with some kind of detector.

"That sabotage near Tomortei," Freeman asked before going to bed, standing resplendent in a patchwork silk robe of vibrant squares, each one emblazoned with the logo of an American football team. "Any reaction from the Chinese?"

"Internal, sir. Intelligence has heard murmurs of a punishment detail—three trucks near Huade—but nothing on the trace. The truce is holding, General."

"Yes," Freeman answered, "for the present."

"Harvey Simmet was right, General. There's a typhoon on the way—miles across. Ground'll be mush. Cheng won't be able to move his T-55s or T-72s for long."

"All right," Freeman answered, "but keep the trace reports coming in. We'll be without SATREP until that typhoon has passed us. Once it starts to rain—"

"Yes, sir. We'll keep our eye on it. Goodnight."

"Night."

Inside the small eight-by-four room of the headquarters Quonset hut, the general went through his nightly ritual. He kneeled, his West Point ring pressing hard against his forehead as he prayed that he might "vanquish my enemies and uphold the freedom and honor of the United States," got up, broke open his pump-action Remington 1200 shotgun, checking the double 0-load, closed it, and leaned it up beside his bed and checked the Sig Sauer 9mm Parabellum beneath his pillow. There had already been two attempts on his life.

In bed he took up his copy of *The Art of War* by Sun Tzu, which he kept by his Bible that he always read before going to bed, liking best the part wherein an army was described as having to be like a river having to adapt its course as it comes across the opposition, the kind of measure that always separated out those who had initiative from those who did not. It reminded him of Douglas MacArthur's strategy in the Pacific where MacArthur had simply bypassed several strongly held Japanese islands and attacked others, cutting off the ones he left behind from all supply. Next he put one of the earphones from his Walkman on, letting the other one lie on the sheet so that one ear could always hear the alarm on the shelf above his bed. On the tape he heard the voice of John F. Kennedy awarding Churchill honorary citizenship of the United States, talking about how Churchill had "mobilized the English language and sent it into battle."

"Best damn speech he ever made," the general murmured, and turned a page of *The Art of War*, as he did every night, like an athlete always in training, to remind himself of that which could rob you of victory—of how the simplest lack of vigilance could have dire consequences— that one must never underestimate the opposition.

At that moment ten Chinese divisions, 150,000 men, set their sights on the desert around Orgon Tal, the division equipped with East Wind hovercrafts. Sand, mud, or water—it didn't matter—the hovercrafts could attack at over ninety kilometers per hour.

Freeman could hear the rain drumming sonorously on the metallic roof, it making him feel warm and safe just as it did when he was a child in Missouri. But how much rain would there be? Freeman lifted his phone.

"Duty Officer Burns, sir."

"Burns, get Harvey Simmet up here."

"Yes, sir."

"On the double, Burns."

"Yes, sir. Right away."

CHAPTER SEVEN

"*TASHI DELAG,*" THE Tibetan said, smiling, his earflaps giving him a slightly comical look.

"*Tashi delag,*" the other traveler, a European, answered. The Tibetan nomad's smile alarmed the European. Was it merely a good-natured greeting, or was it an "I know why you're here" look?

It had taken months for the man, a Dutchman named William Hartog, to receive the necessary visas to enter Tibet as a health researcher looking for alternate types of medicine and in particular at the effects of AMS—acute mountain sickness—which affected so many tourists, afflicting them with everything from acute headache to dizziness and on occasion death if the AMS victim was not kept warm enough. His company, Royal Dutch Apothecary, was, he said, looking more closely now at the holistic medical systems practiced by the Tibetans, including the nomads who inhabited the enormous plateau at a height of fourteen thousand feet, the plateau stretching from the Kunlun Range to the north southward to the Himalayas. In between there was desert and occasional grassland and salt lakes.

Hartog was interested in various herbal remedies, golden needle acupuncture, and in particular moxabustion, in which small tufts of moxa incense were burned atop a needle so that the warmth could travel down and affect the nerve point. He was also looking for plants that could not only be used to prevent and/or reduce the effects of mountain sickness but could prove curative for a plethora of Western afflictions and diseases. Hartog's curiosity was equally aroused by the Tibetans' insistence on there being a balance between wind, bile, and phlegm, that is, the three humors that the Tibetans believe must be in balance if disease is not to gain the upper hand.

Hartog had already watched the fine and intricate art of pulse diagnosis in which various pulses provide a readout, as it were, of the various parts of the sick body. By paying homage to the Tibetan medicines—now called Chinese medicines ever since China had invaded the country of two million in 1950—Hartog was more respected by the locals and was not especially harassed by any of the 120,000 PLA troops stationed throughout Tibet or, as the Chinese preferred to call it, the "autonomous region." He had become fairly well known in the markets and often advised a PLA member to try this or that remedy for any proffered illness, but always he would take the medicine himself to show good faith. Hartog was one of those patient explorers. He took the time to make copious notes and photographs of the various herbs.

But underneath, Hartog's pulse wasn't steady, for he was a very frustrated agent of MOSSAD who, because of Chinese sales of ICBMs to Muslim countries, wanted to know all they could about the missiles ever since the Swedish seismologist had recorded an underground nuclear explosion near the Xinjiang border with Tibet. There was a strong suspicion that, following the B-52 destruction of Chinese ICBM sites on the roof of the world earlier in the war, a new site was now in Tibet. The savings in fuel, launching from fourteen thousand feet above sea level, for example, was enormous. But where the site was, neither satellite nor other ELINT—electronic intelligence—had discovered, much of the movement up the Lhasa Road from the province of Qinghai past Lake Nam having been done either at night or under heavy cloud cover.

The only way, MOSSAD decided, was to get humint—human intelligence gained by someone whose human senses and initiative might prove more successful. After all, an infrared blur could, as General Cheng well knew, come from a hot thermos and yet register on the satellite film as a hot jet motor. Hartog's job was to pinpoint the Chinese ICBM sites in Tibet.

It was lunchtime, and snow was falling again. It would be melted quickly by the sun, but with the sudden drop of temperature so typical in Lhasa, Hartog headed for the taxi stand across from the market, heading east along Xingfu then left, up Linkuo Lu to the telecommunications office where he sent a cable to Amsterdam asking for more money that he could change into Foreign Exchange Certificates. It was a signal that he had found out nothing about the ICBM sites. The amount he asked for told them the number of weeks he could remain under his visa.

After exiting the communications center he took a rickety cab south and went along Xingfu Xilu to the Lhasa Holiday Inn. Before going into the hotel where he'd registered for three days, Hartog visited the Xinhua Bookstore next door, and there he bought a cassette of Tibetan music, along with some postcards. Coming out, walking back toward the hotel, he heard the usual hissing and "Change marney?"

"No," he said sternly, without being rude. He suspected that at least one of them might be a Public Security Bureau man—from the foreign sector. If you changed money with them you'd get a good rate and a night in jail for doing it, and then you would be in real trouble.

In the Lhasa Holiday Inn he felt guilty for wasting time and spending it in such comfortable surroundings and knew that soon he would have to risk going off the beaten track for a while and stop along the way at the various army camps where for a few yuan they were known to put you up for a night. The question would be, however, whether it was an ordinary base camp or a special secret camp that served the hidden ICBM sites, wherever they were. He wouldn't know until the date section in his Rolex watch–cum–Geiger counter began advancing rapidly and noiselessly. And it hadn't happened yet.

Well, he decided, he might spend only two nights at the Holiday Inn, then he'd rough it, and he knew it would be rough. For a start there would be the wild packs of dogs around Lhasa that were known for their ferocity, and he decided the best idea would be to travel along with the Chang Tang nomads who had survived the wildest parts of Tibet, a place of stark mountains and even starker plains in the north for over a thousand years.

While shaving before going down to the dining room, he put the Tibetan music cassette in his Walkman and played it through the two small square speakers. He thought it terribly discordant. He thought too about ICBM sites, of where they might have been moved to after the crushing B-52 raid against their old sites in Turpan. He thought also of how it wasn't really in Israel's interests to go poking around fourteen thousand feet or so above sea level looking for them. But in part MOSSAD's mission was a payback due the Americans for their rapid help with the Patriots in the Iraqi War and a sign of good faith between Israel and the United States that he knew would be reciprocated if Tel Aviv needed it.

He rode down in the elevator with a PLA major whose satchel was marked "Major Mah, Camp Nam." Lake Nam, where the camp was situated, was northeast of Lhasa and, if he remembered correctly, was a huge bird sanctuary. Hartog and the major smiled at each other, the major saying something about the weather. Hartog agreed. As they pulled up at the second floor he glanced from habit at his watch. The date had advanced ten days. Like the Russians, the Chinese, for all their newfound expertise, were still notoriously lackadaisical about safety parameters. Hartog made a show of patting his vest pocket for his wallet as if he'd forgotten it and at the ground floor stayed on the elevator and went back to his room. He had to work fast so as not to arouse any possible suspicion by the PLA officer. He pulled the toilet chain and went to work.

When he arrived down in the lobby ten minutes later, he dropped off a postcard to Amsterdam, his forehead glistening in sweat. The Chinese officer looked up from one of the dining room tables and motioned for the Dutchman to come over. Smiling, Hartog produced his wallet from his vest pocket. "Under the bed," he said.

"Good," the officer said, pleased he had found it. "Would you care to join me for dinner?"

"Yes," the Dutchman answered, noticing a large bottle of Tsing Tao beer already emptied. He immediately ordered another two and talked about how changeable the weather was in Lhasa.

"You have been here long?" the officer asked.

"Only two days in Lhasa—two weeks in Tib— the autonomous region." He had almost said "Tibet." The officer was starting on his second large bottle of beer, and loosened his belt.

Hartog inquired of the major whether his camp, near Lake Nam northeast of Lhasa, was one of those that would put up trekkers for a night at a modest cost. "Yes, you could stay at our camp," the major said. "Ten yuan."

It was high by Chinese standards, but for Hartog a godsent opportunity.

"I might take up your offer," Hartog said, adding, however, that it "depends which way I go—east along the Zangbo or back past Lake Nam."

"Well if you go back past the lake ask for Captain Ling. He's my executive officer."

"Thank you, but I may go east along the Zangbo."

"There would be less rain than back north along Nam."

"I'll see," Hartog said noncommittally, raising his glass for yet another toast. "First I want to go and see the Potala Palace."

"Ah," the major said, looking around. "I understand everyone loves to go to the Potala." He wasn't too drunk, but nevertheless he couldn't help employing the official Chinese tone of disdain for the Buddhist monastery.

On that note they said good-bye, and at the desk Hartog gave the clerk a Tibetan folk music cassette for the next morning's post and sent a fax to Amsterdam, struck at once by the irony of being so close electronically to the West but so far away in reality. He read the fax out to make sure that the desk clerk understood.

The herbs which I have found so far should be alphabetized under ISNLNCIEAABTAKMMEREM. Am trying to get more details on Tibetan acupuncture. Willi.

The major ordered more beer be sent up to his room and asked if Hartog would join him. The Dutchman declined gracefully. "Perhaps then," the major said, "I will see you at breakfast."

"Yes," Hartog said, and they waited, watching the floor

needle above the elevator doors. They did not speak together going up in the elevator, the major yawning and Hartog watching the floor numbers light up, standing relaxed at the back of the elevator, trying desperately not to show his excitement. Sometimes in the game it was like that: You worked your butt off for weeks and months in godforsaken places all over the world, looking for a clue, and nothing, then you walk into a hotel and what happens? The wristwatch goes crazy. If the Chinese major hadn't actually been working on or near an ICBM site, Hartog wasn't a Dutchman.

CHAPTER EIGHT

Khabarovsk

THE KNOCK ON Alexsandra Malof's door in the hut that she shared with several other prisoners who had been rescued by the SAS/D teams startled her at first. It was just past midnight. But the moment she remembered she was in an American refugee compound at Khabarovsk she felt safe, having dropped off while working on a draft of her U.N. speech on behalf of all those Jewish and non-Jewish residents of the JAO. Even so, she did as Aussie Lewis had told her and looked out the hut window first, catching a glimpse of the Special Air Service berets: "Who Dares

Wins" in the moonlight. And she went to the door with the gun, a Beretta 9mm that Aussie had told her he'd liberated from the ugliest Chinaman he'd ever seen on the SAS/D dune buggy raid against the Chinese guns.

"Yes?" she asked cautiously.

"Miss Malof?"

"Yes."

"Captain Lourdes." He held up his tag identification. "We've been told by Freeman's headquarters to escort you to the airstrip. General Freeman says you can bring anything you want but make it snappy."

"And this?" She showed him the Beretta.

"No problem this end," he said. "What New York authorities will say is up to them. We'd like to take off before dawn, miss, just in case the Chinese do put up a few aircraft."

"A few what?"

"Sorry, miss, didn't mean to frighten you with talk about enemy aircraft, but it's not just that really. There's a typhoon on the way and the pilots would like to outskirt it if possible."

"Yes, very well," she said softly, and gathered her bag, already packed, and followed them out beneath the beautiful moonlit sky to the Humvee that would take them to the airport.

They pulled up at the gate, showed their ID, the GI there saying, "Good luck," to Alexsandra.

"Thank you," she said, and as they started off again noted the faint, sweet odor of the spring earth about to break open with a profusion of flowers any day now. She also had a sense of déjà vu, not so much that she'd been in the same place but doing the same thing as a child, her smell memory triggered by the strange odor of chloroform. Well past the gate she felt her shoulders suddenly held back, and felt chloroform-soaked cotton pressed hard against her face. She squirmed and tried to scream but there was no use; she was out of it in seconds, slumped in the Humvee's front seat.

"How long to the Black River?" one of the men asked. He was referring to the Amur, which the Chinese, who had hired them, habitually called the Black River.

"A half hour," the leader said. "Then it's up to the Chinese. All we were asked to do was to deliver her unharmed. Keep her from getting on that plane. Now remember, once we get to the river and hand her over to the Chinks we get rid of this SAS battle dress garb and we're back to being just four Khabarovsk traders busy with our import-export business."

The other three men laughed—they were from Hong Kong, where they had worked for the arms manufacturer Jay La Roche before he was murdered. With the reversion of Hong Kong to China threatening their roles as European entrepreneurs unless they kowtowed to Beijing, they were the perfect middlemen—men without a country, between China and the West.

"Hope we get more business like this," one of the four kidnappers said.

"No," said the man who called himself Lourdes and who was doing the driving. "Not like this. This is a one-time fee from the Chinese. Seems she's important to Nie."

"Lot of trouble to go to for a bit of tail," one of the men in the back joshed.

Lourdes had shifted down as they neared the Amur River that separated Manchuria from Siberia. "No, it's all politics," he said. "They want to put her on trial."

"A show trial," one of the men in the back said. "Better her than me."

"Okay, shush," the driver said. "Remember the trace for

the cease-fire is the river here. American patrols'll be past this point in about ten minutes. Soon as they're gone we send her across."

CHAPTER NINE

"FUCKING HELL!" AUSSIE roared. "Whaddya mean someone's kidnapped her? Who?"

"We don't know, Aussie," David Brentwood said. "First thing we knew about it was she was missing the refugee check this morning."

"Well what about the fucking gate? The guards, for Chrissake?"

"They said the guys who picked her up were SAS—ID and all."

"Right!" Aussie said, grabbing his Heckler & Koch 9mm submachine gun. "Let's get a few fuckin' answers."

The SAS men with him—Salvini, Brentwood, and Choir Williams, among the "bravest of the brave" in Freeman's book—didn't dare tell him he'd just blown his bet about not swearing for a week. The Australian was in a murderous mood. His blue eyes actually seemed to darken as he strapped on extra magazine belts. "Let's go!"

"Where?" Brentwood said.

"To find the fuckers! For Chrissake!" Aussie said.

David Brentwood put his arm on Aussie's shoulder.

"Cool it, digger—the MPs've found an abandoned Humvee down by the river. By now she's in Chinese hands."

The information hit him like a blow to the solar plexus, and he was shaking his head, trying to will it not to be true.

"No, mate," he said to David Brentwood disbelievingly. "Must be some mistake." Suddenly he looked up. This man who was renowned in the troop for not being afraid to face the truth—to give you a realistic SITREP, knowing how to separate hope from fact—was now ashen faced. "The airport," he said. "Maybe Freeman had her moved—"

"No, Aussie. Listen up now! We've checked," Brentwood said, adopting the Aussie's idiom. "She's gone, mate."

Aussie seemed to murmur something, letting the Heckler & Koch fall to the bunk where it bounced, the blankets stretched tightly, as per regulation, as if it had dropped on a small trampoline.

"Freeman wants to see us," Salvini put in.

Aussie looked up hopefully. "Right—what's on?"

Salvini instantly regretted he'd mentioned Freeman, as Aussie in his state had leapt to the conclusion that Freeman had already drawn up some kind of rescue op, but he hadn't. He had something far more pressing.

The problem had begun, or rather had taken shape, some seventeen hours ago when in Lhasa the PLA major had waited for the Dutchman, Hartog, to start out on his visit to the Potala Palace, whose grand, sweeping whitish gray edifice against the blue sky seemed impregnable and more majestic than even the white-topped mountain fastness beyond.

The PLA major, Mah, had asked to listen to the Public Security Bureau's tapes of the foreigner, William Hartog, in

room 206. The tape for room 206 was mainly silent, except
for the sound of the toilet flushing and the tinkling, at times
mournful, songs of Tibet, probably coming from the foreigner's Walkman. He knew foreigners became glued to
their Walkman sets and would carry them in the most inap-
propriate places. Mah, whose job, apart from the other du-
ties he had, was to monitor the tapes for the Holiday Inn,
went into room 1219, one of the two China Travel Service
offices on the Holiday Inn's ground floor.

The men who had been on the last watch were tired but
tried not to show it, sitting up attentively with their
earpieces looking like huge green earmuffs, afraid of Major
Mah's displeasure. He came there on his weekly rounds or
"foreigner check," as they called it.

"He has flushed the toilet six times," Mah charged, as if
it were a personal affront.

The technicians looked at one other—yes, they certainly
agreed it was six times.

"And that Tibetan music," Mah said derisively. "Listening to it at the same time."

"Ah," the technician said. "The music I think comes
from his room while he is doing his business on the toilet."

Mah sometimes wondered where it was they'd got these
troops from to police Tibet. They were country bumpkins,
most of them—not at all like Cheng's elite shock troops or
the tougher "PLA Second Artillery Army," those who
guarded the ICBM sites.

"Why do you think," Mah asked contemptuously, "that
he flushes the toilet six times?"

"Perhaps there was an obstruction," one of the technicians proffered confidently.

"Maybe," the other technician said, "he was full of shit!
Ha, ha!"

Mah turned such an iron face toward the hapless technician that he cringed. "Are you the people's official clown?" Mah asked. Before the belittled man could think of any response, Mah kept on, tapping the man's head as if talking to an idiot. "If there was an obstruction, rock brain, the toilet would most likely have overflowed after it had been flushed six times in a row."

"He's not on the toilet," the first technician said suddenly, surprised by his own revisionist thought.

"Ah!" Mah said. "Now we are thinking. Maybe he's doing something else?"

"He's—he's in the bedroom," the oldest of the technicians said, visibly excited by his deduction.

"Doing what, comrade?" Mah pressed.

"He's recording over the music tape. He's talking very close to it. . . . The toilet is to cover his voice. He must have spoken very softly."

Mah nodded, then picked up the phone, pressing the number for the front desk. "And of course he might have a thing about flushing toilets and the music could mean he likes Tibetan music."

The front desk answered.

"Major Mah here. Last night a foreigner, Mr. Hartog, he gave you a tape to mail."

"Yes, sir, and a fax."

"Has the fax gone?"

"Yes, Major. Almost immediately. It was another of his messages about Tibetan remedies."

"Has the cassette tape been posted?"

"No—it's due to go in another few—"

"Send it to me immediately. And your copy of the fax."

Scanning the copy of the fax—it was in telegraphic style, no doubt to save money—Mah saw that Hartog had instructed the recipients to classify his Tibetan remedies discovered so far under the following letters of the English alphabet: ISNLNCIEAABTAKMMEREM. It was signed "Willi."

Mah now turned his attention to the cassette tape. They all sat silently as Mah had the technician run the tape fast forward. There was a gabble of music—the same as picked up by the room mike if Mah wasn't mistaken—but no voice. They tried the other side and played it fast forward. Fast music gibberish again—no sustained pauses—no European voice. Nothing. Maybe the tape was no more than noise cover with no message at all?

The silence in the room was more intense because of the terrible snarling and nipping and yapping of one of the packs of wild dogs who, because the Buddhist monks would not harm any living creature, strayed wild around Lhasa and the other Tibetan villages. Some of the dogs had been shot for sneaking into PLA camps looking for food. Some had rabies. Mah was trying to concentrate, and told one of the men to have the desk get someone out to disperse the mongrels. Had his mother tongue been English it is just possible that Mah might have disassembled the fax's message right away. He looked at it again. ISNLNCIEAABTAKMMEREM and the last word, "Willi."

What struck Mah as odd was that several of the English characters, or rather letters, were repeated, such as *M* and the two *A*s. If a medicine—if anything—was to be classified, why mention the same letters (M and A) twice? And why Willi instead of William? Was he just using a nickname—or was the Dutchman being economical again by not signing his full name? But if he'd been economical he'd hardly use the same letters twice.

In Tibet it was 8:00 A.M., in Amsterdam one in the morning, but in the small shop on the Osterdok near the railway station out of which Hartog worked when in Amsterdam that fax had already been decoded by his MOSSAD assistant and cleared for Tel Aviv as "most secret" and for "immediate" transmission to UNCOMFARE—U.N. Commander Far East, General Douglas Freeman.

"Willi" had five letters, thus the message broke down into a five-line message, so that "ISNLN" became

I
S
N
L
N

and the message read

ICBM
SITE
NEAR
LAKE
NAM.

Lake Nam, at the foot of the Nyaiqen Mountains, was twenty-five miles long, the largest salt lake in Tibet.

CHAPTER TEN

AND NOW FREEMAN'S Second Army HQ at Orgon Tal had the location given them by MOSSAD. For Aussie Lewis it could not have come at a worse time, but from Brentwood's point of view it was a godsend. It was at least something—a danger to the entire Second Army—that might overshadow Aussie's personal loss of Alexsandra Malof. The revelation of the ICBM sites set alarm bells off all through Freeman's HQ at Orgon Tal and as far away as Khabarovsk, all within striking distance of the latest Chinese DF5 ICBM.

But for Aussie the news that Second Army's big B-52 raid earlier in the war on the ICBM complex at Turpan in western China's desert had not completely taken out China's long-range rocket capacity could not begin to upset him as much as the kidnapping of Alexsandra. The ICBMs were Freeman's problem. Alexsandra was his. In his totally unexpected and absolute love for her the message of the ICBMs paled into nothingness, but for Freeman and the more than three hundred thousand men in Second Army, it was everything, should the truce fail. For the hitherto blasé Australian, the loss of the woman he loved was infinitely more pressing and unbearable. For the first time in his life Aussie Lewis wanted more than sex from a woman.

He wanted to possess her not only sexually but in every other way. He *needed* her.

There was a rumble as the officers, NCOs, and some enlisted men rose in the Quonset headquarters hut at Orgon Tal as Freeman entered.

Salvini turned to Aussie Lewis, hoping to cheer him up. "He's got that look, Aussie."

"What?" Aussie asked, his mind far away on the banks of the Amur River with Alexsandra.

"The George C. Scott look," Salvini said. "Somebody's gonna get shit."

"Fucking MPs should be reamed out." It took Salvini a moment or two to realize Aussie was talking about the MPs who had let the Humvee carrying Alexsandra pass through the gates at the refugee camp.

"At ease," Freeman said, his voice booming off the metallic roof. After the coughing and usual scrabbling of feet had died down, during which Freeman looked out upon them with his remarkable facility for making every single man think it was *he* whom the general was talking to, Freeman slapped his birch switch against the huge wall map of China, Tibet, and the Himalayas.

"Problem—our entire army is under the threat of ICBM attack. With this activity going on, the truce can only be interpreted as temporary at best—the Chinese waiting for the most propitious moment to move and/or build new silos in and around the mountains surrounding Lake Nam. This is the roof of the world, gentlemen. We're talking fourteen thousand feet plus. Now we're going to put more SATRECON over that lake and adjacent mountain area and once we find their mobile launch trucks and/or shelters we are going to send in our Stealths and blow the hell out of them."

There was a hand up—a brigadier general.

"Yes, Tommy?"

"Sir, there was an incident this morning—a kidnapping of one of our refugees which I interpret as an act of war. Am I correct?"

Aussie suddenly sat up, fairly bursting at the general's remark. "That's the way, General," he said, looking toward the brigadier. "Give the fuckers—"

"I concur," Freeman agreed, "but unfortunately—" And here he paused, the birch switch smacking his leg impatiently. "—Washington has strictly forbidden any attempt by us to cross the river despite the fact that the leader of the JAO guerrillas has been taken."

There were murmurs of surprise running through the hall by those who hadn't heard of the kidnapping already.

"But," Freeman said, "I propose a *reconnaissance* party along the Orgon Tal trace this evening to demonstrate our displeasure. A hundred tanks," Freeman added.

Norton leaned forward from the table and whispered, "General, how are you going to explain a reconnaissance of one hundred tanks?"

Freeman was still looking out at the sea of faces, determined to at least maintain, if he could not lift, his men's morale, and he answered Norton without turning his face toward his aide. "It'll be a 'reconnaissance in force.' "

Norton sat back. "Washington'll have a baby if they find out, General."

"Dick, we have to show these bozos that violation of the truce won't be tolerated. Washington won't let me go across the damn river, then it's incumbent upon me to do a bit of saber rattling. We're not here to dance. They're damn lucky it wasn't an American citizen, otherwise I'd be at war with the sons of bitches right now."

"Remember, General," Norton pressed, trying not to be

too conspicuous up on the dais, "our reserves of M1A3s up north won't be down here for another five days."

"Agreed. That's why it's important to show up with a hundred tanks. Otherwise Cheng'll think we're frightened—that they can come across the trace and get away with it."

Norton sat back. He'd done his best. And he had to admit the general had a point. Any sign of backing down, of losing face in front of Asian commanders, could be interpreted as weakness. Anyway, Norton guessed, push probably wouldn't come to shove, as the Chinese would probably not see the American tanks in the rain-slashed skies of the typhoon that was about to strike. Already he, like all those in the Quonset, could hear the drumming of the rain on the roof.

Cheng saw the tanks very well, for he'd posted forward observation points with infrared binoculars along the trace near Orgon Tal where the western end of the front came to a sharp V like the end of a check mark, the right hand or tail of the check mark representing the continuation of the front northeastward up into Manchuria. He knew the American was bluffing—making out he had more tanks than he did. Well, the commander of the People's Liberation Army had no intention whatsoever of waiting till Freeman's M1A3 reinforcements reached him from the north. And now the Public Security Bureau had advised him from Lhasa that the Americans must now know about the ICBMs from the Dutchman's message. Cheng could not afford to wait any longer—to do so would be militarily imprudent as well as politically inexcusable. He told Nie, and the chairman agreed. Cheng gave the order to attack—a preemptive strike.

* * *

The trace east of Orgon Tal was a hundred-foot, mile-long ridge running southeast to northeast where the trace arced up from the V of the check mark–shaped truce line, the Americans on the northern side, the PLA to the south. It was hard, stony gravel that further north a few miles, to where the bulk of the Americans were, turned from stony ground to sand dunes. To the south of the trace the stony ground led back up for two hundred miles into the bush-covered mountains that, along with the dragon-humped Great Wall, formed a protective fastness around Beijing.

The typhoon's *tai feng*, or great wind, at over one hundred miles per hour, was not yet upon the area around Orgon Tal, though already gusts of up to forty and fifty miles per hour were heralding what was in store unless the typhoon lost and exhausted much of its power after hitting land coming from the east out of Bo Hai.

Freeman's tanks went ahead in echelons of five in spear-tip formation, the two tanks furthest back acting as wing-men would in a fighter formation, paying particular attention to the flanks while the three tanks up ahead concentrated more, though not exclusively, on the trace now coming up and on the lead tanks' right-hand side. Inside the lead tank, its commander, Lieutenant R. T. Roper from Philadelphia, wondered if this would be it. The first sign, or rather glimpse, of the enemy trenches way over on the other side of the trace was indicated by coils of razor wire, obscuring any view of the troops, though the Chinese, probably the forward artillery observers, clearly had binoculars on the first tank of Freeman's "reconnaissance in force."

Here and there the Americans, primarily the loader and the tank commander, could spot the muzzle of a machine gun where there was a gap in the wire, and sandbagged outposts beyond that were probably heavy 81mm mortar nests. The men in the tanks were confident and with good reason. They were in one of the best, if not *the* best, main battle tanks in the world. The M1A1 main gun was an M256 120mm smooth bore with one coaxially mounted 7.62mm machine gun, the other 7.62 atop the loader's position in the turret with a Browning .50 machine gun atop the commander's position forward and right of the loader. Left of both the commander and the gunner on the right side of the turret sat the loader, the driver outside the turret steering the behemoth in a reclined position by way of short hand bars. Yet above all the firepower there was the sheer grace of something that was on another level so brutish. Its gas turbine motor was probably the quietest of any, capable of charging ahead at forty-five miles per hour despite a larger heat signature than most, its suspension so superior that its turret remained in the same plane, despite the tracks constantly undulating like pythons as the M1s raced across the uneven ground.

"Remember," Roper said, in Freeman's lead tank, "we take one shot, one friggin' rattle of a spent Chinese bullet on our beast, and we vaporize the mothers." Everyone understood, everyone was tense, but they all agreed that Freeman was right to bring the tanks right up to the trace, otherwise the next thing the Chinese would try would be to send over a patrol and take an American prisoner or two as they had done often enough in Korea. The wind was quickening between forty and sixty-five miles per hour, blowing up small whirlwinds of gritty sand that hailed against the sloped armor.

"So how we gonna know if it's a Chink bullet hitting us or not?" the gunner asked, referring to the noise of the coarse sand and stones being blasted at them by the typhoon's early fury.

"You know what I mean," Roper answered. "Something substantial."

"Yeah, well, if it's that substantial," the gunner said, "maybe it'll just shoot a jet right through us." He meant the molten jet of metal that was formed by the HEAT—high-explosive antitank—rounds that could penetrate the M1's body with a molten streak of metal, creating havoc inside the turret, exploding the tank as it ignited the M1A1's own fifty or more antitank shells.

The commander got on the radio and passed the message along—the haillike sound of pebbles striking the tanks could send off a premature shot from the Americans from some nervous commander further up from the line of M1A1s. Lieutenant Roper from Philadelphia didn't care that he was speaking in plain language and not code, wanting to be overheard by the Chinese. That was in effect the power of Freeman's show of force. He merely wanted the Chinese, with their outdated T-59s and more up-to-date laser-equipped, range-finding T-72 tanks, to know they were there, that if push came to shove along the trace, then Cheng would have to deal with Freeman's one hundred tanks preceded by flail, grader, and demagnetizing-pan tanks that would lead them across the mine field between the two sides, and there the Americans would deal out some heavy high-velocity punishment for any truce violation. Each man in the one hundred tanks had been in the Far East long enough to know that for Freeman not to have responded to the kidnapping of Alexsandra Malof with such a show of force would have immediately signaled weakness to the PLA, and if Washington wouldn't understand it, Beijing would.

Cheng spoke to the fifty men from the Sixty-five and Sixty-six armies based near Beijing who had volunteered to spearhead his attack. He had held up a book—or rather a thick monograph, its hundreds of computer pages on a ring binder. It was an account of all of Freeman's battles, from grand strategy to local tactics, including his background, right down to the fact that in matters of food he did not like sushi, was partial to Tsing Tao beer because it had no preservatives in it that would give you a headache, and that he intensely disliked the American actress Jane Fonda and enjoyed westerns. Cheng told them he had studied it all: the man and his tactics. He had studied how Freeman had studied *his* heroes, from General Sherman to Guderian and Rommel, particularly the Germans' tactics, both in the desert wastes of North Africa and in the heavily timbered mountains of Yugoslavia. As a result, Cheng could tell them that the only thing about Freeman that was absolutely predictable was that he was always unpredictable—witness his present "reconnaissance in force" in response to the Malof woman's extradition despite Washington's ban on any military action.

"Then why, Comrade General," the captain asked, "does Washington not recall him for insubordination?"

"Because," Cheng answered wryly, "he is the best fighting general they have—but I do not think he'll be ready for an attack at the head of the typhoon. Remember the rain will bog him down. The mud will harden within hours of the typhoon exhausting itself over Inner Mongolia, but for those few hours, comrades, it will be a quagmire, a sea of mud and rushing streams for a hundred miles to the south and north of us. Are you ready?"

There was a cheer of a team confident of victory.

"The Americans' eyes will pop out," one of the volunteers said. "Freeman will see his own strategy turned upon him with a new twist. It will astonish him."

"Where did Freeman first use the technique?" another driver asked.

"Up on the Inland Sea," he answered, by which he meant up on Lake Baikal.

"Yes," another put in. "He sent several hovercraft across the ice with commandos to blow up the midget sub base from which the Siberians had been launching missiles then hiding out in the lake's deeps."

"Did he get them?"

"The subs? Yes, and he wrecked the base."

"Well, now it's his turn to suffer."

"You're right," another commented. "You see, the old saying is incorrect—you *can* teach an old dog new tricks."

This elicited raucous laughter and even produced a smile on Cheng's lips. His men were in high spirits—they understood the mission, they understood what they'd volunteered for, and they understood the rewards for the mission.

"For now," Cheng told his troops, "relax as much as you can—as many cigarettes as you want." Then in the thick, smoky air they heard the typhoon approaching, a rattling sound outside the doors of their tents.

The battle-stations alarm was on, and like the diving alarm not loud enough to cause a noise short—that is, noise that could be picked up from outside the sub—but penetrating enough to send every man moving as fast as he could to battle stations, one man heading toward the reactor room in his socks, all the quicker to put on the regulation yellow slippers that he would wear while in the reactor room lest he pick up even the minutest radiation and which he would take off when he left the reactor room.

An unknown ship—"possible hostile"—had been picked up by *Reagan*'s passive sonar array, its engines' pulse and movement through the water now registering on the five-window sonar screen, the purplish blue light around the sonar like an island in the redded-out control center.

"Threat library?" Robert Brentwood asked.

"Nothing yet, sir. Possible merchantman—new registration."

"Or hostile running with baffles."

"Don't think so, sir. Cavitation of screw not baffle." Brentwood knew he could get an exact fix on it if he used his active pinging sonar, but then the unknown ship could pick the *Reagan* up, and the *Reagan*'s mission was to keep hidden from all hostiles, regardless of their size, to be ready for a FLAS—flank assist—to Freeman's land force if needed. Everything on the ship was rigged for quiet—all washers and driers off, drawers secured, stoves off, the next meal, frozen sandwiches, already set to be zapped by the microwave if it turned out to be a long engagement that took them beyond dinner.

At the Bangor base in Bremerton, Washington State, it was 8:00 P.M. and Andrea had organized an officers' wives' "ball-out," a bowling competition. "Course you don't want to play," she told Rosemary. "But come along and watch. Keep score if you want."

"No thanks. My specialty is English literature, not mathematics. I'm afraid I'd make an awful mess."

"Oh rats," Andrea riposted. "So just sit and cheer. Don't even have to cheer. B'sides, if you go into premature labor you'll have a travelin' moms brigade with you. You could have a choice—hospital or number one lane."

"You're impossible," Rosemary said, awkwardly shifting herself out of the love seat in her base bungalow. "Maybe it would do me good to get out. And to be quite honest—"

"What is it?" Andrea cut in, adopting Rosemary's semi-conspiratorial tone.

"Chips—what you call fries. I have a craving."

Andrea clapped her hands in victory. "There you go. We'll pig out on fries, popcorn, and pop."

"And we'll pop in the morning," Rosemary said.

"No, we'll do twenty minutes with Jane Fonda's workout—pregnant ladies excused I guess."

"You don't have a Jane Fonda tape?" Rosemary asked in a tone of disbelief.

"Yeah. I know all the guys hate her for that North Vietnam thing, but hell, that's over, right?"

"Then your husband does object?"

"Object? Honey, he'd lose all his hair if he knew. I've got it hidden—video label says 'Home Cooking.' He'll never know. 'Sides, if he does twig to it I'll tell him it's either the tape or me."

Rosemary looked nonplussed. "You would leave—?"

"Oh hell no. But I'd cut him off for a week or two."

"Oh I see," Rosemary said. "After a long patrol. Isn't that a little drastic?"

"Honey, I cut off one guy for a month!"

Rosemary was appalled, Andrea collapsing with laughter. "You—you really thought—oh Rosie, you're a kick!"

Rosemary wasn't sure what a kick was, but it had been said good-naturedly.

"C'mon, let's go bowlin'," Andrea said, looking for the key to the dead bolt. There'd been a rash of B and E around the base, and it was expected that sooner or later someone, probably local teenagers, would try to sneak over the wire into the base.

By the time Andrea and Rosemary arrived at the bowling alley the USS *Reagan* had let the unknown vessel pass over it, and the sub's passive microphone array had registered its noise signature and entered it into the threat library under "possible hostile," as they were too close to the China coast for it to be anything else. They would follow her and get a nighttime infrared periscope view, as this might confirm exactly what kind of ship it was.

Some of the men, the ship's noise signature having been put over the PA system, were betting it was a Taiwanese destroyer making a fast run down the one-hundred-mile strait, half of this being ROK water and not PRC—a fine distinction neither side was paying much attention to these days.

"Sonar?" Rolston asked, starting his watch as officer of the deck. "What's your guess?"

"Gunboat, sir. Hydrofoil with vanes down."

"Vanes might give us a baffled noise?"

"Yes, sir."

"How far away is he now?"

"Three thousand yards."

"Periscope depth at two thousand yards."

"Periscope depth at two thousand yards, aye," the confirmation came. The men were still at battle stations.

"When will the rain hit us, Harvey?" Freeman shouted against the wind.

"In about a half hour, General."

"Sure as hell making a goddamn noise out there." The pebbles were hitting the Quonset hut like marbles, and several windows were already broken and were being boarded up.

In Beijing there was no wind—none. In the eye of the storm there never is, and people walked across Tiananmen with a brisk urgency that seemed to belie the uncanny stillness that pervaded the city. Soon the storm's center would pass over and it would be possible to breathe again, and for many the terror of the typhoon upon them would be preferable to this unnatural quiet wherein even the noise of the bicycle bells had fallen off as people, faced by the typhoon, were more interested in putting their bikes in the nearest parking lot, grabbing their ticket from the granny, and heading inside, many going to the military museum on Changan Avenue, its massive concrete structure and high ceilings making it one of the safest in the city.

In revetment areas all along the trace, Cheng ordered his tanks to stay dug in, in hull-down defilade position wherever they were, and to ready themselves to lay down an artillery barrage before the first wave of troops began to cross the truce line.

"I believe," Freeman said, his knuckles now supporting his weight over the table map of Beijing and environs, "that Cheng is going to attack."

"In a typhoon?" an incredulous Norton asked.

"In a typhoon," Freeman responded, a note of urgency in his voice. "Norton, I want you to encode for the tanks— withdraw a hundred yards from the trace and dig in."

The general saw Harvey Simmet looking at him worriedly. "Well," Freeman said by way of explanation, "you're telling me, Harvey, that it's going to rain buckets for a while, aren't you?"

"Yes, sir."

"Then I don't want my tanks bogged down and vulnerable. This way only their main guns will show."

And the main guns of the hunkered down M1A1s were just visible, but ample reference points for Cheng's fifty East Wind one-man hovercrafts. Actually they were three-man hovercrafts of the same arrowhead shape that Freeman had used on Lake Baikal, the sharp, streamlined, fifteen-foot-long, six-foot-waisted wooden hulls, with an eight-inch skirting below, driven by a ten-horsepower, four-cycle vertical shaft mower engine that moved the hovercrafts across sand, mud, or water between forty-seven and fifty-five miles per hour. It was based very much on the early UP design series of hovercraft in the United States.

The early winds of the typhoon were now gusting at fifty miles per hour, giving the East Winds an additional fifteen miles per hour so that some of the hovercrafts actually had to brake hard, by deceleration and tail flap, in order to maintain stability at around fifty to sixty miles per hour. The space in the cockpit behind the perspex windshield usually occupied by two passengers either side of the driver was now packed with two hundred pounds of TNT and jelled high octane, a napalmlike explosive mix that if it hit the M1 tanks would kill them by incinerating the tank crew.

In the slashing rain and wind-driven squalls of rock and sand on this, the outermost fringes of the Gobi, the laser range finders of the M1A1s became segmented by airborne debris. As a result, the rounds fired by the Americans at the small, fast hovercrafts fell long or short or even wide of their targets.

The constantly fast weaving and jinxing of the sharp-bowed hovercrafts, looking no bigger than wedges of cake at two hundred yards *if* you could see them, made direct hits against them by the M1A1s virtually impossible, and within four minutes of the swarm of fifty hovercraft shooting across, indeed skimming across, the mine field, only one lost power at this critical juncture. Nose-diving hard into the typhoon-whipped earth, its nose detonator exploding instantly, the heat and enormous concussion of the huge, two-hundred-foot-wide napalm fireball took out another three hovercrafts that had been running more or less together across the mine field—the sudden overpressure exploding several more mines.

"Jesus!" Lieutenant Roper said. "Fire into—" Instead of finishing his order he used the gunner's override and pressed the button himself, blowing up some mines, but by now most of the hovercrafts were across the DMZ, racing toward the tanks. The tanks' main gun depression at ten degrees was better than that of most main battle tanks, but Roper and every other tank crewman knew at some point they could depress the gun no lower.

"Machine guns!" Roper yelled over the radio. "And break out for maneuver. Now!"

In the swirling maelstrom of the withdrawal and now the deluge of rain, tracks spun and slewed but still gripped hard enough to back out of their stationary hunkered down position atop the ridge as tank commanders and gunners flipped open the cupolas, the Browning .50 and 7.62mm machine guns respectively in the Israeli position, that is, the commanders' heads were visible above the cupola and would have made perfect targets for the hovercrafts had the latter been fitted out with machine guns themselves. But they were not, the hovercrafts' only defense, though a considerable one, their bobbing and weaving motion with only two hundred yards to go. Only Roper and a few other echelon commanders had guessed the truth—that the mini Chinese hovercrafts were kamikazes.

In the fury of the storm, the acrid stench of cordite filled the air with wet dust, and four other hovercraft disintegrated, vaporized by their own napalm hit by a .50mm Browning on whose belt every fifth shell was a tracer. Then without the wind increasing, its wild banshee sound was punctuated by the staccato sound of machine guns, but the forty-two remaining hovercraft were on the tanks, slamming into them at fifty miles per hour plus, the Americans screaming as each fireball engulfed their tank, the tank exploding in mustard-colored eruptions of earth and two hundred pounds of TNT and jelled gasoline.

Out of forty-two suicide hovercrafts that hit, only two failed to explode, but that left forty tanks—160 Americans, the latter no more than charred corpses, their ID tags melted in the furious heat of the fireballs, the burned and sweetish stench of their bodies blown westward by the typhoon's ferocious wind.

Now Cheng ordered three armies, the Sixty-third, Twenty-seventh, and Sixty-ninth, originally from the Beijing area, to swarm across the trace. Chinese T-59s amassed during the storm provided covering fire, first to clear a path through the minefields and then firing to create a creeping barrage under which the three armies—over ninety thousand men—advanced on the American lines, overwhelming the American defenders who of necessity had been spread too thinly out along the trace, the sudden Chinese attack creating a huge bulge in the right side of the check mark–shaped front. And into the bulge Cheng poured as much armor as he could possibly expend, most of this being the light, eighteen-ton amphibious type-60 tank, its main gun an 85mm. Weighing three and a half times less than the 63-ton M1A1, it presented a mobility in the water that the M1A1 did not have. But here, a hundred miles northeast of Orgon Tal, the bulge met no American armor, most of it being collected around Orgon Tal for what had been Freeman's grand plan of a dash south to the city.

Behind the T-60s, in reality in large Soviet PT-76s that had been used to good account earlier in the war against Freeman, thousands of PLA regular frontline troops moved like so many ants through the downpour of the typhoon, which did not inhibit the amphibious T-60s but hindered the retreating Americans who, devoid of tanks to protect them in this sector, relied on the lightly protected Bradley fighting vehicle. However, the Bradley's superb mobility and speed of forty-one miles per hour was reduced by the typhoon's headwinds, and once again targeting via laser became obscured by airborne debris.

Worst of all for the Americans was the fact that their TACAIR was grounded, the only aircraft venturing forth being a squadron of A-10 Thunderbolt IIs, or "tank busters," as they were affectionately known after their brilliant performance in the Iraqi desert. But despite the bravery of the pilots in flying down into the typhoon, they could not shoot at what neither they nor their infrared goggles could see properly. In any case by now the ground troops of the two sides were engaged in hand-to-hand fighting, and no satisfactory ID of friend or foe could be made from the air.

"For God's sake!" Freeman thundered. "When is this weather going to lift, Harvey?"

Because of the general's tone, Harvey felt personally responsible for the typhoon.

"Another eight to twelve hours, General." Freeman looked along the trace of the map. It was simply too long a trace to cover in any depth. If you rushed through here and there, another bulge would quickly appear to your rear. Freeman was in no panic, but he knew he was getting clobbered. He had earlier believed his M1A3s would be down south before the Chinese—presumably waiting for better weather—would attack. But he did not realize by how much he was being beaten, until exactly one hour after Cheng had ordered his surprise kamikazes, killing Lieutenant Roper of Philadelphia and the crews of the thirty-nine other M1A1s. Suddenly there was an advancing rush of air, like the *chuff-chuff*ing of a huge locomotive only speeded up, as Chinese DF5s fired from Lake Nam by the PLA's Second Artillery or ICBM arm began landing, albeit with conventional warheads, on Second Army positions around Orgon Tal and northward, cutting into Freeman's supply line.

At first the peripheral concussion of just one of the DF5s—designated CSS-4s by the Americans—was so powerful it killed more than fifty-three men outright, the core explosion of the missile killing another seventy-three, the latter members of a marine detachment at Orgon Tal.

The red marker pins of Chinese positions advanced relentlessly across the trace. In some places Chinese infantry had simply swarmed across the DMZ, mines killing scores of them, their bodies, or rather the parts of them, forming a bridge of dead men as stepping stones of flesh for the others behind them.

The blue marker pins of the Second Army were pulling back, not only in the northeast and at Orgon Tal but in the mountains of Manchuria as well—all along the trace.

"If we can just hold," Freeman said, "long enough for the weather to clear—well, hell, we'll hit 'em with everything that can fly. Harvey?"

"General?"

"Your best guesstimate is another eight hours of this nonsense until the typhoon blows itself out?"

"At least eight, General—maybe twelve."

"Damn it, I'll have to give ground."

"I agree," Norton said, "but I don't see any other alternative."

"But damn it, Dick, we can't let them go on like this. This isn't a withdrawal—it's a goddamn rout. In forty-eight hours I won't have any cohesiveness left on the trace. Tell everyone to dig in where they are. We'll resupply."

"Resupply?" Norton ventured. "How?"

"By chopper—at least we can drop supplies through all this muck." But Freeman knew he had to do more than dig in and resupply. The Chinese had the bit between their teeth—damn it! He knew what he needed. So did Norton and Simmet: to take out the ICBM sites at Lake Nam in Tibet. If the missiles kept coming, he didn't stand a chance. Immediately he contacted his Khabarovsk airfield. Surely the Stealths, with the Dutchman's general target designation of Lake Nam, could find out the *exact* positions of the Tibetan ICBM site via infrared and SEV—starlight enhanced visuals. And when they did—well, they could start using their SMART bombs.

After sending in the request and getting a confirmation that Stealths were already on their way with in-flight refueling over the South China Sea before the inland leg of their mission, Freeman felt a bit better, but not much. He was fighting a two-front war—that son of a bitch Cheng sending across division after division of expendable infantry, while he, Freeman, was being kicked in the butt by the ICBM launchers out of Tibet. The babble of voices, the screaming of the wind, the high screech of radio, and the constant chatter of intercepts were buzzing all around him.

"Quiet!" he bellowed. Everyone stopped talking and turned toward the general. Was the old man cracking up after all? Had he met his Waterloo in Cheng?

"While the Stealths are getting ready, what *we* need is a diversionary tactic to draw some of Cheng's troops out of the bulge he's made in our line."

"You got anything in mind, General?"

The general lowered his head, walking thoughtfully toward the huge wall map of China, his shadow dwarfed by its size. "Norton, ask Khabarovsk how long our boys'll take to organize in-air refueling and how long to knock out that ICBM site up at Nam—if and when they find it." Some of the officers wished he'd used the full name "Lake Nam" or "Nam Co"—"Nam" alone was an impediment to the American psyche. It reminded every man there how a war in Asia could start, look as if you were winning it, then eat you up. Like now!

"Wish to hell it was called Lake Iraq," someone said.

"Don't worry about it," Freeman said, breaking out in a morale-raising smile. "Our boys'll go in there with a surgical strike. Those goddamn Chinks in Tibet won't know what hit them. These Stealths'll know what to do."

Somebody mumbled something about the lack of enough Stealths being part of "Clinton's cock-up."

The four Stealth, or "Wobbly Goblin," pilots were Iraqi veterans and, providing the weather was clear enough over the mountains towering around Lake Nam, they knew very well what to do with their pitch black, twelve-and-a-half-foot-high F-17A Nighthawks. They knew, for example, that the best Chinese radar would be unable to track them or even glimpse them as they came in.

As pilots mounted the long stepladder into the cockpit behind the five flat one-way glass canopy windows, they knew their ATO—air tasking order—called for an ICBM site to be hit at Lake Nam, each of the four Stealths carrying two two-thousand-pound bombs equipped with nose-mounted Pave Track laser guidance kits that would steer the fourteen-foot-long bombs via laser-guided movable vanes, allowing the bomb to slide down the laser beam for a bull's-eye hit. There would be no fighter escorts for the Wobbly Goblins as Chinese radar would be unable to get any fix on them because of the 117's flat, angular shape reflecting any incoming radar upward rather than back at the radar. And the two General Electric turbofan engines were set deep within the wing roots to rescue their infrared signature, while the exhaust was cooled and baffled so as to deny any heat or infrared signature to the enemy.

With a maximum speed of only Mach .9, the Stealth was by no means the fastest plane in the American arsenal, but in having to fly over other countries' air space en route to the mountains of Tibet, it was deemed highly desirable to send in the Stealth if the mission was to be kept a secret and U.S. diplomats spared notes of outrage from half a dozen governments, which would have been the case if other American airplanes that could be seen on radar were used.

The only thing holding the mission back was lack of good SATRECON—satellite-reconnaissance—photos of the area, and to reprogram the K14 satellite to take a flight path high over Tibet was extraordinarily expensive and time-consuming. And in any case, once the Chinese got a hint of the spy satellite's new orbit they would not fire any missiles from the site while the K14 was in geosynchronous orbit overhead. But of course the four Stealth pilots would be able to see burn marks produced by the ICBM backflash at the launch site. And so it was finally a matter of waiting for the weather to clear over the roof of the world.

"Send Harvey up here, damn it!"

"Yes, sir," Norton answered. Simmet apparently was going to be held responsible for the locked-in cloud cover over Lake Nam and the surrounding mountains. What particularly annoyed Douglas Freeman was the fact that, knowing he was in the right, he had said a prayer for good weather, but cumulus cloud remained glued to the mountaintops despite his incantations.

"Maybe the Chinese are praying, too, General," Simmet suggested.

Freeman swung about from the map. "Chinese are goddamned atheists."

"The leadership perhaps," Simmet answered, "but not—"

"Don't contradict me, Harvey. I know the leadership are and that's who I'm talking about, not the people. Why do you think I've given express orders to everyone in Second Army that I won't tolerate any vandalism or 'collecting memorabilia' from temples, et cetera. When we win I want the Chinese to be a help in the reconst—"

There was a sound above the drumming of the rain like that of a roaring train, and instantly the three men hit the deck of the Orgon Tal headquarters hut. The earth shook, the noise the most terrifying and sustained roar Norton had ever heard, so much so that his knees were shaking as he got up, half stunned, Harvey Simmet almost falling over because of the concussion-produced imbalance in his inner ear.

Behind them, further down "Radio Alley," dust was still falling, but the babble, momentarily silenced, was now back at full volume, a tone of new urgency, even excitement, detectable, and for those who had felt the close wings of death about them, this moment was exhilaratingly alive.

It wasn't the same, however, for Three Armored Corps's fifty-five tanks fighting a desperate action to stem the tide of Chinese following on from the suicide hovercraft attacks and the creeping barrage of the T-59s. Three Corps HQ would undoubtedly have been overrun had it not been for the M1 overreach. Its 105mm cannon had a range of four thousand yards, two thousand yards better than the Chinese T-72s and three thousand yards better than their T-55s. It was this overreach and only this overreach that prevented the Chinese from pummeling Three Corps HQ at Orgon Tal, an HQ that was caught up in the frantic business of readying for withdrawal. But it was far from a one-way fight, as the Chinese-like amphibious T-60s were now paying the price for their lack of armor. With the rain still pouring down, the M1s could see the Chinese even if the rain cut the laser beams, and it was fire at will. Within twenty-three minutes, seventy-five of Cheng's tanks were tin cans, blown apart bodies, or rather body parts, scattered across the wet, stony ground, one tank, driverless, still rolling forward until another APDS—armor-piercing discarding sabot—round hit it and blew up its ammunition supply in a spectacular explosion of bluish white and red.

But if the Chinese had been stopped around Orgon Tal, Three Corps supporting forces, from gas tanker trucks to signals, were smoking ruins with over two hundred men killed and 312 wounded by just one warhead from a DF5 missile. Freeman immediately gave orders to retreat northwest some thirty miles back to higher ground toward the Mongolian border. Even so, now that Freeman's Second Army on the whole had recovered from the initial surprise in the typhoon, the Chinese were meeting with more sustained and coordinated resistance from MLRs—multiple-launch rocket systems—which found their targets via forward artillery spotters who could now call in U.S. howitzer fire without fear of "blue on blue"—or friendly fire—hitting the retreating Americans. With twelve MLR units firing simultaneously, 144 rockets were sent screaming into the screaming typhoon, raining down twelve miles away on the Chinese positions, and, while not hitting any ChiCom tanks, were filling the air with white-hot shrapnel.

But Freeman knew that while he was now undoubtedly putting up a more coordinated retreat, it was still a retreat and would remain so until the weather, by which he meant the cloud cover more than wind or rain, lifted at Orgon Tal, allowing his A-10s to go in low. But even with this, as long as the ICBMs coming out of the launch site in the Lake Nam area kept coming, he would be run out of China's northeast Liaoning province and would not be safe anywhere in what was for now Second Army's territory.

Tactical rockets, though with nothing like the range of the DF5 being fired from the Tibetan site, were now coming out of Beijing. Their accuracy, despite their shorter range, was paradoxically not as good as the DF5s' coming in from Tibet, and while many of them were landing among the Chinese frontline troops as well as the Americans, Freeman knew there'd be no letup in the Beijing rocket barrage because Cheng could afford thousands of his men to be killed as the cost for killing hundreds of Americans.

Shortly before dark the weather lifted briefly as the worst of the typhoon passed over and the "Warthogs," the A-10 Thunderbolts, came in low, their GAU-8 Avenger 30mm seven-barreled rotary cannon spitting out a deadly stream of heavy depleted uranium that went through the Chinese tanks like ball bearings through glass, their white-hot fragments setting off the tanks' ammunition and fuel tanks, creating great blowouts of orange-black flame.

The Stealths did not give any active radar signals, for this would be to obviate their whole purpose, and so they depended entirely on what they could see, either visibly or through the infrared and starlight goggles. The moon bathed the Himalayas and the mountains to the north in a beautiful, ghostly light, the summit of Everest clearly in sight but the lower parts of the mountain packed tight with snow that looked uncannily like bluish white cotton batten.

Everest was now well to the south on their left and out of sight, clouds shrouding its summit, but below they could see the steep valley formed by the mountains behind Lake Nam off to their right, the mountains furthest to the west faintly visible through scudding cloud. Suddenly there was a blossom of orange light that faded then kept on only with a lower intensity—an ICBM lift-off. Both the leader and his wingman got a fix and dived, laser beams streaking out into the night at the target: the light source. Then the light source disappeared, leaving only an infrared patch of the ICBM's backblast, the residual heat waves washing about the base of the mountain as if it were a mirage in the desert.

"Christ!" the pilot of Nighthawk One murmured, talking to himself. "It's a steel door. The bastards have the missile sliding out on a rail." Only now did he break radio silence and tell the other three what he'd seen, ending up with "We go for the door," and with that his computer, via infrared and laser information, quickly got the exact range and told him he could pickle off the bombs. One slid down the laser beam, and all four Stealth Nighthawk pilots saw the explosion as the two-thousand-pound bomb hit. The four Nighthawks made two runs each, dropping the second bomb amid a sky now pocked with triple A—antiaircraft artillery—the red traces coming so fast, probably one in four, that it seemed as if continuous red lines were shooting up through the night sky, an enormous pile of ice and rock debris about the huge door, heat coming from it like a smoking quarry.

They got out before any of the searchlights that came alive in the valley could zero in on them. Three hours and seven minutes later, Freeman's Six Corps, up near Manchuria's Harbin, took direct hits from three DF5 warheads and, falling back in disarray, reported over three hundred casualties. The number of dead were not yet known, human remains strewn about the trace, and the commanding officer missing, either captured in the aftermath by advancing Chinese infantry or killed, blown to pieces so that his fate might never be known for certain.

A half hour after that, Second Army intelligence—with a noticeable lack of surprise—was reporting to Freeman that closeup computer-enhanced photos from the Stealths showed that a huge steel door had possibly been dented somewhat but that the door, obviously a superhardened entrance to a superhardened silo or the interior of the mountain, had suffered only minor damage.

Stereoscopic blowups from the Stealths' videos revealed lines about 1,435 millimeters apart: rail tracks. The ICBMs were apparently rail mounted for firing, the launcher then shunted back quickly behind the immense armor-plated door.

"Very clever," Norton said. "If the Stealth with laser-guided bombs can't take them out, what can?"

"An A-bomb," Freeman said.

Norton's face drained of color.

"Don't worry, Dick," Freeman told him. "I'm not that crazy." Norton exhaled heavily with relief, but the problem still remained.

The only answer was to get someone down inside the mountain—to blow up the launcher platform.

"Special forces?" Norton proffered.

Freeman nodded. "It's a hell of a thing to ask them, but it's our only chance. Have to be the most experienced men we have, Norton," and the general's aide knew straightaway that Freeman meant Second Army's elite: the SAS/D British Special Air Services and American Delta combination team that had served him so well before.

"It'll be risky, General," Norton said. "Going into a narrow valley between twenty-thousand-foot peaks."

"I know. But goddamn it, we have no choice. We have to take out the ICBM site or we'll lose this war. We have to get someone on the ground, and Brentwood and Co. have HALO and HAHO experience." He meant the parachute troops' high-altitude, low-opening and high-altitude, high-opening missions involving high-altitude drops into the heart of enemy territory.

"Notify Khabarovsk," Freeman told Norton. "We'll need KC-135 in-air refuelers. I want them here and ready within twelve hours. We'll use fighter-protected Hercules for transport. Fly from here to Lake Nam—via Mongolia if necessary to avoid Chinese radar and triple A. Thank God we've got air superiority."

"The Mongolians might have something to say about a U.S. overflight," Norton cautioned.

"If they do," Freeman said, already drawing in the route from Orgon Tal to the Tibetan ICBM site, "I'll turn Ulan Bator into a parking lot."

Norton was on the scrambler to Khabarovsk.

In his dream Aussie Lewis couldn't hold her any longer. Her hand was reaching for his, but in the quicksand there was nothing more he could do. He felt her fingers touching his—he reached, strained to grab her, but she was gone.

"Aussie!" David Brentwood was speaking in an urgent but subdued tone, trying to bring the Australian out of the dream sleep gradually. With the commandos of the SAS/D trained for hair-trigger response, more than one orderly had ended up on the floor with an SAS/D man atop him, chest knife drawn before the commando realized where he was.

"Aussie—"

Suddenly Aussie was sitting upright on the edge of the bunk, staring at Brentwood. "Alexsandra?" he said, expecting, hoping for, some news of her.

"No," Brentwood said. "Sorry, chief—it's not about her. We've received orders from Freeman. An ICBM site is cutting our boys to pieces. We're going in."

"HALO," Salvini added from the next bunk, already checking his oxygen mask.

"How many?" Aussie asked.

"A squadron of us," Choir said, meaning eighty SAS/D

troops would be involved in the drop, broken up into four troops of twenty men each.

Aussie nodded and, trying to shuck off the weight of his worry about Alexsandra, commented wryly, "Be a bit chilly. What's the altitude?"

"We'll go out at fourteen thousand. Night drop of course, NV goggles—the lot."

"Weapons?" Aussie asked.

"Each to his own. Somehow we've got to get inside a mountain where the Chinks have their ICBMs stacked to send out on a rail launcher. Once we're inside we blow it up."

"Oh, that all?" Aussie said. "I thought this was going to be something difficult."

"Nah," Salvini said, adopting Aussie's nonchalant mood and glad to see his comrade in arms fight his way out of his depression about the woman he loved. "If it was difficult," Salvini continued, "we wouldn't have asked you along. Right, Choir?"

"Right, lad," Choir said, loading the magazine for his thirteen-inch-long Heckler & Koch MP5K submachine gun with 9mm Parabellum cartridges, the gun's rate of fire nine hundred rounds a minute.

"Each of us will command a stick of twenty going in," Brentwood told them. "Regroup soon as we land best as we can."

"We got any pics on this?" Aussie asked.

"Yes," David Brentwood said, dropping a manila envelope of high-quality "fax-fotos" onto the bed. "Sent up from Orgon Tal. Beautiful scenery."

"Fuck the scenery," Aussie said, pulling out the photographs. The valley between the peaks looked to be about a mile across but would appear as nothing more than a scratch at fourteen thousand feet, the mountains towering above it.

"We'll go in the northern end of the valley, which is a mile or so wide," Brentwood said.

"Bound to be high winds," Aussie said.

"That's the fun part," Salvini said. No one laughed.

Outside, the Galaxies, Hercules, and fighters were readying for the flight to Orgon Tal HQ.

Hartog was exhausted from climbing the hundreds of stone steps of the Potala Palace to reach the thirteenth story of the 406-foot-high Red Palace its majesty highlighted by the wings of the older White Palace on either side. The Dutchman walked quietly through the seven mausoleums of the Red Palace, seeing the salt-preserved remains of the nine Dalai Lamas, their tombs lined with gold, silver, and jewels—stunning even in the monks' poor candlelight. Respectful of tradition, he was careful to walk clockwise around the holy shrines but wondered how long it would be before China desecrated this place, too, the Chinese having already built an unsightly jumble of brutish, modern apartments at the base of the palace, the style of the apartments, if one could call it style, owing more to the Stalinist school of architecture than to Tibet.

Before he set off down toward the Dragon King Pool on the north side of the palace, he glanced across at the Iron Mountain, Chagpori. Once a prestigious medical school that was destroyed, like so much else in the "Cultural Revolution," it was now a cavernous fortress. It had enough supplies of ammunition, frozen food—primarily meat and rice—and winter uniforms to fully supply the garrison for months of seige, which might happen, Hartog thought, if ever the two and a half million Tibetans rose against the occupying Chinese as they had in 1959 when they were viciously repressed.

As Hartog began walking down to the north exit, tired after seeing inside only twenty of the one thousand rooms and hundreds of shrines, the Chinese major at the Holiday Inn dialed 22896, the number of the Potala Palace. It was answered by a monk who was in fact a member of the Gong An Bu.

It wasn't until he reached the seventh level that the monk, all but breathless, caught up with him and told him he was wanted in one of the lower rooms. Hartog looked down in the bright sunlight that was below him, his senses alert to the smell of alpine flowers, from which direction he couldn't tell—or were they crushed flowers near a shrine? The only thing he was sure of was that a group of monks below him with their drab oxblood-colored shawls about their saffron robes suddenly looked strange, advancing hostilely up toward him.

More monks materialized behind him from dark corridors and dimly lit rooms. What had they been told? That he had violated one of the Dalai Lama's *chortens*, stealing the gold and inlaid jewels that decorated each crypt? Surely all of them couldn't be Public Security men. And why not? he thought. There were enough genuine monks to hide a large number of security men if the Chinese wanted to do it. He looked down over the thirteenth level, the people ant-sized below, and all about him shaven heads closed in slowly, with a deliberateness in their eyes that did not evoke salvation but rather damnation.

CHAPTER ELEVEN

Orgon Tal

"ALL RIGHT," ROBERT Brentwood called out, his voice echoing in the hangar to which the Galaxies and Hercules had taxied after the hop from Khabarovsk, "everyone listen up. We're using the GQ three-sixty chutes and going in HAHO." He meant the high-altitude, high-opening technique as opposed to high-altitude, low-opening, or "HALO." High altitude, low opening meant you were in free-fall up to two to three minutes at two hundred feet per second. It got you to the drop zone much more quickly than HAHO, but they wanted to avoid going straight down onto the ICBM site for fear that the triple A would chop them to pieces on the way down and that the PLA guards at the site would be onto them before they could break free of their harness and unlash their drop pack of extra ammo, food, etc.

Even so, Aussie Lewis, a veteran like David Brentwood, Choir Williams, and Salvini of high-altitude, low-opening, preferred to free-fall for two minutes then open the chute. Very few ground troops, he had found, could respond in under five minutes. But Brentwood said it was the CO's idea to go high-altitude, high-opening two miles north of the ICBM site and therefore away from most of the triple A that SATREP revealed was clustered in the valley about the site. Besides, the slopes between the range of mountains and Lake Nam being only three to five miles wide meant that for such a high jump there was always the possibility of wind shears moving off the sides of the twenty-thousand-foot mountains. Freeman had decided that they should have high-opening, for this way they would have more time to steer themselves down, and also the drop planes could then turn off and so not encounter the worst of the triple A that festooned the ICBM site further along the southern end of the valley.

As Choir Williams was checking his nine-cell Ram-Air GQ chute, which had cross-port venting as well as both inside-outside stabilizers to help steady the chute in cross-current turbulence, Aussie Lewis made some disparaging remark about HAHO. "Oh, I don't know, Aussie," Choir said. "I prefer a little time going down to catch the scenery."

At twenty feet per second, the high-opening descent from twenty-five thousand feet could take up to twenty minutes to half an hour, depending on how much glide was involved.

"We'll be old men before we get there," added Aussie, who was checking his insulated Gore Tex battle smock and trousers before getting into his overlay of SAS/D gear.

"All right," Brentwood said, going down the checklist. "Oxygen masks, wrist altimeter, tether line . . ."

There were a hundred and one details that had to be checked, particularly the oxygen masks which, because of the danger of altitude sickness, would have to be used not only on the way down but for many on the ground as well after the freezing descent. David Brentwood was finishing getting into his all black SAS/D antiterrorist gear with his

combination SF/10 respirator with oxygen tank behind.
Even the eyepieces of the mask were blackened so as to
withstand the flash of the famous SAS stun grenade. As
well, he was sporting a Kevlar vest in black, a black
Browning high-power thirteen Parabellum shot pistol, and
his stockless Heckler & Koch MP5K belt kit of pouches
holding extra magazines, stun and smoke grenades. Now he
pulled on his Danner boots. He was pulling on his black
leather gloves and checking to make sure his upside-down
knife in its sheath was hanging properly from its tether in
the middle of his vest.

"At-ten-*hun*!" Brentwood said, and Freeman, with
Norton following, entered the hangar. There was a special
respect that the SAS/D men had for Freeman. No matter
what Washington said, he was a hands-on, at-the-front commander, and they knew that if he had his way he would
have been leading the attack on the ICBM site. But the fact
was that he somehow had to stabilize the military situation
on his fast-disintegrating front east of Orgon Tal.

"Wish I could come along with you boys," Freeman said,
and they knew he was telling the truth. Choir had told the
youngest of the commandos how Freeman had led the night
raid on Pyongyang in North Korea and on Ratmanov Island. "That was a party, that was," Choir said. Ratmanov
Island was now part of the Freeman legend—how he'd led
his men on the drop over the barren wastes of the Bering
Strait and fought the special CIS Spetsnaz troops to a standstill in the tunnels.

"He likes tunnels," another paratrooper said as they
waited for Freeman to reach the impromptu dais made up
of a wooden loading pallet.

"You think there'll be tunnels on this one?" a trooper
asked.

"Oh no," Salvini answered. "Don't think so. What would

they be doing with tunnels? Nah, they can just disappear whenever they want. They make themselves invisible, see, and walk straight through the fucking mountain."

"Hey—no need for the fucking sarcasm."

"Gentlemen!" It was Freeman, putting on his reading glasses and pulling out an extension pointer that, recessed, looked like a .45 bullet casing. ". . . your attention."

Salvini checked the magazine release catch on his HK MP5 and looked at the seven-by-four-foot stand map Freeman was pointing to. The general placed the pointer on central Tibet then let it slide to latitude 30.4 north and longitude 90.62 east near Mount Nyainqemtanglha Feng. Immediately to the south of Lake Nam there was a fifty-mile-long east-west range of mountains twenty thousand feet high running parallel with the lake, a small town called Damquka on the other side of the mountains on the China-Lhasa road. The whole map shuddered and dust spilled from the prefab hangar as more heavy Chinese artillery or a warhead from one of the ICBMs exploded in the distance around the Orgon Tal railhead. ". . . Between this part of the mountain range that runs southwest to northeast," Freeman continued, "is a narrow slope that is the land between the mountain range and the lake. The lake is fed by streams from the mountain range, hereafter referred to as the Nyain Range. What we have to do is come down in the valley and head along the base of the mountain until we find the launch site. Once the big door opens, we go in."

"Sir," Aussie called out. "Have they got any ground sensors? If so, they'll hear us coming for miles."

Brentwood was glad Aussie asked the question. It was at least getting his mind off Alexsandra.

Freeman shook his head. "Don't worry about it, Lewis.

Only sensors they have up in there in that godforsaken place are a yak or two." There was laughter.

"What we depend on, men," Freeman said, "is surprise and speed. We'll be in and out before they can get any PLA to us."

"Why isn't their PLA camp near the ICBM site, General?" another trooper asked.

"They're not stupid," Freeman answered, "that's why. That'd be a dead giveaway to SATRECON. No, the nearest PLA camp is at Damquka—on the other side of the mountain range. Away from the site but close enough to help with helo gunships. But remember this—it will take them time to realize what's going on and to send troops over in choppers. That's twenty thousand feet of mountain they have there, and choppers will have to weave their way carefully through any of the passes, particularly if there's any overcast. Anyway, the PLA site is over there not so much a guard for the ICBM site, which we weren't supposed to know about, but rather to keep an eye on the Tibetans along the Lhasa Road. PLA are always hurrying them on through the valley—don't want them messing around or camping too near the lake and seeing a missile launch. Besides, Beijing has an obsession about Tibet. It wants enough troops in there just to show them who's boss."

"Minor question, General." It was from Aussie. It was a measure of the standing of the elite SAS/D corps that a man from the ranks could address the general in such an informal tone.

"What is it, Lewis?"

"Suppose we bring it off. How are we going to get out?"

"Trust the Aussie," Freeman said. "Worried about getting home." There was a general smattering of laughter. "You making book on this, Lewis, or you got some young filly you're keen to get back to?"

There was an awkward silence, but Freeman, with all the cares of command, could hardly be expected to know how Lewis had fallen head over heels for Alexsandra Malof. Even so, Freeman, with that sixth sense of command, knew he'd made some kind of blooper. Salvini intervened diplomatically. "He's making book on it, General—as usual."

The polite laughter among the old SAS/D troopers—about forty out of the eighty—eased the tension, and Norton was speaking softly to Freeman about Alexsandra Malof. Freeman nodded. "Good question, Aussie. How do we get out? The answer is by chopper. We can get MH-53J Paves with drop tanks and in-air refueling."

"How about triple A fire, sir?" David Brentwood asked.

"Let's look at the map," Freeman said. "Now, left to right—southwest to northeast—we have eighty miles of mountain wall. We're talking here about peaks of twenty thousand feet plus." There were a few low whistles. "Now the space—the valley between this line of mountains and the lake just to the north running parallel to them—varies between five and seven miles wide with a lot of short, fast-flowing rivers coming down from the mountains into the lake.

"The lake is salty, by the way, and it's already four thousand meters high, so some of you might need oxygen from your tanks during the attack.

"Another thing—the bases of these mountains, as you can see, are splayed out like so many long, bony chicken feet reaching down toward the lake. SATRECON tells us that all of the AA is between two of these fingers—that is, around the ICBM site. Once we finish and get back out from between those two fingers and behind another one just next to it, their AA will be useless. It can't fire around corners.

"Also, I want you men to know I wouldn't have asked

you to do this if there were any other way, but remember that after all the hoopla during the Iraqi war we learned that over 70 percent of all bombs dropped on Iraq failed to hit their target. And that, gentlemen, was in a desert, not in a chain of mountains like the Himalayas. We've got no other way of doing it. You have to go in there and take it out. You'll be given fighter escort and support as far as weather allows. Triple A boys want to compete, then our boys' 30mm cannon and ATG missiles can deal with them. Your job will be to get to that door—blow it open and make one godawful mess of that place. If you hit the large fuel tanks—also under cover inside the site because we can't see any of them outside—you won't have to worry about anything else. That'll do the job."

"And how about us, sir?" a recently graduated recruit ventured.

"You run, you silly bastard!" Aussie said.

There was raucous laughter that brought a smile to Freeman's face. He couldn't ask for better morale. The ability of the Australian to spring back from his low mood about his woman and to get his mind back on the task ahead was just the kind of quality he, Freeman, expected in the SAS/D, and they had never disappointed him.

"Very well, gentlemen. Godspeed and good luck."

CHAPTER TWELVE

ONE HUNDRED MILES off the mainland, Admiral Lin Kuang waited with his Taiwanese fleet, not only because the last of the typhoon had yet to pass through the strait but because he knew that as long as the Tibetan ICBM site was intact, any attack by him against the mainland would result in his fleet being rained upon by the conventional warheads of the ICBMs. On one hand he felt that he was letting his allies, the Americans, down, for what they needed now was an attack on China's southern provinces by Kuang to draw divisions away from Cheng's offensive against the trace. And the admiral, or rather his envoys, had promised Freeman support. But it was a matter of timing. There was no point in risking the fleet now until Freeman's forces had silenced the hidden launch site in Tibet. And if Freeman's men failed, then what use would the fleet be?

He asked for SITREPs from his agents in Beijing and was told that despite the martial law imposed there, people seemed generally well behaved. But how much this good behavior was merely for show and not real could not be easily ascertained. The admiral knew that his mainland brothers and sisters had had long training in self-discipline and in parroting the official party line if they knew what was good for them. Many of the older ones had passed through the "Cultural Revolution," an orgy of spite, envy, and hatred that swept the land like locusts, and attacked religious shrines and, among millions of others, had victimized and killed those who dared make the slightest protest against Mao's line.

The other reason, the agents suspected, for the acquiescence of the population, not only in Beijing but even as far north as Harbin, was the ruthless efficiency of Chairman Nie's Public Security Bureau. But Admiral Kuang knew if all the secret dissidents managed to come together simultaneously, and then were given some real encouragement, they would pose a considerable problem for the authorities in Beijing. But now—following the calamitous typhoon—a spirit of cooperation was alive and well as people began helping one another rebuild some of the worst-hit areas. It was for this reason Freeman had warned his air force not to bomb Beijing or any Chinese city for that matter. He knew that with high-explosive bombs ripping the earth up all around you, you do not care who is dropping the bombs, only that whoever is doing it is your enemy.

Such cooperation between workers and students, however, worried Nie, who hadn't rested easily since Tiananmen Square on the night of June 3, 1989. What had worried him and the "old men" running the party was that for the first time in a long while workers had marched with, and not against, the students. And it was workers in the main, not students, who had killed the trapped members of the PLA. Thus a prime aim of Nie's internal policy was to drive a wedge between the students and workers, to spread lies and set one against the other. If only he could make the Malof woman publicly confess her crimes as a foreign agent provocateur, then her role as a rallying point for the dissidents, be they workers or students, would vanish. For Nie it would be a major victory. He would feed her well and have the experts from the Beijing film studios make her up as if no pressure had been applied—*if* she cooperated.

As he walked, hand behind his back, past the solitary cells, his eyes began to water from the astringent odor of urine and feces. When the guard opened number seventeen cell, the light barely penetrated from the few small holes in the brick high on the stone wall. Immediately, Nie struck a match and lit his American cigarette to try to smother the stench.

Alexsandra had never smoked—she had neither the desire nor the money when she worked as a waitress in the Jewish autonomous region—but right now she craved a cigarette—to taste something, anything other than the fetid vegetable slop she was given once a day and the polluted water from the rusted-out plumbing of the prison that officially had been slated for demolition ten years ago. Her legs were bloody, as female prisoners were issued neither tampons nor even the large sanitary napkins available to the better-behaved prisoners. They had thrown her some rags, and now in the corner she held her legs tightly against her, yet her eyes were as defiant as those of a trapped animal.

"It is your wish to live like this?" Nie said very formally, blowing out a long trail of smoke, its dark and pale blues streaming in strange currents about the cell. He heard her breathe in the smoke and savor the alternate odor.

"Would you like a cigarette?" Nie asked. "And good food, eh? This would be nice."

She told him he was a turtle and that all his forebears had been turtles. Nie was so incensed by the insult he threw down the cigarette on the cold wet flagstone of the cell, stamped it out, and yelled, "You will not have this cigarette or another. You will not have—things to keep your wretched body clean. Or fresh water until you confess. I—I could beat you!"

"Then beat me!" This was a brave but foolish thing for Alexsandra to say, for her having challenged Nie in front of the guard meant that Nie must now follow through with his threat or lose face.

"Beat her!" he ordered the guard. "Do what you like with her." But the guard was no fool, which is why he had been put in charge of looking after such an important political criminal. The guard understood that what Chairman Nie meant was, beat her by all means but not about the face or forearms or anywhere else where, during the trial that would follow her public confession, bruises could be seen by the cameras. That she would yield, the guard had no doubt. As the echo of Nie's footsteps faded, Alexsandra turned her face to the wall. She wanted to cry, but tears would not come—it was beyond that.

The guard returned—a tall man for a Chinese—and he brought her a whole packet of tampons and a bucket of fresh water. "Clean yourself. You look disgusting." She grabbed the tampons, clutching them to her. *"Gundan!"* —Go away!—she ordered.

"Ha!" he laughed. "Ha!" But her tone had had the desired effect. "I'm going now," he said, looking down at her, and then with a most childish gesture he wiggled a finger at her. "But I'll be back!" And with that he used his other hand to massage his groin. "Okay?"

She raised her head from the bucket, which she had leaned upon with one arm, using the other to sweep her long hair away from her face. She thanked God she still had her hair, because she knew that as long as they left her hair alone she would be alive. They daren't have her with a shaven head in a show trial, for it would tell the gallery how far they had humiliated her before bringing her to trial.

"Is that," she began, looking at the guard's obscene gestures, "what Comrade Mao taught you to do to women?"

"Ha, ha!" the guard said, in a forced tone of *fuck you,* adding, *"Comrade Mao is dead."*

"His sayings also?" Alexsandra pressed gamely. "Are they dead, too?"

"Ha, ha!" he said, and was gone. If he came back to rape her, she knew he would bring others. That last "ha ha" about Chairman Mao's sayings would need some strength through numbers to overcome any scruples he might otherwise have. The fools—did they really think raping her would make her confess? She had been raped before in the jails at Lake Baikal and in Harbin. She had almost starved to death, too, but had survived by going through her feces to extract the undigested pieces of corn. Who did they think she was? See how the bully of a guard was shamed into leaving a moment ago? In any case she knew he would not assault her while she was still bleeding. He meant later, after her period had passed.

Within an hour of Freeman's speaking to his eighty SAS/D troops, the long-haul C-130H-30 Hercules was roaring down Orgon Tal's marsden matting runway, the plane's four four-and-a-half-thousand-horsepower Allison 501 turboprops nearing full throttle, its crew of four strapped in for takeoff. The eighty SAS/D troopers, forty to a side, sat facing one another, each man thinking about the mission, about whether or not he would get it, or the man opposite him, or perhaps most of them would get out, perhaps all of them would get out. Sure. They were all experienced in high-altitude drops, but never over such terrain as they would be in Tibet in eight hours time, depending on the head winds over Mongolia, the western province of Qinghai, or in Tibet itself. The mission involved many more planes, F-15E Eagles and F-18 Hornets as fighter cover, and a logistics nightmare of carefully coordinated in-flight refueling for the fighters.

CHAPTER THIRTEEN

IN THE IRON Mountain, opposite the Potala Palace, they had the Dutchman, Hartog, under interrogation. They kept asking him why he was in Tibet, and he kept telling them he was interested in holistic medicine, especially in moxabustion, which could warm the affected nerve.

"We have another nerve treatment," the major said. "In order to take away pain from one area of your body, we place the pain elsewhere."

"Sounds interesting," Hartog said.

"Yes," the major said, "but we don't use needles." Hartog said nothing. The major barked out an order, and within the minute a pair of long-nosed pliers was brought in and placed on the bare table beneath the naked bulb.

"Now, Mr. Hartog," the major pressed, "we both know what will happen."

"Do we?"

"Oh yes. You will withstand pain for some minutes, then you will be unconscious. We will repeat the process, and in the end you will give us the names of your Tibetan contacts. Who sent you? The CIA?" The major put his face down so close to Hartog's, the Dutchman could smell it. "Why resist when you know you will tell me the truth sooner or later?"

The major affected disappointment as he told the guards to begin. Two men held Hartog, even though he was tied securely in the chair, and one began pulling out his fingernails, tugging, twisting a little, then tugging some more.

The major said he would be at the Holiday Inn, and left. He was not at all convinced that the Dutchman knew anything. He, the major, had certainly not given any information out about the Lake Nam site, but why then had Hartog sent a fax with what had seemed to the clerk a line or two in it in some kind of code? On the other hand, it could have been nothing. By the time they had pulled out the second fingernail, the Dutchman had fainted, just as the major had predicted. *"Zhaogao!*—Damn it!" the man with the pliers complained. "This is going to be a long night."

"Come on," his comrade said, slapping Hartog's face and pouring cold water on his head. "Wake up, you bastard!" But the Dutchman made no sense, talking as if he were half-drunk, his fingers curled up, paralytic with pain, the slightest breath of air on the red, raw, exposed roots where his nails had been an indescribable agony. In addition he had contracted giardiasis, an intestinal bug that only the drugs Tiniba and Flagyl would remedy and which the Chinese garrison in Iron Mountain either did not have or would not give to him—until he talked. Outside the prison could be heard the baleful howling of packs of wild dogs and the sound of firecrackers being set off, whether to frighten off the curs or for some kind of celebration Hartog had no way of knowing, but dogs howling seemed to him the most terrible and forlorn noise he had ever heard.

* * *

The moon was a huge, golden disk over Inner Mongolia, made so by the dust blown up by the typhoon.

"Bogeys ten o'clock high!" The warning didn't come from any of the fighters riding shotgun for the Hercules but from an E-2C Hawkeye, a hundred yards aft of the main force. As two F-15 Eagles, Angels One and Two, made the first cut hard to the left and right, one of the bogeys, a Fulcrum-29, had already fired a Soviet-made Acrid air-to-air heat seeker, and straightaway the F-15 that the missile was going for started dumping flares out the back.

The action suckered the fourteen-hundred-meters-per-second Soviet-made Acrid infrared or heat seeker. But the other Fulcrum was on Angel Two, firing a radar-seeking missile, and clumps of foil were being jettisoned as the second F-15 made a defensive turn hard left toward the Fulcrum and fired its cannon. The Fulcrum went straight up, and Angel One fired a Sidewinder, saw the Fulcrum tailslide, but it was too late, the missile hitting the Fulcrum's left wing, creating a ball of flame. The second Fulcrum disengaged.

Out of chaff, or foil, to dummy a second radar-seeker missile fired by the second Fulcrum, Angel One released its lure, a small, cable-attached decoy emitting strong false echoes. The Fulcrum's missile made a sharp left and slammed into the decoy in an orange-black ball that roiled and rolled upward into the night.

The Hercules pilots felt well protected but began veering away from their original course deeper into western Mongolian airspace so as not to give away the previous vector, which, because of fuel considerations, they had drawn straight to the target in Tibet—still hours away.

"Bad sign," the copilot said.

"What is?" the pilot asked.

"Well, I mean we're out just over an hour and to get picked up like that."

"Ah, don't sweat it," the pilot replied. "Probably saw us on local radar—had to send up the bogeys to have a look see. Nah, they'll figure we're on a resupply run."

"Where to, Mongolia?"

"You worry too much."

"Yeah, I know."

"Relax. How'd you like to be those poor bastards back there?" He indicated the rear of the plane. "Going for the big bungee jump into the pitch dark. Freeze your balls off for a start."

The copilot said nothing, so the pilot pressed him for morale's sake. "Come on, where would you rather be? Up here with the defrosters going or in the middle of fucking Tibet?"

"Up here," the copilot said.

"All right, then, let's get it done."

They saw two F-15s going up behind the tanker, saw the tanker's "shuttlecock"-tipped refueling boom arcing down, the small pinpoints of light for the final few seconds of the hookup, the lights out, and beyond them the moon so bright it would have given triple A a perfect shot, radar or not.

"Relax," the pilot repeated. "The moon'll be covered by cloud where we're going."

"Then how we gonna see?"

"Why is it that you have no confidence in instrument flying? You're qualified."

"Yeah, sure, but I like to see where I'm dropping my cargo, that's all."

"Relax, Mel. They've been in cloud before. This isn't some weekend sky-jumping gig, you know. These guys *drive* their chutes."

"Yeah?"

"Yeah. SAS and Delta boys can do it in their sleep. Man, you know what kind of training they go through? Tough as fucking nails. Out on their own, days at a time in stinking below-zero weather—can stay concealed in shallow trenches—can even shit and piss in those trenches and not move they're so good at it. You remember the Falklands War?"

"Yeah."

"SAS first in—blew up an Argentinian squadron on the ground. Every one of them can take an eye out of a needle with a submachine gun."

"Yeah, how about the needle? Anything left?"

The pilot pursed his lips and shook his head. "Not much, Mel."

"You stupid bastard," Mel said, grinning, and felt better in the warm near-darkness of the instrument panel. He *was* worrying too much—it'd probably be a milk run.

Thousands of miles away across the Pacific it was early morning, and Rosemary Brentwood was sleeping fitfully, her dreams of childbirth at once reassuring and frightening—reassuring because Andrea Rolston kept looking out with reassuring smiles and holding Rosemary's hand as the contractions increased, and then just as vividly in the dream a terrifying metamorphosis would take place as her kindly face was replaced with the indistinct face of a stranger—a man who did not smile but who pursued her and who seemed Oriental. Always in the background of Rosemary's dream, fading in and out of view but always present, was the man's implacable stare, extending his hand in friendship, only to have him grasp the baby by the throat, at which point, as she did now, Rosemary would sit bolt upright, sweating, immediately feeling her stomach and then suddenly relieved as she felt the baby kicking.

She was a competent teacher, with all the self-confidence that that entailed, but as a mother-to-be she felt entirely inadequate and, without Robert, more alone than she'd ever been. She had the sudden urge to ring Andrea, saw how late it was, and decided instead to make a cup of tea. She thought she heard something moving in the kitchen and froze, and then heard the squeaking of a dolphin paperweight, the white dolphins in the blue sea inside the transparent weight making their crying sounds if the slightest movement vibrated the paperweight. Rosemary had never intended them to be an alarm, but something the baby might like in the crib. Slowly she pulled out the service .45 from the drawer in her bedstead, flicked the safety catch off, as Robert had told her, and called, "Who's there?"

All she could hear was a light breeze that through the trees of the base outside sounded like running water. "I'm armed!" she said, with as much menace as she could muster, which was hardly any at all. Her hands shaking, she thought of telephoning base security, but then whoever was there, if there *was* someone there, would have an advantage, as she knew that having to use one hand for the phone would mean she couldn't hold the .45 still enough.

She heard another rush of wind through the trees, and then the dolphins squeaked again. She approached the hallway leading to the kitchen. It took her a full thirty seconds before, heart pounding and hands trembling, she reached the hallway and immediately saw the push-out window above the sink hadn't been closed to the last notch, and so the window frame was being blown against the ledge above the sink, causing the dolphins to squeal. Still shaking, weak with relief, she returned to the bedroom, put the gun back in the drawer, and went to the kitchen to make tea.

For a moment of ice-chilling fear she suddenly felt she was being watched again, but by whom and from where she didn't know. It was five A.M., and she picked up the phone to dial Andrea, decided it was too early to impose her prenatal jitteriness on her American friend, and instead replaced the phone down in its cradle. "When the wind blows," she remembered, "the cradle will rock."

Turning back toward the kitchen, she gave herself a dressing down. All right, Rosemary, enough of the hysterics please. Get a hold of yourself. Whatever would Robert think. Really—

And the dolphins squeaked again, and it was little wonder, Rosemary thought, with all her walking and bumping around. She'd make herself a nice cup of "char," breathe easily, and wait patiently for the morning. As an extra precaution she walked all about the bungalow to see whether all the locks were on. They were, and she felt safe.

CHAPTER FOURTEEN

IF LENIN'S FAVORITE dictum, that in war quantity has a quality all its own, was to be seen in action it was on the hundred-mile Orgon Tal–Honggor section of the front. Though a straight line could be drawn between them running northeast from Orgon Tal nearly one hundred miles, the actual line with bulges made the front more than 150 miles long, the bulges consisting of four Chinese armies made up of elements of the Sixty-ninth, Sixty-third, and

Twenty-seventh infantry and two armored divisions, consisting not only of infantry and the usual ninety-six tanks per army made up of three tank regiments with thirty-two tanks each, but nine regiments of reserve armor—in all, 2,815 tanks, half of which were T-72 laser-sighted.

With militia included, Cheng had fielded over 153,000 men against two U.S. infantry divisions: 36,100 men plus 732 M1A1 tanks. Both in numbers of men and tanks the Chinese had an advantage of almost four to one against the Americans.

Under cover of the typhoon, Chinese infantry, who, an old wives' tale had it, didn't fight well in the rain—particularly the militia units around Honggor—had made more headway than expected, the blinding dust and then rain degrading the laser sites on the M1s and making it possible for the militia to penetrate here and there to harass the already-overextended American supply line. Had it not been for the typhoon, U.S. TACAIR's A-10 Thunderbolts could have inflicted grievous losses on Cheng's troops, but grounded by the typhoon and with more than seven U.S. airstrips having been mortar bombed from the typhoon-obliterated perimeter, TACAIR was in no shape to render any assistance. The weather then had worked in the Chinese favor, or rather had been used by them as an advantage.

Tanks were often working blind until almost atop one another, with deadly close-order battle meaning that the M1A1's overreach of at least a thousand yards meant little. What caused the most surprise among the Americans was the sheer tenacity and fitness of the PLA infantry. They traveled light compared to the Americans and knew the ground better.

Whatever the reason for their punching gaps through the American line, Freeman knew he would have to stem the flow quickly, not only because he feared pincer movements on his lines of supply north of the Orgon Tal–Honggor line, but that any general Chinese breakthrough might give pause to Admiral Lin and his Formosan forces. If, on the other hand, the Orgon Tal–Honggor line could be held, then the admiral, or rather his superiors, would see the staying power of the American Second Army and attack, making it a two-front war, not including the Lake Nam launch site, which had not let up its pounding deeper into the American sector.

At times, a warhead struck its own troops, but Cheng, with a four-to-one advantage, could afford "blue on blue"— "friendly fire." Besides, he had resources of over half a million he could draw on almost immediately from the south who were being held there only because of the possibility of Taiwan attacking.

Again as on their drive south, Freeman's men found the Chinese method of clearing a mine field insane and devastatingly effective, as one PLA soldier would use the bodies of his fallen comrades as stepping stones through the field until he either made it or was killed himself, in which case he became the next stepping stone. What was holding the Chinese up, however, were those M1s, which, once they ran out of ammunition, got close enough to ram the enemy, the ramming power of an M1 against a T-55 or 72 resulting in a demolition derby in which Chinese welding had much to answer for.

Second, the Americans, taking Freeman's repeated warnings about the truce merely being a resupply device by the Chinese, had dug in as well as any marine had at Khe Sahn in the Vietnam War. And of primary importance in this were the prolific and well-dug American grenade sumps.

Under Freeman's direct orders, all officers and NCOs down to and including section leaders were told that when they dug in they must be sure to dig what was in effect a dry moat about their feet so that the earth they stood on for firing positions was in fact a raised rectangle of earth that sloped away on all sides. It meant that when the Chinese tossed their stick grenades, which, being more offensive than defensive grenades, had more blast than shrapnel, many grenades simply rolled and/or were kicked away down the sloping firing platform into the deep grenade sump trench which contained the explosion. The worst off was any American who was wearing contact lenses, as the flash would throw up fine dirt that would sting and temporarily blind a man in the trench.

Lacking enough mobile artillery to cover such a huge front from Orgon Tal to the Manchurian-Siberian border, Cheng relied heavily on the plentiful supply of grenades for the infantry. The American grenades, however, being primarily defensive, as ordered by Freeman, were made less to stun than to spray dozens of splintered fragments acting like scythes among the Chinese who advanced en masse again against the dug-in Americans. And in more than one foxhole, the steam of urine rising in the typhoon's cold air gave evidence of yet another marine cooling down his machine gun barrel as the Chinese kept coming from Orgon Tal, now designated the "ant heap" by those Americans of the Third Division's Second and Sixth Infantry Battalions who had been stemming Cheng's advance.

Now quantity was starting to tell as the American supply line, severed in more than one place, was unable to keep up with the wastage at the front. Of all that he hated most, Freeman hated giving an order to retreat. But if he was "shot through," as Wolsey said of Thomas More, with pride, he was not profligate with his men, and if he could save one American life he would do so, as Cheng had learned from Freeman's insistence during the truce that the

Chinese hand over a lone SEAL, by the name of Smythe.
Smythe was still being held in Beijing jail as a spy because
he "bore no proper uniform when caught at the Nanking
Bridge," which the SEALs had blown before the truce.

With Freeman's retreat to another line twenty miles to
the northwest, Chinese poured into the gap, but here the
mechanical aspect of the U.S. Army outdistanced the Chinese now overrunning the U.S.'s abandoned positions. The
Americans, as Cheng well knew, loved wheels and would
not go anywhere without transport, reminding Cheng of the
French troops in the counterattack at Verdun in '14 who
were driven out from Paris to the front in thousands of
taxis. But Cheng did not care that so many potential American POWs had escaped. What was important to the Chinese commander was that he had won a decisive battle,
forcing Second Army to yield over two thousand square
miles of territory, even if, as Nie was fond of saying, the
territory was fit only for Gobi Bactrian camels, who, because they were so perfectly camouflaged in the desert, had
been used by the Chinese hauling up tons of supplies to the
front, for even the lightly outfitted Chinese soldier needed
ammunition and rice resupply to press home the fight
against Freeman's "imperialist warmongers."

The news flashing across China and—courtesy of
CNN—across the world was that a great victory by the
People's Liberation Army had been won all along the
Orgon Tal–Honggor line, and the Americans were in full
retreat. In the Mideast, millions took to the streets of Iraq
and Iran to cheer the Chinese victory, and in the United
States, antiwar protests were appearing outside the White
House.

For Freeman, one of the worst blows was the discovery
by the Chinese of dozens of blivets—enormous, water bed–
like containers of fuel—buried at strategic points in the des-

ert in the event of his armor—Bradleys, M1s, and armored personnel carriers—having to fall back. Much of the soil used to hide the blivets had been blown off by the typhoon, revealing bald patches of earth where a section of the blivet was visible.

The Chinese immediately set fire to them so that many of the M1s returning to what they thought was a hidden fuel depot found there raging fires going up in orange-black flames hundreds of feet high. Some of the blivets were used to refuel the PLA's T-62s, and entire blivet dumps were ignited by the warheads from the Tibetan ICBMs. At Honggor, the U.S. Seventh Corps under General Meisen were badly mauled, caught in a Chinese outflanking movement coming up through the dunes, and over three thousand Americans were taken POW.

In the United States, talk of recalling Freeman and suing for a peace treaty was growing louder with each newscast of the withdrawing Americans. Reporters continued to get it wrong, including CNN, by repeatedly referring to army personnel carriers as tanks and creating the impression that U.S. armored losses were catastrophic, whereas the truth was that the M1s had acquitted themselves magnificently, but without gas they were merely heavily armored coffins.

"Goddamn it!" Freeman thundered. "We've got to get back into the fight. How far away from Lake Nam is the SAS/D detachment?"

"A half hour, General," Norton said. "Chinese radar probably has them on screen now—"

"But we've got Wild Weasels running countermeasures, haven't we?" Freeman pressed.

"Yes, sir. Just hope it works."

Over the remote town of Kormeng seventy-five miles northeast of the drop zone, the planes had picked up an active Chinese radar signal, and so the countermeasures began from the Wild Weasels, and the fighter cover began sending out powerful active signals of their own, so powerful that instead of seeing the dot or dots of incoming enemy planes, all the Chinese saw was a wide, incandescent cone that they knew contained American planes but that was so fuzzy and wide that no one plane could be spotted, nor a general bearing ascertained. As well as this jamming of the Chinese signal, two of the F-15Es detected at the widest part of the Chinese signal a side lobe, like the outer rings of a ripple, the fighters producing strong return signals in the lobes that misled the Chinese radars by creating what seemed to be a signal bouncing off the American fighter but was in fact a ghost signal from the side lobe, thus giving a false bearing—a case of the F-15Es using the ChiCom radar against the Chinese.

"Get ready!" the jump master was informing the troops by placing both palms of his hands toward them. David Brentwood and the other seventy-nine SAS/D men rose in two lines of forty each. The jump master had his hands on his chest as if he were holding two suspenders, then the jump master's right arm dropped to a forty-five-degree angle signifying "Stand by door—prepare to jump." The warning light had gone from red to warning yellow.

David Brentwood waddled to the door like a pregnant bear in his antiterrorist hood and his seventy-pound drop bag of equipment. The light went green, and he was gone— into the swirling, icy darkness twenty-five thousand feet up. It was déjà vu. He was over a five-to-eight-mile gap between the twenty-thousand-foot-high mountain range and the vast salt lake somewhere off on his right, but he was also back over Ratmanov Island, the clouds whistling past in various shadows through his infrared goggles, their cold wetness and insubstantial forms wrapping around him like wet cloth so that soon he felt everything had frozen solid, barely hearing the quickness of his breathing, like a trapped animal, as he pulled the rip cord, felt the sudden jerk, the uprising, the descent again, and the punch in his stomach that he and every other man on the mission felt as they tumbled into the howling vortex of screaming wind and felt the concussion of heavy AA exploding. But by then the Hercules had already turned with its fighter escort, and the troopers were parachuting, or rather gliding and steering their way down in the night.

Aussie Lewis lowered the right toggle of his chute, pulling the right side of the arcing, rectangular chute down in the rear and so in effect braking it as it turned right. Then, in a clear, moon-flooded sky between stratus clouds at eighteen thousand, he pulled the right toggle down to his waist level, putting himself in the tightest possible spiral turn, which was pulling him away from the lake, a vast, polished blackness far down on his right, hoping that he was moving more toward the base of the mountain range on his left, but not too far, otherwise he would be on the side of a mountain.

No one could know if any of the eighty troopers were lost until they reached earth and could use their beeper transmitter and hand-held Magellan 3 GPS—geosynchronous positioning system—accurate in placing a man's position with a maximum error of ten feet.

As Aussie descended he heard his heavy breathing like a pilot pulling four Gs over the banshee howling of the high Tibetan wind. Each man carried four hours of oxygen for both the oxygen-starved jump and the fact that Lake Nam was three thousand feet higher than Lhasa, and even in Lhasa there was often oxygen starvation bad enough to produce both benign and malignant AMS, or altitude sickness. It could start with headache, unusual behavior, dizziness, nausea, and vomiting, the malignant form ending in coma and death. Even the Acetazolamide 250mg tablets every eight hours, which the SAS troopers had with them, were only marginally useful in reducing the headache, but for the more serious cases of AMS, the patient, failing to get enough oxygen, would breathe faster and the blood would thicken. Needing six liters of oxygen a minute, the SAS drop packs on the end of their twelve-foot tether line carried two additional small high-pressure O_2 tanks.

Triple A was now coming in *their* direction, now that the planes were gone, enough metal about the paratroopers to give off faint radar echoes.

Glancing at his wrist altimeter in the fleeting moonlight, Aussie, through the infrared goggles, saw that he was at six thousand feet. He wouldn't put down his tether line and pack until he was three hundred feet above the ground. At the moment, his "infrareds" revealed nothing in the swirling grayness beneath him, only the odd streak of tracer more than a mile away. Then suddenly the sky seemed to explode, filling with a volcanic roar and a pulsating whitish gray in the infrared goggles—in reality a crimson-orange glow that streaked heavenward, a DSS-5.

Those lower than Aussie, having been dragged down faster than they would have liked by wind shear, got a good infrared fix on the missile's plume, and had its point of liftoff cross-referenced to a position plus or minus a mile. It was the height of Chinese contempt for the enemy. Knowing it was unable to be bombed, so confident in the impregnability of their mountain redoubt, the Chinese had simply dismissed the appearance of paratroopers on the screen as yet another futile Allied attempt, and had rolled out the rail car base platform to fire off yet another missile that would strike Second Army over two thousand miles away.

* * *

As their packs hit the soft snow and the chutes collapsed, the commandos were already extracting their weapons, and section leaders were taking stock of how many had landed. In all, seven were unaccounted for: three, including Aussie, from Aussie Lewis's troop of twenty, and four from Salvini's troop. They all knew the rule: no one would wait for the seven, but all would proceed as quickly as possible to the target area. No one man or small group of men could delay the attack, because for every multiwarheaded missile fired, the equivalent of ten enemy missiles being launched at once, more Americans would die.

"Just my friggin' luck!" Aussie said as he hauled in the chute, quickly rolling it up and burying it in the snow. From the plume of the missile he had reckoned he'd been "sheared" two miles northwest of the missile site, two high ridges between him and the site, the ridges forming part of the mountain range's foothills.

He clipped a banana-shaped magazine of thirty 9mm Parabellum cartridges into the 12.8-inch-long Heckler & Koch MP5K, set it for three-round bursts, and then, putting on his winter-white–sheathed pack, he began heading southeast toward the missile site. Clouds of wind-whipped snow streamed off the ridges, creating whiteouts.

After walking for about five minutes, Aussie paused and knelt to tighten the white overlay hood that fitted snugly over his National Plastics ballistic composite helmet and to pull down on the Velcro tab of the Kevlar vest's groin panel. As he got up he saw the imprint of a boot. He couldn't tell whether it was a Vibram sole or a Chinese imprint because of the powder-drift snow that had all but filled in the indentation.

Pulling down his infrared goggles, he began following the tracks, which he could tell belonged to only one man and not a patrol. But he could be in between a patrol's forward scout and the rest of the patrol, and so he made sure to walk in the tracks so as not to alert any patrol further back to his presence. He was struck by the coincidence that whoever he was following must be about the same build as he was—the footprints remarkably similar to his—until he consulted his wrist compass and discovered that in the whiteouts he'd gone full circle, had in fact been tracking *himself* for the last five minutes. "You fucking zombie!" he told himself, chagrined at the ribbing he would take if any of the SAS/D comrades ever found out.

The bullet that hit him threw him back six feet into the snow, the impact of the 7.6 round ripping open his snow-white camouflage overall but absorbed by the plasticine layers of the vest. Within a second of hitting the snow he had the HK on fully automatic and got off a spray, hearing several of the bullets striking hard rock beneath the flecks of snow.

He rolled fast left—could see a blob—and let the HK have its head. The blob shivered into a blur and fell on the snow. Clipping in another mag, he ran to the right of the body now lying about forty feet from him. As he got near he could smell human excrement and turned the man, who was dressed in Mao padded winter issue. There was a bloody hole where his chest used to be, and Aussie guessed he was the point man for a ChiCom patrol. The others couldn't be far away, coming up behind him from the direction of the missile site. He and they might be less than a hundred feet apart, hidden from one another's view by the whiteouts.

The thing that infuriated the Australian was that here he was, slated to lead his troop into the main attack, and instead he had landed nowhere near them and run into a patrol to boot.

The best he figured he could do was take off his helmet,

don the earflap Mao headpiece the ChiCom was wearing, and put his helmet on the dead ChiCom. After this he put the empty mag back into the HK and took the AK-47. Lewis then put his HK in the man's right hand and put an HE grenade under the man's right thigh, pulled the pin—the ChiCom's weight holding down the spring clip—and moved off to the left of the man's trail behind several snow-capped forty-four-gallon-size drums and waited with the AK-47.

Within a minute he could hear the tired shuffle of boots through the snow. They weren't lifting their feet up and placing them down "smartly!" as the SAS sar'major would say. No, they were obviously regular army troops out patrolling the godforsaken perimeter of the site, probably convinced—until they'd heard the exchange between the HK and AK-47—that they were thankfully out of the fighting that they could now hear two miles back over the two snow-covered, treeless ridges.

The moment they saw the body, covered in its winter overwhites as they were, its head covered by an Allied special-forces helmet, a Heckler & Koch SMG by his side, there was a celebratory call for their forward scout.

"The HK is mine," one of the Chinese claimed, and as the others fanned out slightly, still calling for their point man, one of them put his foot under what he believed was the dead American's torso. He glimpsed the grenade and the snow-covered face and turned to run. It was too late. The grenade exploded, killing him instantly. But Lewis wasn't watching him.

Instead he had already thrown two other grenades, and as they detonated in flashes of brilliant purple, cutting down the tail end Charlie and the two men nearest him, Lewis moved the AK-47 to the remaining two, who were running for cover, one tripping in the snow, his partner brought

down by a single shot from Lewis sixty feet behind him.
There was a click from the Kalashnikov. Without hesitation
Aussie Lewis drew his thirteen-shot Browning .45 and
started running, unclipping a flash-bang stun grenade now
his HEs were spent.

The man who fell never got up as Lewis fired two shots
on the run from his Browning automatic. The last man
swung around, out of breath. He looked like a polar bear
enraged but at a distinct disadvantage. He was up against
one of the SAS who had spent hundreds of hours in calm
to gale-force winds pursuing one another across the wild
moors and in the Black Mountains on the Welsh border. If
you weren't fit enough to run miles at a time and fire accurately on the run then you failed the course. The last
ChiCom sprayed left to right with his AK-47. Lewis hit the
snow, used both hands to fire, and hit the ChiCom, and in
his mind's eye saw the mustachioed SAS regiment's sergeant major berating him, bellowing, "You bloody wastrel,
Lewis. Queen pays for your board and keep and you go
wasting bullets. Pull yourself together, man. One target, one
shot!"

Lewis was too busy to celebrate his one-man ambuscade.
Picking up his HK and helmet, he only hoped that he
wasn't missing out on the action at the missile base, and
then there was the small matter of "extraction"—getting out
via the Pave Low choppers after the raid.

He began a steady, loping, long-distance run toward the
two ridges, fervently hoping that all the troopers who'd
made it near the target were as lucky as he had been.

They weren't.

The mountain cave that had been selected by the Chinese
for expansion into a bomb-proof shelter for the launching
of its ICBMs was at the bottom of a north-south V that was

formed by two enormous toes or foothills coming out of the twenty-thousand-foot mountain range opposite Lake Nam.

Back-checking on the Pentagon computers had ascertained that it had been the site some years earlier of a Chinese underground atomic test for which, taking advantage of a natural fissure in the rock, had been excavated a hole a mile into the base of the mountain range. A hundred-ton rolled steel door on left-to-right slider rails blocked the entrance of the cave and was opened only long enough for the rail-mounted missile-firing rig to be wheeled out, or rather shunted out, by two locomotives, just long enough for the launch. It was this out-in launch procedure that had given birth to "Cuckoo Clock," Freeman's code name for the attack on the Chinese ICBM site.

"Jesus," one of the men in Salvini's team said, "we're the ones that are cuckoo." He was looking through Salvini's infrared binoculars, and the door, even half a mile away, did indeed look impregnable. But that would only be the start of it. If they could blow it, they would still have to go inside and wreak such damage on the site that it would be permanently out of action.

The Second Artillery—Chinese nuclear arm—was renamed the "Strategic Rocket Troops" in 1984, but many of the older commanders like General Wei still knew it as the Second Artillery and referred to it as such in their communiqués.

To protect the massive cave site, Wei had two hundred specially trained mountain troops from the Damquka base from the other side of the mountain range, and upon one of their patrols' report that at least fifty, possibly a hundred, enemy paratroopers had landed, Wei sent a hundred of his mountain troops out to deal with them, leaving a hundred in reserve inside the cave.

Wei knew that an attacker needed at least a three-to-one advantage if he hoped to make any headway at all, and even at that it would be tough going. Besides, his mountain troops and his one-hundred-man company of regular troops were already acclimatized, anyone who had suffered from altitude sickness having been weeded out and returned to the lower-altitude regiments. Wei expected his men to make short work of the enemy paratroopers, who had no support akin to that of his own troops.

Despite the multilayered nature of their uniforms, from polypropylene underwear, quilted polyester pants and jacket to the white Gore Tex camouflage hooded parka and pants over their black antiterrorist uniforms, the SAS troopers moved easily in the snow, and in the starlight-activated binoculars, David Brentwood could see the huge, one-hundred-ton door now one mile away. Then through the infrared binoculars he could see two streams of heat waves shimmering like a summer mirage as two lines of PLA soldiers, only their body heat visible, exited somewhere beneath a high mantle of snow well above and back from the door.

It meant that there must be exits atop the complex, for at least twenty, maybe twenty-five, came out each side, quickly disappearing into a jumble of snow-covered rocks and boulders that trailed off either side of the solid steel door that now glistened in the starlight goggles as a green sheen, covered in a sheath of solid ice in the minus-thirty-degree weather.

With radio silence a must, a runner from Salvini's troop, another from Aussie's, and the last from Choir Williams's troop, gathered around David Brentwood, who could now see that the originally envisaged plan of attack to blow out the huge reinforced steel door was impractical as well as foolhardy, given the sudden appearance of about fifty enemy troops, and these were only the ones they'd seen exiting through what must have been holes bored through the solid granite roof, exits that not even the Stealth bombs could penetrate.

Brentwood checked his Heckler & Koch and told the runners that a frontal assault on the door was pointless. "The best way in is where they came out. Whoever's in charge in there must be a rocket man—he sure as hell isn't an infantry commander. Shouldn't have deployed his force so quickly—now he's given away two exit-cum-entrances, one high left of the door and back, ditto for the right side. Now I want my troop and Aussie's to take the left flank, Choir Williams and Salvini—" There was a whistling through the air. They all hit the deck and felt the crunch of a heavy 81mm mortar exploding about a hundred yards off, sending up a white spume of snow and ice rising high in the air, a sign of just how deep the snow and ice layer was. It immediately told Brentwood that neither side would be digging in unless they had a front-end loader, and so it would have to be a bounding "overwatch" advance, using the snow- and ice-crusted rocks that had been used to excavate space for the door as cover and that now lay about the cave entrance as massive boulder debris.

Aussie Lewis had reached the top of the first ridge, which was about a hundred and fifty feet high. Despite the absorbency of the Gore Tex overlay, he was sweating profusely and knew he couldn't afford to pause for long lest the perspiration quickly turn to ice in the minus-twenty-to-minus-thirty-degree weather. He checked his HK. It was a beautiful submachine gun, its constituent parts engineered and turned by the best German industry had to offer. However, like so many precision instruments, if one section was even slightly out of kilter the whole was endangered. But all felt well as he moved from the three-round-burst position to full automatic.

There was now about a mile to go—down the side of the ridge onto the summit of the next—and then below him he should see the missile site—if his boys hadn't already penetrated it.

At the top of the next ridge, its summit more acutely angled than the last and subsequently much icier, he could see nothing but fog, creating a complete whiteout. Then for a few seconds it lifted, and he glimpsed a parachute flare, its stuttering light revealing what seemed to be a massive sheet of ice, like a frozen waterfall, about a mile away, and infrared hot spots bleeding from atop it on either side. He guessed it must be exits above the door, but in the dying light of the flare the sheen of ice took on a darker sheen like black ice, and he couldn't be sure it was the door. Now everything was black again, and the wetness of the fog clung about him like a heavy web. He heard a noise—a tumble of snow—and froze, sensing someone was moving toward him but unsure from which direction he was coming. He readied for a full 360-degree swivel. Then he heard a voice that told him whoever it was must have a bead on him. The voice came again. "Who goes there?"

He was so relieved he let his HK go loose for a moment as he said, "Princess Di goes here!" and suddenly realized it could be an English-speaking ChiCom. The HK came up again.

"Son of a bitch! It's Aussie!"

It was one—no, two Americans, both lost souls from Salvini's troop who, like Aussie, had been blown off course. When they emerged close enough for him to see, he recognized one but not the other.

"Was it you doin' all that shooting back there?"

"Yes," Aussie said. "Ran into a ChiCom patrol!"

"You outflank 'em?"

"Outflank, fuck. They sleep with the fishes!"

"What fucking fishes?" the younger of the two whispered.

"Fishes in the fuckin' lake," Aussie replied.

"How many?" said the older one, the man Aussie had recognized.

"Seven of 'em."

"Seven? Shit—you get the Kewpie doll?"

"What's a Kewpie doll?" the younger trooper asked.

"Jesus Christ, Morely. Where you been?"

"All right," Aussie said. "Let's cut the social chitchat, boys. Nice fast run down to the main show. Watch out for loose boulders. If I remember correctly there was a lot of debris indicated on the SATRECON shots—when they blew out that great bloody hole for the missile site. Friggin' mountain blew out toward the lake, making a kind of boulder-strewn valley between."

As they started off, Lewis leading, ready for a 180-degree arc, the second man, Hogan, pointing his weapon left, young Morely with his weapon pointing right but ready for a full rear traverse, Morely whispered to Hogan, "What's a Kewpie doll?"

"Be quiet!" ordered Aussie, who knew that as they approached the drop zone they'd have to be careful not to spook anyone. He was also figuring out the best way to go at what he was sure was the door. But first he'd have to confirm that it *was* the door with Brentwood, Choir, and Salvini.

"Aussie?" a voice came in the darkness.

The three of them stopped, Hogan almost hitting the Australian's backpack.

"Yeah?" Aussie answered.

"Over here, sir. Captain Brentwood wants to see you."

"Right," Aussie said. "I want to see him. Where's Choir and Salvini?"

"Down there," the trooper said. "We're all down there—'cept for you guys and I think four more."

"Yeah," Aussie said, "well we got 'sheared' off, didn't we?"

The trooper sensed the Australian's annoyance. Morely whispered to Hogan, "You asshole—no such thing as a fuckin' Kewpie doll."

"Fuckin' *is*."

"Take me to your leader," Aussie commanded the trooper from Brentwood's group. "I've just had a bloody brain wave!"

"All right," Brentwood said, after hearing Aussie out, "but we'll still have to prepare for overwatch."

"No sweat," Aussie said.

Now the Chinese had four more mortars on the go, but from a mile away—trying to zero in for a kill zone on the mile-wide stretch of snow-covered boulders and ice that separated the SAS/D troopers from the launch site.

"All right," Brentwood said. "My troop and Aussie's will go first." He turned to the other runners. "You tell Salvini and Choir Williams to cover us. When we're settled we'll give you a green flare, then you move to the next overwatch position and we'll give you cover and so on until we can get as close as we can. Keep going as long as you get green flares from me. One red flare and we stop everything."

"So when we get near the door," a trooper said, "instead of going for it we go for the exits, right?"

"Right!" Aussie cut in. "The exits—that's our ticket." It was then that Brentwood heard through the darkness the distinctive unoiled squeak that was either a bicycle or a fifty-ton tank.

The new boys, about six of them, in Aussie's seventeen-man force, looked at one another and tried to smile. Aussie Lewis had commanded them to smile whenever they saw a tank—said that it helped overcome the natural terror of seeing the monster bearing down on you and made you remember that if you did it right, if you kept your nerve, one man could kill a tank.

"T-59 probably," Aussie said. "Fucking tin can. We'll take care of the bastard."

The mortar attack had eased off—the ChiComs had either found the killing zone they'd zero in on should the SAS/D attack, or they might have wanted to avoid hitting Chinese infantry that might now be halfway across the two-mile-wide, boulder-strewn gap between the lakeside and the mountain fastness towering in front of them.

"Arpac!" Aussie called out. He was calling for the disposable French antitank missile and launcher. The launcher was small—forty centimeters long with a bore less than three inches wide and weighing just over three pounds with a range of one hundred yards, so small in fact that an old SAS joke was that if you weren't careful you'd lose it in your pocket.

Once the trooper with an Arpac came up, Aussie told him, "We'll have to get a lot closer, mate. But just be ready. If we advance quietly and fast enough and nobody shows their noggin, the Chows won't see—"

They all heard the crack of the hundred-millimeter cannon.

"Down!" Aussie yelled as an HE shell slammed into a boulder fifty yards behind him.

"Shit!" one of the troopers said. "Bastards must be on infrared."

"Okay," Aussie said calmly, "let's draw 'em out a bit. He's at the maximum of his range now."

"Christ, Aussie, we can't draw 'em out much further. How far back can we go?"

"To the fuckin' lake if necessary."

Now they could see another two tanks joining the one that had just fired. "They can't climb boulders, son," Aussie assured the SAS man with the Arpac. "They're going to have to come closer if they want us."

It was a stalemate—the SAS/D could go forward with its leapfrogging or bounding overwatch advance, but the ChiComs' three cannon and six machine guns—three coaxial with the cannon—formed a formidable barrier unless the SAS could get closer, which meant dodging behind boulders and emitting infrared signatures that meant you might as well wave "a bloody flag," as Aussie told it, and yell out, "Here I am!"

Some of the younger Turks in the four troops were sorely disappointed. Nearly all the training they'd done was for hit fast, hit hard operations: rappel down the side of a building, stun grenade through a window, take out terrorists, clear the room. Quick, fast, furious, and efficient.

"What the hell are we sittin' on our butts for?" one said.

"You want to die?" Salvini said. "Then just stick up your head and that T-59 will oblige."

"Where the hell's all the infantry we saw piling out?" another asked.

"Doing what we're doing, sport," Salvini answered, "keeping behind cover, and when they do move, staying right behind the tanks. Where would you fuckin' be? Want to try to rush 'em? SAS/D 'who dares wins'—is that it?"

"Well it's better than 'he who sits, shits.'"

"All right, Joe, when we move in," Salvini said, "you can lead. Right?"

"Right!"

"Okay?"

"Okay!"

"You want it like the movies," Salvini said.

"I want to do something, not just stay out of range and freeze my nuts off."

Salvini gave him a wicked grin. "Oh, don't worry, sport. You'll get your chance. You can be tunneler one."

"What?" There was a chattering of 7.62mm opening up again and long, orange flashes of tracer in the blackness.

"You can be tunneler one."

"We goin' down a fuckin' tunnel?"

"No, you asshole. We're going *into* one, and you can lead the way. Attach the infrared goggles and take us in."

"Where?"

"The mountain, for Chrissake."

"When?"

"When Aussie's got it figured out, that's when."

"He's not figurin' anything out. He's still yakking up there with Brentwood. Think they should have planned better right from the start."

"Oh, spare me," Salvini said, getting mad. He didn't mind the open give and take that NCOs, officers, and privates had among one another—it was the same in most elite units where mutual respect was earned in the tough, gut-wrenching, mind-building training, but it was still a team effort, and this kid *was* opening his yap once too often. He was from Brooklyn, like Salvini.

"We didn't have all the info, did we?" he put it to young Brooklyn. "If we'd been told exactly what to expect, exactly what was here, we could have planned it better. We didn't know. You never know the whole story so welcome to the fucking war."

Aussie, Brentwood, and Choir knew as well as Salvini that they were in a stalemate situation. "Both looking down one another's throats," Salvini explained.

"You think," another trooper asked, a black Kentuckian, "they'll be firing another rocket soon?"

"Aha!" Salvini said. "Give the man a cigar. That's the sixty-four-thousand-dollar question, buddy. Longer we hold them up, more time our boys back along the DMZ will have without being dumped on every half hour."

"Well, hell," young Brooklyn said, "we're not gonna stop 'em sittin' here, are we?"

"Maybe you're right," Salvini said.

"Well, Jesus, man, we oughta just break radio silence—pull out the four phone, spring open the satellite aerial, and call for pickup."

"Where would you suggest?" Salvini asked.

Young Brooklyn looked hard at Salvini. Was the troop leader taking the piss out of him or what? He seemed serious, so young Brooklyn said, "Down by the lake'd be the best place to get us out."

"I agree," Salvini said.

"You want me to make the call?" young Brooklyn pressed.

Salvini smiled. "You do and I'll blow your fuckin' head off."

A trooper from further down the line walked in, crouched down behind the row of boulders, and hissed, "Can anyone tell us what the fuck we're doing?"

"We're waiting to see if they'll fire off another rocket," Salvini said.

"What if they don't?"

"Then we've done our job."

"All right—what if they fucking do?"

"Ah," Salvini said, "now that'd be different."

Over in Choir Williams's troop, made up of most of the Delta contingent of the SAS/D force, Choir was quietly humming the stirring "Men of Harlech." Gwyn Jones joined in, and a cockney from Kilburn said it was nice to be serenaded "before we all die." David Jones, no relation to Gwyn, said that maybe if the Chinese heard Gwyn Jones sing it one more time they'd surrender. They were all on edge—they'd wanted to hit hard and *fast*, to do what they were trained to do. This waiting around was the worst kind of enemy—gave a man too much time to count the odds.

Salvini lifted the flash protector on his watch and saw it was 0420 hours. At 0425 there was an enormous rumbling sound like the echo of a storm way to the south toward the Himalayas. It was the hundred-ton door moving.

CHAPTER FIFTEEN

IN LHASA THE half-starved wild dog packs were howling and on the prowl.

"You have surprised us," Major Mah conceded. "You've held up remarkably well."

Hartog was curled up in the fetal position, in shock, all his finger- and toenails torn off, making him look in the dim, depressing bulb light as if he had painted his nails with bright red nail polish. Though his whole body trembled, his jaws were clamped so tightly that he had broken a tooth, and this too was bleeding.

"Now of course," Mah said, his voice rising as if Hartog

couldn't hear him properly, "there is no point. Freeman has sent paratroopers to the site, the site *you*, Mr. Hartog, told them about."

Hartog remained silent, his demented gaze fixed on some point on the cell wall beneath the bars, one of whose shadows bisected his face. It seemed to the major that Hartog was on the fine line between utter madness and possible recovery. But Mah also knew they would never find out.

When the guard came in with the placard of the type criminals had to wear and be paraded in during the Cultural Revolution, the major helped the guard put it over Hartog's head and put a large dunce cap on him. "Get up!" the major said. "Otherwise this will hurt."

Hartog put his hands out, looking like a man just cut down from a cross as they helped him to his feet. He was so weak he had to be carried down, screaming each time his feet or a hand got in the way.

They left him sitting at the entrance to Iron Mountain, from where he could see the holy Potala Palace from which he'd been dragged. They covered him with blankets to keep off the lightly falling snow, his guard having explicit orders that he was not allowed to parade the prisoner until dawn— until the Tibetans were about their business.

For Hartog, the snow was a gift from God. Each flake he let fall on his feet numbed him a little more, freezing out the pain, though he was no fool, knowing that when the snow stopped and the temperature rose by even a degree or two—or worse, if it was a sunny spring day—the unbearable pain would return. He thought of the orange groves of Israel, how they had borne fruit from the desert, and he could see the bright green leaves, so green they looked as if they were polished, and at that moment he promised that no matter what humiliation he would have to bear if they led him through town like a common thief, the Tibetans would be on his side anyway, and he would not break, he would will himself to survive, to be exchanged for one of MOSSAD's prisoners. And then he would see the orange groves again.

The huge door seen through the infrared scopes was slightly open now, moving only inches at a time to the left and revealing a vertical split of darkness that was nevertheless awash from heat waves emanating from inside the enormous underground site, the gap the door was creating growing with each minute. The door was sliding, opening faster now, and soon the large black mouth, fifty feet wide and fifty feet high, was revealed as the cave's entrance became visible in the infrared wash against the colder background of the mountain, and now another white, wavy pattern emerged on the infrared scopes, coming out of the mountain.

"Rifle flares!" Brentwood ordered. "Three."

There were three thumps, and night became day, revealing an enormous rail platform on which a steel-webbed firing cradle rested, and on the cradle was a huge multiwarheaded DF5 East Wind missile, shrouded in a mist that rose in consequence of the warm hydraulic lines and the like meeting the minus-thirty-degree outside temperature. The tanks opened up with an HE round from each, and there was another chattering of the machine guns. Flitting shadows could be seen as regular Chinese guard troops—in white overlay—dashed from one boulder to another closer to the tanks.

"All right, all right," Aussie said as he pulled back the bolt of his troop's Haskins M500B rifle. "We'll keep our heads down, don't worry."

The missile platform, a long, reinforced flatcar, stopped about a hundred yards from the cave mouth. The door began to close, and the massive missile rose gradually up from its rail flatcar like one of the great Paris guns of World War I. Aussie guessed it would be another five minutes before it was in its vertical position amid what looked like a huge Mechano-set-like platform that rose with the rocket to form a gantry.

The Haskins M500B rifle, like the Haskins M500, had a weight-reducing fluted barrel that made the barrel cooler after a shot, an adjustable stock with bipod, a ten-power telescope and sight, and a muzzle brake that reduced the kick of the rifle. It wasn't a beautiful weapon to look at, for it had been made for utility, not for looks. But it could hit a target the size of a man at two thousand five hundred feet—almost half a mile away. Like the Haskins M500, the 500B had a bolt action, but unlike the M500, it had a six-round magazine instead of a single-shot mechanism, and was mounted with a Kigre KN200F intensifier image sight that could be used night or day.

Aussie checked the magazine of six .50 caliber rounds, each round designed to take out a vehicle and/or smash into an aircraft's vitals, the 1.5-ounce bullet having more than four times the whack of a 7.62mm round and capable of punching through four inches of armor with a hardened tungsten-carbide penetrator in the bullet, the rest of the bullet hard packed with high explosive and incendiary material.

"All right," Aussie told his runner. "Keep your ass down and tell Brentwood and his boys to open up for 'overwatch.' Tell him we need to get a half mile from the cave. It'll take us within the T-59's range, so I'll want everyone with an Arpac ready to go."

In his troop, Salvini turned to young Brooklyn. "Right, sport, you can pack an Arpac and lead the way while we make our overwatch move. Let's see whether you can bust a tank."

Suddenly the boulder-strewn, two-mile-wide strip between the mountains and Lake Nam was filled with noise as Brentwood's troops, most equipped with the HK11A1 light machine guns, let rip as they moved toward the three ChiCom tanks, which in turn opened up with cannon and machine guns, the echo of the cannon's booms causing loose snow to fall down over the steel door like curtains of salt. A T-59's shrapnel flagellated the air, hitting two troopers, one with arm lacerations, the other a bad gash in his thigh. Despite his top physical condition, Aussie, under the camouflage overwhites and polyester, was still sweating, as were most of his troops as they ran forward for a second time after Brentwood, Salvini, and Choir provided a hail of covering fire, the battle joined by Chinese infantry clustering around the tanks.

And now the heavy Chinese mortars were "getting in the act," as Aussie noted, their kill zone about a thousand yards in front of the tanks. The mortars were in fact much more deadly than the T-59 high-explosive rounds. Once the high-explosive round went off in the boulders and spread its shrapnel, that was it, most of it ricocheting skyward or at least over the heads of the SAS/D commandos. But when the Chinese mortars struck in relatively open ground, their shrapnel proved much more deadly, the Chinese mortars using time-fused rounds that often went off in air bursts, showering *down* amid the SAS/D men, four of them being hit, two killed outright, the other two severely wounded.

Now Salvini's group moved up as Brentwood and Aussie and Choir provided covering fire. Amid the earsplitting cacophony of machine gun, rifle, cannon, and rifle grenade fire and the crash of mortar rounds, the night alive with tracers, Aussie reached a point two thousand meters—over a mile—from the launch rail car. He centered the crosshairs on the lower half of the missile, which now looked like an enormous redwood tree in his scope shrouded by mist rising like dry ice about the rail car, the two railway engines used to shunt it out now going back into the cave where the door was closing.

Aussie could hear the high whine of the hydraulics lifting the big missile to the vertical position, as he breathed in slowly, trying to ignore the adrenaline rush, exhaled only half the air he'd taken in, and squeezed rather than pulled the trigger. The crack of the Haskins, no more than a finger-snapping noise within the sustained roar of battle between the Chinese and SAS/D troops, would not be heard till after the bullet struck its target. Aussie did not take his eye off the telescopic sight and was first to see the small glow, like a dandelion shedding its seeds, yellow suddenly filling the scope, and then a crimson red flash. "Jesus Christ!"

The base of the missile, not yet free of the gantry but still manacled to it, shot out, or rather blew out sideways after trying to shoot up from the cradle. Instead it ripped the gantry to pieces like a wild animal tethered to its cage. Ignited fuel spilled, roared in a river of fire, surging about the base of the great sliding door, buckling the ball-bearing runners, the warhead section of the rocket tumbling to earth amid snow and boulders like some huge cone, and then the feral roar of the second stage fuel igniting filling the air, its hot blast dry as the Gobi Desert. Several Chinese were aflame and screaming horribly until taken out either by SAS fire or their own comrades.

Brentwood fired a green flare, and his and Salvini's troops formed one line, making their way quickly, snaking through the boulders while Aussie Lewis's and Choir Williams's troops formed the second line of advance, but they were not firing, conserving ammunition for the next overwatch if there was going to be one, unless Brentwood thought enough damage had already been done. Brentwood signaled to his troop to continue covering fire and ran fast on a curving track through the boulders till he reached Aussie Lewis.

"Congratulations!" Brentwood said.

"Haskins are beautiful, aren't they?" Aussie said, patting the weapon like an old friend.

"Yeah, but d'you think it was enough?"

Aussie Lewis wanted to shout yes, of course it was enough. He wanted to break radio silence and ask for the pickup by the helos that the U.S.-led forces had acquired with some arm-twisting on the border of India after the SAS mission had already left. He wanted to say yes and get back as fast as possible and do what he could for Alexsandra. "No," he said, "it's not enough. If they have a spare gantry inside, behind that bloody great door, they could be back in business in a day or two."

"Well, if we went forward and blew up the rail lines?"

"Same thing, Dave—they could replace it in a matter of hours. Besides, there's got to be a whole bloody store of missiles inside somewhere. We'll have to go in."

David Brentwood nodded his head. "You're right I guess. But we'd better do it fast before they move in troops from Damquka on the other side of the mountain range."

"Right," Aussie said, and took aim at the nearest T-59's infrared searchlight mounted to the right of the cannon. He blew it apart, then did the same with the other two.

"Why the hell didn't you do that before?" someone asked.

"I've got two mags of point fifty sniper rounds, buddy. Missile had the first priority."

"All right let's go!" Brentwood said, and with that he returned to his men and another green flare shot in the air as a signal, not as a light, for the commandos had all the illumination they wanted in front of them in the burning fuel whose flames were silhouetting the Chinese as they dashed from boulder to boulder. Even so, the SAS lost another three men in a fifty-yard dash, and counting the four still missing since the drop they had seventy-one out of the original eighty.

A half mile from the roof exits high on either side of the door and back in the snow, much of which had been melted to ice by the fuel fire, the SAS/D saw more Chinese coming out—shot two of them, which kept the others' heads low.

"Let's concentrate on one exit!" Brentwood yelled.

Aussie disagreed. "You and Sal take the left—Choir and me the right."

"Roger!" Brentwood acknowledged. "But be damned careful of shooting our lot once we're inside."

"You too," Aussie said, and the seventy-one men split into two groups of thirty-five and thirty-six. All they were waiting for was to take out the three tanks.

Young Brooklyn had got to within a hundred yards of the nearest T-59, and he lifted the French-made Arpac, steadying its small tube against a rock, waited till the T-59 filled the peep sight, inhaled, held his breath, and fired. The sliding barrel recoiled, and the missile's motor blasted from the tube at 247 feet per second without any telltale flash. The tank exploded. Again Aussie almost wished he'd told Brentwood that one DF5 missile blown up was enough, for he knew that in this close, the fighting must soon be hand to hand, and even veterans had no stomach for that.

In Lhasa it was dark and still snowing, despite the fact that it was officially spring. This was not that unusual for the Tibetan capital, nor were the wild dog packs that were congregating about the base of Iron Mountain. Its radio mast, which had received the signal that told the major that the attack on the missile site was taking place, was no longer visible in the snow, and the guard wasn't sure whether the Dutchman was suffering from hypothermia or whether his shivering was because of the beating. A bit of both, he thought.

As the snow eased, more Tibetans could be seen emerging from their cluttered buildings onto the street. The major told the guard that Hartog was free to go. The guard prodded him with his bayonet and Hartog half fell, half scrambled down the stone steps. The dogs had not eaten, for the human feces they often lived on were covered by snow, and instead it was the smell of the Dutchman's wounds that drew them, slowly at first, but then when the curs realized no Tibetan would help the downed man—the Chinese squad ready to deal with anyone who would try—the dogs moved in and tore the Dutchman to pieces, his screams drawing a large crowd, the placard proclaiming that he was an enemy of the people sodden and torn asunder by the dogs in their frenzied attempt to get at his vitals. A Tibetan monk was objecting, lecturing the Chinese on nonviolence until the major drew his pistol, and the monk's colleagues hurried him away.

CHAPTER SIXTEEN

DESPITE THE FLARES' flickering light, mistakes were bound to be made by both sides in similar-looking white camouflaged overlays. The problem for the SAS/D—Brentwood's troop on the left and Aussie's on the right—was to climb up the flanks of the door to get on top of the cave. This meant that they would first have to negotiate the piles of snow-covered debris that was the excavated soil either side of the cave and then somehow climb almost sheer cliffs of over a hundred feet that stood like ramparts either side of the door, ramparts that were ChiCom high ground protected by at least four machine gun nests. The 7.6mm guns were set back from the cliff edge out of direct sight from below, but not so far back that they couldn't rain down their fire on most of the boulder-strewn apron that spread beyond the railhead where the mangled gantry now sat, still so hot that it was vaporizing the snow falling on it.

"One, two for me!" Aussie yelled to Brentwood, indicating the two machine gun posts atop the left side of the cave and the door, and "three, four, for you," pointing to the two 7.6mm nests atop the right-hand side of the cave.

"Roger!" Brentwood answered, and the two lines of commandos moved forward.

With the element of surprise expended, the SAS/D troopers understood and accepted, however reluctantly, that speed—dashing out, guns blazing in the boulder-strewn area about the cave entrance—would only bring certain death. But to go too slowly would give the ChiCom battalions at Damquka time to reach the cave—then the SAS/D would find itself sandwiched between two ChiCom forces. Immediately, however, both Aussie Lewis and Brentwood saw that for the four enemy machine gun posts there would be a "no-fire" zone of about twenty yards or so directly beneath the top of the door, the ChiCom machine gunners unable to depress their weapons at a more acute angle. It was this ground that the SAS/D force would have to reach and hold.

Quickly Aussie and Brentwood passed the word—no more flares, wait till all flare light had subsided, then attack, home plate being the front of the cave's closed door.

But the ChiComs weren't cooperating, still sending up flares from behind boulders, and the flames from the burning hulks of the knocked-out T-59s were lighting up the area. Brentwood knew that to rush out would be to have his men mown down. And so once again, all the SAS/D could do was wait, yet to wait was to give the Damquka garrison more time to respond. In civilian life it was called being between a rock and a hard place. Brentwood turned to his runner. "Tell Salvini and Choir to spread out far right flank, far left. Mimic a charge and maybe we can get the ChiComs to use all their flares."

The messenger nodded, repeating the order. "Simulate flank attacks to dummy Chinks into using up flares."

"You've got it," Brentwood said. "Go!"

Rosemary had made sure that all the windows were latched as well as having slipped the dead bolts, and had been sitting, sipping her tea in the kitchen, when she'd heard the dolphins squeak. Vibrations from the wind. She wanted to throw the blasted dolphins away. No, she couldn't. Robert had bought them for her—well, for the baby really. And besides, dolphins were the submariners' logo. It would soon be dawn, but it was still dark outside. The important thing, she told herself, was not to let her nerves get on edge now she was so close to having "toughed it out," as Robert would say. By herself. She hadn't panicked—well, a little, and she may have lifted up the phone, but she hadn't used it, that was the point. And she knew it was precisely these little victories that gave one the courage to see it through—well, Andrea would accompany her to the hospital when the baby's time came. But what would happen if Andrea couldn't—if her child was sick?

"Then, my dear," she told herself aloud, "you'll just have to do it solo."

"What the hell you on 'bout?"

She had tried to yell, but no sound would come—only a gasp as if she'd been completely winded. He was big—over six feet, black, and the knife blade caught the living room light. "You scream, I'll cut your fuckin' head off, lady. You unnerstand me?"

"Yes," she said, sitting on the edge of the chair, her knuckles white with fear. "I haven't got any money—" she began, her throat so dry she couldn't finish.

"Don' you give me that shit, lady. Old man's credit cards."

"He has them," she said.

"Oh sure. Listen—don't leave home without 'em!"

"Th-that's right," she said.

"Where's he gonna use 'em lady—bottom of the fuckin' sea?"

"I'm telling you the truth—truly—"

"Then give me yours, honey." He was so close now she could smell him—cigarette smoke and beer—but she didn't think he was drunk. He moved too quickly for that. "Gimme yours," he told her. "Hurry up!"

"They're in my bedside drawer."

"Well what the fuck you standin' here for? Go get 'em! I want your bank cards and your secret little number."

She heaved herself out of the chair, heard the dolphins squeal. "I'll get them," she said.

"That's right, momma, you get 'em."

As she walked through the door from the kitchen into the hallway toward the bedroom, she remembered what Robert had told her: Try to get your breathing under control—if it isn't, your aim will be off. You've got to hold the gun steady enough. She knew he would kill her if she didn't get him first. She knew it—not because she knew credit cards would be of no use if she were left alive to talk, but because she'd seen it in his eyes. And all this time she'd been worrying about the Chinese sending agents to eliminate or terrify the wives and families of—

"Move yo' ass!" he said.

By the time she reached the bedroom she was perspiring heavily, her hand on the metal knob of the bedside table. She suddenly became ice cold, focused on what she had to do.

The phone rang.

"Fuck—you got a message machine?"

"No," she said.

"Shit—how come you got no fuckin' machine?"

"I've—we've just moved onto the base. I haven't—"

"Shut up. You answer. Say you're in the bath. You'll ring back."

"A bath?" she said. "At five in the morning?"

"Shit—shit—"

The phone stopped ringing.

He was staring at it, went over to rip it out, then changed his mind. "Fuckin' phones. If it rings again—" He wasn't sure how to play it. "Just hurry up. C'mon—cards—and gimme that fancy ring on your finger."

She still had her hand on the cool metal handle and opened the drawer. She made a quick move with her right hand and froze.

"This what you lookin' for, honey?" He pulled the gun from his hip pocket and with one swipe, pistol-whipped her to the bed, blood running down from her cheek. He kicked at her legs. "You fuckin' bitch—stay on the bed." She was on her stomach, and he grabbed her by the hair, the gun in one hand, the knife in his pocket so he could clout her about the head a couple of times, she whimpering in fear and trying to cover her face from the blows. He reached over, tore open her nightdress, grabbed a breast, and squeezed it roughly. She gasped in pain.

"You like that, huh?" he said, his breath all over her. "You makin' me hard, white trash. You want it, huh—you askin' for it?"

"No, no, I—please, the baby!"

"Fuck the baby. Fuck you, little smart ass. Now you got five seconds to get your cards else I'll kick you right in the gut. How's that? You like that?"

She heaved herself off the bed, went to the closet, and was barely able to reach a shoe box.

"Hey," he said, "wait!" But it was too late. The lid was on the floor and the box's contents spilling out. He started in fright, but there was no gun, only traveler's checks.

He picked up a wad of five-hundred dollars in American Express. He saw they were the double signature types either spouse could sign. "Hey, Rosemary, now we're cookin'.'" She was slumped by the closet, barely able to stay upright, he standing in the doorway between the bedroom and the hallway. Rosemary was trying to hold up the top of her nightdress, and he was staring at her breasts rising and falling with fear. He pocketed the gun and, after picking up the checks, started to fondle her breasts, and she was stiff with fear. She knew without the slightest doubt that he was going to kill her. What use was the robbery to him if he could be reported?

"Hell," he said, "you ugly everywhere else with that bun in the oven, honey, but you got nice tits. Kneel down in front of me. Here, I'll sit on the bed, tell you what we're gonna do—"

The shot crashed through glass and hit him in the left shoulder, flinging him toward the bedstead. For a split second Rosemary saw the gun sticking out of his back pocket and grabbed it. She fired once, twice—she fired till the chamber was empty, the bed and wall splattered in blood and bits from his head, an artery gushing blood like a burst pipe. She dropped the gun and didn't hear the knocking till a few seconds later. When she let Andrea in, the second mate's wife looked calmly at the carnage. "Good girl, Rosie. That's the way. You killed the bastard."

"No!" It was a scream of pain from Rosemary, the service .45 she had been holding dropping to the floor.

Andrea embraced her. "Now, honey, you have a damn good cry. I'll call the MPs. You sit—c'mon in the living room."

"How did you know?" Rosemary began as Andrea dialed.

"Easy. Couldn't sleep. Usual, first few nights after they go out. Saw your lights go on and phoned. No answer and I just knew there was trouble. You did good, Rosie—don't worry about it."

For some inexplicable reason, Rosemary, the English teacher, almost corrected Andrea—"You did well." She hated the ungrammatical "did good" when they meant "well." She said nothing, still shaking. "Andrea?" she called.

Andrea was on the phone.

"Andrea!"

"What is it?"

"The baby—I think—"

"Uh-oh—you better hurry with that ambulance, ma'am. I think we've got a premature baby on the way. What? Yes, ma'am, a mother in premature labor. And she's in shock. So you hurry!"

Rosemary had never felt as ill as she did now—pain from the blow to her cheek and so sick in the stomach she just wanted to pass out, but she didn't and could hear the ambulance siren wailing in the distance.

The flares were finished and it was down to killing by moonlight because there was no place to run—a hundred yards here, a hundred there, and then there would be a collection of new boulders. And in the darkness atop the cave a few triple A guns brought forward so they could be depressed to shoot down in front of the missile cave couldn't do so for fear of hitting their own troops with ricochets.

The Chinese were brave. Ordered out to hunt down the SAS/D, they couldn't contain the American and British commandos, whose morale, fitness, and equipment were superior. As the SAS/D shot their way past the tanks, the range was often point-blank, and here the small, thirteen-inch-long HK MP5 submachine guns firing at nine hundred rounds a minute were better than the longer AK-47s, pumping out two hundred rounds in less than a minute. Some SAS, however, carried AK-47s, it always being useful to have the enemy's 7.62mm ammo as well as your own at your disposal.

More than a dozen Chinese were felled by the chest-sheathed knives of the SAS/D teams, and several of the SAS/D troopers had the Browning High Power 9mm pistol as a backup, the magazine holding thirteen rounds of hard-hitting Parabellum. In the din of the battle, huge, flickering shadows crisscrossing the boulders could be seen as a result of the light from the missile's dying fuel fire. Now and then a scream would pierce the air as another SAS/D chest knife found flesh and bone. Even so, nine more SAS/D were cut down, reducing the original force of eighty to sixty-two, counting the four who had not made the rendezvous after the jump.

Aussie Lewis's and Salvini's men were first to reach the open ground before the cave, the ground now littered with the smashed gantry, looking like some monstrous metallic stick insect that had crashed and fallen amid the flames, exposing its ribs.

Unhesitatingly Aussie Lewis began scaling the rocky cliff by the base of the door off to the left, searching for finger holes or anything that would help propel him up and lead him to the exit from where he'd seen the Chinese come.

"Hey," someone said in an urgent but subdued voice. "Use the bloody ladder."

Lewis dropped to the ground, catlike, and on the swing around, his infrared picked up a long, white blob, a Browning 9mm High Power preceding it, on the rungs of a ladder cemented into the sheer wall, previously hidden by the snow. Then he heard the rip of an AK-47—Chinese or SAS/D he didn't know until he saw the blur of the 9mm Browning dropping after its owner to the ground, and above the blur a bold white stick pointing out and down:

the barrel of an AK-47. Aussie sprayed nine millimeter at the stick and lobbed a stun grenade up and over.

There was a tremendous metallic crash as the grenade exploded, and in the five seconds it took Aussie to get up the ladder and spray over the top before he had his foot on the last rung, the Chinese was on his knees, appropriately stunned. Lewis kicked him in the head, then with one swift movement, his Browning High Power in his left hand, he pulled the soldier to the edge of the thirty-foot cliff and pushed him off.

"Jesus, Aussie!" It was Salvini below, trying to get up the ladder, only to feel a close rush of air as the body passed him. "Don't recycle the bastard!"

"Sal?" Aussie called.

"Yes?"

"I can see the exit." What he meant was that he couldn't actually see it but rather its heat signature—obviously it served as an air intake as well for the cave. But when they got there, he and four other SAS/D men following, two turning to take up the rear defensive position, Aussie failed to move the exit cover by pulling on its ring bolt. "Fucking thing's closed from the inside."

"Blow it!" Sal said, and in seconds a whole seam was packed with donutlike C4.

"Everybody back!" he yelled before he detonated the plastique. There was a tremendous explosion, shards of ice and small pebbles bouncing off the boulders below, and from those that the men on top had used for cover. When they went back the seam had been ruptured here and there, but it still held.

"Shit!" Aussie declared. "Okay—let's go again." But as no one in the small group had any more of the explosive, he yelled, "Plastique! Left exit!" A volley of fire erupted from below as five Chinese around the burned-out shell of a T-59 fired in the Australian's general direction. It was a bad mistake, as the volley of fire they got in return from the flanks and above killed all five.

"Room service!" Salvini yelled, helping three members of his troop up the ladder and sending them and their plastique over to Aussie.

The second charge exploded, the exit's seams now turned up and curled back, blackened and scarred like chapped lips, but the steel core of the exit still held, though Aussie could see through a crack about three inches wide down into the cave and could feel the freezing air being sucked down into the mountain's interior where he saw panic— blur upon blur of men trapped—and though some of them were undoubtedly among some of the most brilliant nuclear scientists in the world, they had no idea what to do about their predicament.

"Right!" Aussie said, hunched over the edge of the exit's twisted steel. "Won't take the fucking easy way then we'll do it the hard fucking way. CS tear gas rounds—quickly!"

Each man pulled out two or three 37mm black rounds of CS gas from the thigh loops on his uniform and gave them one by one to Aussie, who put them in the baton stick and fired them, or rather dropped them, into the huge interior through the three-inch hole, finally plugging the hole with his white overlay hood, which he cut off with the knife. "Let's see how the bastards like that."

Suddenly a giant tremor shook the mountain.

"The door!" Salvini said. "They don't like that CS."

"Aw, shit!" a trooper said in mock sympathy. "And they wanted to have more fun with their missiles. Aren't we fucking awful!"

"Jesus," one of Salvini's troop cut in. "Does this mean we have to go down that friggin' wall again?"

"No, it doesn't," Aussie answered, seeing David

Brentwood's troop over to his right fighting it out halfway up that side of the door. "Choir's troop'll take care of the ground floor and—" Aussie stopped speaking, then ran to the edge of the cliff, shouting down, "Hold your fire! Let 'em go, Choir! Hold your fire!"

The Chinese—most of them in heavy, padded Mao suits—were streaming out, choking from the gas, tears running down their cheeks, handkerchiefs over their faces then putting their hands up one or two at a time, whatever they could manage. Only a few, realizing precisely what was going on, were able to lose themselves amid the boulders either side of the rail track that extended out from the cave.

These were the men, scientists mostly and some soldiers, who knew that if any shots penetrated the liquid fuel tanks stored inside, then the whole mountain cave would become an inferno, consuming them. The warheads would probably not go off, but the rocket fuel surely would.

Choir was tired of searching the evacuees for arms, but those who had surrendered had to be checked out as a matter of routine.

Aussie, two of his troopers, and two of the prisoners donned their S6 gas masks and made their way back to the cave, Aussie ordering the Chinese prisoners to show them the door controls. When they found the wall panel that operated the door, they began to close it again until there was only room for one man to slip in or out at a time. The sky began to pass from blackness to a moonlit, suffused gray, and Aussie knew that dawn would soon be on them and it was still a three-mile trek to the lake for the helo pickup that Brentwood had ordered.

Having reached the right top exit–cum–air intake, Brentwood had followed Aussie Lewis's method of dropping down CS canisters. Aussie and Salvini volunteered to stay behind until everyone was out of the way. Then Aussie with the Haskins—Salvini to provide covering fire if necessary—would finish the job, after which they would make for the lakeshore.

There was to be a delay, however, for Salvini, further in the cave than Aussie, had made a gut-wrenching discovery. Deeper in the mountain, beyond the stand of half a dozen missiles, the huge cave narrowed like the interior of a goat's horn, this secondary cave much smaller in diameter, but one along which a narrow-gauge rail track ran, disappearing into the dark bowels of the mountain. Salvini had ventured only thirty feet into the tunnel when he saw the first storage room filled with fuel drums and a row of lights that seemed to go on forever inside the mountain.

Soon Aussie and two other troopers joined him. Following the rails for another hundred yards, Aussie experienced a gnawing apprehension that around the next bend in the tunnel they would find more Chinese regulars. They didn't, but they did discover dozens of storage rooms hewn out of the rock, and that the railway line snaked around several sharp S curves that acted as blast protectors.

To ensure maximum destruction, Aussie saw that they'd have to jury-rig an explosive line of gasoline drums so that an explosion at the cave mouth could in fact negotiate the S bends and take out the string of thick-walled storage rooms of fuel, ammunition, food, and rocket supplies as well.

From one such gasoline dump—drums stacked to the ceiling—Aussie ordered two troopers with him and Salvini to puncture as many drums as they could and to roll these down along the narrow-gauge rails toward the cave's mouth, the gasoline spilling between and around the tracks. In addition, he ordered some drums to be rolled down to other, nonfuel, storage rooms, punctured there, and rolled in and out of the other rooms so that finally he had created a gas-sodden path along the rail track toward the cave's mouth several hundred yards on as well as having created gas-sodden tributaries, as it were, from the main line into each storage room. When he and the other troopers, five of them, emerged from the cave mouth, the others, as agreed, had already left for the lake.

"All right," Aussie said, "let's head into those boulders—'bout three hundred yards from the cave."

"Roger!"

A quarter mile beyond the missile complex, Aussie looked up through a gap in the clouds to see a sparkling array of stars, then they were gone. He had no need of starlight, however, nor did he want to risk using a flare anywhere near the mouth of the cave. Through the infrared scope on the Haskins he could see the racks of missile fuel clearly enough, standing up at the rear of the gargantuan interior like huge stovepipes. He pulled back the bolt and fired an incendiary.

The explosion was immense, bigger than he or Salvini had ever seen—like a sudden sunburst, its feral roar escaping the cave in a one-hundred-yard-wide dragon tongue of flame, the ensuing rivers of flame issuing forth from the secondary storage explosions.

"Chri-i-st!" Salvini said, looking back at the sight, but Aussie couldn't hear him, for the noise of the explosion had been so loud it left the Australian's ears ringing. He tapped Salvini's S6 filter as Salvini stood mesmerized by the spectacle. "Come on, let's go to Lake Nam."

"I don't like that name," Salvini said. He had to say it again before Aussie could hear him.

"Why?" the Australian asked.

"Reminds me of *Viet*nam."

"So?"

"Spooky, man."

"Bullshit. It's a salt lake in the middle of nowhere."

"Right," Salvini said, and they set out—neither walking nor running but in that slow, commando jog that wouldn't exhaust them yet would get them, they hoped, to the lake in time for the pickup.

CHAPTER SEVENTEEN

EVERY OFFICER AND guard in Beijing Number One jail was in a foul mood because, with the missile threat removed, the United States, with local guerrillas involved here and there, was counterattacking all along the Orgon Tal–Honggor line.

Although they were only recapturing territory they had lost, the very fact that the Americans had turned and regained the initiative in some areas bespoke a commander who the Chinese knew would be loath to surrender. And in that way that it always does, despite official prohibition against it, the news of the American turnaround was already known by most of the prisoners. Only those in solitary, like Alexsandra Malof, had failed to hear the news, but the guard assumed she had.

"So, your guerrillas help."

"Wo bu dong"—I don't understand—she said.

"Your guerrillas help."

"Help what?"

"Ah, you think Chinese authorities do not know."

"Know what?"

The guard stepped forward and punched her in the face. "You think guerrillas will—" He punched her again.

She flailed at him with her hands. "Get away from me. . . ." He enjoyed the fear in her eyes. He hit her again and felt his excitement rising. "We will kill all Americans!" the guard yelled. "All guerrillas."

Grabbing her prison dress, he pulled it up about her waist. She tried to fend him off, kicking at him, but, laughing, he wedged his left thigh between her legs and kicked her with his right boot and she collapsed. He hit her again and again, and she knew if she didn't yield he'd kill her, but he took her sudden servility as encouragement. Beneath all her hysteria, he told himself, she was just like the other women prisoners—she wanted it. Not being on the outside for a while, she missed it. He felt her legs give way, and she lay like a compliant dog as he huffed and puffed his way to ecstasy. It was short-lived, and when he heard the heavy door clanking open all he saw was the gun, and it was the last thing he ever saw, his body knocked off her, his temple a fountain of spurting blood, and astonishment on his peasant face as his head crashed into the stone wall. The reverberation of the pistol shot and the acrid bluish gray smoke were still in the air.

The moment Nie had looked through the judas hole and seen what was happening he'd ordered his aide, Captain Shung, to fire.

"Get him out of here!" Nie said, his voice even but its timbre vibrating with anger. He took one look at the prisoner's face—bruised and bloodied by the fool of a guard. "After you get rid of him," Nie added without looking at the captain, "get her to first aid. If she has to go to the prison hospital I must personally sign the transfer order. Understood?"

"Yes, Comrade Nie."

"Thank you," Alexsandra said quietly, realizing as she did so that the guard had knocked out one of her top teeth.

"You," Nie said, "are becoming an embarrassment. You *must* confess!"

Then she understood—there hadn't been an iota of sympathy in him for her in what the guard had done, only extreme annoyance that his most prized captive had been beaten about the face so badly that it would be awhile before he could make her look presentable in any show trial. In any event, he told Shung that he wanted the *China Evening News* producer and the best makeup artist from the Beijing Opera to see the Malof woman immediately and give him an estimate of how long it would take to make her presentable in court.

Shung was also instructed to tell the replacement guard on the wing that he and his family would be summarily executed if so much as a scratch was found on the prisoner once she had been bandaged and returned from medical treatment. Nie had told Shung the very same thing, assuring a trembling Alexsandra before he left the cell that "We will certainly kill you as a spy if you do not cooperate. If you confess, your death will be quick—a public execution. But if you do not confess . . ." He threw up his hands in a gesture of hopelessness. "Then the guards can have you—do as they wish."

There was growing pressure on Nie by the Politburo to have a public confession from Malof as an enemy of the people before they killed her. The effect of confessions, particularly among the peasantry, was much underrated by

Western observers and intellectuals, who thought the mass of Chinese were as skeptical as they were about such confessions.

CHAPTER EIGHTEEN

FREEMAN WAS PLEASED his forces had been able to rally significantly from the massive Chinese ground attack and to regain some lost ground, but the victories he'd expected from the close air support against Cheng's main battle tanks were not forthcoming. The Chinese had made excellent use of smoke cover after the typhoon had passed, and, combined with the dust, the smoke not only obscured large areas of the battlefield and cut the Americans' bombing and sighting laser rays and thermal sights, but made IFF—identification friend or foe—a near impossibility. Several M1s, mistaken for enemy tanks, had been taken out just south of the railway at Orgon Tal.

"At least the missile problem's licked," Norton said.

"For the time being," Freeman answered. "Oh, it'll take them quite a while to set up shop again, but we have to do something in the meantime, Dick—something so spectacular that it'll short circuit the whole war."

"Anything in mind, General?"

Freeman seemed not to notice Dick Norton's voice. "I

wonder whether young Brentwood shot those goddamned scientists."

Norton was genuinely shocked. "You don't mean that, General?" he said, but it was more a question than a statement of fact.

The general glanced at him and sighed. He was bone weary from lack of sleep. "No, Dick, I probably don't, but have you ever thought of how we gain air superiority?"

"By more of us shooting down more of them I presume."

"Planes or pilots?" Freeman asked.

It made Norton pause.

"Australian air ace," Freeman continued. "Man called Caldwell used to shoot the German pilots in their parachutes in WW II. Said if he didn't, the bastards'd be up the next day shooting down more of his buddies." With that, Freeman looked up at the map and smacked Tibet. "Chinese scientists are same as the pilots. Long as we have them running loose they can build more missiles."

"General," Dick Norton said, "you once told me that no war is black and white—all have a gray area—but you said the degree of grayness is what separates us from them—an American from a totalitarian."

"Did I?" Freeman said.

"Yes, sir, you did."

"Well, Dick, don't worry—just wishful thinking. I didn't order the scientists shot. We'll find out when Brentwood gets back. A few taken prisoner wouldn't hurt."

"Won't know till he's here, sir." Dick Norton looked at his watch. "The three evac choppers should be reaching that Lake Nam pretty soon."

"What are our casualties?"

"No word yet. Brentwood just used enough air time to send in the call for pickup."

"What are we using?"

"Pave Lows."

Freeman nodded approvingly. The MH-53J Pave Lows were superb NOE—nap of the earth—fliers. Just the kind of machine they needed in the bad weather swirling down from the twenty-thousand-foot mountain range.

"Air cover?" Freeman asked.

"F-15 Eagles on their way now—drop tanks and tankers."

"Good."

"We shouldn't have any trouble with ChiCom fighters," Norton added. "Eagles'll eat a Shenyang alive."

"Thank God for that. Listen, Dick, I've got to get some sleep." He slapped his aide on the shoulder. "Otherwise I'll get so goddamned tired my judgment will start to go. End up shooting scientists." He winked.

Norton smiled. Sometimes even Norton couldn't tell whether Freeman was kidding or not. The general *did* have a point: The way you got air supremacy was to shoot down pilots, not just planes. The missile site near Lake Nam had been taken out, but how long would it stay that way? How long would the Chinese take to get it going again? Freeman was right; Second Army had to do something spectacular in order to shorten the war before missiles started raining down again.

Before he fell asleep, his Winchester 1200 riot shotgun by his bed, the Sig Sauer 9mm beneath his pillow, Freeman read again those sections he'd underlined from Sun Tzu's *The Art of War*. The master had said surprise was a good tactic. Well, hell, it didn't need a Chinese sage to tell you that. He made a note in his diary to the effect that one of the reasons Second Army had not collapsed along the Orgon Tal–Honggor line stemmed, he believed, from the simple fact that the U.S. soldier normally fires about 4.7 times as much live ammunition in practice as his Chinese counterpart. With all the modern weapons of war, it gave him a sense of pride that, like the long rifles of the American Revolution, American marksmanship was probably the best in the world. Even so, he was outnumbered, and he knew the U.S. front couldn't hold forever without urgent resupply along lines that were stretched, straining to the limit, all the way from Khabarovsk to Orgon Tal.

He knelt by his bed and prayed for all his men and that he might be given a chance for victory.

On the shores of Lake Nam the SAS/D detachment was met by the four paratroopers who had not made the rendezvous. With them they had brought six Chinese prisoners, four of them scientists whom they'd picked up on their way down to the lake after they'd heard the enormous explosion and figured correctly that the missile site had been blown and that the best they could do was to make the rendezvous for pickup at the lake.

"Well stone the crows!" Aussie said upon seeing the four SAS/D men. "About time, fellas. Where you been? Wanking yourself off by the lake? Lovely!"

"We damn near drowned in the lake," a corporal said. "Damn lucky we made it to shore."

"Where'd you find this lot?" Aussie asked, swinging his Haskins in the direction of the six forlorn-looking Chinese, their padded Mao suits the worse for their escape from the inferno.

"Here," the SAS/D corporal said. "They were here by the lake. When they spotted one of our guys with an AK-47 they thought it was Christmas—till they saw our mugs."

"They don't look too fuckin' happy, do they?" Aussie observed. The laughter started to build, and in the relief following the enormous tension of the mission, Aussie's wry comment took on the aspect of one hell of a joke, then one man slipped and fell, butt first, on a pile of bird droppings that were all around the edge of the lake, it being a bird sanctuary. "Oh, shit!"

"That's right," Salvini said, and some of the commandos were laughing so hard, tears were streaming down their faces.

"Okay, settle down," Brentwood said. "Remember Pave Lows will have their hover coupler on to bring 'em to this exact GPS spot through all the cloud and mist. But if the weather closes in, the choppers won't risk landing when they can't see the ground—it'll be standard hover coupler procedure. Means they'll be about forty or fifty feet above us. They drop the rope ladders and we go up to them. Divide yourselves up into three groups of around twenty each."

By now three ski platoons from the PLA's Damquka camp on the other northeastern side of the twenty-thousand-foot mountain range had been dispatched via six Shenyang-made M1-4 fourteen-seat helicopters over the pass and on down toward the direction of the lake, but they were still airborne a good two miles from its nearest shoreline.

"Why don't the bastards come right on down?" someone asked. Aussie Lewis had his Haskins and eight incendiary bullets ready. If a chopper got much closer he'd have a target that would fill the scope. Another commando readied one of the two Stinger ground-to-air missiles.

"Come on, you pricks . . ." Aussie said, "come closer." But that was as far as the Chinese would come, and it puzzled Brentwood.

"Hey Aussie," Salvini called out, "they must have heard about your sharpshooting with the jolly Hask."

"They don't want my Stinger," one of the two antimissile missile commandos called out.

"Kawowski," Aussie quipped, "nobody'd want your fucking Stinger! Dunno where it's been."

The six Chinese helicopters disappeared from view in mist that suddenly swept down through the pass and hid everything, including a good part of the lake.

"I don't like it," Brentwood commented. "Not coming closer like that."

"Neither do I," Aussie concurred. "Bit bloody queer isn't it? I mean, it'll take them a good half hour to get here by foot. By that time we should be outta here."

"Maybe," Choir Williams said, "they're worried about our fighters jumping them and they want to stay close up there by the mountain range. Harder turning for a fighter."

"Maybe," Brentwood said, unconvinced. "Anyway, we've got to get to work on the defensive perimeter before they get here and—"

The trooper next to him was lifted off the ground and flung back with the force of the AK-47's burst, and the next second another SAS/D man was dead.

"Down!" Aussie yelled, and in the scramble for cover behind the nearest boulder he dove into the snow, which packed the end of the Haskins' barrel with ice. He put the muzzle brake at the end of the fluted barrel into his mouth, inhaling then exhaling into it, like giving a drowning victim the kiss of life.

He had made an understandable but disastrously wrong estimate.

The ChiComs from Damquka camp on the other side of the range weren't regular mountain troops—they were ski troops. In a mogul-jumping advance that would have pleased any professional skier, they had cut the normal hiking time between where they had landed and the lake's shore by more than a half. What would have been a twenty-minute or half-hour journey for an average hiker in good condition was slashed to five minutes via the speed of collapsible skis, telescoping poles, and Silvretta step-in bindings—and, where they needed them, light, tough magnesium snowshoes, their camouflage overwhites as effective as those of the SAS/D contingent. In another four minutes the fresh eighty-four ChiCom ski troops were all around the little more than sixty SAS/D troops.

Brentwood prayed that the three Pave Lows wouldn't show up for a while, as an attempted evacuation by helicopters now would prove suicidal. Brentwood had no sooner clipped a new magazine into his HK MP5K submachine gun than he heard two fighters overhead.

"Our Eagles," one man in Salvini's group proffered.

"Don't know," Brentwood said. Then they could hear the steady chopping of the air that marked the approach of helos in the mist.

"Everybody," Brentwood ordered, "defensive positions." Within seconds the SAS/D had all but disappeared between the rocks along the foreshore, or in their white overlays were lying inert against the snow.

"It's all right!" Brentwood shouted. "Must be the Paves." There were three rope ladders dangling from the mist. Aussie and the other SAS/D men materialized from their hiding places to go up the rope ladders, the mist and fog rolling down the mountainsides and mixing in a bone-chilling whiteness that completely obscured the sight of the helicopters that were hovering in the pea soup, presumably no more than forty feet above them.

But the ChiComs from Damquka could be heard—a kind of eerie shuffling noise—obviously hoping to kill the Americans before they could get anywhere near the rope ladders and disappear into the churning mist and fog, the deadly stutter of Chinese T-85 submachine guns complimented by a lot of shouting. The sound of a Chinese bugle and the chatter of older but effective Soviet-made PPSh-41 submachine guns that filled the air was coming closer with dramatic suddenness. The initial wave of fifteen or more Chinese was cut down by the defensive circle of SAS/D troopers, but at the cost of four men from Salvini's group.

The second wave, taking advantage of the first wave's shock, took protective positions amid the many rock spills and boulders that lay covered in snow. Brentwood grabbed the radio and warned off the Pave Lows and the fighters, even as he was struck by the irony of having the world's best strikers above him while he was unable to call them in as TACAIR, given the close proximity of SAS/D and ChiCom troops. And he knew that the longer he waited to call in the helos the more fuel they'd burn up, to a point where they would have to turn back as their fuel was consumed in the waiting.

Meanwhile, the Chinese were lobbing stick grenades all over the place. A few SAS men tossed the grenades back, but in all it was mainly a game of bluff on both sides—neither knowing exactly where the others were. Now the fog and mist became thicker, and Brentwood didn't hesitate. "Withdraw to purple!" he called, and fired the flare, guessing the distance at about a hundred yards—nearer the edge of the lake. Reverse overarch—that is, retreating in stages of overarching protective fire—was something the SAS/D troops had rehearsed and performed elsewhere many times. The fog made it more difficult and dangerous, but still they could do it, and in squads of four they began the withdrawal to the purple smoke—a purple halo in the falling snow, the sound of the choppers near but out of the purple corona and glow that would have given them away to the Chinese.

Seven more SAS/D men were lost during the pull-back, but those that made the purple were next to two SAS/D from Salvini's troop—or rather, what was left of it—and were pointed in the direction of the hanging rope ladders just beyond the penumbra of light cast by the flare. In another five minutes most of the remaining fifty-three SAS/D troops had made it to safety beyond the surreal purplish world of swirling snow, whiteout, and the deafening sound of rotors, approximately seventeen men allotted to each of the three Pave Lows. In another ten minutes they should be safe.

"After the swelling goes down," the makeup artist told Chairman Nie, "I'll need four—perhaps six—hours."

"I can keep the cameras far enough away," the "All China News" producer added. "No closeups of course."

"But *when*," asked Nie, "will the swelling go down?"

The makeup artist shrugged. "I'm no doctor, but I'd say four—six—days. Good food—fresh air."

"All right," Nie said, decidedly unhappy about the turn of events but seeing that he couldn't do very much about it at the moment. The trouble was, the Politburo was becoming impatient. There had been widespread reports of "hooliganism" in Harbin and to the south in Fuchow province just across the straits from Taiwan.

"Hooliganism" was now even a wider net, meaning anything from reading a capitalist newspaper from Hong Kong to actual insurrection. It could also get you shot.

Nie needed a confession coming from her own lips. That was the propaganda he wanted. Instead of her starvation diet they would feed her well, fatten her up a little, get her looking healthy. In Harbin they had captured four undercover conspirators, and in Beijing jail they still had the American SEAL, Smythe. If she did not confess he would have the four conspirators and Smythe all shot in front of her, not at once but as the questioning proceeded.

* * *

That evening one of the night nurses on her rounds came to the prisoner's bed and could not see her. The nurse panicked and had almost sounded the alarm when she thought to check the lavatory, and found the Malof woman there. All her bandages were off, and she had a gruesome black eye that she did not have before.

It was self-abuse, they told Nie, to get more time in hospital, the action of a coward.

No, Nie said, it certainly wasn't the action of a coward but of a "brave enemy agent." Yes, she no doubt had given herself a black eye and unbandaged herself to delay her recovery, to delay her questioning, and that told him that she was afraid of something happening, that finally her will would break under the pain.

Aussie and the two men with the Stingers waited till last before they began their climb up into the mist, voices lost to the wind under the roaring of rotor blades. As he began his climb, Aussie heard a sound like firecrackers in the distance and then mortar fire, not toward him but out on the lake. Beneath a long tongue of mist he could see water spouts as mortar rounds hit the lake, and then a strange mist—or was it fog?—seemed to rise up from the enormous lake to join the mist above.

Salvini, Choir Williams, and Aussie Lewis were the last three to approach the last Pave Low, ten men having gone before them, one badly wounded and bleeding profusely. The trooper beside him gave him a shot of morphine from his helmet pack then proceeded to make a tourniquet out of his belt.

"Last three!" Salvini yelled up at the two chopper crewmen at the door. One of the crewmen, despite the strain, the expectation that any second a wild burst of ChiCom machine gun fire from the pickup zone might riddle him and the chopper, still found time to laugh, calling out to the other crewman, "These guys might be tough 'uns, but they sure as hell can't count!"

"Whaddya mean?" the other man shouted back, barely audible over the noise of the rotor slap. The other crewman pointed down. "There are four of 'em, not three."

The other trooper shrugged—what did it matter? long as they didn't leave anybody, and they could only wait another five minutes before the fuel gauge would dictate they head out.

Aussie was carrying the Haskins sniper rifle, weighing twenty-three pounds, and in the swirling vortex of wind caused by the prop wash he was trying to make sure that the last trooper, below him, wasn't bothered by the muzzle brake and the end of the barrel, which had a tendency to swing a bit like a pendulum in the high wind, despite its weight.

"You okay, mate?" he yelled down.

There was no answer. "Hey buddy, you okay?" Aussie yelled, letting the barrel tap the man's helmet. "You in trouble?" Suddenly he saw a black blob pass him into the open door. He heard a shout from above and saw the grenade come out again, bursting open about ten feet below him, and felt a hot sting in his right buttock. By now realizing the man below him was a ChiCom, he let the barrel of the Haskins swing in close directly above the man's white overlay hood. The ChiCom's right hand came up to push the rifle away, his left hand holding another grenade.

"You—" Aussie began, and pulled the trigger on the Haskins, sending a .50 depleted uranium slug right through the ChiCom helmet, exiting from the man's chest in a crimson cloud of pink snow, the man, or rather his corpse, falling quickly to the ground, already lost to view in the snow.

"Cheeky bastard!" Aussie yelled as he was helped aboard the Pave Low, saw the rope ladder coming up after him, and felt immediate relief. Then as the Pave Low started off along with the other two southwest across the lake and began climbing, he sensed a sudden tension inside the chopper. He heard a bump, then another, and could feel the Pave Low yawing hard to the right, and he could hear the pilot's voice. "Go for height, damn it! Height!" His voice shouted with urgency, and Lewis could hear another pilot's voice but was unable to make out what he was saying over the sizzling noise of static. Then he heard, quite clearly, "I'm going down." Seconds later there was a muffled explosion.

"She's gone!" Brentwood said. There were several more bumps hitting the fuselage. "Gone where?" Aussie asked. There was no answer, and Aussie made his way through the tightly packed troops to the pilot and copilot's cabin. Beyond the windscreen was nothing but an impenetrable whiteness. It was a complete whiteout, but the radar was speckled as if a pepper shaker had been passed over it and all the speckles alight.

"Birds," the copilot yelled, seeing his puzzled expression. "Fucking thousands of 'em. Lake's a fucking bird sanctuary."

"Jesus," Aussie said, "is that what's hitting us?"

"You've got it." He'd no sooner spoken than another impact hit the chopper, and a spray of blood and feathers was smearing over the perspex window. The wipers began to whine. They threw out anything and everything they could to lessen the weight and gain more altitude, including the Haskins, minus its bolt action, and eventually they were high enough that the iridescent dots on the radar became less and less but were still a threat. They heard the F-15

Eagles streak past high over them and then a Mayday from one of the pilots, then a gut-wrenching explosion.

"Christ, his intakes must be jammed with 'em," the pilot said. "And at that speed, man—"

Lieutenant Reid had seen the "telephone post," the Soviet-made SAM streaking up toward the F-15C Eagle, and had dropped down to get below the SAM. When the Eagle was below it, Reid pulled up harder, the SAM following but unable to make the acute upturn in time, going harmlessly past the Eagle. Then suddenly, triple A had exploded halfway between the plane's right-side 20mm Vulcan cannon and the speed brake actuator, tearing the plane apart. Reid had ejected immediately, the Douglas ACES 11 seat suddenly in the sky, full of rushing wind and dirty black puffs of triple A fire exploding all around, and the chute opened, drifting down silently amid the mist and fog, Reid doing everything possible to steer the chute away from the lake but realizing it was mainly up to fate. The black puffs of AA smoke seemed to decrease, and Reid was pretty sure that the chute was being blown over the mountain range toward Damquka.

For several seconds Aussie could see parts of the F-15 Eagle sliding down the Pave's radar screen. Both remaining Pave Low pilots wanted to go down and try to rescue some of the men from the downed chopper and, if possible, the pilot of the F-15 if the pilot had had time to eject, which was highly unlikely. But they both knew the rules. If they went back down into the mass of birds, which the Chinese had deliberately panicked and set to flight above the lake, then they too risked crashing—then everybody would be gone.

Lieutenant Reid landed northeast across the mountains down toward the Damquka-Naggu road. She knew her chance of being rescued by the choppers on the mission was nil, but momentarily at least she was pleased that if she had to be shot down it was triple A and not the result of making the wrong cut in a dogfight. There was no way she or the best pilot in the world could evade triple A by maneuvering—it was simply a matter of bad luck. But that satisfaction—that she was as good as any man—a conviction perhaps essential to the first woman combat pilot in any theater of operations—was short-lived.

In what was a whiteout, Julia took out her compass and headed north to where her military fold-out map of Tibet had "numerous nomad encampments" marked. It was a calculated risk, to go north, further toward China rather than south toward Lhasa, but with Tibet overrun by the Chinese she decided that keeping away from Lhasa, where there were thousands more Chinese than native Tibetans, would be the preferable risk.

In addition to her emergency rations and kit, which included a Nuwick forty-four-hour heat/light candle, she had what pilots called the "tit," a small, arctic-type pup tent just big enough to lie in and zip up and have room for the candle. She could try a purple flare, but it was only a low probability that any of the aircraft, including choppers, were anywhere in the area—anyway their flight plan had called for them to fly south toward the Indian border, not north. And in that case the purple flare would only be an invitation to the Chinese. She felt, too, an added pressure—as the first female combat pilot. If she could tough it out in this godforsaken clime and somehow escape, then her fortitude would be another victory against the prejudices of those who didn't want women in combat. History had also taught her that if she was captured by enemy troops, rape was a high probability. Far down on the white, icy north road she could see a black dot—a roadside shack, or something moving? A vehicle? She couldn't tell. She would have to get closer. Just then she experienced a whiteout and felt a surge of fear—told herself to settle right down and took out her compass. If she walked north-northeast she should meet the road.

For Aussie Lewis and the other returning SAS/D troopers it was a somber helo trip back via the Indian border, and it remained so all the way to Khabarovsk.

Freeman's dreams the night after the SAS/D returned were seamless, each running naturally into the other, despite the fact that in one dream he was at Trafalgar, where, after the broadside of just one naval engagement, all the men on the gun deck, as often happened, were permanently deafened. And he dreamed of the Russians, who had pioneered paratroop drops but without chutes when in winter they had to crawl out on the wing and drop off into the snow. Many were injured or killed, of course, but many were not and were quickly in action against the Wermacht. He dreamed of Hannibal crossing the Alps—of Napoleon's retreat, how the Russian fastness soaked up the French like blotting paper soaked up ink—and he dreamed of the first land defeat suffered by the Japanese in 1942 at Milne Bay and of MacArthur's triumphant return.

Suddenly he was awake and, hearing a noise outside, immediately reached for his shotgun. It was a mournful, keening wind fresh out of the great Gobi, and in its wolfish howling there seemed to be a warning that if he did not do something soon, the sheer weight of Cheng's numbers would determine the outcome: China would absorb him as Russia had the French. It was in that moment that he realized what had to be done. Of course it was a gamble, but if it worked it would be a decisive blow—no, *the* decisive blow. He got up, ordered in coffee, and told the duty officer that as soon as the SAS/D team got back he wanted to see the four troop leaders.

"They'll be pretty tired, General, after—"

"Tired! Don't give me tired, son. Just get 'em here. They've had fourteen hours sleep on the flight back from India through Japan," Freeman said. "Besides, these are SAS/D, Major. They're the best we've got. So don't give me tired."

"No, sir."

Studying the SATPICs of Beijing, Freeman could see what looked like headless bodies along the east-west Changan Avenue and also in the square. Higher magnification showed the people's heads were covered by a kind of muslin bag. Others, street sweepers, were busy with long straw brooms and wearing surgical masks against the dust. Freeman pointed to the stretch of dirt that had no doubt once been a grassy meridian. Or at least that he knew had once been a grassy meridian.

"In the fifties," he explained to Norton, "the Chinese government, with faultless Marxist logic, decided to do something to get rid of the millions of birds feeding off the city and defacing statues of the Heroes of the Revolution, and so the authorities encouraged the people to kill all the birds. Only problem was, with all the birds gone, there came a plague of insects that most of the birds had fed on. The insects destroyed the plants, and then the winds blew away the soil with no plants to anchor it. So now in addition to the west wind bringing all the dirt out of the Gobi, we've got the dirt from the city mixed in with it." It was a yellowish pollution—a mixture of dust and grit from the deserts.

"Dick," Freeman ordered, "get Harvey Simmet up here." Norton glanced at his watch. It was three A.M., the time when most people die.

"Yes, I know," Freeman said. "He's probably having his beauty sleep, but get him all the same."

"Yes, sir."

"And get the aerial photo wiz."

"It *is* late, General. Can it wait—"

"No! I don't give a goddamn what time it is. You think Cheng shuts down past midnight? At night, Major, he moves entire divisions—thirteen thousand men at a time. The Chinese are a sea around us, and we'd better do something mighty quick before we drown."

"Yes, sir."

What in hell, Dick Norton wondered, was the general up to now? Had a little snippet of Chinese history—another point of the minutiae he knew about China—changed his mind about the strategy of the attack?

In fact, General Freeman was thinking about the night of June 3, 1989, when the PLA's Twenty-seventh Army used a lot of tear gas at the Muxidi Bridge in Beijing.

Julia started out and anticipated feeling nauseated from altitude sickness until she got used to the relative lack of oxygen at fourteen thousand feet. But whether it was her training in the centrifuge, the tight compression at high Gs, or the fact that she was in superb physical condition, she experienced little of the shortness of breath that they'd been briefed about before the mission.

She still couldn't tell what the black dot was, only that it must be moving away from her at the same rate she was following it.

For minutes at a time the dot was completely lost in the sudden windstorms of snow and even hail that beat down, then just as quickly disappeared to reveal the denuded landscape of Tibet's Chang Tang, a land of sky-blue lakes and vast green treeless grassland, pierced here and there by precipitous treeless mountains of somber, mustard-hued beauty.

The black dot seemed to break into several parts, and she could see it was two or three animals, stopped now, and another figure—a man—possibly walking with them. Should she wave or not? Would they be Chinese or Tibetans?

Most Tibetans, Julia knew, hated the Chinese since the PLA's takeover in 1950 and the fleeing of the Dalai Lama nine years later. After the Red Guards' mad "Cultural Revolution" was over, after they'd murdered monks, forced them into labor camps, and destroyed over fifteen hundred Buddhist monasteries, there was a legacy of oppression that ran deep. Julia knew if it was a group of Tibetan nomads or *drokba* who lived from one campsite to another on the seventeen-thousand-foot-high plateau that was the Chang Tang, or north plateau, then she might be lucky. The *drokba* had suffered as much as any of the Tibetans in Lhasa and the towns. Often they'd fared worse, the Chinese insisting that Tibet was theirs, forcing many of the nomads into communes and confiscating the yaks, goats, sheep, and pasture grounds upon which the *drokba* had traditionally depended for their livelihood.

As she got closer to the yaks she saw smaller animals, sheep probably, and some goats milling about—now about half a mile away down the road. It had not been a heavy snowstorm, and the black coats of the yaks had only a dusting of snow, as if someone had thrown talcum powder over them, and they were mostly still, nuzzling through the light spring snow, eating the rich grass below.

Whether it was her anxiety about just what kind of reception she'd get—some of the poorer nomads had collaborated with the Chinese and become richer—the shoulder holster holding her service .45 was rubbing against her bra and she had to loosen the shoulder strap. She prayed she wouldn't need the gun but that if she did, she wouldn't hesitate, she would fire it the way she flew—with total concentration, the kind of concentration that had made her the first American woman fighter pilot to down two of the enemy: a Chinese Shenyang and a MiG Fulcrum.

None of the male pilots in Khabarovsk had taken any notice of her downing a Shenyang, common opinion being that if you couldn't down a Shenyang with one eye closed you were a piss-poor pilot. The Fulcrum—well that had made the boys sit up and take notice. Not many had downed the brilliant Chinese-bought CIS fighter.

She had heard, "Bogey five o'clock!" and made the first cut hard left, she dropping speed, he increasing, till for a second they were all but parallel. Then she was climbing and started a barrel roll right, going for the Fulcrum. Next minute she couldn't see him in front, the next they were in rolling scissors. She had him in her sights for less than a second and had the tone from the Sidewinder. It was all she needed—releasing the missile, the latter streaking forward with its nose locked onto the Fulcrum's exhaust.

The Fulcrum tried to drop fast and outturn the Sidewinder, but the missile disappeared up his exhaust, blowing the Fulcrum apart in a yellow sheet of flame—no chute.

It had lasted less than a minute, but after her downing of the Fulcrum, the ribbing suddenly ceased. And if in the world of split-second, fly-by-wire warfare she could get another three enemy fighters she'd be an ace. Some of the guys she knew would celebrate her; some would be eaten away by jealousy. Tough. But before any of that could happen she had to get back, and next to the north and south poles, she was in perhaps the harshest place on earth, where you could experience the four seasons in one day, so unsettled and everchanging was the weather on the roof of the world.

Now she could see that several yak-hide tents had been put up, and already there was smoke wafting above them, the yak-dung fires giving off an unexpectedly pleasant odor. She went through her emergency pack again, looking under the wafer-thin but highly absorbent tampons to the phrase book. Unfortunately it had only Chinese—Mandarin and Cantonese—phrases. If none of the nomads spoke English it would all have to be done with sign language.

As she approached the nomads' camp, several *naki*— sheep dogs—began barking, their bluish black coats in marked contrast to the light dusting of snow, and several children in filthy clothes gathered around one of them while staring at this apparition—this long, lithe Westerner that might well have come from one of the mountain gods. One of the children, looking at her fixedly, called out, presumably to someone in the tent, but Julia couldn't tell for sure as the child's stare had been unbroken while he ate what looked to be a kind of yogurt from a small, decorated bowl.

Then abruptly the child went inside, followed by one of the dogs, and a man dressed in trousers whose bottoms were sewn into a pair of Reebok shoes and whose torso was covered by a dirty sheepskin jacket, wiping his nose on the sleeve, came out of the yak tent, smiled, and waved her inside, saying something in Tibetan that she hoped meant "You're welcome."

"What the—"

"The general wants to see you, Harvey."

"You know what time it is?"

"I do. The general still wants to see you."

Harvey Simmet could barely raise himself from his bunk. "What does he want?"

"Don't ask me, sir. I'm just the gofer."

Harvey almost left the tent without his helmet.

"Better put it on, sir," the duty officer told him. "The general has a standing order about that—even have to wear them in . . ."

" . . . When we go to the latrines. Yes, I know. Eighty-dollar fine, right?"

"Right, sir."

As he bent his body against the Gobi wind, Harvey was wondering what was so urgent that the general had to dig him out of a warm bed at this ungodly hour.

"Ah, there you are, Harvey. Hope I didn't wake you up. Coffee?"

"No—yes, sir. Coffee, yes."

"Clear the cobwebs out, Harvey," Freeman said, handing his meteorological officer a steaming mug. "Spring has sprung and we've work to do, gentlemen."

"What do you want to know, General?" Harvey asked.

"First things first, Harv. This dust storm from the Gobi. Will it be short?"

"Could last for days. Bad for our air cover."

"And theirs, Harvey."

"True." Harvey was starting to come round with the coffee. "I'd guesstimate three to four days."

"After that?" the general asked.

"It'll settle down. You'll have your close air support again. Warthogs can prowl at will."

"Perhaps, but that's no consolation if Cheng's troops start using that goddamn smoke cover again. Impossible to make IFF."

"True," Harvey said, pulling the blanket around him.

"So it's three to four days' dust we have."

"Yes—maybe longer, but three to four I'd figure."

"Now, Harvey, this is important. How strong is the wind going to be?"

"Thirty, maybe forty miles per hour. Forty at the outside."

"It's more than that out there now."

"You're right, General, but it still sounds worse than it is. In any case it'll be down around thirty miles per hour in four days—maybe less."

" 'Scuse me, sir, Major Norton." It was the duty officer.

"Yes, Major?"

"Photo recon boys are here."

"You have that computer model ready yet?" Freeman cut in.

"Working on it, sir."

"What the hell does that mean? Is it ready or not?"

"They're working on it, sir."

Suddenly Freeman slammed his fist against the map, knocking off several armored divisions. "Goddamn it! What's the matter with you people? You think it's time to sleep?" He was so loud he even drowned out the radio babble outside his room. "We haven't got time to *sleep*! We're going to counterattack! We are going on the offensive, gentlemen. And I don't mean holding our positions. We are going to eat Chinese alive."

"That's no good," Harvey Simmet whispered to the duty officer. "Eat a few and you're hungry again."

"Is that clear?" Freeman bellowed. "I want this team to think *attack*. Defeat starts in the mind and I won't allow it!"

Harvey Simmet took another sip of coffee. He wasn't in the mood for Freeman's Follies. Damn generals were all the same—except that George C. Scott here did have one quality that always earned him a lot of forgiveness. He was prepared to be out on the point with his men when it counted, and he had proved it from Korea to Ratmanov Island to the Never-Skovorodino road.

Freeman put everyone in the tent on a need-to-know status. He didn't want anything to get out, otherwise the entire operation would be jeopardized. He decided to do the mock-up himself. Computing three-dimensional stereoscopic printouts was fine, but to see it actually built in front of you—something you could touch, move things around a bit—was the best. Besides, the truth was, Freeman wasn't all that good on a computer—strictly a two-finger basher. "Slow as a wet week," as someone had said. With Play-Doh he was adept and fast.

When they played taps for the five-man crew of the Pave Low and the seventeen SAS/D men aboard it who had gone down over Lake Nam, as well as the pilot of the F-15C—no chute had been seen—Freeman's eyes flooded with tears, for he was as moved by the death of those who served under him as he was proud of them in battle, and it wasn't until ten minutes later, when he had time to compose himself, that he had the remaining thirty SAS/D men into his headquarters hut.

Thirty out of eighty. A unit with that kind of loss was usually taken off the board, but Freeman had work for them to do. He expected no complaint and received none. Aussie Lewis, slightly wounded in the butt from the ChiCom grenade, Salvini, Choir Williams, and Brentwood told him they were ready. Aussie was still thinking about the fact that had he not had the Haskins sniper rifle and waited till last to climb aboard, he would have been in the first chopper—the one that went down. He knew it was illogical, but this knowledge made him feel that he owed something special to the unit, to the men who had gone down.

"Gentlemen," Freeman told the thirty SAS/D men, "you're going to be up to full strength again and then some. Eight squadrons in all, a hundred and sixty of you.

You lot have done a magnificent job at Lake Nam, but we have to capitalize on that victory *now*. We can't assume that your action will stop the missiles for more than two weeks or so before they rebuild."

He stopped and decided to illustrate his point with a true story of how the Chinese in the Sino-Japanese War sabotaged a train track. "Now we use explosives," Freeman said. "But back then the Chinese didn't have enough and so they brought out a whole town. Thousands of them. Every man, woman, and child stood in a long line, and then at one command they all upended the track by its sleepers so that it just buckled and pushed right over. We don't even *think* like that because we've never had that kind of population. But they can—they've got the manpower—so we can't assume that now we've given them a black eye at Nam they won't be ready to go again with more missiles in a few more weeks. Which is why it's imperative that we act within the next ninety-six hours. That should give you time to re-equip and learn your part till you think and breathe it. Harvey Simmet guarantees a break in the winds on the fourth day. We'll move out at twenty-three hundred hours the night of the third. We'll chute in at plus or minus zero one hundred hours. In the first place they won't expect us, and even if they did, they would figure dawn, not pitch darkness, as the time of attack."

When he pulled the cloth off from the Play-Doh model everyone knew what it was immediately. Freeman was either bonkers or brilliant.

"We're going for the brain, gentlemen—we're going to paralyze their central nervous system. Without that, the body politic will have no center and we'll see not one China but many who will join us to throw out Nie and the whole State Council."

The SAS/D team gazed down at the model. Freeman had

even found a small newspaper photo of Mao and had put this at the entrance to the Forbidden City, looking out from on high over the vastness of Tiananmen Square, the largest square in the world.

A few blocks further west along Changan Avenue, well to the left of Mao's picture, Freeman had sculpted out the Zhongnanhai compound where the State Council members, and, most importantly, the entire military commission, were housed and guarded.

"Everything," Freeman said, "depends on our speed and ferocity. Simultaneously we will be launching the biggest counterattack yet along the Orgon Tal–Honggor front. But it's here—in the heart of Beijing—where we must succeed. If we seem to be winning there, we'll have others follow— the Malof guerrillas up north, the Democracy Movement in the south, and, if we're lucky, Admiral Kuang in Taiwan will move across the straits. If that happens the ChiComs'll have a two-front war into the bargain."

Most of them were still watching the mock-up of downtown Beijing—the sheer audacity of Freeman's plan only now sinking in.

"We go right into the square. Fan out from there from the Statue of Heroes of the Revolution. We'll keep ferrying in more troops as we can, but our one hundred and sixty will be the point."

"Our?" Aussie Lewis said. "Are you coming, General?"

"Unless," Freeman replied, "anyone has any objections." The effect on the men's mood was instantaneous.

"Lewis."

"Yes, sir?"

"Your troop with me. We'll hit the Zhongnanhai compound. Capture who we can, shoot who we can't. Williams and Salvini."

"Sir?"

"Great Hall of the People. Brentwood."

"Sir."

"Underground railway—including the secret escape line they don't think we know about that runs from the Zhongnanhai compound to Xishan military base."

"Yes, sir."

"Right. You'll form the core, and with the replacements we'll gather strength. Choir, I want you to take charge of the radio tower, or rather what's left of it." Choir was about to interject, but Freeman stopped him. "Not now. I'll go into more detail in the final briefing later on. Meanwhile I'll leave choice of weapons up to the individual, but remember, it'll be short-range for most of it but I'll need twenty snipers to spread about. Take some Haskins." For Freeman it would be the Winchester 1200 with fléchette-packed cartridges. The enormous implications of Freeman's plan excited Aussie Lewis. He turned to Brentwood. "Say what you like, the old man's got balls."

"Lewis!"

"Sir."

"Over here."

"Sir."

"Lewis, I don't want to hit this one too hard, but intelligence reports tell us that Miss Malof is in the same Beijing jail as Smythe. Soon as we take the square, you take a squad to liberate it."

"Bloody right," Lewis said.

"General?" Salvini asked. "How about the Chinese garrison? Beijing has the Thirty-first Army ready."

"Not in the middle of the city—on the outside perimeter. They're expecting an armored thrust through the Great Wall. We'll feint there of course, but our main force'll leapfrog the son of a bitch."

His confidence was infectious, but even so, Norton, Har-

vey Simmet, and others knew that it would be touch and
go. If he lost, they'd drum him out of the army. If he won,
well—they'd have to wait and see.

CHAPTER NINETEEN

INSIDE BEIJING AND the other big Chinese cities from
Harbin to Shanghai, the sirens of military convoys were
constant, many of them two to three truckloads of soldiers
going to yet another public execution of "hooligans" and
those suspected of being "fifth columnists."

In the Beijing prison yard, where the first blooms of
spring had popped up along the wall, the killing posts were
chipped and scarred by the seemingly endless procession of
Nie's firing squads.

From her drab hospital bed in a ward that in any other
country in the world would have been condemned under
the Health Act, Alexsandra could see those being
executed—mostly men but women, too. A day or so after
Alexsandra had arrived they had done away with any cere-
mony, not even bothering to blindfold them—just made
them kneel, their hands tied behind their backs, and one
shot through the base of the skull.

Alexsandra tried to pull the blinds closed. The blinds
were removed, and her bed and side table wheeled closer to
the window in such a way that she could not help seeing

the daily executions down in the courtyard. Nie was determined that she should daily observe what happened to those who did not cooperate with the Party. After her beating, Nie had said her sentence could be commuted to life if she confessed.

Two Chinese group armies—a total of one hundred thousand reinforcements—were on their way to Orgon Tal-Honggor from the Beijing military district as well as a tank division, two artillery divisions, and four engineering regiments, the latter called up because of serious flooding of the rivers following the typhoon. Also, the Chinese had a problem with their bridges once they got outside the greater general metropolitan area. Here many old bridges simply could not take anything bigger than a fifty-ton load, and the engineers were there to ply emergency spans across swollen streams and irrigation channels that had become rivers in the spring storm.

Alexsandra knew that the further north you went the worse the bridges became. As she was thinking about the bridges as a metaphor for her own journey, how she had crossed the Black River so many times from the Jewish autonomous region in the north into Manchuria, she wondered if she had come to the last bridge of her life. A confession would allow her to pass from certain death to life and hope—if the Americans won. But she knew she would not cross the bridge if the toll for it was a confession against her comrades. She sat forlornly watching another "conspirator" die. When first she'd entered the jail a few days before, they had only tied the condemned prisoners' hands. Now they had gags on as well.

"Why are they gagging them?" she asked the young

nurse on duty. The nurse was busy writing reports, and she did not look up. "They call your name!"

For Alexsandra, those few words were like being struck again by the guard who'd brutalized her. But the sorrow she felt, the humility, the realization that people were dying with her name on their lips, undid her, and she wept, the tears starting down her cheek and stinging the ugly purple-red bruises on her cheekbone. The nurse, a short, pert woman—a no-nonsense air about her—told her to be quiet or she would have to sedate her. If she didn't keep quiet it would set off an unruly protest by the other patients. Alexsandra didn't care now what they did; the bravery of men and women dying for her cause and theirs had stripped her pride utterly.

"Very well," the nurse said, and came bossily behind the screen with the hypodermic of ten millimeters of Diazepam. She also placed a kidney basin on the small bedside table and in it a white strip of paper. She pointed to the paper as she brushed Alexsandra's arm with a swab of cold cotton wool smelling of alcohol. Alexsandra turned over the paper. It said simply, "1:00 A.M. Be ready."

With that the nurse injected Alexsandra, put the hypodermic in the kidney basin, and walked curtly away. The Diazepam wouldn't knock her out but would calm her enough so that she might get an hour or two's sleep. She buzzed the nurse and asked her assistance to go to the toilet. Despite the Diazepam coursing through her veins, she was still alert and said simply but very quietly, "You must tell our friends to blow all the bridges."

She knew it would make little difference to Freeman's army, for its replacement tanks were already too heavy to use most of the China bridges and would have to be either airlifted over or put across on bridges of their own, but the bridges were still strong enough for the lighter Chinese tanks, and if they were blown, it would cost the Chinese divisions crucial time in trying to stop any American counterattack.

CHAPTER TWENTY

FREEMAN'S SECOND ARMY was as ready as it would ever be, and the speed with which his new armor had arrived on the scene within the last few days once again owed something to his legendary attention to the tactical details as well as the strategy of war. In having fired a young logistics officer for not knowing the difference between the Siberian and Chinese railway gauges, which could have caused a defeat at the rail terminals, he had served notice to the logistics officers and engineers to get busy adapting rail cars for the shorter gauge. The resulting smooth transition from ship to railhead southward proved a crucial factor in Second Army's logistical buildup, and it was clear to the Chinese, having to move cautiously through rain-swollen creeks, rivers, and other conduits, that a major American counterattack was under way.

The shape of the attack was that of an arrowhead or triangular formation, the widest part or baseline being the line between Orgon Tal and Honggor, the intent of both ends to meet in an arrow tip of overwhelming mobile force near Badaling on the Great Wall, forty miles from Beijing and then on through the Juyong Pass, past the western hills to the city thirty-five miles to the southeast.

On the map of the city, Freeman connected the targets that would form a rough V shape. The left top of the V was Beijing University, at the bottom of the V, Tiananmen Square, the Great Hall of the People on the left, or western, side of Tiananmen, as well as the Zhongnanhai compound, which housed the "Central Authority"—the top party officials—and to the northeast, or top right-hand side of the V, Shoudu Airport.

Regular Second Army paratroopers would be dropped over the airport to secure it for Second Army, but if they could not take it then TACAIR would go in with the tarmac-busting air-drop mines that would both pockmark and booby-trap the runways, preventing the Chinese from using or repairing them. But the main business of the 160 men of the SAS/D force in the inner city was to take the Zhongnanhai, built around two lakes next to the moat-protected Forbidden City, the ancient imperial capital of China.

"Remember, our main job," Freeman told his SAS/D men, "is to take the Zhongnanhai. Officially its name means 'central and south seas' because its residences and offices are built around two connecting lakes—Lake Zhonghai, the central lake, and Lake Nanhai, the southern lake. The two are about a mile long and vary in width from a third of a mile to the north to three-quarters of a mile wide at the southern end. Now there's reconstruction and new building going on with new sauna baths and enlarging some of the residences here and there. We don't know exactly what bungalows are being worked on, nor if the families of the Party bosses will be there. You'll need to be very careful when clearing rooms. This'll mean flash-stun grenades rather than HE to be thrown by the first pair. But quick response to anyone you see, and remember to shout a challenge in any possible IFF mix-up. The Zhongnanhai, as you can see, is to the west of you if you're in Tiananmen Square looking north at the Gate of Heavenly Peace where Mao's photograph is hung.

"Zhongnanhai is walled, and so once we get in, the wall can serve as a protective barrier from any PLA coming too quickly to the rescue—we hope. Anyway, our job is to take out the leadership and to hold until relieved by our main forces attacking through the wall at Juyong Pass, thirty-seven miles north."

"How about the PLA *in* the compound, General?"

"A small force—possibly two to three platoons at the most. They always have the two white-gloved sentries at the gate. Here inside the model you can see there is a series of walks and bungalows—luxurious bungalows—for the exclusive use of the Party bosses. While we're going into the Zhongnanhai, pamphlets will be dropped into the Beijing and Qinghua universities to explain how we've come to liberate the city from the old Communist bosses and to return the goddess of democracy to her rightful place. That's powerful stuff for people, especially the younger ones, who still remember the massacre by their own troops in eighty-nine in Tiananmen Square.

"Intelligence indicates we have a virtual underground army waiting for the means and help to overthrow the detested old men like Chairman Nie. But what the regular army will do we don't know. That's why I want the whole military commission captured as soon as possible. After that I don't know what will happen—we could get a backlash of patriotism despite the hated Communist rule." Freeman paused. "For that reason this is a purely voluntary mission. It's risky—a dice throw—but if we can pull it off—"

"Sir?"

"Yes?"

"You mentioned Admiral Kuang during the first briefing. Do we know for sure that he'll attack across the strait and tie up the southern forces which would otherwise be used against us? And how will he know that we're attacking?"

"Hopefully he'll attack," Freeman answered, "and as to your follow-up question, the moment our armor hits Badaling he'll know. So there it is in overview. Anybody want out?"

No one did. Freeman nodded knowingly. "Didn't think so. I can promise you this, boys. If we pull this off it'll be one hell of a coup! You'll read about yourselves in the history books!"

"If we're alive to read any," one of Aussie's group murmured.

"Well," Salvini said, "you going to bet on this, Aussie?"

Aussie said he wouldn't. He was a gambler, sure, but he wasn't a fool. Freeman's plan was brilliantly conceived, but absolutely too close to call.

In the wind-riven high country of the Chang Tang, Julia was obliged to stay with the nomads three days before she could move, or rather had to move. She had been suffering from hypothermia when she had reached the nomad's tent and sat down to warm up by the dung fire, the smoke exiting from the smoke hole high up in the dark yak-hair tent looking like a rectangular marble column, its boundaries sharply defined by the sunlight flooding the smoke hole. But the presence of the sun did not carry any promise of warmth, for outside a blizzard had been sweeping across the snow-covered pass between the mountains whose summits had been lost to a swirling mist created by the howling winds.

Everyone had sat smiling, the man in his fifties perhaps and a woman whom Julia took to be his wife in the same kind of dirty sheepskin coat that so many of the Tibetan nomads wore. And two children, around ten or twelve, she guessed, their noses running from the cold and open-mouthed at the arrival of the stranger whose flight suit seemed nothing less than miraculous. But the gun she wore—or rather had now taken off and put by her side—the gun put her in perspective. They had seen guns before, of course, but mostly the old flintlock muskets that were still used by the nomads. The kind of gun and the pouch she wore, however, were like those the Chinese had brought up and down the Lhasa road.

They offered her yogurt and tea with *tsamba*—roasted barley flour. She found the yogurt bitter but steeled herself for the sake of good manners, and in an effort to win their friendship she smiled approvingly at the yogurt. This evoked laughter from the two children and a reciprocal smile from the parents. She had told them she was American. They made bobbing motions with their heads, followed by long *ahhhs*, but Julia wasn't sure they really understood.

After unzipping her flying jacket, she had pointed to the sewn-in panel of cloth made up of the American flag and beneath it, sewn-in printing in several languages—most East European, the panels having been made during the old cold war period. Translated, the panels asked all the nationalities represented to assist the wearer of the panel back to the United States forces and promised a thousand-dollar reward for doing so. It had been one of Freeman's ideas put to use earlier in the war, but the languages included only three Asiatic tongues: Chinese, Japanese, and Korean. The languages of South Asia, from India to Bhutan, had been omitted.

* * *

On the third day an elderly man—in his late sixties or early seventies, Julia guessed—came into the hut but ignored her and sat down by the fire and began fanning it with goat skin bellows that squeaked each time he pumped. Grateful to have found warmth and food, Julia was nevertheless anxious to be getting on, to get out of Tibet and China somehow, but she knew the Chinese were everywhere in Tibet, that it was a political fiction to pretend Tibet had any autonomy. The Chinese were here to stay.

The old man, whom Julia took to be one of the grandparents, said something to the younger. The younger man nodded agreeably, and pulling up his sheepskin jacket, he pointed to his watch, which read 5:00 P.M., and held up his fingers to denote twenty more hours, and by a mixture of smiles, head shakings, and grunts of approval managed to convey the message that someone would be here in twenty hours who would speak her language. At least that's what she thought he meant. Or perhaps he meant something entirely different.

The frustration of her predicament was made worse by the strong probability that she had been reported as MIA—for when her chute had opened she'd not seen any trace of her wingman in the thick cloud. If they thought her dead, then why send anyone else out to look for her? Deciding she could do no more, she curled up on the sheepskin mats and went to sleep—at least confident that she was among friends. She pulled the gun under the sheepskin rug.

When next she woke she heard the straining of ropes against the tent. All the others were asleep except the tent's owner who had first welcomed her. The fire cast a flickering glow across the man's face, one minute hiding him in shadow, the next revealing his smiling teeth. Cocking herself up on one elbow, she saw by her watch that it was 8:00

P.M.—which meant she had to wait another seventeen hours before the arrival of the man—she presumed it would be a man—who could speak English. Or perhaps he spoke only Chinese?

Lying down to sleep again, she was aware of something crawling over her skin beneath her breasts. She turned, now facing away from the fire, and peered down her khaki T-shirt to see if she could see any bug on her. She couldn't, but still felt itchy. She tried not to scratch, tried to think of something else to take her mind off it, off everything for a while. Was it lice? Could they live in such cold?

It was then, as she reached under the sheepskin, down further about her feet, up higher, both sides of her, that she realized the gun was gone. She turned about abruptly and looked straight at the tent's owner sitting by the fire, but he was nodding off to sleep. Or had he simply closed his eyes?

CHAPTER TWENTY-ONE

THE AIR FORCE brass disagreed strongly with Freeman's refusal to bomb Beijing into submission, and Freeman was appalled by the air force's narrow view.

"My God," he told the air chief, "we want to *win over* the Chinese people—not alienate them. What you guys have to remember is when some son of a bitch is dropping bombs on you you don't care whether they're democratic or totalitarian—you hate them. No, damn it, the whole point of this SAS/D raid is to cut off and capture the head of the snake, not the body. We want to leave Beijing to the new forces of the Democracy Movement. So what I want you to do is to keep hammering away at Cheng's armor up near the trace. I know it's tough with all this damn dust and rubbish in the air from the typhoon, but try to keep his armored force locked up with your A-10s. Remember, I don't want any of your planes over Beijing unless I specifically call them in for pinpoint clearance duty. Besides, if you bomb the crap out of Beijing I'll have a vast rubble that my tanks can't get through and we'll be Molotov-cocktailed to death."

Turning to the map, he pointed to the Bo Hai Gulf. "And as for the possible launching of Tomahawk cruise missiles from off the coast, the problem there is that the Chinese, learning from the mistakes of Saddam Insane, have put up tents and huge cutouts from the Peking Opera throughout the Zhongnanhai compound and the main square. This is to confuse cruise missiles' terrain-contouring programs, which are made up from recent SATRECON shots. And if a cruise is confused about its target it's likely to hit anywhere in a city, killing civilians.

"Hell, the Beijing Hotel is only a five-minute walk up Changan Avenue. Not a very good policy," General Freeman told his air chief, "to litter a place with dead civilians then tell the rest we've come to liberate them."

The nurse due to go on duty at Beijing Number One jail's hospital from midnight to dawn cleaned her desk, or at least put the relevant yellow sheets of paper in either "incoming," "outgoing," or "pending." She had made a joke with the other two members of her cell in the Democracy

Movement that the Malof file should strictly be in the "out" tray that day, but she had been sensible enough to leave it in "pending."

The fact that it had taken so many weeks to get the democracy group ready was a matter of getting false papers for a planned journey from Beijing to the seaside resort of Beidaihe, 160 miles east of the capital, where it was still too early for holiday makers to be bathing off any of the three beaches. From one of the three—East, Middle, or West—it might be possible to get her away via a U.S. sub through the Bo Hai Gulf, as any northern journey from Beijing would have to pass through Cheng's divisions spread out northeast from Orgon Tal and China's Inner Mongolia to Manchuria.

It had also taken weeks to set up, because many of the Democracy Movement's underground cells of three had been penetrated by Nie's agents posing as eager recruits. The nurse, Meiling, knew that after the disappearance of the prisoner Malof she and the other two members might also have to leave the city lest they be hunted down and killed by Nie's men.

It was a sacrifice each of them had to make, for parents and relatives would suffer, most of all Meiling's, because she would be the person who, arranging for Alexsandra to hide under the dirty linen in the big two-wheeled baskets, would have to bribe the janitor to look the other way when the prisoner was transferred to a waiting vehicle. The janitor could always reasonably say he had seen nothing and be believed, but Meiling, the prisoner's bed nearby, would immediately be suspected and her family and relatives questioned—probably tortured. But it was something that Meiling had long been determined to do. No one had asked, and she'd told no one but her parents, that one of the so-called "hooligans" and "antistate bandits" who had been shot on June 3, 1989, on Changan Avenue when the Twenty-seventh Army moved in with tear gas, clubs, AK-47s, and armored personnel carriers, had been the man she had wanted to marry.

She looked up at the clock. It was 1:10 A.M. She walked over to Alexsandra Malof and, remaking the bed, whispered, "Call me to assist you to go to the toilet at one-twenty. I'll unstrap you and walk down there with you. You understand?"

"Yes."

Alexsandra had almost said "Thanks," but she had had so much betrayal in her life she always harbored a suspicion that she might be betrayed again. Even when the SAS/D commandos had cut her free from the Chinese guns in the climactic battle at Orgon Tal before the truce, she had thought that the Allies might torture her.

At one-twenty she jerked the cord pinned to her pillow and it rang the bell. Meiling ignored it for a while, then answered crossly for the benefit of any other prisoners listening and unstrapped her, allowing her to use a walker to go to the toilet. Though still weak from the guard's beating, she could have walked, but this was better, for using the walker would mean that none of the other prisoner patients would expect her back for quite a while as the toilet was way down the hall and off along a more poorly lit hallway to the right of the hospital ward.

In a small *hutong* where the smell of cooking wafted up not far from the hospital and where the houses were no more than holes in the wall, two men were trying to keep warm on the brick *kang*, its charcoal smoking below.

"We better go now—you have the tickets?"

The other man drew the tickets—two of them—return tickets to Shanhaiguan forty miles further on than Beidaihe,

but one of the men—a student from Beijing University—
and Alexsandra Malof would get off at Beidaihe rather than
Shanhaiguan as a safety precaution, then take a later train
for the remaining one and half hours to Shanhaiguan.

CHAPTER TWENTY-TWO

FREEMAN WALKED INTO the psychological warfare
section of Second Army, a unit that the general usually had
little time for. He said they ought to have reduced Noriega's
sentence for putting up with all that "damn rock 'n' roll"
the psych unit played at him through the loudspeakers in
Panama. "Let's see the pamphlets we're going to drop," he
said.

Dick Norton had already picked one up from the table
and handed it to Freeman. The general took an immediate
liking to the cartoon of the detested old men in Beijing
kicking peasants and workers. "Good. I want something
the people can understand—won't have to be highly educated to get the drift. All the minorities will understand
the Chinese symbols, but wasn't it the Chinese who said
that a picture is worth a thousand words?" He looked up
at the psych officer, asking, "Have you made a cartoon
for each minority—you know, different national dress, et
cetera?"

The CO of the psychological warfare unit shifted uncomfortably. "Ah, well, we thought that Han Chinese being the most . . ."

"There you go again!" Freeman cut in. "If I've said it once I've said it a thousand times—you keep thinking of China as one cohesive bloc. It *isn't*! *Never was!* Why do you think the Great Wall was built? To keep those who wanted in, *out*! The minorities are our natural allies— millions of them—as tired of the Beijing empire as the Gauls were of the Romans—as the republics were of the Soviet Union. You don't see the minorities or hear them in the mass of the Han, but they're there—waiting to be free."

"Yes, sir," the psych major said.

"Right, now make a note, Major. The text is good, telling them we've come to free them from Beijing's yoke. They'll all understand the Chinese script even if they pronounce it differently, but as well we must have the cartoons drawn so as to appeal to every different minority."

A captain from the psych unit who was affronted at Freeman's assumption that he knew more about the minorities than the psych unit asked, "Exactly *which* minorities did you have in mind, sir?"

"Everyone," Freeman said, and then he gave it to them, from memory and with both barrels. "The Hui, Manchu, Daur, Oroqen, Ewenki, Tujia, She, Li, Miao, Bai, Zhuang Dai Yao, Yi, Tibetan, Uygur, and Xibe. All right?"

The captain, indeed the entire psych unit, was silenced, and Dick Norton couldn't help a smile—he knew that news of the general's performance would spread through Second Army like wildfire, and within hours there'd be another notch in the Freeman legend of a man who, as usual, knew and had studied his enemy in meticulous detail.

"Norton."

"Yes, General?"

"Get Harvey Simmet up here. Fast. Tell him I want another update on the next *five* days' weather."

Harvey was relaxing, or rather in the process of relaxing, on his bunk when after some initial static on the tape he settled down, hands crossed in a funereal position, to hear the first few bars of Sinatra's "My Way" when the PA crackled to life. "Would Major Harvey Simmet report to . . ."

The latest from frontline SITREPs—situation reports—told Freeman that his forces were holding their own against the massed T-59s and T-62s south of Orgon Tal, with only two of every one hundred U.S. tanks "tits up"—down—because of some mechanical failure. But up around Honggor, the other terminus of the front, the situation was grim. The PLA's salvos of mobile-type 54-1 122mm howitzers thudded away at the dug-in American positions of Five Corps as screams from the swarms of T-70 130mm rockets rent the air as the rockets crashed down in deadly unison.

In defilade hull and turret positions the Americans' M1A1s held their own, but on this, the northeastern end of the trace, the battle took on a strange and unexpected aspect of trench warfare from the days of World War I and the Korean War—both sides in a rough equality, Cheng's armies having more men and more guns, the Americans fewer men and guns but much more accurate in their fire.

There was an attempt by Cheng's army to ford a swollen irrigation ditch in the desertlike terrain here with fifty-one of his fifteen-ton type-77 AAVs—amphibious armored vehicles—but the American M1A1s, able briefly to see through the windblown dust and debris, wreaked a terrible vengeance on Cheng's amphibians, with only seven making the shore, and of these, two simply conked out, their armor pierced by the molten jet from an APFSDS—armor piercing fin-stabilized discarding sabot—shot and leaking all over.

Bravely the Chinese commanders opened hatches and manned the 12.7mm AA gun, and fourteen of the sixteen men from each amphibious vehicle poured out only to be caught in a cross fire between the American tanks' coaxial 7.6mm machine gun and other 7.6mm atop each tank's turret, not one of the Chinese infantrymen making it.

More fifteen-ton T-77 AAVs were sent across the muddy swirl of about a hundred yards wide. Again the M1A1s came up from the hatch-down defilade position and the amphibians were slaughtered. But Cheng knew what he was doing, having ordered the amphibians across, confident that, sending them en masse, a dozen or so would make it and be free to race toward the Americans' dug-in positions. And so long as there were targets for them, the tanks of the U.S. Five Corps had no option but to use their fifty rounds apiece. Meanwhile swarms of Cheng's fast motorbike interdiction teams, armed with 85mm, 18.8-pound, rocket-propelled grenades, raced through the dust and over narrow footbridges to sever Freeman's overextended supply line.

Freeman's engineers worked the wonders that they are all too often forgotten for, but they couldn't perform miracles. The supply line they'd laid for the gasoline was a long, plastic hose plowed under a few inches of ground to bring gasoline to the front, but once a fissure in it had been made by a Chinese 81mm barrage it burst skyward in a long, thin finger of fire that served as a marker for all ensuing 81mm attacks in the sector.

Soon the line containing two blivets—the big plastic underground tanks—was like a giant water bed suddenly pierced with multiple needles, and the fuel set afire by backflash from the first mortar-created fire burned fiercely in the desert, as demoralizing to the Americans in the trenches as it was to those inside the tanks where ammunition was running low.

It was then that Cheng unleashed his regimental T-69s. The relatively light thirty-seven-ton, 580-horsepower tanks raced at fifty kilometers per hour, sweeping forward in arrowhead-shaped echelons, their laser range finders, which had been cut by the dust, of no concern because the fuel fires now illuminated the American M1A1s in turret defilade positions.

It was now that quantity—over one thousand T-69s against the two hundred M1A1s—had a quality all its own, as M1A1s that had run out of ammunition, having stopped many of the 69s dead in their tracks, were now themselves destroyed, many out of fuel as well as ammunition as they were finally overwhelmed by Cheng's tanks.

Dragon missile antitank teams managed to make some of the Chinese main battle tanks pay for the victory, but there were still 838 Chinese MBTs left to advance on the dug-in Americans.

"Send in the A-10s!" Freeman ordered. "Use our fuel fires as flares. And undo those T-69s that are crossing or near the severed fuel line." The A-10s, taking their cue from Freeman's order, used the fuel fires now as identification friend-or-foe flares and killed over a hundred more of the Chinese tanks.

The Warthogs' pilots were ecstatic, one of them reporting joyously, "We got the mothers—a hundred of 'em," to which Freeman's wry reply was, "Good—that only leaves seven hundred and thirty-eight."

The American infantry, at first dug in and now withdrawing from the positions south of Honggor without sufficient armor cover, were slaughtered by the ChiComs' 12.7 machine guns both on the tanks and those of the YW531H-type armored personnel carriers of Cheng's—many of the Americans simply run down and killed by the treads of Cheng's vehicles. In some instances, the Chinese rested their machine guns, many of them having got too hot because of the rapid fire, and used cannon to clear a trench, which left nothing but a bloody conduit of mashed bone and flesh that only further greased the treads of the Chinese tanks and gave off the peculiar copperlike odor of blood, adding to the smells of involuntary defecation, cordite, and dust.

"Dick," Freeman announced, "we have to hit them with a second front."

"What about Admiral Kuang?"

"He hasn't moved yet and I can't afford to wait."

"What do you have in mind—something on the coast?"

"Good man," Freeman said. "Great minds think alike. Yes, let's have a marine air-ground task force. And call in a carrier from South Korea to provide close air support."

Norton wondered where the MAGTAF would be used. "*Where* on the coast?"

"Beidaihe!"

"Ambitious," Norton commented, in what was one of the understatements of the war so far. Beidaihe had been chosen by Freeman because not only was it 150 miles east of Beijing but it was the summer fun place for all the high-ranking cadres and their lackeys. Deng's fortresslike villa was at Beidaihe. It was where all the top Party members and "worker heroes" of the People's Republic and selected military personnel went to escape, and those workers suffering from lung disease and nervous disorders went to Beidaihe's sanatorium for the peace and the salt air. Now in spring the fishing village was quiet, but it had three good beaches and had a good road as well as a railroad to Beijing. It was also the cadres' favorite resort. It used to be said that he who owned Beidaihe—not Beijing—had the mandate of heaven. Since Mao's victory in 1949, they simply said, "He who owns Beidaihe owns China."

"They get wind of it before we're ready, General, and those beaches could become an abattoir for Second Army."

"Well, Dick, it'll be our lot's job to make damn sure they don't know. We'll make a feint of hitting the coast up north first. Meanwhile at Beidaihe we'll send in SEALs by submarine. That skipper—young David Brentwood's older brother—Robert Brentwood. He's proved his mettle. We'll send a SEAL team in with his sub to scout the approaches. They can wrap underwater demolition charges around any obstacles to a landing and we can blow them in unison later by remote control."

"*If* Kuang doesn't come in and we need to send in the MAGTAF," Norton said.

"You've got it. At the very least it'll frighten the pants off of Cheng, having a beachhead attack to worry about. He'll have to divert at least two divisions—more—from the Beijing Military Region. If the marines get pinned down we can always pull them out, and us attacking Beidaihe might light a cracker under Kuang's ass and get him moving. Then China could have four fronts to contend with—the Orgon Tal–Honggor front, the trace north of Beijing, Beidaihe to the east, and Kuang to the south. That's when I'd expect all the Chinese minorities to take the cue. Hell, even if they don't, we have to take the pressure off our boys around Honggor. They're getting clobbered. We'll have to move in a carrier force from South Korea to Bo Hai—bomb the crap out of the Beidaihe beaches before and while our MAGTAF is going in."

Norton saw the weak link in a flash, and he was about to say something when Freeman conceded the Achilles' heel of the operation. "Yes, I know, PLA's navy is a brown navy. Haven't got a pot to piss in when it comes to deep water, but here we're talking about coastal defenses and they have scores of hydrofoil and fast-attack surface-to-surface missile boats for coastal defense. Well our carrier's screen'll have to deal with them."

"Washington isn't going to like the expansion of this 'reconnaissance in force.'"

"Well, Dick, I have a choice—see our boys chopped to pieces around Honggor, or take the pressure off with a MAGTAF. Hell, that's what a MAGTAF is all about—self-contained emergency force ready to move anywhere. If this isn't an emergency I don't know what in hell is." He paused. "Did I call it *that*—a 'reconnaissance in force'?"

"You did."

"Hum—needs a new title, Dick—with something U.N.-ish about it—'police action!' By God, that's it! For Khabarovsk press releases."

"Yes, sir. You do know the press are crying foul about you prohibiting them from the front."

"For their own safety," Freeman said.

"They'd take that risk, General."

"Yes, by God, I'm sure they would. And some son of a bitch'd take a faceup snapshot of one of our dead, and next thing you know we'd have every damned liberal from here to Waco telling us how we *should* have done it. No, Dick. No press—not now."

"Yes, General."

Within a half hour the MAGTAF was notified, and Captain Robert Brentwood, skipper of the Sea Wolf II class combination Hunter-Killer–ICBM sub USS *Reagan*, was ordered to take a SEAL team fully qualified from Coronado and San Clemente, the latter an open-water school at San Diego, and the airborne school at Fort Benning, Georgia, and have them carry out a BLS—beach landing site—survey of the central beach off Beidaihe.

As Alexsandra was pushed out of the prison exit into the darkness in a large bamboo hopper, she almost threw up from the noxious odors of the hospital's filthy linen, but it was her way to freedom, and within a half hour she had been transferred from the hospital truck to a *hutong* not far from the railway station. From there, after a change of clothing and bowl of meat-laced rice, she found herself aboard the six-and-a-half-hour train to Shanhaiguan, the university student accompanying her telling her that it would take only five hours to Beidaihe. If everything went all right, they would arrive close to dawn.

It was still several hours before dawn as Julia Reid was awakened by the baaing of sheep, the wind howling about the tent still sweeping down upon the Chang Tang unabated. Despite the soft sheepskin rugs she had been sleeping on, her body ached all over, and what had been a small bump on her left cheekbone, caused during her eject, was now a dark bruise. The smell of the dung fire, surprisingly pleasant, mixed with that of sour yogurt and cheese in the tent, gave a cloying quality to the air.

The strangeness of it all, the constant moaning of the wind and the pull on the tent ropes like a ship straining to be free, all reminded her of how far from home—how far from civilization—she was. She could hear the grandfather and the man who'd been watching her snoring like motor mowers, the sound so loud that at times it even subdued the wailing of the wind. Used to living in shared quarters at

Fairchild Air Force Base in Washington State, she wasn't normally bothered by the snores and other nocturnal sounds in barracks, but now they irritated her to the point of sleeplessness, and she pulled the sheepskin over her head. It was worse, her sense of isolation exacerbated. How long could she stay with the nomads?

From the little she'd been able to understand, it seemed as if they stayed only long enough for a pasture to be grazed and then moved on. Given this and the snow, she guessed they'd be on their way within a day or two. But to where? Further into the vastness of the Chang Tang plateau. Yet what else could she do? Turn around and *walk* to Lhasa, with Chinese troops looking for the pilot of the downed F-15? Or perhaps they couldn't reach the wreckage, wherever it was—perhaps it wasn't even visible, burned somewhere in the high mountain snows.

Someone in the tent broke wind, and a malodorous cloud permeated the smell of unwashed bodies, yogurt, and yak dung. Next time someone told her women weren't fit for combat she'd tell them to go find a yak tent. Beyond the immediate noises of snoring and the wind, Julia thought she could hear snoring from the next tent, which she knew was impossible.

The more she listened, the more convinced she became that it was a motor. No sooner had she deduced this than the flap of the tent seemed to implode, and silhouetted against a flurry of snow was a man. From where she was lying he looked to be over six feet, and in his sixties, his face leathery from the harshness of the climate. He immediately began talking. Julia had no idea what it was about, but from his tone she could tell it was urgent. The snoring stopped abruptly, and in the dim light of the fire's coals she could see the shadow of the grandfather, then his son or son-in-law.

The children woke and started crying. The man who had entered the tent so abruptly came across and tapped her on the arm. He raised his arms as if he were holding a rifle, then made driving motions, pointing beyond the tent. "Chin-eze," he said, "Chin-eze," and motioned her to follow him, handing her a sheepskin coat and hat. As she stumbled over the bodies in the darkness, she felt the grandfather grabbing her and thrusting something hard and warm into her hand. It was her service .45.

Out in the freezing darkness the snow was still swirling down. It was a light snow, the howling wind whipping it across her face, making it seem much denser than it really was. There were two yaks standing still as statues, and she wondered why she hadn't heard them coming up to the tent. The man indicated she should get on the nearest animal, which she thought would be easy until the yak, sensing her hesitation, moved, and it was more difficult to mount than any F-15.

"Chin-eze," the man repeated.

"Yes," she replied. "I know—Chinese."

He nodded to confirm that she understood. "Chin-eze," he said again, and headed off into the snow, the yak Julia was riding tethered to the first. Julia could still hear the motor sound she heard just before his arrival. Suddenly she was struck by a bone-chilling apprehension that he was not taking her away from the nomad encampment for her safety but to deliver her to the Chinese for what she knew must be a substantial reward for a downed American pilot. She just as quickly dismissed the idea as absurd. As far as she knew, the Tibetans hated the Chinese.

Of course there were those who didn't, who, during the madness of the Cultural Revolution in the sixties when Mao sent out his Red Guards, had collaborated. The Chinese had forced the nomads into communes, and those who had wealth had their animals stolen, their silver earrings torn off, and other goods confiscated. The nomads were branded "class enemies" of the people and as often as not were evicted as outcasts, even from the lowest level of the communes. During this time, some of the very poor had become powerful officials of the Chinese. Then after the Cultural Revolution had faded, the old order of nomadic society had reasserted itself, to the relief of nearly all the nomads. But there were still those who, once having had the power of the Chinese behind them, wanted it again and would do anything to ingratiate themselves with the Chinese.

What bothered Julia most was having had her .45 revolver stolen—if only for a few hours. Perhaps it was a local custom to share anything new brought into the camp.

It was like instrument flying in bad weather. She could see nothing through the darkness. Having placed all her faith in the guide, all she knew for certain from her watch-compass was that she was headed east into the wilderness of the Chang Tang.

She could hear the sound of the motor about a mile away, she thought, behind them, and it kept getting louder. Then abruptly it stopped. The old man turned to her in the saddle, pointing back toward the camp. "Chin-eze."

Then the old man slid off his yak and, still holding its rein, came back to her and motioned for her to get off. As her feet touched the snow, the old man pointed down at their track marks. They were discernible at least twenty to thirty yards back, the snow not falling heavily enough to fill in the yaks' footprints. The old man now indicated that they must walk with the yaks. It would mean more but lighter footprints, which the snow would fill in more quickly. At the campsite, the woman in the tent had given her a beaded necklace of carved bone and stones, said to ward off evil spirits that lurked in the mountain passes to trap the unwary. She fingered it like a rosary as they went higher into the Chang Tang.

Aboard the USS *Reagan* in the South China Sea, the high-speed burst message received gave Robert Brentwood his orders from Freeman, CIC Far Eastern Forces. Eight SEALs would be parachuted over a rendezvous point, their purpose a beach survey. It wasn't Robert Brentwood's favorite occupation. You never knew when your sub might be the victim of magnetic, or worse, nonmagnetic, mines activated by the sound print of the sub, depending on how good, how current, the PLA's threat library of sound prints was. Since China had purchased some Russian subs after the collapse of the Soviet Union when the minorities rose there, there would now be more need to update the *Reagan*'s threat library of sound prints given off by the PLA navy, particularly as the *Reagan* entered Bo Hai gulf.

On this mission Robert Brentwood wouldn't be part of the SEAL team as he had been before the cease-fire fell on the Yangtze. His job now was to insert the team of eight "surveyors," one officer swimmer and seven other members, off the middle beach and then extract them four hours later after the SEALs, equipped with bubble-free Draeger rebreather systems, "cased the joint," in the words of the chief of the boat, Petty Officer Rowan, by which Rowan meant they would go in in four pairs, a hundred yards from one another.

The SEALs would drop their lead-weighted sinker line every twenty-five yards to get the depth, which would be marked on their plastic thigh plates. Then they would work in grids to check systematically for any undersea obstacles, making a note of these on the slate and getting their exact position by waterproof GPS, or global positioning system.

The divers could then place a magnetic pinger, with a battery life of at least four days, or they could use malleable lumps of C4 plastique with primacord inserted. Then all the primacords could be attached to a master detonating cord.

It was a long, painstaking job in the darkness, particularly as the men found a fence of "hedgehogs"—six-pointed steel tripods, Chinese versions of the old Normandy landing's Belgian gates—where a wall of twelve-by-twelve-foot cross sections of steel girders was supported by a large, backward-sloping, and flat-based system of girders. With floating contact mines attached to the top of the obstacle, they could blow a landing craft right out of the water. While the officer made his way toward the so-called "shark" net—in reality a sub net—the other seven swimmers in his team found over fifty of the China gates that made up an almost solid line of obstacles across the deepest channel at high tide.

The officer in charge had crossed the shark net of the middle beach and threaded it with primacord and Hagensen packs of C2 explosive and affixed his primacord to the master cord, which in turn was attached to a subsurface floater or bladder buoy, which would not be bobbing around on the surface but which was anchored by means of a Danforth anchor and which would be marked on the grid system as the detonation point for any incoming force.

When they returned to the sub—they had been out for over four hours—every SEAL was dog tired reentering the chamber, which had to be pumped free of water before they could dry off and earn a well-deserved rest in the sub. When the last man let go of the hatch too quickly and its bang resonated throughout the sub, the passive sonar operator tore his headset off. "Jesus Murphy!"

Brentwood heard it, too. In fact he doubted whether anyone else on the watch hadn't heard it. There was one, the assistant cook, but he'd had his head stuck in the freezer, moving around heavy lumps of frozen beef.

The Chinese Navy had heard it. It wasn't one of their few nuclear subs that had picked up the sound racing through the water at four times the speed it would have in air, but the *Perch*, a refitted diesel electric, one of the early Russian clankers known as "honeymoon machines" for all the noise they made—like a toolbox on the move. Normally the *Reagan* would have picked her up had she been under way with her diesels, but the Chinese sub was still, on station, diesels shut down, maintaining her position only by means of her battery power. As such she was silent as a tomb, much quieter than the pump of the nuclear sub *Reagan*, which had to be kept on at all times.

The question for the Chinese captain was whether the other submarine would give off any more noise "shorts." And yet his battery power would last for only another hour. Should he move in closer to shore or wait? It was unlikely the other sub would be going in any closer to shore but would rather be egressing into the gulf.

He decided to wait. Meantime, all his torpedo tubes were loaded with warshots. Besides, the gulf was relatively quiet, so that subsurface sea clutter should be at a minimum and make any unusual noise easier to detect.

When the ship's writer let it be known the familygram burst messages had arrived, the atmosphere aboard the *Reagan* immediately seemed infused with a festive air as crew members eagerly, yet trying not to seem overly excited, waited for news of home. All they needed to hear was that the family, wife, or sweetheart was fine. "Everything's fine" was all their psyches needed. Anything else—a newborn having put on weight, a student getting honors, a football team in good spirits, victorious or not— was what the officers and men of USS *Reagan* considered the icing on the cake. "Puss in boots is waiting" almost ousted Andrea Rolston's anonymous "I need meat. Can you bring home the bacon?" as raunchiest 'gram of the month.

When Rolston saw a duplicate of it, unsigned, pinned up on the notice board as 'gram of the month, he shook his head, tut-tutting, "Geez, what some gals will write. Disgusting."

"Oh no, sir," a torpedo man first class said. "That's beautiful."

"You're sick, Mulvaney," Rolston joshed.

"Well, I'd sure like to meet whoever the gal is."

CHAPTER TWENTY-THREE

IT WAS TOO bad it wasn't summer, the young man explained to Alexsandra. "In summer you can go to Kiessling's." It was a delicatessen where you could get pastries and scallops.

"Have you ever been to prison?" she asked him, her taut body tired and swaying rhythmically in what was for the young man a seductive way in tune with the clickety-clack of the rails crossing the sleepers.

"Once," he replied.

"For how long?"

"Ten days. It's all they could hold me on if they had no charges that would stick."

"What were the charges?"

"Hooliganism," he said proudly. "I was accused of writing some of the *dazibao* at Beijing University, but there were dozens of such notices and proclamations of our solidarity and support for the goddess of democracy and they couldn't prove which one was mine."

"Did it matter?" she asked him, her voice fatigued.

"I don't understand," he said. "Did what matter?"

"Whether they could prove it or not. If they wanted to keep you they would have—proof or no proof."

"Ah, but not this time," the student said. "Some of the *dazibao* said 'Arrest without proof is fascism!' This shamed them."

The prospect of Nie's followers being ashamed of anything struck her as being peculiarly unlikely. It made her nervous in fact, and for the first time since being trundled out with the dirty linen she was alert to a possible danger—that the boy was a plant, a collaborator who had exchanged a long prison term for being an informant. To talk to her—to have her confess to him anything she had done against the PLA—and then they would have a star witness.

He was not a worker's son but one of the middle class that wasn't supposed to exist. They cracked much more quickly than most, she knew. Put a middle-class kid in a cell overnight, take away his shoelaces, belt, anything with which he might hang himself, leave the light on all night, stale rice and water, a bucket for a toilet, and you never saw morale collapse so quickly in all your life. It was as if they were on another planet. It was the way the Public Security Bureau and indeed so many other police forces throughout the world got so many confessions. Everyone felt guilty about something they'd done in their life, and it was this free-floating anxiety that interrogators gave shapes and names to.

He saw the concern in her eyes and immediately divined her alarm. "You can trust me," he said. She nodded. Another hour and they would be near Beidaihe.

What else could he say, she thought, if she'd shown she suspected him?

"I would do anything for you," he said, and she knew that what he meant was that, apart from anything else, he would like to have sex with her. Puppy love. She smiled gracefully but beyond that did not answer, thinking of Aussie Lewis, of how she longed to be with him and under his protection. She was so weary of being the champion of the minority, the June Fourth Movement, and the Goddess of Democracy Movement. She wanted her own champion to take away *her* fears, *her* constant anxiety from being hunted.

"Come here," she told the boy, and the next moment he was sitting stiffly, flushed, by her side. She put her arm about him and drew him to her, his eyes closing as his head rested on her bosom. They sat like this, rocked to and fro by the mesmerizing action of the train. She was looking out the window at green rice fields and beyond toward the sea. "Have you betrayed me?" she asked softly. "Hmm?" she said, pulling him even closer to her. "Have you?"

For a moment he couldn't speak, the tears rolling down his face. He nodded. "They told me my family . . ."

He couldn't go on.

"Shhhh," she told him. "I know. They want to discover who my Manchurian friends are." She paused. "And the nurse?"

He said he didn't know about her. She seemed genuine, he said, but no one could be sure of anyone, he said, excusing his own weakness. Alexsandra ignored the plea for pity, though she did pity him. "Then we must leave the train before Beidaihe," she said.

"Will you come with me?" she asked him. "It may mean punishment for your family if we are caught. You don't have to."

"I must," he said, his face creased with worry. "What could I tell them if I don't come with you? What could I tell the Public Security Bureau—that I let you escape?"

He was sitting up, wringing his hands and snuffling. The train began to slow in the predawn sky, some of the stars above the gulf so bright one could almost touch them, the wind having shifted, coming from the east now, blowing some of the Gobi dust back to where it belonged.

Alexsandra rose and pulled the padded Mao suit around her and did up all the buttons except the very top one. "Are you coming?" she asked.

"No. Yes. Yes," he said, and made to hop up from the seat.

"Have you any money?" she asked.

He gave her three yuan, his eyes avoiding hers.

"If you don't come with me," she said, "you *will* be punished. This way if we're caught you can say I did all the planning."

"When do we jump?" he asked.

"Don't be silly," she said, her tone schoolmarmish, but she was so tired, so utterly tired of betrayal, that it had given an edge to her voice when she meant none. She longed to have Aussie with her. At least he was someone you *could* trust. "We'll get off at the station before Beidaihe."

"But—but," the boy stammered, "we'll still have to go through Beidaihe if you are to go north."

"Yes, but don't you understand they'll be looking, waiting, for us at the train station. We won't go near it."

CHAPTER TWENTY-FOUR

MAGTAFs—MARINE AIR-GROUND task forces—come in different sizes, but the one General Freeman ordered in from Korea was a MEF—marine expeditionary force—a total of fifty-one thousand men, forty-eight thousand of these marines, fifty amphibious ships, and armed with everything from sixty Av-8 short-takeoff and -landing Harrier jets, forty-eight F/A18 fighters, twenty A-6E all-weather night-attack aircraft, twelve KC-130 refuelers, sixty Chinook 46 medium-lift and assault choppers, twenty-four attack helicopters, Hawk surface-to-air missiles, and at least eighty Stinger surface-to-air missile teams.

The MEF also contained seventy MBTs, over sixty-five heavy mortars, 150 TOW antitank missiles, plus 216 assault amphibious vehicles, over one hundred 155mm howitzers, and other medium mortars. Such a force could not easily be hidden, yet without the element of surprise it would take at least a four-to-one marine advantage to be able to secure the beach. Air support of course would be telling in their favor, but two or three ChiCom divisions drawn south from the Orgon Tal–Honggor line could soon engage this force of Freeman's at the beach. And what Cheng lacked in air cover for his own troops would be made up for in having at his disposal the largest coastal navy in the world, its northern fleet headquartered at Qingdao. But surely the Chinese would pick the MEF up at sea on radar.

They did, but Freeman, in another brilliant stroke of strategy, had the naval force set its heading, under Major General Strachan, south to the Formosa Strait and notified Admiral Kuang of the ROC—Republic of China—Navy accordingly.

"Two birds with one stone," Freeman explained.

"You think they'll fall for it?" Norton said. "If they send too many divisions south, Kuang could be in for a nasty landing." Freeman had no sympathy for a man who was indecisive. If Kuang was holding his men off for no good reason, then he deserved a fright. And if Harvey Simmet was right that another monsoon was building over the South China Sea heading into Fukien province across from Taiwan, then the marine force racing south could turn about under cover of bad weather with Kuang meanwhile thinking the Americans were coming to his aid. Once on the beach, Kuang would be as committed in Fukien as the marines would be north at Beidaihe—if they had to land. Norton didn't like it because it smacked of pulling a fast one on Kuang—it was playing politics, he bravely told Freeman.

"Balls, Norton! Every Tom, Dick, and Angela whines about something being political when it's not going their way. When it *is* going their way they call it foresight, brilliance, tactical skill, anything but politics. Man is a political animal, Norton. Ask Cheng and his crew holed up in the Zhongnanhai. Those gentlemen are going to get one hell of an education in politics, in—" He paused and looked at his watch, which was not on top of but under his wrist so that in action there would be no unnecessary glare. "In about six hours," Freeman continued, "providing Harvey Simmet is right about the bad weather." Freeman's face suddenly lost all its lines of happy anticipation. "By God, if he isn't, the Chinese'll see the MEF heading back up north."

"Quite possible!" Norton said nonchalantly.

"Norton."

"General?"

"Get Harvey up here. On the double."

"Yes, sir."

Harvey had his gloved hands around the tin cup of strong coffee when he saw the rain cape approaching: Norton. He poured the coffee out, muttering, "Goddamn it!" Norton felt bad about it. He didn't think for a moment that Simmet's forecast was wrong or needed updating—the barometer was still falling for all to see, and even CNN was saying there'd be monsoons over the South China Sea as far north as China's Bo Hai Gulf—but Norton hadn't been able to resist planting a seed of doubt in Freeman's mind. A little uncertainty did wonders in deflating a prima donna's ego and for making him think twice. Besides, hadn't Freeman himself told Norton that if he, Freeman, ever got too cocky to remind him of the Never-Skovorodino road where the fake Siberian tanks had suckered *him*?

"Harvey!"

"General."

"Harvey, you boys down there at the met office are doing a crackerjack job."

"Thank you, General. I'll tell the men."

"Harv!" Freeman said, putting his arm round the met officer. "Norton here tells me that this monsoon could lift—give away the position of our MAGTAF. Is he right?"

"Well if it lifts it could—if they have their coastal boats out that far, but I doubt they'd do that in heavy seas, General. Monsoon is traditionally tie-up-at-the-docks time."

The general was reassured but not convinced.

"But you would say we're in for bad weather."

"Very bad."

"Thank you, Harvey."

"Landing in a monsoon," Norton said, thinking ahead about Beidaihe, "would be considered foolish by some commanders, General."

"That's precisely what I want Cheng to think, Norton."

"General, there could be one heck of a lot of men sick as dogs on those landing ships while we're playing chess with them."

Freeman nodded. He was looking due east as if he could see through the terrible fighting now in progress near Honggor, where one of Freeman's Bradley fighting-vehicle battalions had made a stunning counterattack using TOW missiles and their rapidly firing, armor-piercing 30mm cannon. He was looking as if he could see through the dust wall and mountain fastness of Manchuria all the way to the sea. "Dick, have you ever been seasick? I mean truly seasick, when even the very thought, the merest suggestion, of food made you want to throw up? Where the seas were so mountainous, so full of piss and fury that you could imagine death as the only release?"

"Can't say I have, General—not that sick."

"You know that's how many of our boys felt on D day, after that June storm." He turned to Norton. "You realize that Doug MacArthur threw up his guts the night before Inchon?"

"No, sir, I didn't."

"Well I do," Freeman said, and put his hand on his subordinate's shoulder. "Dick, let me tell you something. When you feel like that, the thing you pray for, desire most in the world, isn't a good woman or a good cigar or a good plug of Southern Comfort. Dick, all you care for is land, to set foot on dry land, muddy land, it doesn't matter. You crave land. You make deals with the heavenly bodies—Buddha, Allah, God, Muhammad, your ancestors—anything. 'Please get me to land where I can stand—and end this agony.' By Christ, Norton, three days in that monsoon and those boys'll turn into razors if I deliver them up to terra firma."

"And if not?" Norton proffered.

"Then they'll have to be sick."

One such individual was PFC Walton, who was at that very moment on his knees at the stern of the eighteen-thousand-ton Iwo Jima–class amphibious assault ship. The smell of gasoline from the tied-down CH-46 Sea Knight and 11 CH-53 Sea Stallion choppers mixed with the smoke belching from the stack had caused him to vomit one more time, but there seemed to be nothing left to discharge. Every morsel of food, every dribble of liquid, had been heaved out of him, and he was the shade of stewed celery. Already on his knees, he promised God that if He spared PFC Walton he would fight the godless Communists that kept this vast land in subjection. At this point his eyes had no real focus but seemed to be rolling with the ship. Certainly he was only dimly aware that his buddy, Sergeant Hamish of the thirty-man rifle squad, stood next to him, his left foot looking smaller than his right as he fought the pitch and yaw of the ship.

"Hey, you look ill, man!"

Walton made an indecipherable kind of moaning sound that ended in "go away," accompanied by his right hand waving his comrade back. Instead of helping his friend, Hamish ignored PFC Walton's request to be alone. "Look, man, you've got nothing left in your gut. No wonder you're sick." He had to repeat this as the wind at the stern stole his first sentence of advice. "Listen, man, this is nothing—old man says we're in for a monsoon proper in the next forty-eight hours. A real mother of a storm."

PFC Walton emitted a great gorillalike groan that ended in a heartfelt "No!"

"Fucking yes!" Sergeant Hamish said. "Come on down below and—"

Walton shook his head in abject defeat, wiping his mouth on his arm. "I'll be . . . I'll be . . ." But whatever it was, he couldn't finish.

"Okay, okay," Hamish said. "Stay up here if you like, but I'm bringing you some chow. What do you want—coupla eggs? Milk?"

Walton gave a great heave and vomited bile, and his head rested or rather lolled across his wrists from left to right and back again with the roll of the ship. His whole body was a definition of defeat. "Fuckin' monsoon!" he bellowed into the wind.

"Freakin' right," Hamish answered. "A monsoon *soon*. Get it?"

If PFC Walton could have, he would have killed Sergeant Hamish right there on the deck, but there was no strength in him.

As the task force sailed into the frenzied wake of the typhoon, thousands of miles eastward Rosemary Brentwood, in premature labor brought on by the shock of the intruder, was having her baby by cesarean section because it was in the breach position. On top of the trauma of having shot the intruder dead, it was a nightmarish experience for her as she had a bad reaction to the local anaesthetic Marcaine used for the epidural, which produced hallucinations of such terrifying proportions that Andrea Rolston, out in the waiting room, could hear her friend's primeval scream.

Twenty minutes later, a hospital-gowned nurse, her mask

still on, came quickly through the door, taking the premature baby, a boy, into the intensive pediatric care ward. "The baby all right?" Andrea asked.

"Don't know," the nurse said abruptly as she rushed by, heading toward the IC unit in which Andrea then saw the nurse hooking up the baby to various tubes, assisted by two other nurses. Andrea immediately thought about the familygram Rosemary had sent her husband—before the break-in, the shooting, and now this. "Everything fine," had been her last two words.

CHAPTER TWENTY-FIVE

AS DAWN BROKE, Major Mah and twenty-one privates aboard a Zil-151 truck arrived at the nomads' campsite and began screaming at people. But if the Tibetans, already up attending to their animals, understood Chinese, none admitted to it, and they stood silently, some open-mouthed, gaping Chinese provincial style at the soldiers.

One of the children was rolling a snowball, rounding and tapping it so expertly it looked like a huge, white, round stone in his hand. He threw it at the truck, and Major Mah started screaming again—signaling impatiently for the interpreter, who then proceeded to tell them all that if they'd been found to be hiding American criminals—"pirates of the air" being the literal translation—then he would shoot one person from every tent, then burn down the huts.

All Tibetans by now, Mah said, should understand that the PLA loves the people and the people love the PLA. The child who had thrown the snowball was making another when his mother—despite her offspring's resistance—took it from him and crumbled it. The child began to cry, and a pet goat from the nearest tent suddenly ran out, causing Mah to step back, drawing his pistol before he realized what it was. This evoked great laughter from all the Tibetans and a few of the troops. Enraged, Mah fired into the air.

"What's he doing?" a little girl asked her father.

"Shooting at air pirates!" the father said.

By now Mah's men had been through all the tents, causing no small confusion and panic among the pets who scattered every which way as bayonets were thrust into piles of blankets.

"If we find you have been hiding anyone we will take all your salt!" Mah warned them, upping the ante. This caused a rumble of resentment and fright among the nomads, for their salt packs filled from the salt pans of the salt lakes were precious, not only for their personal culinary use but as tender for bartering. One of the Chinese soldiers left the main body and, walking about the camp, looked through the scope of his rifle. It was infrared capable, able to pick up the temperature differentials even where snow had fallen but where a footprint had recently been. He called out excitedly to Major Mah—he had found tracks, two yaks probably heading away from the camp—not very old tracks, perhaps a half hour at most.

Mah left five men with the truck—which could climb no higher—to stay in the encampment should anyone return to the tents. He placed himself with the remaining fourteen soldiers and began to follow the man with the infrared scope.

The sonar operator aboard the Chinese sub *Perch* did not hear the distant thud of another hatch being closed and so stayed on station but decided to surface, for it was time to get a resupply of air and run awhile to recharge its batteries.

The periscope revealed nothing but a scud of dirty cloud to the east, and indeed when the *Perch* broke the surface and had lookouts posted the scud seemed just as dirty and a lot bigger through the binoculars. "Well at least we don't have to put up with bad weather," the captain told his officer of the deck. "Once it starts getting rough we'll pop below where it's nice and calm." It was the one great consolation of being a submariner.

He kept the sub on an easterly heading, not using his active sonar for fear of giving away his position but merely going slowly and watching what, if anything, was coming in on the green screen out of the passive sonar array. All the sonar operator could hear was a frying, sizzling sound, the noise of millions of shrimp mating—either that or a very good imitation of it put out by an enemy sub. The lookouts were attentive to their tasks as the fresh, bracing sea air awoke them from the kind of torpor that overtakes submariners short of oxygen and with their lungs full of hydrocarbons from the diesel fumes.

The starboard lookout shouted that he saw something. When the captain fixed his binoculars on the horizon he saw only another scud of cumulus, and the lookout had to concede if there had been anything there it had disappeared. The captain shook his head as much in amusement as disappointment. Being a lookout was no easy business. Most people, in the way they saw faces or forms in the clouds, tended to see what they wanted, or expected, to see if you left them there long enough. The trick was to give as many men a turn as possible as lookout. In any case, everyone getting a turn in the fresh air did wonders for morale.

The Sea Wolf sub USS *Reagan*, traveling at fifty miles an hour, was sixty miles due east of Bo Hai Gulf when Brentwood ordered a twenty-two degree turn on the right rudder. The helmsman pushed in the wheel slightly and executed the turn. This would put them on a heading to meet a U.S. carrier force now steaming south from South Korea to join the Marine Expeditionary Force on its way to the Taiwan Strait. The sub would surface briefly to transfer the mine-field and obstacle intelligence that had been gained from the SEALs' survey of the Middle Beach at Beidaihe, a beach whose obstacles the SEALs, aboard USS *Reagan*, were ready to blow once the carrier-centered force got close enough to provide support for the amphibious landing vehicles—*if* they were used and remained a feint to draw more ChiCom forces away from the Beijing Military Region.

Aboard his Intruder aircraft-laden carrier, Admiral Lin Kuang was handed the decoded message flashed to him by the ROC—Republic of China—agents who, like him, had remained determined to one day bring down the Communists:

American invasion fleet heading south for possible beach landing off Fukien.

"Possible beach landing off Fukien," the taciturn admiral repeated. "Where else could it be? Where else do we have big guns like those we have on Amoy and Quemoy islands to give us cover on the beaches?"

It became not a matter of prudence or of the inclement weather building up, but rather it came down to an old-fashioned, bone-deep matter of pride. Kuang was determined that the first soldiers that should land on the Communist mainland from the sea must be Chinese troops—his troops. To all his ships and aircraft he flashed, "Summer Palace." The invasion of mainland China from the sea was under way, as the war within China, inside her northern borders, raged along the bends and hills of the Orgon Tal–Honggor front.

Admiral Kuang was suspicious the moment he received the message from his forward AWACs—Air Warning and Control Aircraft—that there was unusually heavy sea traffic up and down the Formosa Strait. Junks were reported strung out from as far away as Fuchow to the north, south past Xiamen to the other Communist special-economic-zone port of Shantou 240 miles across the strait from Taiwan.

Kuang's fleet of one attack helicopter carrier, an A-6 Intruder bomber carrier, and fourteen armed troop-carrying ships, together with over fourteen destroyers and frigates, under the umbrella of thirty-five ROC F-18s, was put on special alert. The AWAC estimated there were over a hundred junks plying the strait between the South China and East China seas. Admiral Kuang was surprised—he had expected opposition much earlier.

The other thing that surprised him was the reports from his underground operatives that thousands of members of the June Fourth Movement had seized the opportunity to strike against Beijing's forces already. They had exceeded the admiral's most optimistic expectations, having attacked and cut the rail junction 120 miles inland at Zhangping in the Guangzhou military district, thwarting any hope of the PLA quickly reinforcing its sixty-eight thousand members of Thirty-first and Forty-third Army Corps stationed on the coast around Xiamen.

Admiral Lin Kuang had also expected the PLA's East China Fleet and planes out of Fuzhou to attack him before he was halfway across the strait. Again he had proved too cautious, for his own air force commanders in Ching Chuan Kang in Taiwan had confidently predicted that the low-level, radar-confounding, predawn strike by their F-15 Eagles, each carrying a twenty-three-thousand-pound bomb load, would all but obliterate the Communists' opposition, destroying most of the PLA Shenyang F-7s on the ground at Fuzhou.

In any event, the few Shenyangs that did get airborne carried a maximum of only one ton of bombs, as opposed to the American-made Eagles' ten tons, and were 345 kilometers slower than the Eagles. And the American-made planes were piloted by American-trained Taiwanese who had always, correctly it appeared, regarded the PLA pilots as brave third-raters in fourth-rate machines.

But if the Taiwanese Air Force was cocky as it continued to patrol the skies above Lin Kuang's invasion fleet, the admiral himself never underestimated the mainland's enemy forces. He told his captains to ignore the boasting of the air force and to keep their eyes peeled for the fast Haunan Hai Kou and the hydrofoil Huch'uan attack boats that formed the bulk of the PLA's coastal "Great Wall of Iron," not all of which had been destroyed either at dockside or by the air force's attacks against the giant Shantou Base.

Many of the attack boats—it was estimated over forty— had not been accounted for, along with one of the Communist Chinese navy's three old nuclear submarines armed with modern missiles. Reconnaissance showed that most of the PLA's elite naval forces had in fact been deployed in the north off Manchuria rather than in China's southern military regions that bordered on Laos, Burma, Vietnam, and India.

No doubt some of the naval forces would turn south to meet the Taiwanese threat and, if they saw it on their radar, the American Marine Expeditionary Force, but they had over a thousand miles to come down from the Yellow Sea where the bulk of the best boats had been patrolling from the mainland bases at Luda, Lushan, and Quingdao. Also Lin Kuang knew that the bulk of the guided-missile destroyers, the PLA navy disdaining bigger ships because of its commitment to its primary role as a coastal defense, were also deployed in the north. And so even if elements of the PLA's Northern Fleet did leave Korean waters, heading south, the PLA's fastest vessels, the heavily armed patrol boats, would not reach the Taiwan Strait for at least thirty hours. By then Lin Kuang hoped to have his invasion force of over a hundred and twenty thousand crack assault troops firmly established on the beachhead.

Everything was going so well in fact that Taiwan's joint chiefs of staff believed that with Taiwan's two tank divisions, eighteen motorized infantry divisions, one parachute division, and tactical air army—in all, over a quarter million highly trained, superbly American-equipped men—Taiwan might well defeat the three-million-strong, but much more poorly equipped, People's Liberation Army—or, as many after Tiananmen called it, "the People's Liquidation Army."

Even so, Lin Kuang would not be swayed into taking shortcuts. He had always prided himself on being a realist, and because of that he was sticking to the original plan: to establish a beachhead and, with aerial superiority, press inland in a fan-shaped advance along the 120-mile Shantou-

Xiamen axis. Such an advance was not only capable of being under a constant ROC air umbrella but could be constantly reinforced by ships coming in stream from Taiwan, less than twelve hours across the strait. Then and only then, Kuang believed, would his invasion prove a rallying point for the millions of disaffected Chinese civilians of the post-Tiananmen generations who, with the minorities, had been biding their time, waiting their chance to strike and overthrow the oppressive Beijing regime.

Lin Kuang's strategy was further based on the fact that not only were the PLA's two hundred divisions not nearly as well trained as the smaller, better-equipped Taiwanese divisions, but the two hundred divisions that the PLA boasted were spread all over the Chinese vastness—from Vietnam in the far south to Siberia in the north.

Fifty miles from the mainland, Lin Kuang felt the excitement mounting, some of the PLA's shore batteries already exchanging fire with the big Nationalist guns on Quemoy, others firing beyond the line of junks on Kuang's advancing Nationalist patrol boats, Kuang's destroyers opening up on the lines of what they were sure were Communist patrol boats disguised as junks. From the junks, over twenty percent of which were hit by the first salvos of Lin Kuang's destroyer escorts, bright orange flames erupted skyward, and behind the dense white clouds of smoke that could be seen pouring forth from them, creating a screen, squadrons of the two-hundred-ton Huangfen attack boats maneuvered adroitly against the oncoming fleet.

As streams of thirty-millimeter fire raced out from the high, thimble-shaped gun housings of the Huangfen boats, HY2 surface-to-surface missiles could be seen streaking from the two angled-box housings on each side of the patrol boats. Admiral Kuang's observers also saw the wakes of several long twenty-one-inch-wide torpedoes just visible through the confusion of spray and smoke that was being penetrated by others in the flotilla of PLA attack boats, including at least a dozen Huch'uan hydrofoils speeding in zigzag patterns, bows high, closing and traversing in excess of forty knots.

In the ensuing chaos, the air filling with the thump, thump, thump of heavy-caliber machine gun fire and the churning noise of the fast patrol boats that occasionally ran into "friendly fire," the hydrofoils tore open the sea, their wakes crisscrossing those of Lin Kuang's destroyers, the latter trying frantically to avoid being hit by the torpedoes while throwing everything they had at the Communist boats.

Though not yet at the edge of the smoke cover themselves, a handful of officers on the bridge of one of Lin Kuang's forward picket frigates noticed through their binoculars that the crews of the fast patrol boats were not only wearing goggles against the spray but what appeared to be gas masks. Minutes later, Lin Kuang's advance screen of destroyers, entering the smoke proper, experienced the most debilitating attack of all, the destroyers' crews blinded by the gas. Then it was frigates floundering as a flotilla of eight fast-moving Huch'uan hydrofoils closed on the frigates, the latter wallowing and most of their officers dead.

Next one of Kuang's frigates was hit by three torpedoes, two of them striking it forward, the other immediately aft of midships, causing the ship's stern to lift clear out of the water. With its back broken in two, its aft section slid out of sight amid a boiling sea, the frigate's forward section following soon after. All 195 crew were lost, either sucked down by the vortex or already dead or dying from the poisonous gas.

But Admiral Lin Kuang had been planning this invasion all his life and was as prepared as any commander could be for such a contingency. While not about to launch his chemical-biological shells, his restraint moved not by any humanitarian concern but because the wind was coming from the shore to the sea, favoring the Communists, he ordered all ships sealed.

Within minutes automatic "flush pumps" were in action all over the ships, spraying down the contaminated decks, the ships' chemical-biological warfare filters kicking in while every combatant of the hundred-and-twenty-thousand-man-strong invasion force in the transports donned CB masks.

Some filter systems in the hermetically sealed, air-conditioned ships failed, and these vessels had to be pulled out of the line. Among them was one of the heavy transports carrying over two thousand soldiers. In the close conditions 'tween decks, the troops were victims of greater concentrations of the highly persistent gas, which even over the sea failed to dissipate quickly and which, being a derivative of Sarin nerve gas, killed its victims with a massive attack on the central nervous system within three minutes, creating involuntary defecation, vomiting, and acute seizures.

The admiral saw the wind shifting to the north, a gap opening two miles off his port quarter. He ordered the fleet to it at full speed, all the while calmly giving muffled and nasal-sounding instructions through his mask in the large, armor-plated and insulated combat control center aboard the carrier. So calm was he that it was difficult for some officers, were it not for the heavy thumps of the guns on Quemoy and the brisk movement of the fleet's model ships on their own ship's magnetized operations board, to realize that a decisive battle for China was in progress.

More Communist Shenyang fighters appeared, but their attempt to intercede, though brave, was as ineffective as their attempts earlier that morning—the American-trained Taiwanese pilots enjoying a kill ratio of five to one. For those who bailed out, on either side, there was no mercy, most of them raked by machine gun fire, a few obliterated by concentrated triple A before they, or what was left of them, hit the churning waters of the strait. A dozen or so pilots, Nationalist as well as PLA, did escape the withering fire and whistling shrapnel of the naval battle only to die horrible deaths in the gas cloud that clung low above the sea in a vast, suffocating sheet, despite the wind shift.

Once through the gap to the north, Lin Kuang's destroyers, much lighter and faster than the troop ships, began to lay down salvo after salvo on the Chinese shore, adding to the bombardment from the big Nationalist guns on Amoy, pulverizing the PLA's bunkers in preparation for the landings. And as the green "go" flares burst skyward through the gas-streaked and shell-rent air, there was a cacophony of noise that terrified even the hardiest of the best-trained assault troops who, as the big transports moved in closer, began boarding the LSTs that would roll down the stern slipways of the troop ships for the final run to shore.

It was then that Lin Kuang saw the first troop ship quite literally blow up, bodies spit through the massive explosion like tiny charcoal toys, and he realized that he was on the verge of disaster. Though floating mines had been cleared by his preinvasion ROK SEAL team, the junks, in the last forty-eight hours, must have sown the offshore waters with hundreds, if not thousands, of the heavy, Russian-made plastic anechoic—that is, antisonar coated—pressure mines. Dropped overboard, attached to weights and nonmetallic cables, often nylon rope, the mines lay hidden well beneath the sea's surface, set to explode only when ships of a certain tonnage—in this case the ten-thousand-plus troop ships—passed over them.

Another troop ship, carrying two thousand assault troops with all their supporting amphibious landing craft and M-1 tanks, erupted in a huge, flame-slashed V, going to the bottom in less than four minutes. It was only a mile or so from shore, the Communists having chosen the area well, for here the wrecks would effectively form a barrier to the on-coming ships. From the bridge of his chopper/Intruder carrier, Admiral Lin Kuang saw PLA patrol boats coming in, machine-gunning anyone still alive in the water.

Also at that moment he realized that the ubiquitous mine, so easily manufactured on mass assembly lines—the cheapest naval deterrent any poor nation could hope for, and which, most importantly, such nations could easily make for themselves—had suddenly proved as devastating as its proponents in the PLA said it would be when they, like "traditionalists" elsewhere, had argued against the devotees of high tech. The latter had ignored the promise of the humble mine, not because it was ineffective, but because it wasn't sexy—a mere slug in the flash crackerjack world of air-to-air, fly-by-wire and laser-designated targeting. The fact that the mine had been so successful both for the Arabs in the Persian Gulf during the eighties and for the U.S. blockade of Nicaragua had taught them nothing.

"Admiral, what do we do?" the captain of the carrier asked, having already rung the telegraph for "full astern" and ordered the entire fleet to maintain position. It was a turning point, and they all knew it. Except Admiral Lin Kuang.

The vision of burning down Mao's villa, of bringing down the Communist god, was too powerful to give way so quickly. Without turning to the carrier's captain, he ordered, "All ships re-form. Behind me. We are attacking. Air arm to strike with HE bombs ahead of the carrier." Their explosions, he explained, would create the pressure required to detonate the mines.

"Quickly!" he ordered.

Then, having already anticipated that few of the fighters would be "bomb racked," most of their armament load being made up of cannon ammunition, he ordered a flight of twenty A-6E Intruder bombers from the carrier, each carrying 18,000 pounds of ordnance on five external hard points, to "blast out" a corridor, two hundred yards wide, a mile into shore.

As Kuang's F-15 Eagles flew cover for the Intruders, which rose from the carrier at the rate of one every fifteen seconds—except for the four lost to AA missile fire from the patrol boats—240,000 pounds of high explosive were dropped over the next twelve minutes, turning the sea into a boiling cauldron. Even so, Lin Kuang knew the odds were that not all of the pressure mines had been detonated. He ordered the sixteen Intruders and his choppers back to Taiwan, then told the carrier captain to proceed "slow ahead."

There were seventeen more explosions directly under and around the carrier, and she was going down, the shore less than a half mile away. "Full ahead," he ordered, also ordering all hoses to be played on the magazine, thus enabling the carrier to cover as much of the gap as possible before it would start to go under.

Soon the big ship was listing at more than twenty degrees to starboard as Kuang, on being informed the hoses couldn't keep the temperature of the magazine from rising, ordered all her cocks opened. If the magazine went while the ship was even partially afloat, the concussion alone from the carrier would be enough to kill many of the men in the LSTs that were now coming down the ramps of the troop ships only two to three hundred yards behind. If the carrier could be scuttled earlier, then Lin Kuang knew any explosion from the magazine would be minimized.

Most of the carrier's crew, including Lin Kuang, were rescued by the lighter frigates and destroyers. As it transpired, the magazine did not blow, and the first of sixteen thousand assault troops were soon wading ashore from the gaping mouths of the LSTs. The return fire from the Chinese, stunned by the sustained prelanding bombardment from Quemoy and the Nationalist warships, was sporadic, and within an hour a perimeter a half mile wide and a quarter mile deep had been established by the Nationalists as F-15 Eagles, refueling from Taiwan, kept mounting a new sortie every forty minutes.

And the Intruders, pregnant with bombs from Taiwan's west coast Chin Chuan Kang air base, returned to widen the safety channel through the mine field, making it safer for the dozens of resupply ships already en route from Taiwan. To the south of the invasion zone, hundreds of villagers risked death from shrapnel, if not direct fire, by coming out in sampans to harvest the thousands of tons of fish floating stunned or dead in the water.

Now, Lin Kuang knew, the hard part would begin: waiting to see whether the anti-Communists on the mainland would continue to join him in sufficient numbers in his crusade against Mao's heirs. Or would Beijing's patriotic appeal to defend the motherland overcome the disaffecteds' hatred of the Beijing regime? Speed was of the essence.

It was now that Douglas Freeman issued his call for operation "Spring Tea," when the brown envelopes were opened from the safes of every ship in the U.S. Seventh Fleet. It was a *request*—not an order—to support as much as possible the landing by Kuang's ROC forces. Even the normally astute Norton had had no prior knowledge that this would be part of Freeman's idea of a "reconnaissance in force," or, more latterly, the tarted-up "U.N. police action." On one hand, the general's idea of dummying the ROC into an invasion he wasn't prepared to join himself until the ROC attacked from the sea first was by far the hardest-hearted thing he had seen Freeman do.

"What if they hadn't gone in?" he asked Freeman.

"Kuang's troops? Then *we* would have."

Norton still wasn't sure. "Where?"

"Beidaihe."

"So do we go into Beidaihe now?"

"In a manner of speaking, yes," Freeman said. "Send in Brentwood on the *Reagan* to blow up the mines so—"

"Cheng thinks it's a preparation for another invasion."

Freeman smiled. "Plus a few of our merchantmen and a cruiser or two on the horizon to add to the feint. Yes. That way we'll draw some of his forces away from Kuang in the south. You see, Norton, I'm not such a son of a bitch after all!"

They both knew the battle was far from over, but if the Communist Chinese yet overwhelmed Freeman, Norton knew that it wouldn't be for the general's lack of strategic and tactical skill.

CHAPTER TWENTY-SIX

"I WILL NEVER," Rosemary said, "go through that again!"

"Honey," Andrea answered, "a C section is supposed to be the cat's meow. I mean unless you're one of those strain-your-guts-out natural types. Personally I prefer good ole morphine when push comes to shove."

"I mean that . . ." Her face drained of color. "I killed a man. I killed another human being."

"And good riddance, I say. Lordy, I thought you were on about that spinal injection they gave you. You sounded godawful, Rose, and that's a fact. Thought you were dying in there."

"So did I," Rosemary said, but Andrea saw by her friend's eyes that she was still talking about the trauma of the break and entry—the shooting.

"Well you're bound to be upset for a while. Wouldn't be normal if you weren't. But you got a lot going for you, kiddo—good husband, little boy's doing fine. Bit small, being so premature and all, but hell, he's out of the woods now. Next thing you know—well I just bet he's going to be another Arnie!"

Rosemary looked nonplussed.

"Schwarzenegger," Andrea explained.

"God forbid," was all Rosemary could say.

"Now Rosie, don't you go bad-mouthin' Arnie. He's my pinup boy. Met him at a USO concert. Sent my blood pressure soaring, I can tell you. Love his movies—'sides, he's a Republican." Andrea paused but asked anyhow, "You a Democrat, Rose? I mean the party?"

"Sometimes."

"Course you've got royalty—I love all that pageantry."

Rose didn't answer. It bothered Andrea that not once had Rosemary asked about her baby—but at least, Andrea thought, for the moment she wasn't dwelling anymore on the rat that she shot. Or was she?

A beeper in the intensive-care unit started up, and nurses came rushing from everywhere. When Andrea went out and walked up to the glass she saw it was little Arnie, as she'd begun calling him. It was the second crisis in as many hours, but what could she tell Rosemary? Even worse in a way—did Rosemary care?

On the other side of the world, Lieutenant Julia Reid was experiencing the first symptoms of mountain sickness—a dull headache that promised to increase in intensity and a vague feeling of being unwell, a feeling that she could not isolate as affecting any one part of her body in particular, but a feeling that seemed to move all over, one second here, the next somewhere else. She took her pulse rate and found it had increased alarmingly in the last half hour—since they had begun yet another climb over yet another ridge.

Pride kept her going, that and the plainly obvious—that the further she and her guide got from the camp the better chance they had of eluding their pursuers. She hadn't been sure whether or not they were being pursued, but for the old man there was no doubt as he'd stopped, sniffed the wind, and tapped his nose with his finger and said, "Chineze." She believed him. She'd heard how the Vietnamese had said they could smell the different body odor of the Americans far off, or maybe it was simply the old man hearing the shots from the encampment.

Whatever, finally her top-gun pride had to face common sense. If she kept on at this rate she'd pass out and be even more of a burden on the old man than she was now. She began to tell him in sign language that she couldn't—shouldn't—go on when he astonished her, the voice coming from his rough woolen scarf announcing matter-of-factly, "You tired?"

After she recovered from her surprise she nodded, "Yes, I'm tired." Was that all the English he knew, this old man to whom altitude did not seem to matter? Or did he know much more than he was letting on? For some reason she could not fully explain, his utterance of English alarmed rather than comforted her.

CHAPTER TWENTY-SEVEN

Orgon Tal

"SIR?" IT WAS one of Choir Williams's troop, a Chinese American, during the final briefing. "How about the broadcasting building?"

Freeman nodded at Norton, a sign that the SAS/D man had impressed him. "You know where it is, son?"

"On Fuxingmenwai Dajie—the main drag, sir."

"You've been to Beijing?"

"Yes, sir."

"In what capacity?"

"Tourist, sir. My mother and father were born there and took me back on holidays—that was in—"

"All right, son," Freeman cut in good-naturedly. "Don't need your biography." There was a smattering of laughter. "Fact that you're in the SAS/D is good enough." Freeman looked out at Choir Williams. "Mr. Williams, you keep that boy real close to you."

"I'll handcuff him to me, General."

More laughter.

"Better idea," Freeman said. "Cuff him to the radio." Freeman turned to his next topic and waited till the men had settled down. "I know as a prerequisite for SAS/D force every man here has to have a working knowledge of one language other than English. Now most of you swear in at least a dozen languages and we have some jokers from down under who harbor the belief that they speak English."

"Bloody right, mate!" Aussie interjected, and was hooted down. Freeman didn't mind the fun, for when they took off in the C-47 Chinooks for the capital of the most populous country on earth, into the very heart of communism, their mood would be somber enough.

"Right!" Freeman continued. "Listen up, now. How many Chinese speakers have we?"

Out of 160 men who would be put down in Tainanmen Square, eleven spoke Chinese.

"Mandarin?" Freeman asked. "Not Cantonese."

Six hands went down immediately.

"Very well, gentlemen, you five will stay so close to radio operators that you'll look like their shadows. Shadow one, two, three, four," Freeman said, indicating Aussie Lewis, David Brentwood, Choir Williams, and Salvini, "will stay with the respective troop leaders. Number five, you'll stay with me. Now, everyone, watches—time is now ten hundred hours. We leave at oh four hundred. We should be in the square before dawn."

"Air cover?" someone shouted.

"Pessimistic bastard," Freeman replied, and this got the biggest laugh of what would be a final half-hour-long briefing.

"Comanches!" the general answered.

"You mean Apaches, sir?"

"No, I do not mean Apaches. I mean Comanches. Second Army gets the first batch of fifty."

"All right!" a tall, black Tennesseean said.

"Let's hope we don't need any," his buddy countered.

"Dreamin', boy. You're dreamin'."

"As to the original question," Freeman said, "about the broadcasting building. You're right, Private. Damned important target—same as the telegraph office east on Xichang' An Jie. These targets as well as other railway overpasses and bridges will be hit by cruise missiles. We don't want to destroy anything in Beijing, however, unless it's of military importance. We expect a number of students and workers to rise and help us. Like ten thousand or so. We don't want to bomb them. Our mission is to become a rallying point for our attack on the compound."

Freeman reached in his top left pocket and extracted one of the leaflets he'd had printed. "This pamphlet, drawn with the goddess of democracy in the background, promises that Second Army is here only to wrest control from the Communists so as to turn the government back to the people, to the goddess of democracy, the June Fourth Movement, et cetera . . ."

Next Freeman walked over to a large table that was covered in a khaki sheet backed by a row of enlarged black-and-white photos of China's top leaders. "Now, gentlemen, I want you to pay attention to this more-detailed mock-up of our target." And with that, Freeman, with the flourish of a Houdini, pulled the khaki sheet aside in one movement, revealing the central area of Beijing in detail. Even the model size of Tiananmen Square drew whistles of surprise. Its vastness was evident even on this scale, representing almost a hundred acres of cement. "All right," Freeman said, opening his telescopic pointer. "You've had time to study the map since the first briefing. I'm facing north and standing in the middle of the square. What's immediately to my rear?"

The answer from 160 throats sounded like a roar. "Statue of Heroes of the Revolution!" The pointer now slid north across Changan Avenue.

"Tiananmen—Gate of Heavenly Peace, and," Freeman added, "entrance to the Forbidden City, which is two hundred and fifty acres and where we do not want to go unless we absolutely have to. We're not here to shoot up their ancient buildings, monuments, or artifacts. If any of you land in error or have mechanical failure that puts you down inside the Forbidden City, head south immediately and get out through the Tiananmen Gate and join us in the square. All right, I'm still standing in the middle of the square. On my left-hand side to the west?"

"Great Hall of the People."

"Correct. To the east—right-hand side?"

"Museum of the Chinese Revolution."

"Correct."

"Behind me, beyond the Statue of Heroes of the Revolution. To the south?"

"Mao."

"And dead as a doornail," Salvini said.

"You bloody hope," Aussie cut in. It got a laugh, but not from Freeman, who, Norton noticed, rather sternly slid the pointer to the northwest corner of the square, immediately left of the Forbidden City.

"Zhongnanhai—Snakes' Compound."

"Good. That's our target, so as soon as you get down in the square you get yourselves together into four troops of forty men each and head for the compound. Now I'm not going to feed you any bullshit so you might as well understand that because the buildings in the Zhongnanhai are residences as well as the offices of the elite Communists there will be women and children present.

"If it were simply a matter of killing them all we could send in a cruise missile there as well, but then we, the U.S., would knowingly be killing women and children. That's not our way—that's what makes us different from them—from the Communist hardheads. This is why you SAS and Delta have been asked to do the job. You're specially trained in the split-second decision making on clearing rooms in hostage situations—so as dawn breaks let's clear them out as carefully and as quickly as we can. Same rules as I mentioned before—choice of weapons is yours but has to be okayed by your troop leader.

"Remember, the only people we're interested in are the State Council—Chairman Nie, Cheng, and the others on the State Council whose photos we have on the board up here. While we're in the compound, more troops will be landing in Tiananmen. I'll only give orders when I think our one-two-three—one, go in, two, get them, three, get back to the square—has met any unusual or unforeseen obstacles. Other than that it's up to you to follow your four troop leaders—Brentwood, Salvini, Aussie, and Choir Williams. Any questions?"

"Sir," Williams asked, "will the main attack against the wall at Badaling and down through the Juyong Pass coincide with our attack on the compound?"

"It will," Freeman said, remarking that the Zhongnanhai complex "is almost as big as the Forbidden City, including the area covered by the two lakes. And I should tell you that we've been flying nighttime nap-of-the-earth chopper missions in and already dropping leaflets, so hopefully our entry in the Chinooks won't elicit too much interest on their radar even if they do pick us up on screen. But everything will ultimately depend on surprise and speed. Before that, darkness and bad weather are our best camouflage."

"Piece of cake," Aussie said, making an eye-rolling Groucho Marx face that belied his ironic tone.

"Very well," Freeman said. "I have one more comment to make. It's no use glossing over the opposition. We know neither how many we'll run into nor, if our luck holds, how few. But one thing we do know is that we'll be at the heart of the dragon. Chinese still think they're the center of the world—closer to heaven than anyone else. If we get the State Council out of there, if we take the mandate of heaven from them, yours will be the greatest single blow ever against the world's last great Communist bastion. I believe if we succeed the whole edifice will fall as it did in Soviet Russia in ninety-one, and freedom'll have a chance. You remember all those faces you saw on TV in eighty-nine—in the Tiananmen massacre? Hell, they're on your side before you even land." He glanced around at his audience of one hundred and sixty, and with a look of determination that harbored no anxiety, not even the slightest doubt, he proclaimed, "That's all. Good luck and God be with you."

"My MP5'll be with me," Aussie said. At thirteen and a half inches long, the submachine gun looked more like a huge pistol with a front grip, but it was perfect for confined spaces, whether you were trying to take out a hijacker in the narrow confines of an aircraft or in a large room. Like everyone else in the SAS/D team who cost two and half million dollars each to train, the men who fired the MP5 didn't use the gun sight but fired more by intuition sharpened by hundreds of practices in "killing houses" in Wales and in the United States at Fort Bragg, trying to conceive of every possible situation. But Freeman knew that *this* situation was one they could have only partially been readied for, because it had more unknowns than most missions.

After the briefing, Norton mentioned to the general that he hadn't seemed too pleased when Aussie Lewis had made the comment about hoping Mao was dead.

"Well I'll tell you, Norton, first, you're damned observant—as usual. Second, Mao's memory is one of the unknown factors in this. I believe I'm right in assuming the minorities are with us, and a good many of the Han Chinese even though they're in the majority. But I don't underestimate the power of myth—the myth of Mao. He's beyond death—he's a god for the godless, and invoking his name alone may cause an otherwise rebellious Chinese to hesitate. That's why it's so damned important to keep civilians out of this as far as possible—I mean not out of it, but no mass bombing over any Chinese town—to make it clear to them that we're only going for those corrupt warlords who call themselves the Communist leadership."

Freeman's uncertainty gave Norton a pulse-jarring moment, but Freeman was still the gambler, the general who had turned a number of different situations here and abroad to his own advantage, from Ratmanov Island and the Dortmund-Bielefeld Pocket to Lake Baikal. In any event, Norton could see it was too late to abort, even if the general did have second thoughts. Like most great battles, at one point one is too far inside the enemy territory to pull out, even if you want to. They were too deep into China, and the awesome bureaucracy needed to coordinate the separate attacks as one offensive was too far along to stop, for it had, like all bureaucracies, attained its own momentum. It was either win this battle or Cheng would have time to get his second wind and redirect his three-million-man army to devour Second Army piecemeal.

At Orgon Tal, Three Corps was already preparing for the offensive that would be launched simultaneously with the SAS/D attack on the Zhongnanhai, and at Honggor three divisions limbered up for an advance, the star players being those halfway along the line, for these would bear the frontal attack on the Great Wall nearest Beijing, the forces at Orgon Tal and Honggor sweeping in from the west and east respectively to close about Beijing in a giant pincer movement.

The backbone of the forces at the midpoint was comprised of the eighteen-mile-range towed M198 155mm howitzer and the self-propelled M109 155mm howitzer with a range of eleven miles and a speed of thirty-three miles per hour that made the monolithic weapon the most versatile of the heavy field guns in the U.S. armory, the turret having a full width bustle in which twenty-two rounds of ammunition could be stored, including HE, chemical, smoke, flare, and, if needed, nuclear.

Anticipating massed infantry charges after initial penetration by ChiCom armor and/or artillery, Freeman had made sure that all battalion commandos in the area had the six-barrel Vulcan antiaircraft guns for both antiaircraft fire, at three thousand 20mm rounds a minute, and the reduced one-thousand-rounds-per-minute rate for enemy infantry. Mounted on an armored personnel carrier, the gun could be moved at forty-three miles per hour, and it was hoped that modification on it since the Gulf War, where it performed well, would allow it to operate with the same efficiency in the snow and rain conditions of the northern Chinese spring.

In addition, engineer battalions were not only ready to lay marsden matting for airstrips that would have to be bulldozed out of the desert regions south of the Orgon Tal–Honggor front, but would also help in grading minefields, pushing the mines either side of an enormous plow blade, to be dismantled later. As the time for the battle neared, the men's nerves were taut, and the monsoon, though not at full force, was already strong enough to blow the sand across both the Chinese and American forces.

The M1 main battle tanks started up, the smell of their exhausts quickly blown away by the monsoon and inhaled by the American infantry boarding the APCs, Vulcans riding nearby and motorcycles probing the chosen attack routes for possible mine traps. But here Cheng's forces had not had sufficient time to make the elaborately hidden traps that had earlier caught Freeman's tanks unawares.

The U.S. carrier battle group proceeding south from Korea was what the French call "triple layered," that is, the carrier, being the heart of the force, had a protective screen beyond it for 213 miles in any direction. At a distance of two hundred miles from the carrier, Robert Brentwood's Hunter-Killer/ICBM Sea Wolf II, the USS *Reagan*, was on outer escort duty for the carrier force. A hundred miles closer in to the carrier there were the surface ships, an Aegis cruiser, two destroyers, and four frigates.

Further in, in a tighter defensive ring ten miles from the carrier, were another cruiser and two destroyers, the whole two-hundred-plus-mile defensive rings covered by an aerial umbrella of Hawkeye early-warning aircraft. In addition there were three pairs of combat fighters forming CAPs, combat air patrols, to intercept any enemy planes before they had the range to fire antiship missiles. The CAPs extended to seventy thousand feet.

To increase her security, the carrier the USS *Carl Vinson* had gone to "switch off," wherein all the active radars on the ship were turned off, no active pulses being emitted that could give any enemy radar the carrier's position. For information on any enemy approaching her, the Aegis cruiser's radar acted as the eyes of the carrier, feeding her with an endless stream of information while the carrier simply remained invisible to enemy radar screens over the horizon. But she was still vulnerable to a sub attack if the sub had also forsaken sending out active radar pulses to gain echo bounce-back and instead was simply listening on passive radar mikes.

On the *Perch*, her air supply replenished, the second last lookout on the starboard quarter saw one of the second zone's frigates. She waited, hearing the bigger game of the carrier, the powerful pounding of its engines sending sound waves through the sea at five times sound's speed in air because of the sea's salinity.

Now on the green vertical roll of the Chinese sonar screens sine waves began and were repeated and repeated again, giving a good enough sound print. It wasn't particularly good seamanship that the Chinese sub had managed to find out the carrier's approximate position. It was luck, the kind of luck that the skipper of the *Perch* had had in mah-jongg. He was known for it. All his tubes were loaded with warshots, and if the carrier kept up its present heading it would pass within two miles of the *Perch* in a matter of hours.

The officer of the deck had already done the computerized trigonometry, the readout on his computer giving the *Perch* the most advantageous vectors for the four fish the *Perch* was willing to expend on the carrier. If only the American leviathan kept on the same heading, the skipper of the *Perch* needed only the smallest, quietest of tones on silent running to realign—at five hundred feet in the subsurface currents—what could be his kill shots.

That evening Pin Dao, a member of the university's June Fourth Movement and one of those who believed the Americans were coming, by which he meant they would probably make a frontal attack on Beijing from the northern plain, was a passenger with two others in the back of his brother's three-wheel pickup. Beside him he had one of the AK-47s that the students had snatched from the PLA in the Tiananmen massacre in '89, and each of the other two had, from the labels at least, a twenty-six-ounce bottle of Tsing Tao beer, but the bottles were in reality filled with gasoline and a petrol-soaked rag.

Slowing in traffic by the Zhongnanhai gate, Pin Dao could see the two immaculate, white-gloved guards. He lifted the Kalashnikov and shot them both in two quick bursts at practically point-blank range. He immediately ducked, and the other two threw the lighted Molotov cocktails through the gate.

"Go!" Pin Dao's brother yelled—but already a bevy of Public Security men were running out the gate through the crowd, a siren wail coming immediately after them.

The two Molotov throwers jumped out and disappeared

in the river of people flowing down Changan. Pin Dao kept firing at the gate, felling a second guard, then he too abandoned the vehicle and ran into the crowd. Several pistol shots were fired, then a scream, and there was pandemonium across and along the Avenue of Eternal Peace.

Two hours later a pirated and, under Chinese law, thoroughly illegal videotape was shown on CNN's French channel and picked up by all CNN feeds. From Beijing it was reported that criminal antisocial elements had attacked the Zhongnanhai. Arrests were expected soon. Meanwhile all women and children of high-ranking officials would be taken to the country, which all Chinese knew meant "out of the way."

General Freeman's headquarters was stunned.

"The stupid bastards!" Aussie Lewis said. "They've fucked up the whole plan. After moving their wives and kids out, they'll be the next to run."

"No they won't." No one had seen Freeman enter the barracks, glued as they were to CNN.

"Turn that damn thing off!"

"Yes, sir."

"If you think the Chinese leadership is going to vacate Beijing because a couple of guys tossed in a Molotov cocktail and shot two guards, you don't know much about the Chinese. They leave Beijing now and they lose face, my friend. They lose that, they lose it all."

A slow smile now spread across Freeman's face. Of course everyone knew the general was right, but then Aussie quickly pointed out, "They're bound to have reinforced security though."

"Yes," Freeman said coolly, almost dispassionately, and Norton detected in the general's tone a kind of resoluteness that had never wavered in the face of odds. "Would you expect a commando attack after that?" Freeman asked the assembled SAS/D men. "I sure as hell wouldn't. Would you, Aussie?"

"No, sir!"

"Which is precisely why the raid's still on. See you at the choppers."

"Jesus, he's a cool one," one of Salvini's troop of forty said.

"He's nuts, that's what he is," said another, a first-timer. The men who had served with Freeman before reserved judgment. "If he loses, everybody'll call him nuts. If he wins, it'll be ticker tape down Fifth Avenue." As Freeman had once told them in an attack on Ratmanov Island in the Bering Strait, "When you're in charge it's either hoots or hosannas and you'd better get used to both."

He had then quoted Douglas MacArthur, who had listened to all the arguments against landing at Inchon in the Korean War: Inchon had the world's highest tides and at low tide the harbor was a vast mud flat, both conditions disqualifying it from the highly complex business of amphibious assault by seventy thousand marines. MacArthur, Freeman reminded them, had listened patiently to all the objections and replied, "The very arguments you have made as to the impracticability involved will tend to ensure for me the element of surprise. The enemy commander will reason that no one would be so brash as to make such an attempt. . . . Surprise is the most vital element for success in modern war."

"Yeah," an SAS/D trooper said. "Is that when he threw up?"

CHAPTER TWENTY-EIGHT

THE ROLLING THUNDER that was Freeman's Second Army pressing its counterattack hard all along the Orgon Tal–Honggor line was only six miles from Badaling and the Great Wall. If they reached and took the twenty-foot-high, fifteen-foot-wide wall at Badaling—at three thousand feet— then at the long, narrow cleft of the Juyong Pass running northwest to southeast they would be forty-eight miles from Beijing. But if they could not bash their way through the pass, then Freeman had ordered them to dig in and maintain positions.

It would give the Chinese an initial advantage in that if Harvey Simmet was right and the monsoon kept up, the U.S. close air support would be unable to distinguish between friend and foe in the swirling fury of the monsoon coming off the Bo Hai Gulf. But the weather was all important to the SAS/D mission, and now it became clear as to why, the plans calling for a drop of eighty men to secure an LZ—landing zone—on the east side of the Statue of Heroes of the Revolution. The worse the weather, the easier it would be for the four Chinooks to hide, despite the *wokka-wokka* sound of the blades.

Freeman waited to see everyone else aboard before he walked up the ramp of the first of the four Chinooks. After an LZ was secured by the SAS/D team in Tiananmen then another forty choppers, each carrying up to fifty fully equipped regulars, would come into the square, but before Freeman could even hope that this might happen he knew he had to capture the State Council, preferably alive but dead if necessary.

Now the Comanches came into play, not as troop carriers—that was the Chinooks' role—but as Stealth-skinned, heavily armed choppers riding shotgun for the Chinooks, the Comanches having less than 2 percent of the Chinooks' radar cross section and a speed of two hundred miles per hour. Taking off from desert pads twenty minutes to the rear of Second Army's Orgon Tal–Honggor front, the RH-770 Comanches were state of the art for the seventy-mile, twenty-minute dash—across the edge of the northern plain and up over the mountains down into Beijing.

The Comanches made the celebrated Apache of Iraqi War fame passé. Where the Apache was a superb tank killer, as it had proved around Orgon Tal against Cheng's T-62s, it was not designed to penetrate by itself deep into enemy territory, and while the Apache was relatively easy for an enemy to detect on radar, the radar cross section of the Stealth-sheathed Comanche was 1.07 percent of that of the "standoff" Apache and other light attack helos. This tiny radar cross section, together with the nap-of-the-earth flying by pilot and copilot, meant that unlike the Apache, the Comanche could penetrate further into enemy territory undetected.

With its chin-mounted, remote control, twin-barreled 20mm Gatling gun sticking out beneath its infrared Starlite sensor's nose, the chopper would be formidable in any of its four modes, from armed recon up to heavy attack, deep strike, and air combat. Its two retractable claw mounts carrying four Hellfire antitank and two Stinger air-to-air missiles, the much faster Comanches in diamond four formation would be riding shotgun for the four Chinooks and if necessary would drop decoy chaff and/or flares to draw off any ground- or air-launched Chinese missiles fired at the Chinooks. And the Comanches, their exhausts from their twin three-foot-long LHTEC-T-800 engines cooled by sucked-in air through tail vents, would not give off sufficient heat to attract heat seekers themselves.

In addition, the sound of their engines would be muffled by the antitorque fan in the enclosed tail, with its five- instead of four-bladed rotors, the latter reducing tip speed, thereby reducing the Comanches' noise signature.

Two more squadrons of Comanches would follow on, escorting as many men as it might take to secure the landing zone in the square and finally, if all went well, with a maximum of 20 percent casualties, the square itself. The element of surprise depended on the twenty-minute run-in.

The Chinooks with their twin machine guns forward and one heavy machine gun on the open ramp would fly low, over the vast, sprawling city, their pilots hoping that the helos' noise would be attributed by the populace to the Russian-made Hinds that had flown over Beijing during the Tiananmen Square massacre, dropping leaflets on the people and students below, pamphlets proclaiming, "The people love the PLA. The PLA loves the people," before they had begun machine gunning the people down.

"We all set, Captain?" Freeman asked the Chinook leader.

"Yes, sir," she answered.

"All right, take us to Beijing."

The four Chinooks rose, creating a ministorm within the storm of the monsoon, and headed out into the dust-stinging blackness of the Orgon Tal–Honggor front.

* * *

The colonel in charge of the Zhongnanhai was now a junior lieutenant, ten years of promotions demolished in two minutes as Cheng humiliated him. The fact that two Molotovs had been thrown was bad enough, but the failure to close down the block on Changan Avenue and to recognize the "hooligans" on the video feed from the lamppost-mounted cameras along the avenue only compounded the error in Cheng's view.

Apart from losing face over the incident, the worst insult not only to the colonel but to the two hundred men responsible for the security of the Communist elite of the State Council, was the news that spread like wildfire that Cheng had announced, endorsed by Nie, that from now on security of the Zhongnanhai was to be the responsibility of Special Security Unit 8431 under the direct command of the Central Military Committee.

SS Unit 8431 was the toughest of the tough, used to going anywhere to immediately douse "ideological fires" or "demonstrations" that got out of hand. The commander of the unit 8431 was asked defiantly by the recent colonel what he, the commander of 8431, would have done to resolve the Molotov incident.

"Two armored vehicles would have been dispatched immediately," the commander answered.

"To do what?" the disgraced colonel pressed.

"To annihilate the antisocial vermin immediately."

"Oh? And how would you have distinguished them from the mass of people moving past the Zhongnanhai section of Changan Avenue?"

"It would not be necessary to make that distinction," the CO of 8431 said.

"You would have killed them *all*?" the ex-colonel asked incredulously.

"Every one," the commander answered. "Without hesitation." With that, Commander Hu of unit 8431 contemptuously dismissed the one-time colonel and set about arranging the new security for the Zhongnanhai.

No one would be allowed to use the two lakes, he said—all boats were to be housed in the boathouse by the gazebo in the center of the south lake. He did not expect the Americans to be so foolhardy as to attack the Zhongnanhai, but in the event that any other social degenerates might try to breach the compound he would have divers carry out round-the-clock underwater inspections as well.

All the same, Hu realized that a wall that defended you could also box you in, as the Americans had found at their famous Alamo. Originally arrangements had been made for the entire State Council to be moved, in a time of war, via the supposedly secret subway station in the Zhongnanhai, to Xishan military base. For years it had been assumed that no one outside the State Council knew about this escape route from the Zhongnanhai, but then a map showing it was found on a June Fourth Democracy Movement cell leader.

Besides, Commander Hu had concluded that if the Americans ever did reach the capital, the line to Xishan would be one of the first blown up by the Democracy Movement traitors. Accordingly, Hu decided he would need a space in which to put the State Council, to give them visibility so the populace would know they had not deserted the city, and yet one that was capable of being defended in depth if necessary.

Julia Reid had never seen a snow leopard, period, let alone one in the wild. Yet here was the beautiful, lithe creature stock-still, the left front paw extended, the right slightly bent, caught in a moment of indecision, the old man either not having seen the animal or, if so, ignoring it with a mountain man's sixth sense about such things.

Julia felt inside her sheep wool coat for the .45, its grip giving her enough of a sense of security that she steeled her nerves and managed to pass within fifteen feet of the leopard, the yak she was riding keeping up a steady pace, either pretending that he did not see or smell the potential enemy or, thought Julia, perhaps the yak knew there was no way he could defend himself from the leopard. When she looked ahead at the old man she was surprised to see him staring at her, his mouth hidden by the thick cashmere scarf but his eyes so alive that for a moment he seemed much younger. Only now did she discern that the look was a warning, not of her sexual attractiveness to him but a warning not to draw her pistol. "One shot," he said, and then passed his ancient hand across his throat, "An' Chin-eze."

"Yes," she said. "I understand."

He turned from her, his knees motioning the yak on, and through the fine-grained but stinging hail he led her higher until she had to tell him by the appropriate sign language that her headache was so severe she couldn't go on. It humiliated her more than she could have imagined, and in her mind's eye she saw lines of tormenting faces—all male, all pilots, the bovine grins on their faces saying, "We told you women couldn't hack it!" She was feeling dizzy and nauseated as well. Either she was weakening, or the nomad had taken her too high, albeit gradually.

He nodded knowingly, and sliding off his yak, he approached and motioned for her to unbutton her coat. She hesitated. Was he smiling? She couldn't tell. He took her hand and, taking a step closer, placed it over his heart. She nodded that she now understood that he was only being solicitous of her health and wanted—no, needed—to feel her heartbeat. She pointed to her wrist. He shook his head vigorously, his fist now on his own heart and him making a wheezing noise through his scarf. Ah—he wanted to listen to her chest. "Quick! Quick!" he told her. It amazed her how specific he was with his English, given that he apparently knew so few words.

She undid her sheepskin coat and he quickly put his ear to her breast. In the icy blast of the snowstorm she felt frigid, despite her other sweaters and flight jacket. Whatever, he seemed to take an inordinately long time listening to her. As she was about to say something, he abruptly finished, nodded knowingly, and said, "The wheeze." Her head was pounding as if an iron band were tightening about her. He turned his yak into the storm and, though she couldn't be sure, it seemed to her that they were going back down the mountainside, but it was difficult to tell, her vision blurring, her disorientation increasing with white upon white, the rain of small hailstones coming at her like tracer, taking her back to the dogfight with the Fulcrum, another time, another world away.

In the near distance, about fifty yards away, beyond which she could see nothing, an outcrop of rock appeared, the old man driving the yak toward it. Everything went black, and she felt herself pitching forward, losing the reins, vomiting, falling.

As the choppers entered the rain of the monsoon, the noise against their skins grew to a sustained roar, even the *wokka-wokka* of the Chinooks' rotors subdued by the noise. The pilot of Chinook One was already sweating, and she didn't care if Freeman saw it. There wasn't one visible fix you could see, only the rain-filled darkness, the helos having to fly by instrumentation alone. The only thing that gave the Chinook pilots any comfort was that even though they were flying nap of the earth, by virtue of the infrared contour sensors, their noise would be muffled by the banshee howling of the monsoon.

"They'll never expect a raid in this weather," one of Aussie Lewis's troops aboard the second chopper said.

"Fuck *them*," his buddy replied from across the aisle. "*I* never expected a raid in this freakin' weather."

"Just so they don't drop me in that fuckin' moat," another said, referring to the moat that separated the Forbidden City from the Zhongnanhai on the latter's eastern side.

"Fuck the moat," Aussie Lewis put in. "You'd better hope they don't drop you in the friggin' lake."

"Which one?" another joshed. "The central—the Zhonghai—or the south lake?"

"Neither of the fuckers. I can't swim."

This got a great laugh, for SAS/D troopers were required to swim with weapon and several clips of ammunition, their training the most brutal in the world.

"Bullshit, man," the Tennesseean said. "We ain't going in no fucking lake. I was told we were on a fast rope insertion."

"Yeah, fast rope right in the fuckin' lake."

"All right, you guys," Aussie yelled. "Pay up or shut up. Five to one someone lands in the pool?"

"Some friggin' pool."

"Come on," Aussie pressed. "Five to one—" And out came his small black book from his vest and a small purple indelible pencil from his first-aid pack under his helmet strap. He gave the pencil a lick, looking for all the world like a bookmaker's tout.

"Put me down for two bucks," a trooper said.

"That's two bucks you've lost already, Aussie."

More bets were shouted, Aussie writing quickly.

"Hey Aussie," called out the Tennesseean—the tall black soldier sitting by the ramp. "What if you get hit, man?"

"Come on," Aussie riposted. "Get real. I can't get hit. It's against the fuckin' Geneva Convention. Besides, I have a plan for which there is no known defense. It's called the Aussie Auxiliary!"

"Jeez—you're full of it, man," the Tennesseean replied, half the forty troopers in the Chinook clapping Aussie, the rest waving him off.

Aussie flashed the book at the Tennesseean. "So how about it, Tennessee? You game or not?"

"Mr. Lewis," the black man said with mock formality. "How long have I known you?"

"Too fuckin' long," someone else said.

"The gentleman's correct," the Tennesseean acknowledged. "Too long. And that's why I'll not bet a cent." He turned to the soldiers nearest him, raising his voice. "You'll notice he said 'pool,' but what particular pool does he mean, gents? The *lakes*, the *moat*?"

This started a flak of spirited questions directed at Aussie, who held both hands up. "The lakes only," he said. "Right? Fair enough? The lakes."

In preparation for fast-roping it down into the square, they were all pulling on their gloves, and those who already had them on pulled them on that much tighter. The Tennesseean did the same thing. Quite irrationally there was something that made one feel invulnerable, pulling leather gloves on tightly, flexing the knuckles, seating each finger snugly. Aussie looked across at the black man, a longtime friend and colleague. "Thanks a lot, you fucker. *What* pool? Christ, nearly had a riot."

"Keep the riot for the Zhongnanhai," the Tennesseean said good-naturedly.

Up front in Chopper One Freeman held up his hand. "You boys ready?" There was a unified and boisterous response. It could have been a football game. And going out into the darkness each man had the same gut-tightening experience.

"Ten minutes!" Freeman announced, holding up the fingers of each hand to underscore the point, and everyone fell silent, most watching the red five-minute warning light and feeling the Chinook's buffeting by a dying monsoon.

David Brentwood, who stood behind Freeman, the general's backpack pushing against him as they dropped suddenly in an air pocket, had been quiet for most of the trip. He was thinking of Georgina, his wife—how they'd been honeymooning in the Canadian Rockies when he was recalled to Second Army. A master's degree in political science from the London School of Economics and Political Science meant she knew much more than David about the political situation and intrigues that so often led to war, and it had taken awhile for David to accept the fact that she was more intellectual than he and wasn't talking down to him. It was her British accent that created that impression. She spoke so beautifully that he worried about what he figured would be the inevitable clash between Georgina and his friend Aussie. Well maybe everything would be all right—maybe the same thing that happened to the Australian once he'd met and fallen head over heels for the Alexsandra Malof woman would occur and he would show his politely spoken better half. Or was that the better half? Once they landed on the square that rougher side of Aussie would help get the job done. They would all have to be uncivilized if they were to go in and take the Zhongnanhai.

"That's what I heard," came a voice on Choir's chopper, a first-timer from further down the line. "Chinks don't like to fight in the rain."

"Ferris, you'd believe any fuckin' thing."

"I'm just tellin' ya what I heard. Right?"

"Yeah, yeah, you know that's the same kind of shit they gave us about the Japanese."

"What?"

"Said there was no way a Japanese could fly at night 'cause his eyes were too fucking narrow."

"Yeah, well, hell—that's just plain dumb!" the first-timer said.

"That's right. About as dumb as believing Chinks won't fight in the rain."

"Well," the first-timer said, snorting with superiority, "you know the kind of shit you hear from the grunts."

"Yeah, well just remember the moment you hit terra firma you're a Delta commando. Remember what you've been taught." He paused. "You'll be okay. Hell, we've been through that mock-up ten times at least, right?"

"Right."

"Five minutes!" Freeman called aboard Chopper One, holding up his black-gloved hand and making his way back from the pilot so that he would be one of the first to go down on the ropes. The worst part about fast-roping it was the downwash of the rotors—like a water bed on your head it was so powerful.

They had been flying over the city's outskirts for some time, but there were few lights. Not only was the city normally dimly lit by modern standards, but Cheng had put a blackout in effect the moment he broke the cease-fire.

Up in the cockpit before he'd taken his place by the left-side door, Freeman had seen through the infrared binoculars that coming in from the northeast they'd already passed over Purple Bamboo Park, avoiding the high chimney between the park and the Beijing Zoo, and had started a right-hand turn above Xizhimen Railroad Yards, over the Xinhua printing plant and the bird and fish market where they saw the infrared blobs of white faces looking up at them from a gray wash of background—the market people being early risers along with the farmers and fishermen. They were passing by the chimney before the old Presbyterian church and everything went crazy, the sky lighting up in deceptively lazy-looking traces of green-and-red tracer and over the sound of the passing monsoon the steady bump, bump, bump of triple A fire.

Straight ahead the pilots could see the bell and drum towers across the Houhai, the top of each tower alive with triple A streaming from it, then both towers exploded from Hellfire missiles as the Comanches came into play. Now all they could hear was the rain and the explosion and the Comanches leading the Chinooks over the art college before turning right again down over Number 101 High School, the Ministry of Culture, Congan Hospital, turning right again over the Post Office and now hovering over the Museum of the Chinese Revolution on the eastern side of Tiananmen. Suddenly there was a terrific bang by the chopper, the scream of its engines, and the pilot's voice: "In your seats—we're going down! In your seats!"

It was a double shock to most—the announcement and the sound of a woman. Men fell backward hard against their packs, cussing and buckling up again.

"We're hit!" the woman's voice came. "We're going down—hold tight!"

"Hold—" Brentwood began, but whatever he said was lost in the crunch of the chopper buckling over its landing gear.

"Out!" Freeman yelled as the ramp went down, slamming hard on the concrete.

"Terrific," Brentwood said, his finger on the H & K

safety. "No damn ropes." Last to leave were the chopper crew: the captain, her copilot, and the three gunners.

In the drumming rain of the metallic dawn the sky above them was pockmarked with black smudges of AA fire, and one Chinook, Salvini's, was ablaze a hundred yards from them. Some SAS/D were fast-roping it as the big, banana-shaped Chinook kept hovering. Only three men made it down, however—Salvini and two of his troopers free of the ropes before the Chinook exploded, breaking in half and spilling men from it like so much burned detritus, their screams heard above the roar of the Comanches attacking every possible AA fire emplacement, one of them sweeping low over the square, flames issuing from its belly and decoying three heat-seeking missiles intended for three choppers now on the ground, fast roping forgotten with surprise having been lost.

Freeman was already in contact with the Comanche's leader, who had flown over the Zhongnanhai to check for any mortar or heavy machine gun positions. He reported none. Repeat *none*. He had come in low, his 20mm Gatling gun ready, and had seen no one. Not on infrared, not on Starlite goggles—not that the rain would permit anything much to show up on them—but definitely nothing on infrared that looked like troops.

He banked the Comanche hard right over the vast Forbidden City, ready for another run over the Zhongnanhai, again to match any infrared images he saw with his preprogrammed threat library. Any matchup between the target seen and the target in the computer would automatically tell him what weapons should be used and would also "prioritize" the targets in order of their danger.

He was at five hundred feet above the Working People's Cultural Palace, then over the Tiananmen Gate as he leveled off from the turn to go over the Zhongnanhai again.

Oh, he picked up infrared neutrals—that is, the heat exhaust from the State Council's furnaces and the like—but there were no guards, no soldiers, a fact he quickly conveyed to Freeman.

"Women and kids are out," Freeman said. "We know that. Maybe they're in some underground shelter in the Zhongnanhai," he posited.

"General, there's no one—Jesus!" The copilot-gunner saw the rocket streak for him and dropped flare and foil decoys. The missile exploded twenty feet from the chopper, but the missile stabilizers or fins had chopped into the pilot's four-axis control unit and slashed open a port-side fuel tank beneath the copilot who sat up and behind the pilot. Simultaneously the threat library identified the AA missile as an AA-6RH Acrid. The Comanche's left-hand-side retractable claws slid out and opened. Within seconds a Hellfire air-to-ground was selected and fired, not at the Zhongnanhai, for the pilot was right—it had been abandoned. The Chinese ground-to-air missile had come from the Forbidden City!

"Comanche leader to S/D leader. They're holed up in the Forbidden—" The end of the transmit was swallowed by the explosion of the Comanche as it fell from the sky like a fiery rock into the south lake inside the Zhongnanhai.

"Aussie?" Freeman called.

"Sir."

"Take a nine-man recon patrol to the Zhongnanhai and see if either of the Comanche crew made it. Brentwood, Salvini, Williams—over here."

"Sir."

"They've holed up in the Forbidden City," Freeman informed them.

"Shit!" It was Salvini. "Fucking place has over ten thousand rooms."

"Nine thousand, to be exact," Freeman said. "But first we have to get over the moat."

The second Comanche came on the air reporting that due north of Tiananmen Square past the Tiananmen Gate there was considerable enemy activity inside the Forbidden City. The pilot's estimate was two to three companies—around 250 to 300 men—most probably, he said, just regular infantry hurriedly trucked in to guard the State Council.

CHAPTER TWENTY-NINE

"HEY—YOU THERE!" It was a local policeman who had seen them on the outskirts of Beidaihe, the official's voice full of officiousness before the tourist season had even begun.

"Are you talking to me?" Alexsandra said upon turning.

"Yes, you. You are a foreigner."

"You're very observant."

"Ha, ha!" said the terrified student who had blubbered to her that he had been forced to cooperate with the PSB, his attempt at ingratiating himself with the policeman taking on the tone of "The police love the people and the people *should* love the police."

The policeman shot a look at the student that would have silenced an entire cell of students.

"Where are your travel papers?" he demanded of Alexsandra.

"In my bag."

"You have no bag."

"I said you were very observant."

"Ha, ha!" the student said, his tone more groveling than before.

Alexsandra kept looking straight at the policeman. "My bag is back at my hotel."

"Ah, a hotel—what hotel?"

"Jinshian Hotel of course." It was the best.

"Your identification then?"

"And yours?" she demanded. The policeman's face went beet red in vivid contrast to the early morning fog that was rolling in from the sea onto Beidaihe's Middle Beach. "I demand to see your identification," she repeated. "Don't you know who I am?" And she added stiffly, "I am here with important officials."

"What is your name?"

"Ha, ha!" the student said, knowing the policeman was either going to draw his revolver or whistle for help.

She thought of all the petty harassment and gross humiliations the Chinese and Siberian officials had visited upon her—degradations unimaginable to anyone in the West. "I demand to see *your* identification," she repeated, taking out a small notepad from her pocket.

"Ha!" the student said. They were both going to be arrested.

"No!" the policeman said angrily. "You must show me your papers first." The policeman's cloudy breath added to the fog.

"Oh all right," she said, and took her hand out of the coat. "Will this do?" She thrust hard, and the switchblade pierced his heart. He stared, wide eyed, at her, making a half-choking, gargling sound and began to pull the knife out. She then thrust her left hand about his neck as if to kiss him and pushed the knife in further. "Keep it, you little bastard!"

"Oh—" the student said. "This is very bad."

"Have you still got the tickets?" Alexsandra said.

"Our tickets?"

"Get a grip on yourself. Yes, the tickets to Shanhaiguan."

"Yes, why?"

"*Why?* We're going there, you fool. Come on, get his gun and cartridges and we'll go to the station." She knew now that, previous plans notwithstanding, she would have to use Beidaihe station after all to get the train to Shanhaiguan.

"Oh!" the student said, shivering with cold and fright.

"I've had enough," she said in rapid Mandarin. "I've had all I'll take. I'm not running anymore." Which of course is precisely what she was doing.

"Oh—this is tremendous," the student said, but he had mispronounced the word in his fright. He meant "This is very bad."

Suddenly she stopped and looked at the student. "The Chinese Communist pigs are at war with the United States. Now whose side are you on?"

"Yours, but my family and—"

"Never mind your family," she said sharply, almost hysterically in her own fright. "Never mind *my* family—the few they left. Whose side are *you* on?"

"I am against the Communists of course."

"Then act like a man, damn you, or give me the gun. Give it to me anyway—it bulges in your Mao suit, padding or not. It'll fit better in my overcoat pocket."

"Yes, of course. Ha, ha. Do you know how to use a gun?"

"Are you serious, Wei Chen?"

"No. Ha, ha." They were both going to die.

She could feel her stomach trembling and tightening, and for a moment she thought she'd black out. Why had she lost her temper like that—why hadn't she offered to go back to the hotel—figure something out on the way? She didn't know. She had been so cool, so calm, so many times to survive in her life—perhaps she couldn't do it anymore? Perhaps something in her had finally snapped and she was going mad.

By sheer luck when they reached the railway station— Alexsandra, silent and hollow eyed from her prison ordeal, the student close to nervous breakdown—their train, the 7:30 from Beidaihe to Shanhaiguan, came rolling in, and the student was engaged in an argument with the ticket clerk, who said tickets to Shanhaiguan were not valid if you stopped off at Beidaihe. The student looked at Alexsandra. "Ha, ha!" Big trouble, he meant—until Alexsandra simply said, "Give her more money."

"You don't know much," she told the student as they boarded the hard class.

"Ha, ha, I guess you're right."

The student kept watching the great clouds of steam curling and swirling up from around the engine, half expecting a squad of police to emerge through them at any time. He looked at her apprehensively, too, wondering, and a steely, hollow-eyed face gave him the answer. By God, she *would* shoot them. Unable to break the tension after another cloud of steam revealed no one, the student excused himself quickly and headed for the toilet. "You can't use that!" a train attendant told him brusquely. "Not while you are in the station. Where do you think you are—at home?"

"Ha, ha! Sorry." His face was grimacing in pain. Suddenly the train shunted, steam poured out and up into the air, and the carriage began to jerk forward, becoming progressively smoother. He made to go in.

"Not till we are out of the station!" the attendant yelled at him.

"Ha, ha," he said, his legs crossed, taking a deep breath and turning spastically toward the window.

Soon the train was out of the station, picking up speed, and he ran in. The noise of the train clicking across the sleepers, amplified by the toilet tube, became a sustained roar.

On his way back to his seat he knew the police would be there. Perhaps he could sit away from her, but the train was full. He passed several families who had already opened glass jars of tea and were eating cold slices of fatty meat. As he made his way further down the aisle he was struck by people's mouths moving and he unable to hear them for the roar of a large goods train passing them toward Beidaihe. Perhaps he was going deaf.

"Feel better now?" Alexsandra asked.

"Yes."

"I'm sorry for being so rude with you. I'm afraid I need more sleep."

"Ha, ha," he said, and this time it meant, I wish you would and give us both some rest. She had closed her eyes but was kept awake by more troop trains roaring by. "Tickets?" came a conductor's voice.

"You show them," Alexsandra said.

"Yes," the student said, but he found his hand was trembling. She took the tickets from him. "I'll do it." He was alarmed—if the conductor questioned the ticket purchase she would probably shoot him.

CHAPTER THIRTY

JULIA FELT HERSELF manhandled off the yak and carried from the whiteness of the hailstorm into the blackness of a cave in the rock ridge.

What she didn't realize was that the old man had been carrying her on a circuitous path on the rocky ridge so that any pursuers following the snow tracks would come to a dead end on that part of the bare ridge in the lee of the wind where only hail and not snow had become wedged in the fractures.

When the old man put her down by the cold remains of a fire she ached in anticipation, but there wasn't to be the slightest sign of smoke—worse still, the faintest whiff of it and the Chinese would be on them. Her headache was bad, utterly untouched by aspirin. She toyed with the idea of a morphine shot in her small first-aid kit but didn't like the idea of it doping her out so that, along with the pain, she'd be of little use to the old man should the Chinese come upon them.

The old man left her yogurt, butter, cheese, and *tsamba*, the roasted barley flour that she could eat dry or with the butter. He motioned to her not to light a fire. She found it difficult to follow his meaning, her headache so pervasive that only part of his message managed to penetrate. By way of an answer, or rather a question, Julia took out the long-lasting Nuwick heat-and-light survival candle and, her sheer will fighting the pressure in her head, explained that it did not give off smoke or any odor.

"I go," the old man said as he tapped his watch. "Come back." She nodded that she understood he would return. Before he left, he bent down behind her, and she could feel the rough skin of his herder's hands biting deep into the back of her skull. Stiffly resistant at first, she now relaxed, surrendering to the old man's deep massage. From the small first-aid book that came with her pack, Julia knew that the nomads had much more hemoglobin in their blood than others, which protected them from altitude sickness, so that she doubted whether the massage would do any good. Surprisingly, however, though it didn't take the pain away, it reduced it to a more bearable level, and she could think straight enough to be concerned that his long fingers were now reaching the top of her breasts. Was this part of the *drobka*—ritual—of caring or was this a straight-out grope? Whether he sensed her unease the further down he reached or whether some other imperative moved him, he stopped abruptly and walked back to the entrance to the cave, which was at the end of a rough, S-shaped corridor at times no more than five feet in diameter. Though she lost sight of him once he passed the S bend, she could hear his fading footsteps.

Five minutes had passed when she heard footsteps again, faintly at first but then growing, making a crunchy sound on the pebbles that had accumulated in the cave. Whoever it was was not yet around the S and so remained hidden. She drew out the .45 and moved to a kneeling position, her hands shaking not only from fear but from the mountain sickness. She released the safety.

* * *

Running the half mile west along Changan Avenue—the Avenue of Eternal Peace—for the Zhongnanhai, Aussie and his reconnaissance patrol caused no interference but only drop-jawed stares of the early-rising citizens of Beijing as they bicycled down the avenue, there being fewer than usual about at this time of the morning because of the rain that had followed the monsoon's tail and that was still falling.

Then from up ahead there came two short cracks and more. Immediately Aussie signaled the reccy patrol to split—five on the southern side of the meridian, his group of four on the right-hand side, both groups moving toward the Zhongnanhai Gate from where the shots had come and where the two guards were lying down for better aim in front of the high, varnished red gates.

Aussie called to the others across the street to take them out with the SAW—squad automatic weapon. The SAS/D trooper stopped, the sling belt of the SAW over his right shoulder, the twenty-two-pound machine gun pumping out a burst of 5.56mm that silenced the two guards.

People were fleeing in all directions, but in a strangely almost habitual way as if this had been a weekly occurrence. The other part of Aussie's patrol crossed the road and joined his foursome.

Someone was clapping and several others joined in. An old man, a red armband to show he was one of the elder brigadesmen—or rather, local snoops—called out angrily, waving his fists, telling those who were clapping that these were "foreign devils," to which the first clapper told him to go to the night cart in his *hutong* and eat shit.

At the gate one SAS/D man braced himself against the wall, and Aussie Lewis took a run up and in one jump, using the man's cupped hands as a stirrup, he put his other foot on the broken glass top a fraction of a second before he jumped down on the other side. He landed on the edge of a pebbled path leading in from the gate, but at the guard-house inside, which was deserted, he couldn't understand any of the Chinese signs. Not wanting to waste time calling over for the Chinese interpreter, he pressed every button he could. A siren sounded and died, but by then he'd pressed another button and the Zhongnanhai Gate opened.

The moment it was open the remaining nine members of the reconnaissance patrol came in, fanning left and right, two men designated by Aussie Lewis to take the left foot-path and check out the little pavilion in the center of the round southern lake, the rest of the patrol running north along the cobblestone pathways to the apartments and bun-galows of the elite.

Even from the pathways it was difficult to see the extent of the buildings, as they were carefully hidden by meticu-lously attended shrubbery, trees, and gardens that followed the contours of the elite's houses. There was no sign of the downed Comanche in the south lake. As they went into one door after another, the signs of a hasty retreat were every-where, from unfinished tea to meals half-eaten, and in an-other building, the heat still on.

It wasn't until the ninth or tenth apartment that they saw the stepladder that had been used by the State Council to climb over the wall and vacate the Zhongnanhai via row-boats over to the Forbidden City across a moat a hundred and seventy feet wide, a moat that flowed around the For-bidden City.

Aussie reached the top of the wall on the aluminum step-ladder, and all he could see was the dark green moat, then the sandstone-colored wall on its far side, and behind the wall the rusty red of the walls of the Forbidden City.

"How'd they get over the moat?" the SAW operator asked.

"That bridge down there has been blown," another SAS/D pointed out.

"Probably had boats lined up ready," another began, poking his head up over the wall. "See, down by—"

He didn't finish, his body knocked from the ladder as if struck by a lance from a horse, the crack of the rifle shot that hit him reverberating against the moat and throughout the great squares of the Forbidden City. The radio "receiving" light came on, and the recon radio patrol operator snatched up the hand-piece. "Recon leader to—" and all he could hear was firing and static on the line. "Say again!"

". . . everyone will proceed to the lounge bar."

"Roger," the recon operator said, knowing that this message was most likely being listened to by the Chinese. "Lounge bar" was the designated code name for the Forbidden City. Not that anyone had thought they would be using it. And "everyone will proceed" meant that the recon patrol, like everyone else, was expected to attack the Forbidden City from wherever they were—most of them being with Freeman, clustered about the Statue of Heroes of the Revolution in the square, and about to advance, original plans having gone awry with the State Council's quitting the Zhongnanhai.

The recon operator was about to report one man down—when he saw Lewis thrown back, rolling over, facedown on the cobbled path. Then two of the other seven men lifted him up to his feet. He waved them off with a nod of thanks. The front of his antiterrorist uniform had what looked like a burn mark through it; the Kevlar vest underneath had hardly a scratch on it.

"Thank Christ," someone said.

"Thank Dupont," Aussie said as he got back his wind

and was figuring out the best way to deploy the reccy patrol. "Tell Freeman we'll move up from along the Zhongnanhai wall and try to sniper out a few if we can. We have a Haskins."

The reconnaissance patrol response was appreciated by Freeman, who had already sent another patrol down the right-hand, or eastern, side of the Working People's Cultural Palace, which came before the Tiananmen Gate, but where they too found the Donghua Men, another bridge, had been blown. In fact all the crossings over the moat had been blown, and the commandos were hearing from another Comanche pilot that tons of rubble now lay where the rear entrance to the Forbidden City—the Gate of Divine Military Genius—used to be. The only way through was via the Tiananmen Gate, and it was toward this that Freeman and the bulk of the commandos were headed.

There was no doubt in Freeman's mind that he had caught them off guard in making his monsoon attack, but the prudence of unit 8431's commander in having moved everybody to a new location had equally surprised Freeman. Indeed it alarmed him, for if they couldn't get the State Council quickly rounded up and back to the square before Second Army broke through at Badaling, the whole mission would be a failure, and with every passing minute Cheng would have a chance to increase the odds against the 125 or so commandos achieving their mission.

What in Freeman's mind was meant to be a hard, quick, if not clean, snatch and grab of the Communist leadership was now promising to be a much longer, drawn out affair.

Freeman and his commandos rushed toward the Gate of Eternal Peace, or Tiananmen, ready any moment to have machine-gun fire rain down upon them from the ramparts where Mao had made so many of his momentous speeches.

Once through Tiananmen, they had to pass through the second gate. Still there was no firing, no opposition.

"I don't fuckin' like this," Salvini said, he and the three survivors of his forty-man troop now grouping with Choir's troop of forty.

"Well," Choir said, keeping up the pace, their Vibram boots silent, ideally suited for the run on the ancient flagstones, "if we don't get any fire from the Meridian Gate"—the actual entrance to the Forbidden City, now three hundred yards in front of them—"I'm a China—"

Suddenly there was the tearing tarpaper sound of multiple ChiCom type 56-1 machine guns opening up behind them, and ten of the SAS/D men went down in a hail of 7.62mm bullets coming from atop the gate they'd just passed through.

"Keep going!" Freeman yelled, leading the way to the Meridian Gate. "SAWs cover!"

Ten squad automatic weapons raked the Chinese high up on the gate's battlement, that is, toward the second gate between Tiananmen and the Meridian that Freeman and the rest of the commandos were making their way toward.

By now ninety-seven SAS/D commandos had reached the base of the Meridian Gate, the entrance to the Forbidden City proper, and were firing at the railings-cum-battlements above.

Two commandos—Harrison and Bernstein—from Choir Williams's troop were ordered by Freeman to use their weapons. It was something Freeman hated to do, but the future sightseers of Beijing would just have to forgive him. Right now he had barely ninety men left, a little more than half of what he'd started out with.

"Go!" he told them, and the two men stood so that the barrels of their weapons were pointing almost straight up, and an instant later two yellow streaks of liquid fire went into the eyes of the brooding Meridian Gate. Within seconds the lacquered red top of the gate was ablaze, and Freeman's sappers—two of David Brentwood's men—were placing satchel charges of pentolite and TNT with a thirty-second fuse up against the huge, closed door of the Meridian Gate. The explosion blew open the heavy doors, not by much, but enough for the SAS/D commandos to pass through with withering machine gun fire preceding them.

"Up the stairs!" Brentwood yelled. "Clean 'em out!"

But Chinese regulars were already coming down, coughing from the acrid smoke of the fires that had been started and easy targets for the SAS/D who cut them down with three-round bursts from their HK MF5s and fire from M-16s.

"Masks on!" someone yelled, and within seconds the SAS/D men who were going up into the smoke had donned masks and continued the slaughter as the Chinese, blinded by the smoke, practically ran into them.

They had been running so hard and so fast that the architectural beauty of the Forbidden City was the last thing any of the SAS/D troopers thought or cared about. For them the overwhelming aspect of the Forbidden City was its sheer size: 720 acres, eight hundred buildings, and nine thousand rooms.

Beyond the Wumen, or Meridian, Gate they came to the five marble bridges over the Golden River, the moat below shaped like a Tartar bow. Here they came under more heavy fire from the towers of the Gate of Supreme Harmony ahead of them.

The SAS/D was giving as much as it was taking, but Freeman knew they needed high ground fast and so ran forward across the central marble bridge and onto the great flagstone square where one group directed heavy fire at the Taihe—the Hall of Supreme Harmony—providing cover for the commandos running to take cover in the Hongi and Tairen pavilions. And once the Hongi and Tairen towers were reached, with six men lost in the process, the men in and around these two pavilions fed long bursts of fire into the Hall of Supreme Harmony.

It was when he reached the hall that Freeman realized what had happened, and his anger at himself stung him with humiliation. The legendary Freeman of Second Army, of Ratmanov Island, the Dortmund-Bielefeld Pocket, the Freeman of the victory in the snows of Siberia and the hero of the brilliant attack on Orgon Tal before the truce, and of the celebrated night raid on Pyongyang earlier in the war, realized that the hunted, by retreating from the Zhongnanhai to the Forbidden Palace, had become the hunters, having lured the Americans inside the moat-bordered palace of 250 acres. As neat a trap as you could have planned for.

In the fog of war, confusion an ever-present player, Freeman had concentrated on going for a quick surgical strike to take out the State Council. But the quarry had been moved into what turned out to be the maze of the Forbidden City, and with them so had the elite members of unit 8431, their snipers buying time for army units to be recalled from the Orgon Tal–Honggor front back to Beijing and the Forbidden City, where the American general would be captured and, with his remaining eighty or so troops, be humiliated before the State Council in the great square of Tiananmen—a world telecast of the Americans in chains. Already Beijing radio was broadcasting reports, picked up and reported by CNN, of the imminent victory over the American "warmongers," who were "vandalizing one of China's great cultural landmarks."

"*Vandalizing!*" Freeman roared. "Goddamn it, they're the ones who are using the place as an ambuscade. Like some gunman running into a church then pleading piety to his enemy. Well, hell, I don't want to violate their national treasures any more than anyone else, but damned if they're going to stop me." He remembered all the men who had been lost trying to take Monte Cassino in WW II—not allowing the Italian monastery to be bombed—until too many men had died. He wasn't going to let the same thing happen here. Freeman looked around the graceful and ancient rooms in the Hall of Supreme Harmony. "Radio!"

Two men held up their hands.

"Over here, son," Freeman said to one. "Now this is what I want you to encode." Next he looked at his grid map of Beijing and gave the operator the coordinates.

Her vision blurring again from the mountain sickness, the .45 trembling in her hand, Julia had nevertheless made the figure out to be that of the old man. He had brought her scoops of hail and snow in a salt bag and made rubbing motions across her forehead. "Headache," he said, gave her another salt bag of ice, and left.

When he returned to where the two yaks were tethered he sniffed at the hailstorm and looked down at the earlier footprints back further in the sea of snow that surrounded the ridge. There had been enough snow and hail by now to obliterate the latest tracks. He walked the two yaks for two hundred yards or so, crossing the wind-blasted summit, and then started down with the two animals, making fresh prints away from the ridge.

In the Bo Hai Gulf the Sea Wolf II–class USS *Reagan*, though submerged two hundred miles off the China coast, was trailing her long VLF—very low frequency—aerial and was receiving Freeman's message via the Khabarovsk relay.

Within seconds of the decode, Robert Brentwood, from

the raised podium of the control room's attack center, ordered, "Man battle stations missile!" and the alarm sounded, water immediately shut off from all showers so that men in them could hear the call. The sudden absence of water meant that at least one man—a steward—had to quickly vacate the shower, his head and shoulders covered in sticky shampoo.

Robert Brentwood's hands gripped the brass railing that girded the bigger search and smaller attack periscope housings. "Set condition one SQ."

This was the highest alert.

"Set condition one SQ," confirmed Rolston, the officer of the deck. No sooner had the OOD said it than the various departments throughout the sub were punching in "ready" status.

"Condition one SQ all set," Rolston confirmed.

"Very well," Brentwood answered. "Mutual trim."

"Mutual trim now, sir."

"Very well. Prepare to spin. Stand by to flood forward tubes one and two, aft tubes five and six." There was a faint sound of rushing water as the tubes were flooded. Tubes one and two forward and five and six aft were already housing 3,500-pound, 28-mile-range Mark 48 torpedoes with contact fuses.

It was a precautionary measure should the sound of the USS *Reagan* firing off Tomahawk cruise missiles be picked up by an enemy Hunter-Killer who might in turn launch an immediate attack against the *Reagan*.

"Missile status report?" Brentwood asked.

"Spin-up complete, sir."

"Very well. Prepare for ripple fire."

"Yes, sir. Prepare for ripple fire."

Throughout the *Reagan* crewmen moved quickly but without panic to their firing positions. The ripple or staggered firing sequence meant that as one cruise missile was being fired on the starboard side, the water rushing into its silo would be balanced by the water pouring into the next silo of the next missile fired, which would be on the port side, thus minimizing the yaw created by the inrush of water on the starboard side and vice versa.

The weapons officer waited. His assistant, with wire trailing from headphones, moved, head bent in priestly concentration, up and down "Blood Alley," the rigged-for-red corridor made up of banks of computers, as he constantly monitored the missiles', in this case the cruise missiles', status.

"Missiles ready," the weapons officer reported after having checked each one's housing to make sure it was ready to pass through its prelaunch modes.

"Flood Tomahawk tubes."

"Flood Tomahawk tubes."

"Tubes flooding, sir." There was a few seconds' delay as the water poured into the vertical housing, filling the space between the elastomeric shock-absorber liners and the Tomahawk missiles themselves. Brentwood inserted his key to complete the firing circuitry, giving his independent authority to launch.

"Stand by for ripple fire," Brentwood said.

"Stand by for ripple fire," the weapons officer repeated.

"Fire one," Brentwood ordered.

"Fire one."

"Fire two."

"Fire two."

"Fire three."

"Fire three."

"Fire four."

"Fire four. All fired."

The Tomahawks rose from their housings, breaking the

water-missile interface protective membrane, and within seconds were through the water into the air, their fiery tails first giving off smoke and looking as if they were skidding sideways for a time, then rising higher and higher before leveling out and going into their TERCOM—terrain contouring mode—in which each missile would sweep in over the Chinese coast, its television eye recording the topography, matching it with that of the target fed into the computer before launch. The missile would not come down until the exact configuration seen by its TV eye matched the preprogrammed picture of the target—like a hand moving toward its mirror image. Having made the matchup it would "down turn" to complete its homing lock-on.

"Where the hell they going?" an electrician's mate, Holmes, asked.

"China, man."

"Yeah but whereabouts?"

"Dunno, man. Skipper got the orders to press the button. He pressed it. Wherever they're gonna land it's *hasta la vista*, baby."

"And now," Holmes said, "every mother within a hundred miles of us knows where we are."

"Hey, man, that's why we're half missile launcher and half HUK." He meant Hunter-Killer. "They want to come for us we can play. Why you think the old man loaded those four Mark 48s in the tubes? He's ready."

"Hope so," Holmes said.

"Know so," the mate said.

The Chinese sub *Perch* heard the launch on its passive sonar but could not fix range unless it used its active sonar, and to use that would be to let the Americans know precisely where *it* was. It preferred to risk surfacing for a quick high-burst radio message to the naval base at

Qingdao, which in turn alerted its flotillas of fast, standard, and hydrofoil gunboats, most particularly the Soviet-built Osa I guided-missiles boats with a speed of thirty-six knots, a range of five hundred nautical miles, and armed with four surface-to-surface Styx missiles and one surface-to-air N-5 launcher.

But the gunboat flotilla wasn't at all interested. It had already been dispersed up and down the coast, concentrating particularly along the 120-mile strip between Xiamen and Putan opposite Taiwan, from where Admiral Kuang's invasion had established a beachhead near Xiamen.

With no interest shown by the Brown Wave Navy, the Chinese sub skipper decided to resume his patrol in the direction of the American Sea Wolf alone. If it missed the Sea Wolf and could no longer hear its water pump, then there was still a chance to take a bite out of the big U.S. carrier group itself. The *Perch* could go to the bottom, cut its engines, and wait, silent, ready to attack on battery power alone.

At Honggor, things were falling apart. The Americans were not overwhelmed by the far more numerous Chinese but were caught in a draw, and a draw wasn't good enough, for ultimately the Chinese sea of armor and the troop and matériel reinforcements being rushed by rail from Shenyang's northern armies in Manchuria must turn the tide against the U.S. forces.

This day the second in command to Freeman, General Leigh, commander to the Orgon Tal–Honggor front, decided that the only thing to do, especially given the snags that Freeman's SAS/D troop were running up against, was to call in the Marine Expeditionary Force. It was time to turn the feint into a reality at Beidaihe's Middle Beach. He was on the radio asking Freeman for permission to call in the marines. "Request Golf Force."

"Permission granted," Freeman said. "Disembarkation at fourteen hundred hours. Repeat, fourteen hundred hours." At the time, no one thought to question why Freeman was so emphatic about 1400 hours. In any case, on hearing "permission granted," the 48,000-strong Marine Expeditionary Force was instructed to execute "Golf Force," to hit the Chinese east flank at Beidaihe. And Robert Brentwood knew he would have to blow the hidden beach obstacles.

As the USS *Reagan* detached itself from the main force and raced ahead at forty knots submerged, the ChiCom sub *Perch* remained on silent station. It came to periscope depth and glimpsed one of the DDG-51-class Flight III guided-missile destroyers only five miles away. The control room was charged with excitement as the *Perch*'s captain, known to his crew as Xingyuner—Lucky—decided to wait no longer for the appearance of an American sub. On the basis of one in the hand being better than two in the bush, he aligned his tubes, running silent on battery power alone, in the direction of the coming destroyer. As he snappily took the bearing, a Sea King helo from the American state-of-the-art destroyer rose from the ship's after deck and began a routine ASW search over a predetermined grid pattern by hovering in the middle of each grid, letting down its dipping sonar, which, sending out an active pulse, could wait to see if there was any sound. It received an echo in 1.2 seconds and, allowing for the local salinity, told the two pilots and two sonar operators aboard the Sea King that there was a sub in the immediate area.

The captain of the helo already had a computer list spewing out, telling him the type and location of all Allied subs and surface vessels in the area. The only one in general proximity was the USS *Reagan*, and it was on a heading thirty-one miles away and only five miles from the China coast. The Sea King notified its destroyer that it was attacking, and dropped a 9.5-foot-by-12.75-inch 805-pound Mark 50 ASW torpedo. When it hit the water it went into active acoustic homing mode, streaking toward the *Perch* at 42.7 knots.

Aboard the *Perch* they heard it coming, and the captain ordered hard to starboard, battle speed. As soon as it turned, the Sea King had its bearing via the dipping sonar mike and dropped the second Mark 50. The first torpedo missed but exploded near the sub; the second's hundred-pound warhead hit the Chinese sub midships but did not explode. Assorted debris popped up from the site of the first explosion, followed by a large bleed of oil.

The USS *Reagan* heard the explosion but kept on toward Beidaihe.

"May just be a fake," the pilot of the Sea King reported. "The oil and debris." But the fleet had no time or torpedoes to waste, for it was critical that the Marine Expeditionary Force make an on-time coordinated attack, and so the Sea King returned to scouting ahead for the frigate, the encounter with the sub logged as a possible sinking of a Chinese diesel sub.

In the Hall of Supreme Harmony there was a bloody and air-shattering firefight between David Brentwood's troop of twenty-seven men, all that remained out of the original forty—and six of the twenty-seven were wounded—and elements of Special Security Unit 8431, who, now that the Americans had been boxed in in the hall, were letting rip from the top of the Gate of Supreme Harmony two hundred yards away with AK-7.62mm and light type 81-1T-74 7.62mm machine guns, their drum magazines interchangeable.

Atop the Meridian Gate two SS Unit 8431 riflemen, armed with 7.62 semiautomatic sniping rifles with four-power telescopic sights, zeroed in on the Hall of Supreme Harmony. They had killed four SAS/D men before Aussie yelled amid the din and smell of cordite for the Haskins. The soldier who had been issued—or "married to," in the SAS troop's lexicon—the twenty-three-pound Haskins M500 came over to Aussie's side. At relatively close ranges, even in the 250 acres of the Forbidden City, the ten-power magnification of the Haskins M500 telescopic sight meant that anything that moved completely filled the cross hairs. With this weapon eight Chinese members of Special Unit 8431 were "lifted"—blasted away—from the wall of the Meridian Gate, two falling headfirst over the balustrade to the cobblestone expanse below, their blood pooling near the five marble bridges and trickling down into the Golden River.

The armored thrust pivoting south of Orgon Tal was doing much better than those about Honggor to the east. While no gain was easy, Cheng's troops contesting every meter, those elements of Freeman's ground force heading for the wall at Badaling—forty-two miles northwest of Beijing—and Juyong Pass six miles further south found the going not as tough. Some would ascribe it to the monsoon being more powerful at Honggor, but the mud and wet sand that had to be negotiated were about the same either end of the trace. All other things being equal it was a mystery— the kind of mystery military analysts are well acquainted with but not at ease with, for it does not lend itself to the cold logic of logistics but belongs more to the spirit, a matter that cannot be easily defined or boxed neatly in DoD compartments.

Some argued it was explicable when one paid close attention to the disposition of forces—in this case, those pivoting about Orgon Tal had been longer under Freeman's command and had been taught that whatever else happens on the battlefield you must keep moving. But those troops at Honggor also knew Freeman's adage, and yet the advance had gone not nearly so well, and not only amid the infantry but amid the armored thrust. At Orgon Tal, Norton was closer to the answer than anyone when he pointed to the long distances the M1s had to be driven east to Honggor before going into action. It was one of the best-kept secrets in the American Armored Corps that the driver's seat, built in the reclining position or what some called the TVRM—TV recliner mode—was simply so comfortable that often drivers dozed off at the wheel.

Whatever the reason for Honggor's poor showing insofar as they were holding positions and not advancing like those from Orgon Tal, the commander of the whole trace was anxious for the marine corps's attack on Cheng's right flank.

"Ready to detonate SEAL packs," Robert Brentwood ordered.

"Ready to detonate SEAL packs. Aye."

"Detonate SEAL packs."

"Detonate SEAL packs. SEAL packs detonated."

"Very well. Sonar—active sweep one eight zero."

"Active sonar sweep one eight zero degrees," the confirmation came.

One minute later sonar reported, "Three obstacles above required CV depth." This meant that for the CVs—surface vessels of the Marine Expeditionary Force—three "China gates" remained intact, but three obstacles was a number that Brentwood knew the marine major general in charge of the MEF could live with. Landing craft carrying the 48,000 marines ashore would simply have to go about the unseen obstacles, the latter's positions indicated by fluorescent red marker buoys being readied for eject from the USS *Reagan*.

Meanwhile the four sleek, eighteen-foot-long Tomahawk cruise missiles went in over the China coast at six hundred miles an hour with a strong tail wind, hugging the beach at an altitude of twenty feet, then beginning their contoured flights over the higher ground, each only thirty seconds behind the next, each missile's terrain contour matching computer, computer-radar-altimeter and inertial-guidance-system steering every second, going around hills rather than over them on their three-hundred-mile, half-hour journey to Beijing. As they passed by coastal defenses some triple A came their way, but they were flying so low that in most cases the triple A gun barrels couldn't be sufficiently depressed to get their fire anywhere near them, and those AA guns that were depressed often as not hit the land forms around which the missiles were turning, causing civilian casualties.

Below the Tomahawks that were speeding at ten miles per minute, the missiles were seen by workers in the rice paddies and seemed to be going as fast as the big passenger jets of China Air. Immediately Shenyang fighters were dispatched, but if the peasants in the patchwork fields saw the Tomahawks easily in the trail of the monsoon, the fighters couldn't. The fighters' radar couldn't help them, for all they were getting back from trying to pick up the missiles, which were rarely more than fifty feet above ground, was ground clutter, one pilot glimpsing them for a moment over the eastern suburbs of Beijing.

The person who got the best view was the French reporter from *La Monde* who, in his Beijing Hotel room, was sipping a Scotch and ice and in utter astonishment saw four missiles flash past his window, the first one making a sharp right off Changan Avenue, the Avenue of Eternal Peace, and slamming into its target, the Gate of Heavenly Peace—the Tiananmen Gate. More tremors were felt as moments later this was followed by the second one exploding in the Meridian Gate by the bow-shaped Golden River and the last two, in what was a stroke of targeting selection genius by Freeman, slamming into the Hall of Preserving Harmony, thus taking out all the SS unit's snipers and others immediately to his front and rear.

In seconds the situation had changed dramatically, and without further ado Freeman called out, "Masks!" and ordered the firing of CS canisters toward the building of the Nine Dragon Screen in order to flush out the State Council believed to be hiding there.

Within seconds the Hall of Supreme Harmony emptied of SAS/D commandos, who made the fast run to the Nine Dragon Screen. Overhead there was the whir of rotors and the constant chattering of machine-gun fire as Russian-made Chinese Hind A choppers mixed it with the Comanches. Not one Comanche was downed out of forty, and the Chinese lost eight Hinds. One of the Comanches coming in on Freeman's frequency reported what looked like a line of officials with a couple of PLA officers among them running from the building designated FC15, the Hall of Manifest Harmony, to FC12, the Gate of Divine Military Genius.

In the few moments of the Tomahawk cruise missile attacks, Freeman saw that now was his chance to take the offensive, which he did by being the first of the SAS/D troopers to fire his CS gas canister toward the Dragon Screen as he made his dash to the Hall of Preserving Harmony, a step closer but still some way from the Gate of Divine Military Genius, the last building on the northern side, from which the members of unit 8431 were pouring deadly fire at students fleeing in the huge parking area below between upturned and burning buses that were being bumped and smashed aside by a T-69 and other tanks arriving from the Orgon Tal–Honggor front.

They could afford to, for the battle of the Orgon Tal–Honggor front had taken a turn for the worse. In short, a disaster had taken place on the American left, or eastern, flank around Honggor.

Here the PLA had successfully constructed a formidable defense of tank traps and tunnels that both halted and confounded the American echelons. The tank traps were crude and effective large pits whose sheer walls prevented any escape by the tank once it had tumbled through the camouflage of soil- and bush-dotted netting. The M1's coaxial machine gun was immediately rendered useless, leaving the .50 caliber atop the tank's cupola but with the "up" angle so acute that the tank commander had to keep down in the cupola in order to fire, and he could not see all about him at the same time.

The result was that ChiComs about the rim of the trap could shoot down at will—which they did, in addition to dropping deadly Molotov cocktails, obliging the cupola's machine gunner to withdraw and the cupola's hatch to be closed, sealing the American's fate. The tunnels there were of the kind Second Army had encountered earlier in the war when Freeman's armored column and his FAVs—fast attack vehicles—had stormed the ChiCom artillery wall at Orgon Tal, but now there was, however, the added danger of the tank traps that would accommodate a FAV, or "dune buggy" as they were often called, as easily as any tank. The crews of the American FAVs had more mobility in that they could be out of their seat belts and firing M-16s and the .50 front-mounted machine gun at any angle. Still, a stick grenade or two tossed down into the trap put an end to that, and in all, over three hundred FAV drivers, machine gunners, and TOW antitank missile operators were killed in that battle alone.

Still it was Freeman's armor that took the worst beating, with seventy-eight M1s and crews lost. The tunnels dug at night during the cease-fire were in fact in front of the tank traps so that the ChiComs could wait until the U.S. infantry, which had been following behind the protective shield of tanks, passed over them. At this point, Cheng's troops would emerge from *behind* the Americans in ambuscades of withering fire.

The result of this penetration behind the moving American line was that Honggor, which was to be the pivot about which the Orgon Tal–Honggor line would sweep, was a shambles of burned-out tanks, dead tank crews, and, most demoralizing of all, on the point of collapse with the subsequent withdrawal of the American front.

No retreat is pretty to watch, but even among the veterans of Freeman's army, men who'd been trapped on the Never-Skovorodino road and who had been with him in Korea, broke and ran to save themselves. There were not many at first, but the pace of a rout is determined by those who are first to bolt, and their speed was such that it terrified reinforcements, some of whom were yet to be blooded and so had been put on a second line of defense. And in the rout they were met by a fusillade of shots fired by the ChiComs' tunnel battalions. In just over two hours 194 Americans were killed and more than three hundred wounded.

At least Harvey Simmet had been right in his prediction of the monsoon, and the wind from the east was strong so that Freeman and his SAS/D troops, by firing their canisters at the northeastern corner of the Forbidden City, saw the

CS gas sweep across the northern sector of the compound like smoke.

Here Cheng's budget constraints, which did not allow for updating to state-of-the-art protective gear, caused his men to be more on the defensive as their masks were of the old American pre-Iraqi style and were neither plentiful in the PLA nor used enough to offer the Chinese any real protection.

Freeman's personal weapon for the attack was his Winchester 1200 shotgun, his ammunition cartridges of twenty fléchettes packed in each of the cartridges, each dart effective up to a thousand yards and best used in open areas such as those between the Forbidden City's buildings. For closer in work, there were cartridges made of a hardened lead slug in a polyethylene sabot or sleeve, the slug so powerful it was used to take out anything substantial up to 450 yards away. One such slug slammed into the door of the Hall of Preserving Harmony, and the door gave way. The last cartridge was followed by CS gas bomblets bursting, the liquid becoming an aerosol on impact and making the large room uninhabitable in seconds without a mask. Now they could hear shouting in the near distance, and though it was difficult to tell exactly where it was originating from, it seemed at times to come in waves from beyond the Forbidden City, possibly behind them from the vastness of Tiananmen Square.

What was happening was that while some of the armies were racing back from Shenyang to Beijing to help what they believed was a general attack on the city, some of their commanders couldn't have cared less whether they arrived later than sooner.

In short, let the Americans finish off the State Council, then take the Americans, and whoever was left standing at the end of the day would win China.

The widespread myth of cohesiveness between the military command was shown to be just that—a myth—as armored columns reached the city's outskirts. Cheng's rivals in the Eleventh, Twenty-fourth, and Twenty-eighth armies were taking their time. Others, however, *were* racing, namely the Shenyang Thirty-ninth, Fortieth, and Sixty-fourth armies, who were keen to get into the fight first, for not only were their commanding officers all related, but the ones who won the day would have the first claim to the booty after the Americans were defeated, and Cheng would be indebted to them for their intervention whether he liked it or not.

Each LCU—landing craft unit—coxswain and his three-man crew of bowman, stern-sheets man, and stoker mechanic were working hard to keep the LCU from smashing against the side as the marines scrambled down the nets of the mother ships into the landing crafts, which, even though they were on the leeward side, were rising and dropping through six-foot swells.

Once the thirty-man complement had been loaded, the coxswain wasted no time shoving off and joining the other circling loaded LCUs so that when they made for shore they would hopefully proceed in waves, the ideal being to have all the LCUs hitting the beach simultaneously, thus giving the Chinese so many targets at once rather than allowing any one LCU to stray too far ahead where it would draw the fire of all the ChiComs dug into the beach's defensive positions.

At least half the men had been seasick, with the ships having been caught earlier by the monsoon. And many, despite all their training, were scared, the sound of the big ships' guns pounding the shoreline bunkers so loud that it seemed as if there were a continuous rolling thunder. Each coxswain had his own way of trying to calm everyone as he stood in the stern, left hand on the wheel, right hand resting on the port and starboard throttles. Members of this MEF, whether they were going to be ferried in by air-cushion vehicles, LCUs, or choppers, were all aware of Freeman's cash prize for the best joke told aboard any landing craft—only one joke per LC allowed as the official entry. Norton had once pointed out to General Freeman that there was no regulation to allow such a contest, especially not in combat. Freeman had agreed, but he said it was his money—besides which it served "one hell of a good purpose" in keeping up morale during that terrible ten-to-fifteen-minute run into the beach.

Private First Class Walton and his buddy, Hamish, were on one of the last landing crafts to go in, one of the last to enter the big circle of LCs waiting until the last LC designated for any one wave of marines had its full complement aboard and was ready to break from the circle for line-abreast attack.

Walton believed he was truly near death, his face a pasty white, his legs trembling like jelly, and the nausea reducing him to a forlorn figure who was repenting of his sins, yet believing such sickness as this couldn't be part of a benevolent god's world.

"Hang on, buddy," Hamish encouraged him. "We're almost there!"

"Where?"

"Freakin' beach, man. Where else?"

"I don't care."

"All right, you guys," the bosun bawled. "Settle down and Harry Lynch—that's me, Coxs'n El Supremo—will get you in. Shit, I'll be surprised if you get the feet wet." Walton wasn't the only one who was sick, and from the coxs'n's platform it looked as if everyone was at prayer.

"Right!" the coxs'n called. "Let's hear a joke."

There was only a groan from the bellies of the beasts—one man throwing up, another trying to get away from the stench. "You dirty bastard!"

"C'mon," joined in the lieutenant of the platoon that the coxswain was ferrying to shore. "Joke!" Suddenly there was a scream just above them. The Chinese HE was a "long" shot, causing nothing more than a high column of seawater to erupt ahead of them, some of the water sweeping over the men. The Chinese had found the range, and from his semaphore leader the coxswain, Lynch, was being told, as were all the boats in his line, to slow down, anticipating the next salvo would be "shorts."

"Jesus Christ!" Hamish said. "That was close."

"C'mon," Lynch bullied. "I want to hear a fucking joke, right, Lieutenant? I'm not goin' back to the big boat without an entry from—" He waited.

"Third platoon, 'Charlie' company," the lieutenant answered.

"All right then," Lynch boomed through his bullhorn. "Let's hear a fucking *joke*!"

A hand came up from the middle of the platoon.

"Go!" Lynch yelled.

"Woman has an orgasm every time she sneezes. Goes to the doc and tells him. He says, 'Well, what are you taking for it?'

" 'Pepper,' she says."

There was a collective grunt.

"I like it," the coxswain bellowed. "Any more?"

"What's the difference—" Another LCU took a direct hit and Third platoon Charlie company could hear a man's scream.

"Go on," Lynch said. Intruders were swooping over low,

bombing the Chinese emplacements. The LCU would be there in about seven minutes. "Go on!"

"What's the difference between—" No one could hear it, the noise deafening.

"Get ready, boys. Ramp goes down in four minutes."

"Remember," the lieutenant yelled, "weapons high and each man give your two mortar rounds to the mortar team—carefully. Just don't plunk 'em down."

"Yeah, yeah," Hamish said. "The boys know that. Right, Walton?"

"Christ," said Walton, "I don't think I can stand. My fuckin' legs—"

"Ramp down—ready!"

There was the run of chains, the splash, and the first men out—up to their waist, the zinging and pinging of bullets and the inefficient but loud slaps of expended rounds. The whole grayness of the world seemed to crowd in with a depressing enormity upon the crescent of Middle Beach, and from the ruins of the broadcasting house on Middle Beach to its hotel, the Zhonghaitau, came the heaviest concentration of automatic fire that Sergeant Hamish or Walton had ever seen. "Mortar bombs!" the lieutenant shouted. "Mortar bombs! C'mon, get movin'! Get those fuckin' bombs over here—here, Ashe—good man, Ashe. Walton, you too."

As the lieutenant hurried to get the mortar bomb pile set up, the mortar crew already had bipod, base plate, and thirty-five-pound barrel set, one man bent over, aligning the site, and within three minutes HE rounds were whistling up and over with a sustained rate of fourteen rounds a minute.

The heavy guns of the fleet kept crashing in, and without them the thousands of ChiCom infantry crowding on and around the much larger East Beach just to the north would have swept down in a green khaki tide. The pocket the marines had secured on Middle Beach was just that, a semicir-

cle three hundred yards in diameter, but each minute the
superiority of American logistics became painfully apparent
to Cheng's warlords, for the American organization was
such that the sheer weight, the density of men and matériel,
kept pushing out the pocket as if it were some awful inev-
itability, a giant amoeba spreading over the beach where
once cadres basked in the sun.

Cheng, who had taken personal command of the reinforcements rushed in by train from Shenyang, could see
only one way out, and when the bugles sounded, the ghosts
of the Korean War rose up in Cheng's troops. And under
the phalanx of red flags and a terrible din they charged en
masse, and it was decidedly not true, as the La Roche tabloids reported, that only half of them were armed so that all
would charge and if one man fell another would quickly
snatch up the downed man's weapon. The fact was, every
ChiCom soldier was well armed with either AK-74s or 47s,
and there seemed to be no shortage of stick grenades.

But against the bravery of the Chinese and their weapons
was pitted the bravery and equally strong discipline of the
American marines in their thirteen-man rifle squad configuration with a squad leader, like Sergeant Hamish, and
three four-man fire teams equipped with the best weapons
in the world. The marines stood firm, unfazed by the mass
attack and helped by the timely arrival of a flame-throwing
tank whose two-hundred-foot-long tongue was, in Freeman's words, the "biggest goddamn dragon those jokers
had ever seen. Hell, barbecued three platoons 'fore Cheng
knew what had hit him."

In the same way it was rumored that the Chinese didn't
like fighting in the rain, the Chinese believed that the
Americans, so enamored, as Chairman Nie put it, with their
high-tech toys, had no stomach for hand-to-hand combat.
Trouble for Nie was that the high-tech "toys" killed faster

and more accurately than those of the Chinese, and that someone had forgotten to tell him about Fort Lejeune, and when cold steel met cold steel on Middle Beach, the Chinese did a bit better because of their light packs, compared to the much more heavily weighted marines, but no discernible dent was made in the MEF's pocket.

PFC Walton was so exhilarated being on land again he knew no one was going to push *him* back into the sea. On one level, like so many, he was drained of energy from the seasickness, but once ashore, the adrenaline of escape and a quickly consumed Baby Ruth bar were more than enough to carry him.

By now the massed landings of the LC craft were supplemented by over a hundred Sea Stallion helos ferrying commando units *behind* the Chinese, the ChiCom troops so tightly packed on and around the rear approaches to Middle Beach that the commandos were using one-shot disposable antitank LAW rocket launchers against congested areas of infantry with devastating results. Twelve helos were lost on such operations, but the success of their behind-the-lines forays was undeniable and sowed more confusion and knocked out almost as many bugles as anything else.

And it was only Cheng—certainly none of Freeman's commanders—who divined the time of attack, 1400 hours, as most propitious for the Americans. Freeman, Cheng realized, had chosen 1400 hours for the beginning of the attack because he knew one thing the Chinese Army was fervent about was *xiuxi*, the two-hour spell-off period between 1:00 and 3:00 guaranteed them by Article Forty-nine of the Constitution. Two P.M. was halfway through the siesta, where most units' efficiency was at its lowest. Pulling them out of it was like pulling a westerner out of his jet lag and telling him to fight.

The battle to breach the Great Wall at Badaling was not

difficult with helo-ferried troops taken over to the southern side of the wall and getting the ChiCom defenders in a deadly cross fire. The Great Wall, as Freeman had predicted, was a great folly in modern warfare, another example of what Patton had once said—namely that "fixed fortifications are monuments to the stupidity of man," that "anything man can build he can just as easily tear down."

The Chinese didn't believe in the wall any more than Freeman. Cheng hoped instead that the American graveyard would be Juyong Pass, six miles to the southeast, where there were particularly steep walled gorges that must be passed through—an ideal trap for armor. But it was there in the narrow confines of the pass, when friend and foe were clearly visible as the monsoon's rain abated, that the A-10 Thunderbolts, or Warthogs, as they were affectionately known by those who flew and serviced them, attacked the ChiComs' T-62s that Cheng, in his first real blunder—or so it appeared—had ordered in to spearhead the Chinese counterattack. The American pilots were left shaking their heads as they took down the planes and punctured tank after tank with the enormous A-10 Thunderbolts' rotary-barreled GAU-8 Avengers, firing their 30mm depleted uranium-tipped bullets. Hadn't the Chinese seen what the Warthogs had done in Iraq—on the road to Basra? As it turned out, Cheng had ordered all armored personnel, including maintenance crews, as part of their training, to go see the CNN footage, which the PLA had copied.

After what could only be described as a slaughter of Chinese armor in Juyong Pass, the Warthogs returned to base, some with photo recon aboard, and declared the winding Chinese column of sixty T-62s dead. The first one to notice something odd about the carnage was Corporal Glenda Lipcott of the photo recon intelligence unit. She reported to her commanding officer that there was something funny about the corpses.

"Oh—what?"

"Well, sir, I don't mean there's anything unusual with the corpses themselves, but I can't find more than one corpse per tank."

"What do you mean? You can't see inside the tanks with photo recon."

"After they're attacked by the Warthogs you can, sir. Opens them up like a tin can—spare rounds inside the tank blow up."

"I know that," the colonel said liverishly, "but what I'm saying is that it looks like a butcher shop inside. So how can you tell?"

"DPBs, sir." She meant distinct body parts—heads mainly, limbs, etc.

"All right," the colonel said, "let's say you're correct. No tank has more than one corpse."

"Ah, all except the first one," Lipcott corrected herself.

"So?" the colonel pressed. Smart women irritated him.

"Well, sir, it looks as if the only crewman aboard each tank was the driver. First one probably had a commander in the turret to direct the driver to the exact spot Cheng wanted them stopped."

"Stopped—what in hell for?"

"Well, sir—" The colonel glowered at her. If she said "Well, sir," one more time—

"Sir, I think the Chinese wanted to be held up in Juyong Pass. It has narrow defiles, and if you jam one road section, particularly if you select one that's not straight but winding, then you have to remove all those wrecks. One by one, cranes'll have to lift . . ."

"Yes, of course you're right. Give me some of those photos will you?" She passed him a folder with ten 10-by-14-inch shots.

When Orgon Tal's HQ—moved sixty miles southeast around Ondor-Sum—received the information they were initially angered by what the A-10s had achieved until they saw how it had been a no-win situation: whether the tanks had been stopped by the U.S. aircraft or had been sabotaged by their own troops they had effectively closed down the road and stopped the drive to Beijing, only nineteen miles to the southeast past the Ming Tombs and the capital's fragrant Western Hills. Norton, chief aide at the Ondor-Sum HQ, enquired as to how the information of one Chinese corpse per tank had been deduced. The colonel, in a self-deprecating manner, confessed that it was the photos that first gave him the idea. Norton made a note of it. It was the kind of thing Freeman would like to hear about those serving him in Second Army. It was quite brilliant of Cheng. At the most he'd sacrificed sixty-one men to hold up the entire Orgon Tal–Ondor-Sum push at Juyong Pass.

CHAPTER THIRTY-ONE

THERE WAS MUCH more firing now from outside the northern moat of the Forbidden City, where students were massing in the thousands while other students and workers massed at the southern end on Changan and the other avenues. It brought traffic to a standstill, and now there was a sea of people in which it was clear that the people did *not* love the PLA and the PLA did *not* love the people. It was a slaughter, hundreds of students either run over by the tanks or flailed by the army's machine guns. But then the Molotov cocktails had appeared, and four T-69s were burning, their crews either shot or battered to death as they tried to escape from the hatches.

At the northern end of the Forbidden City, a crossing leading over the moat had long been blocked by the students, and now, with more buses and tanks, it became even more congested with the arrival of thousands of students around the Dasanyuan Restaurant and Jingshan Park, many of them armed with AK-47s and large improvised Molotov slingshots that kept harrowing the tank line with small-arms fire and a steady rain of the gasoline bombs.

Warthogs appeared overhead, despite the smoke and the bad weather that was following the monsoon, but the crowds had become so enormous all round the Forbidden City, spilling out on Tiananmen Square, that the A-10s couldn't fire at the tanks because of the certainty that if they did the tanks exploding would kill more students than PLA. But then students, seeing the A-10 Thunderbolts diving then having to pull away, thwarted in their attack, began screaming at everyone to get away from the moat in front of which the Chinese tanks were parked.

At first a margin of fifty yards separated the tanks from the still-firing students, some of the tanks belching smoke, having used their cannon to shoot point-blank into the students. Given the margin of fifty yards or so, the few A-10s managed to sweep down and, as if in some fantastic dance macabre, five tanks seemed to be soaking up the golden rain that the A-10s poured down. Suddenly the tanks exploded in a spectacular scene that made the CNN cameraman atop the Statue of Heroes of the Revolution momentarily ecstatic. But the Chinese tank commander was no fool, and within a few minutes he had ordered the remaining tanks to advance more quickly in line into the receding crowd, for in killing the crowd lay his protection.

The tens of thousands of students, many workers joining them, surged from the northern end of the Forbidden City southward to Changan Avenue and Tiananmen Square, some of the thousands already in the square escaping a similar tank charge by retreating behind Mao's mausoleum at the southern end of the square, around Beijing's Kentucky Fried Chicken outlet—two-piece dinner with fries and hot Mao bun, three yuan.

The surveillance cameras on the posts along Changan were smashed in the event that the Americans didn't win and the Public Security Bureau used the videotape to round up suspects as they had done after the massacre of June 4, 1989, when for a time the students, thinking they had won, had heard Beethoven's "Ode to Joy" booming through the loudspeakers in the square.

By now Freeman's remaining radio operator—one dead, one wounded fatally, the SAS/D team down to seventy men—received a transmit that about the same number of civilians and two PLA officers had been seen reentering FC7, the Hall of Preserving Harmony.

"Bastards have doubled back on us!" Aussie said. To ask how was pointless, as despite the neat, methodically laid out plan of the Forbidden City, its myriad hallways and secret doors were in fact a labyrinth.

Turning back, the SAS/D contingent led by Freeman, Aussie, Williams, and Salvini first had to retake FC7, the Hall of Preserving Harmony, and it was here that unit 8431 had collected its strength. Then Brentwood and Salvini, Salvini bleeding from a flesh wound in his upper left arm, saw what looked like a thousand mushrooms coming down over Tiananmen and the Forbidden City. ChiCom paratroopers on a short, five-hundred-foot drop. In Tiananmen it was no trouble. The students swarmed back, placing the paratroopers between themselves and the advancing line of tanks that were moving southward away from the moat on the southern end of the Forbidden City. If many students died, there would be no doubt that most of the paratroopers would also perish, precisely the fate that the paratroopers coming down *in* the Forbidden City planned for the Americans.

On what was now the Juyong Pass–Honggor front, Freeman's strategy was approaching the top of the curve. It was true that the power of the Soviet-made T-72s that Cheng had used around Honggor under a Colonel Soong were a serious threat to the Abrams M1A1. For a start the Soviet-made gun was bigger, 125mm versus the American 120. It was a smooth bore weapon and could fire a forty-six-pound APFSDS—armor-piercing fin-stabilized discarding-sabot round—at eighteen hundred meters per second as opposed to the M1A1 Abrams's 1650 meters per second.

The driver in Colonel Soong's lead tank had switched over to the gyro drive of his TPD-K1 sight. Three minutes later he uncaged the gyro, the red light coming on followed by the green light that told him he could begin traversing. Next the laser range-finder was activated, and he slewed the turret as Colonel Soong, in the same tank but in his independent cupola, was able to traverse. Soong saw the first M1A1 crossing the line and got ready to fire. However, even though the T-72 has an automatic loader and all one has to do is select the type of round from one of the twenty-two ammunition cassettes, the automatic breech must be opened by hand for the first round.

It was only a second lost, but by then the M1A1 had fired, and its laser-locked APDS wouldn't be denied as it hit Soong's tanks just as the Chinese APDS left the T-72. The T-72's shot, however, was not as accurate, for there was no crosswind error corrective in the tank's fire control, and given the other vicissitudes of barrel droop and the peculiarities of each tank versus any other tank even of the same make, the shot missed the Americans. In short, given equal fitness and determination on the part of each tank crew, American and Chinese, it was American technology, which, for example, quickly corrected for windage, that won the day.

But beyond the tank battle that ebbed and flowed at first because of the four-to-one Chinese advantage and their proximity to the crowds limiting what the A-10 Thunderbolts could do, it was the Bradley armed vehicle that sealed the Chinese fate. At twenty-two-and-a-half tons, its speed sixty-six kilometers per hour, with a 25mm gun and TOW antitank missiles and carrying seven men, the Bradley was simply the best armored personnel carrier in the field. But this wasn't because of a lack of enemy APCs that could keep up with it. The British-Chinese coproduced NVH1 also had a speed of over sixty kilometers per hour and weighed four and a half tons less than the Bradley. It too had a 25mm automatic cannon with electrical 360-degree traverse and a secondary coaxial 7.62mm chain gun, and it carried six men in addition to the crew of three.

And there was the type YW309 infantry combat vehicle, which had a crew of three plus eight Chinese infantry and which, while not as fast on land at fifty kilometers per hour, did have a speed in water of six kilometers per hour, its main armament, a 73mm smooth bore, much more powerful than the Bradley.

But it was the Bradley's suspension, with its quarter-inch

hard steel sides and 30mm of appliqué armor on the front as well, that still held the day. The suspension, like that of the M1A1, had to be seen to be believed. While going up and down over the sandy wastes south of Honggor, the Bradley's 25mm seemed to be sitting still while the underchassis did everything but flip.

The Chinese, as usual, were indisputably brave and on more than one occasion simply rammed their vehicle into an American as the only way of stopping it. But once the worst of the monsoon had passed, the Comanches came down and, hovering where the A-10 could not, became the scourge of the battlefield, their retractable claws carrying eight Hellfire antitank missiles and two Stingers, and their cannon having five hundred rounds of 20mm ammunition, the helos having a fuel capacity of nearly two hours on or about the target.

Standing off, guided by their digital map display and high-speed fiberoptic data and sensor-distribution systems, Vulcan II 20mm Gatling guns in their chin mountings, the Comanches killed as many Chinese tanks as did the American M1A1s, the latter being inhibited in areas where mines had been laid, mines that were triggered to be set off by the weight of main battle tanks but not lighter vehicles so that the Chinese might use their armored personnel carriers. It was a fatal mistake on the part of the Chinese, given the ability of the Bradley. And so it was no one weapon system that could take credit for the Americans simply overpowering the Chinese south of Honggor, but rather a concert of high-tech weapons, many already battle tested in Iraq, that carried the day.

When unit 8431 in the Forbidden City learned that the American tanks had reached the Juyong Pass and that the American Comanches were swarming over the Ming

Tombs area seven miles east of the pass, scattering infantry
companies left, right, and center amid the huge carved
stone animals, unit 8431 knew that they might well be protecting a doomed government, and never mind the fact that
it seemed as if the beachheads established by the American
marine force at Beidaihe and by Admiral Kuang were
growing as ton after ton of matériel and more Nationalist
Chinese and U.S. marines swept ashore. But this knowledge only hardened the unit's resolve that the Americans in
the Forbidden City at least must be wiped out to the last
man.

With helo resupply of ammunition and water, the SAS/D
troops were ready for what would clearly be a fight to the
finish inside the nine-thousand-room Forbidden City.

The old nomad was entering the camp with only one
yak. The five Chinese left there and still waiting for the patrol under Major Mah to return immediately asked him
where he had been, and had he seen either the remains of
an American fighter or its pilot? He either did not understand Chinese or refused to speak it if he did. He acted
dumb, his age in the sixties probably but looking much
older. His skin deeply creased by the elements and his im-
becile stare satisfied the Chinese that the old fool had not
seen anything, which wasn't surprising in the storm. The
Chinese huddled back into several tents, cold to the bone.

Meanwhile the patrol was having increasing difficulty
following the hoofprints of the two laden yaks, as even
their pathfinder—the man with the infrared scope—was
hard pressed to see much difference in temperature between
the fading hoofprints and the surrounding snow and hail.
By the time they reached the ridge and snow gave way to
windblown rock, the pathfinder was convinced they'd now
lost the trail, but by spreading out, he told Mah, they might

pick up the yaks' hoofprints as the animals' hooves would have shucked accumulated snow on the hard rock so that by the time the animals had crossed the rock their hooves would sink deeper in the snow. As they began to cross the rock, Mah noticed that there were several caves on the ridge, some little more than depressions and a few others that went deeper beneath rocky overhangs. Mah heard his pathfinder calling out excitedly that his prediction had been correct. He had picked up the yak's hoofprints again in the snow. Mah asked him whether this meant the yaks might have rested on the ridge before stepping off to reenter the snow.

"It's possible," the pathfinder conceded. A rest on the ridge, inside one of the caves perhaps, would certainly explain the freshness of the new hoofprints. Mah looked about at the caves. What would *he* do if he'd found the pilot and wanted to hide him? The caves. But the longer they stayed to investigate the dozen or so caves, the less likely they would be able to find the hoofprints again, as it was still snowing. Mah decided to cover both possibilities: the caves and the new hoofprints they'd found. He told the patrol to move on, following the tracks, and kept one man to stay with him to have a quick look in the caves. The two of them would then follow the tracks of the patrol after they'd finished.

As the twelve men continued following the yaks' hoofprints, unknowingly heading back to the camp, Mah, taking out his Shanghai black, a .38 revolver, pointed to one of the deeper-looking caves. "You take that one," he ordered the soldier. "I'll go over here. I'll meet you back here in five minutes. It shouldn't take us long."

The soldier, unslinging his AK-47, didn't look too happy about his assignment. He had a distinct aversion about going into dark places—and no flashlight, of course. Mah had one, but then majors in the People's Liberation Army did have a lot more than those who served under them. To hell with the major, thought the private. He'd go into the cave a few yards or so, and if he didn't see or hear anything then he'd come straight out.

Mah went into a cave whose entrance was no more than five feet wide. He heard the slow drip of melting snow, shone his flashlight inside, and looked along the beam of light before he advanced any further. The cave took several twists and turns and then ended abruptly, its walls seeping with moisture.

When he reemerged into the outside light he saw the soldier waiting. "Anything in there?" Mah asked him.

"Nothing, Comrade Major," the soldier replied. "It's hard to see without a flashlight."

Mah grunted. "Your eyes get used to it. Wait a few minutes when you enter, then go on."

"Yes, Major."

"All right, comrade, you take that one—it looks fairly shallow. I'll take the one over there. Looks deeper."

"Yes, Major."

As Aussie Lewis, David Brentwood, and thirty other SAS/D men prepared for the second and final rush on the north side of the Hall of Preserving Harmony situated atop a flight of long marble stairways, Choir Williams, Salvini, and Freeman, leading thirty-five commandos in all, ran around the front to the south side and began their attack from the marble stairs that flanked the long, stepping-stone motif of dragons among clouds. Immediately twelve members of unit 8431 opened fire, some of them taking cover behind the balustrade and long flight of steps that bracketed the carved dragons.

A ricochet hit Freeman's Kevlar vest and fell down the

marble steps like a pebble as he crouched and steadied himself and used a slugging shell in the Winchester 1200, its impact such that it blew the door to the Hall of Preserving Harmony wide open, the unhinged door flying back and knocking over a Chinese commander.

The next four cartridges Freeman fired were fléchettes, all eighty of them, and they could be heard like a hum of bees. At this short range they penetrated the steel helmets of the Chinese defenders, and Freeman could hear them screaming, a dart embedded in one man's eye. The Chinese soldiers lost all control for a moment as Aussie Lewis, Salvini, and Choir Williams came in with three-round bursts from their Heckler & Koch submachine guns. Again, as in the field, it was the combination of guts and good gunnery that won the day for Freeman's SAS/D force.

Suddenly it was over, and Freeman could see the civilians—seven, or was it eight?—CS smoke still thick in the air—staggering around, hands up, and two members of the PLA.

"Congratulations, sir!" Brentwood said.

"Yes, sir," Salvini and Choir Williams added—Aussie Lewis and four other men quickly getting the prisoners in a straight line up against the wall. They were all in tears from the CS gas, if not from the defeat, and for fresh air Aussie Lewis obligingly smashed out an ornate window dating back to the Ming dynasty.

"Jesus Christ!" It was Freeman, sounding like an enraged bull, his voice clearly heard in the Hall of Preserving Harmony above the footsteps of thousands now that the students had penetrated the Forbidden City and were gathering like a great blue-and-gray sea about the Forbidden City, around Freeman, the conqueror of Beijing.

It was confusion again, with some of Salvini's men looking around at the huge crowd forming outside, and even though they were obviously friendly, with the goddess of democracy statue carried bobbing and wobbling among them, the noise of the cheering was drowning almost anything that was said in the Hall of Preserving Harmony, so that Freeman had to thunder out his discovery.

"Where's Cheng? Nie? The State Council?"

"You mean—" Aussie began. "Bloody hell!"

"Bloody hell is right!" Freeman thundered. "The bastards were *never in* the Forbidden City. Son of a bitch—" He grabbed one of the civilians, one of the officials who had stood in for the State Council members, drew his 9mm Browning, and stuck it in the man's mouth, the man almost collapsing in fright. "Where are Cheng and Nie and all the rest?" he yelled. "Interpreter!" But there was no need for interpretation, for at least two of the eleven captured officials spoke English, and with the crowd swirling about them they didn't see why they should be the only ones to take the heat.

"General Cheng has gone," one trembling official said, "with our commanders. And Nie. All the State Council. The soldiers. On the train—the airport has been bombed and—"

"Where?" Freeman demanded, pulling back the hammer.

"Gone," the official repeated. "To—to Tanggu."

"Where the hell's that?" Salvini cut in.

Freeman reholstered his pistol, his hands now on his hips. "Son of a bitch and his guards are on the way by train to Tanggu. Closest port to here. A fast boat trip across Bo Hai Gulf to North Korea no doubt. Goddamn it!" Freeman, his head down, began pacing up and down as the smoke was clearing, and outside the crowd was growing even larger, all cheering his name. Suddenly Freeman stopped and looked at Williams, Salvini, and Aussie. "I'm getting on the radio and we're gonna stop that damn train. If it ever left Beijing. Yes, sir, we're gonna stop every goddamn train out of Beijing." He then turned to the operator, giving him the necessary orders for the A-10s and Comanches—who by now had neutralized all airports and runways in the Beijing area—to stop any train from leaving Beijing, but particularly those bound southeast of the city toward Tanggu.

"You boys," he told Salvini, Williams, Brentwood, and Aussie Lewis, "aren't finished yet. I want you to get aboard the first chopper we can get in here. Go to Tanggu and bring back Cheng and Nie. All the State Council if possible but definitely Cheng and Nie. Bring the bastards back in chains!"

It was simply impossible to get a Comanche, Huey, Chinook, Apache, or any other kind of helo to land in the Forbidden City. It was jam-packed with people. The same was true of Tiananmen Square, and the only way that Aussie, Brentwood, Williams, and Salvini could get out was to climb up a swinging rope ladder to a Huey hovering twenty feet above the roof of the Hall of Preserving Harmony, or what Aussie Lewis, after the battle, called "the Hall of Fucking Disharmony."

"Christ!" Lewis yelled over the roar of the Huey's rotors and the crowd below. "I thought we were done for the day. I'm puttin' in for overtime, mate. No bones about it."

The other three commandos—Salvini, Choir Williams, and Brentwood—were either too exhausted or deafened by the chopper and the mob scene below, growing bigger as the American tanks from the Marine Expeditionary Force entered the outskirts, to say anything. Besides, they all knew they needed whatever energy they had left for what they hoped would be the end of the war.

They had no way of knowing that within half an hour,

when the news of the Beijing collapse got through to the southern beachhead at Xiamen, the southern armies would be recalled by the generals-cum-warlords. The north-south divisions in China were probably the oldest in history, and southern Chinese blood was not about to be spilled in defense of Communist Mandarins in the north who had already fled Beijing, the same Mandarins who had declared it was all right to burn briquettes for warmth in your home if you were north of the Yangtze, but not if you were in the south.

There were no trains out of Beijing. There were no trains coming into Beijing. Everything had been stopped by the massive uprising of the underground Democracy Movement and workers pouring out into the city now that the top Communist leaders had fled. The only trains moving, in fact, were those that had left Beijing no later than an hour before, one of these having been the train to Qinhuangdao via Beidaihe.

By now the news of Beijing's collapse, confirmed by CNN, was flashed worldwide and to all parts of China, where local underground movements seized the moment against local Communist administrations. And it was at Qinhuangdao, en route to Shanhaiguan, that Alexsandra Malof's train was met by a huge crowd waving banners of revolution, her Chinese student suddenly filled with courage and confidence and a feeling of some importance that he had been chosen by fate to be escaping with Alexsandra Malof at the very moment of the Beijing clique's defeat. With an air of authority that surprised even Alexsandra, he bellowed and shouted, making way for her through the crowd at Qinhuangdao, a place that, with its oil refineries and heavy chemical pollution, was probably one of the ugliest and most inauspicious places for such an auspicious event to occur.

There were Chinese everywhere at Honggor as Cheng's staff, among them Colonel Soong, continued to fight on in hopes of blunting, if not defeating, the American Marine Expeditionary Force pressing the Chinese right flank. And for several hours at least, with all communications with Beijing cut and by pouring in regiment after regiment of battle-experienced ChiCom troops from Shenyang's Twenty-fourth Army, Cheng's staff was not only able to blunt the MEF attack on the right flank but also managed to attack Honggor successfully on the left. It was there, on the left flank, that Cheng's veteran regiments came upon one of the few unblooded battalions of Freeman's Second Army, and some of Freeman's men ran.

It wasn't picked up by the press because Freeman had done a Schwarzkopf and kept the press well behind his forces. But it was no use, Dick Norton knew, trying to tart up the report to Freeman by saying the men who ran were overwhelmed by the number of ChiComs, which they were, or that they had failed to get proper artillery support or TACAIR—also true—for the fact of the matter was that most of Charlie company—120 men—in Third Battalion broke and ran. What Charlie company's commander had intended to be a shooting withdrawal was in fact a rout, some men even throwing their weapons away.

And as if a malevolent fate was at work, the old saying that "trouble comes not in ones or twos but in battalions!" had come true. Military police had been sent in to help stiffen the company's resolve, to help the company find its pride again, but what the MPs found was a thoroughly demoralized force. On walking toward two of the soldiers in a foxhole, in the hope of getting them up and out and back at the front to help stem the ChiCom breakthrough, an MP, a sergeant, heard, "I can't do it. I can't—"

"Sure you can," came another deeper voice. "Just relax, babe. C'mon, Danny."

"You'll look after me?"

"Haven't I always, Danny?"

"Yes, but—"

The MP then heard a low, moaning noise, and when he looked over into the foxhole he saw one of them—the shorter, Danny he supposed—down on his knees, sucking off the bigger, older man.

"All right!" the MP said. "You two faggots are under arrest. Get on outta there—and surrender your arms."

"You're just jealous," the older man said, remarkably unperturbed. "Isn't that right, Danny?" Danny couldn't look at the MP.

"So, asshole," said the tall, hefty one, name strip SPERLING, J., zipping up. "When was the last time you got it off?"

"One more word out of you," the MP said, "and I'll blow your fucking head off."

"Nasty, isn't he, Danny? We should teach the mother some manners."

In the near distance they could hear Chinese infantry advancing. Danny was already out of the foxhole, having surrendered his rifle. Sperling followed, sneering at the MP, who was terrified the Chinese would come over the ridge any moment. Danny still couldn't look at the MP sergeant. Instead he just kept walking shamefacedly. Sperling mussed his hair. "Don't you worry, sweetheart. It's all right. Be our word against his."

To the MP's relief, an MP Humvee came in sight, having gathered up two or three other forlorn-looking soldiers from Charlie company.

"Is this the faggot train?" the first MP asked.

"No, these boys are runners, aren't you, boys? Yessir, we've got four courts-martial already with this bunch."

"How do *you* like it?" Sperling asked the driver. "Up the ass?"

"Listen, you fucking queer, get in and behave or I'll shoot you myself."

"So what do you boys do?" Sperling said. "Think of little wifey or *Playboy* and wank off?"

"Maybe," said the MP who'd caught them in fellatio, "but we don't do it when we're supposed to be stopping the fucking enemy from overrunning us."

CHAPTER THIRTY-TWO

THE TRAIN CARRYING the State Council and the remainder of unit 8431 looked no different from any of the other trains that had left Beijing in time, and already two had been stopped by the SAS/D helos and inspected by Aussie, Salvini, Choir, and Brentwood, but had yielded nothing.

The first pass by the A-10 was ignored by the next train's engineer and only caused his assistant frantically to shovel in more coal. And so on the second pass, the pilot of the A-10 gave the engine a burst. It exploded not with a bang but rather a sound like hundreds of snakes hissing, its perforated boiler rapidly losing power, the train dying quickly.

When the train stopped, no one got out, and from the air it looked to Aussie Lewis like a short, headless snake. He counted three cars and shouted above the rotor noise, "Not exactly hauling freight, are we?"

"Two bucks!" Salvini yelled. "That Humpty-Dumpty's on the second car."

"So who's on first?" Brentwood put in. Aussie Lewis and Choir Williams didn't get the joke.

"Fucked if I know," Aussie said, moving the clip of his HK MP5 for full automatic and easing his Browning pistol up and down in the holster. "My guess is Cheng and Co. are in number two—bad bastards in one and three, protecting them."

The Comanche escorted the Huey, the attack helicopter's chin-mounted Gatling gun arcing left and right as the copilot followed the readouts of his HUD. But their job wasn't to kill the State Council—especially not Cheng, who, though commander of the PLA, was not in Freeman's view your typical dyed-in-the-wool Red Communist but rather a professional soldier. The Comanche had already dropped more of the surrender leaflets. Anyone who held one up in the air and put down his weapon would be taken prisoner and accorded—

"Hey, they're coming out!" Choir said. "Cars one and three." They were laying down their AK-47s in the yellowish grass by the railway tracks, the engine still groaning like some primitive beast of burden slowly giving up its ghost in thin curlicues of steam, the riddled boiler making lonely clanking noises.

"Didn't think they'd chuck it in so quickly," Salvini opined.

"Balls!" Aussie said. "They know I'm here. No fucking about with colonials, right, Choir?"

"I hear your wee lassie's train's been stopped at Qinhuangdao."

"What?"

"All right, we're going down," the Huey pilot informed them.

Aussie was looking over at Williams. "How do you know?"

"Haven't you been listening to the radio traffic, boyo? Local MFDs"—he meant movements for democracy— "stopped a train at Qinhuangdao. She's on it." Choir shook his head. "No BS, boyo. She's there."

Aussie nodded. "Thanks." By now, fifty yards away from the train, the helicopter's prop wash was flattening the dried grass in shivering waves as the four SAS men got out into a small depression as other Hueys could be seen gathering westward, apparently manned with regular U.S. Army cavalry troops who'd been dispatched to the area to help out.

There was a noise like the crack of a dry stick, and the Huey copilot slumped, blood running down his right arm, his cursing drowned by the sound of the engine. There was another crack, another bullet ripping into the chopper. The cloying smell of gasoline. With that the pilot yelled, "Get aboard!" but the SAS in the depression waved him off, and even as he rose, obscuring them in dust, they were firing at the troops who had suddenly picked up their arms, several of them falling in the SAS's first volley.

The Huey, limping but still aloft and still under fire, came in sideways, its rotor howling, the Chinese soldiers diving under the train cars for protection, but the chopper stayed there for thirty seconds, creating a veritable whirlwind of grit and dust that didn't inconvenience the SAS troops with their masks but played havoc with the Chinese who were blinded by the grit that filled the air like insects, causing the Chinese to lose the initiative.

Aussie Lewis and Salvini gave full automatic covering fire to Williams and Brentwood as they moved in, with Williams and Brentwood repaying the favor and killing another six Chinese. Choir Williams collapsed, rolling about in a terrible agony, the 7.62mm bullet having smashed the tibia in his right leg.

The Chinese had withdrawn from under the rail cars beyond to a gradual drop-off from the tracks to get away from the Huey blinding them. Lewis and Salvini took the second car, one each end. "Go!" Aussie shouted as he took the steps two at a time.

"Roger!" he heard Salvini reply as he too took the steps at his end of the carriage two at a time, his MP5, like Aussie's, on full automatic to clear anyone from the doorway, the glass on the carriage being a smoky one-way mirror for the VIPs and making it difficult to see the whole car. As Aussie and Salvini threw—not tossed—in their stun grenades, the explosion not only concussed every VIP in the railway car but also blew out the windows, several antimacassar embroideries from the velvet seats following.

As Aussie and Salvini came around each end door of the carriage, they could see the stunned, bovine look on each man, Cheng's cap blown off, his hair mussed, while Chairman Nie sat shaking his head as if trying to dislodge something from his ear. From outside Lewis and Salvini could hear the deadly rattle of the Comanche's Gatling gun, called in by the Hueys to finish off the last elements of unit 8431.

"It's over!" Salvini said.

One ChiCom stared stupidly at him and lunged. Salvini clubbed him. "It's over!" Salvini said angrily. "Look!" He waved the muzzle of his submachine gun in the direction of the broken windows. Outside no surrenders had been taken after the little trick that unit 8431 tried to pull a few moments ago, holding up their pamphlets until the Hueys came low enough to shoot at. Now they all lay dead or wounded, the choppers finishing what the SAS/D had begun.

Aboard the train the State Council had been the first to know they were beaten, and they had been the first to flee the Zhongnanhai under Nie's order as supreme member of the council. Cheng had not been happy about it and had not wanted to leave Beijing, but given the direct order by Nie he had little option, though his heart wasn't in it, for as a soldier he had lost face and he knew it and had no fight in him. Nie, however, was full of indignation, refusing to accept the fact that he had lost utterly until Aussie Lewis told him to shut up or he'd shoot him right there and then.

"That is against the Geneva Convention!" Nie fumed.

"Well we're not in fucking Geneva."

To the east, from the direction of Qinhuangdao, there was a moving mass of people aboard a train that was shunting backward, festooned with red flags and with goddess-of-democracy motifs in white crudely painted in the middle of the red flags. It reminded Aussie of pictures he had seen of Mao's triumphant entry into Beijing half a century ago. Even before the train stopped, people were jumping off, and Alexsandra Malof was out on the rear platform waving a quickly made Stars and Stripes at the Americans.

"Hey!" Aussie said, cuffing each of the prisoners with tape as Salvini guarded them. "How about a bloody cheer for Aussie and the Brits?"

"You'll get your cheers, buddy. She'll—" Before he could finish, Alexsandra Malof had hopped down from the train and onto the one containing the State Council with a gun in her right hand. She looked across at Aussie. There was a wan smile and a chill in the air, despite the dust-dancing sunbeams that pierced the broken windows of the VIP car and gave the illusion of warmth. She walked along the row of prisoners and stopped at Nie, one of those prisoners who had not yet been tied and who was still stunned enough that he didn't quite recognize who she was at first, especially out of prison garb. Then, with the carriage absolutely quiet despite the roar of voices outside, he slowly began to realize who she was.

She seemed to be weighing everything in the balance—sheer terror, the hundreds of murders that this man had perpetuated as the most feared man in China. She turned away from him, then suddenly turned back and shot him point-blank, his brain splattering over the antimacassar behind him.

"Jesus!" Aussie had snatched the gun from her, but Nie was dead. She leaned against Lewis as Salvini, equally shaken by her sudden action, started the train of prisoners walking, or rather shuffling, out of the door toward waiting Hueys to take them back to Beijing. On the way Salvini got express radio directions from Freeman, telling Cheng that all of Nie's political prisoners, including the SEAL, Smythe, must be released immediately. And then Cheng was told exactly how his formal surrender to the U.N. would take place the next day.

It was just on dusk as they landed on the helo pad atop the Great Hall of the People.

When Freeman heard about Nie—about Alexsandra Malof's shooting him—he said, "Accidental discharge I suppose," looking at Aussie.

"Yes, sir."

"Thought so. Case closed. Now, Dick, bring me these

two foxhole 'gentlemen.' I want to nip this in the bud before a reporter even gets wind of it. Then bring me Cheng."

"Yes, sir."

Normally, disciplinary measures in homosexual cases might go to battalion or brigade level, but when Freeman, who everyone knew would go ballistic when he heard of the case, decided to deal with the matter himself, he was determined to thwart a huge, divisive press story. The two men were marched in.

"Which one of you was screwing whom?"

"We weren't screwing anybody, sir," Sperling said.

Freeman looked down at the report. "Oh—yes." He pushed the folder away. "Well you listen to me, both of you. I don't care if you fuck sheep—long as you're reasonably gentle with the sheep and on your own time—and so long as it doesn't bother anyone else. But for Chrissake, in a *battle*? Do you have to do it in a *battle*?"

"That's when it's best—*sir*!" Sperling said.

Freeman read Sperling's name off his shirt strip. "I don't care what turns you on, a battle's no time to be flashing your dick—unless you think it might frighten the Chinese."

Norton couldn't suppress a smile. Young Danny—name strip RICARDO, D.—looked the most miserable PFC Norton had ever seen.

"What's your story, son?" Freeman asked. "Did he make you—force you?"

"No, sir."

"That true?" Freeman asked Sperling.

"Yes, sir."

Freeman turned to Danny again.

"Never threatened you?"

"General, he—" Sperling began.

"Shut your mouth!" It was Freeman. He wasn't loud, he

wasn't going ballistic, but he sounded cold as steel. "I could have you taken out and shot right now for cowardice."

Norton said nothing. It would be more complex than that: a pile of paperwork, courts-martial, lawyers, arguments, counterarguments, the *New York Times*.

Freeman turned his attention back to Danny Ricardo—age eighteen.

"Ricardo, you did this of your own free will?"

Danny nodded, and for the first and only time during the interview his eyes met Freeman's. "I like it, sir."

Freeman sat back, shaking his head. There was a long silence. "Well, I've got a billion Chinese to worry about, so you *gentlemen*'ll have to forgive me if I move right on along here. I'm not going to court-martial either of you, but if I allowed every individual to indulge his or her sexual preference whenever they felt like it we'd be overrun in a week. Now you two and a few others from Charlie company are going out on mopping-up operations. There's the odd red Chinese holdout who needs his ass kicked while I'm trying to fashion something workable here in Beijing. I fully expect both of you to distinguish yourselves by closing with the enemy. You start playing hide the wiener and open a gap in our defensive line and I'll personally see you get shot. And I don't want anybody talking to the media. Sons of bitches'll turn it into a circus. I don't want to end up on the 'Larry King Show' arguing the whys and wherefores of poontang. Understand?"

"Yes, sir," Sperling assured him.

Freeman looked at Danny. "File says you're a good marksman, Ricardo."

"Yes, sir."

"Well, we need men like you at the front. You leave right away."

"Yes, sir."

"Sperling, you too. You'll both be assigned for DMZ duty also."

"Yes, sir."

Suddenly Freeman asked Sperling, "Were you wearing a condom?"

"No, sir."

"That's damn irresponsible. Norton?"

"Sir?"

"I want them tested for HIV before they go."

"Yes, sir."

"Dismissed. Now, Dick, bring me Cheng."

Ricardo and Sperling both had the test and an hour later were in action along the new DMZ that ran east-west, south of Beijing.

Danny Ricardo was killed by a mortar shell from one of the last ChiCom units to hold out. Recommended by Freeman, Sperling won the Bronze Star for going out under heavy fire and bringing Danny in. Medics had to wait a quarter hour before the distraught Sperling would give up the body.

The USS *Reagan* was at four hundred feet when Captain Robert Brentwood heard, "Sonar contact, possible hostile submarine, bearing one three two! Range, eleven miles." Brentwood stepped calmly up onto the attack island. "Very well. Man battle stations."

"Man battle stations, aye, sir," a seaman repeated, pressing the yellow button, a pulsing F sharp sounding throughout the ship.

"Diving officer, periscope depth," Brentwood ordered.

"Periscope depth, aye, sir."

Brentwood's right hand reached up, taking the mike from

its cradle without him even looking at it. "This is the captain. I have the con. Commander Rolston retains the deck."

Beneath the greenish light over the sonar consoles the operator advised, "Range ten point seven miles. Possible hostile by nature of sound."

"Up scope," Brentwood ordered. "Ahead two-thirds." He wanted to make sure that the possible hostile sub did not have any surface companion, though he should have heard them on sonar by now unless they were absolutely still in the water.

"Scope's breaking," one of the watchmen reported. "Scope's clear." Brentwood's hand flicked down the scope's arms, and he seemed glued to the eye cups as he moved around with the scope. On the COMPAC screen Rolston could see the dot, moving at about twelve knots.

Brentwood could see nothing topside—no surface ships. "Down scope." He turned to the sonar man. "Range, sonar?"

"Ten point nine miles," the reply came.

"Range every thousand yards."

"Range every thousand yards, aye, sir. Range nineteen thousand yards."

"Nineteen thousand yards," Brentwood confirmed. The possible hostile sub was well within firing range. "Officer of the deck, confirm MOSS tube number."

"MOSS in aft tube five, sir."

"Very well. Angle on the bow," Brentwood said, "starboard four point five."

"Check," the confirmation came.

"Range?" Brentwood asked again.

"Eighteen thousand five hundred yards."

"Eighteen thousand five hundred yards," Brentwood repeated. "Firing point procedures. Master four three. Tube one."

"Firing point procedures, aye, sir. Master four three. Tube one, aye ... solution ready ... weapons ready ... ship ready."

"Fire MOSS."

"MOSS fired and running, sir."

"Very well." Now the MOSS, the torpedo that was rigged to give off a sound signature like a submarine, might or might not draw the fire of the other submarine, which, after Brentwood had checked what sub should be in what area, he knew must be hostile.

"He's fired," sonar reported. They had a fix, as the other submarine fired at the *Reagan*'s MOSS. Brentwood didn't hesitate. "Fire tubes three and four."

"Three and four fired and running, sir." After a few minutes the torpedo officer reported, "Wire disengaged," advising Brentwood that the *Reagan*'s torpedo was in automatic homing mode. "Three thousand yards ... two thousand yards to go ... veering ... veering ..." There was a violent hiccup on the sonar screen, telling them that the MOSS had been hit, but in taking time to fire its torpedoes against the MOSS the Chinese sub had made a fatal mistake and given away its exact position. "Five hundred yards ..." This time sonar put the impact through the public-address system and they could hear the wallop of the Mark 48 torpedo hitting the Chinese sub and then a sound like a popcorn maker as the enemy's bulkheads crumpled one by one and the *Perch* sank, accelerated in its death dive by water pressure to an impact speed of over a hundred miles per hour.

Thousands of miles to the southwest on the high plateau that was the Chang Tang, Major Mah of the People's Liberation Army had exited a cave and looked about for the soldier who was nowhere to be seen. Mah suspected that the man, afraid to enter even the shallowest of caves without a flashlight, was simply sitting somewhere in an entrance, waiting till Mah was finished. He saw something move, and it was the soldier ambling around a rock pile. "Didn't find anything in there," he said.

"Did you go all the way in? There's enough daylight— most of them are only about ten, twelve feet in."

"I went all the way in, Major."

Mah didn't believe him, walked over, and thrust out his flashlight. "Here, take it and make sure you go all the way in. I'll ask for it back if I come across a deep one."

The soldier was clearly much relieved. "Inspect that one over there," the major ordered. "It looks deeper than most. I'll check out these shallower ones."

"Yes, Comrade Major."

Once again Mah drew his Russian Makarov 9mm pistol and started in.

The soldier, with the new confidence the flashlight gave him, had already disappeared into the deeper cave, and almost immediately he heard a sound, like a run of stones. He put the AK-47 off safety and swept his beam about but could see nothing, the sound now further back around the bend in the cave.

He saw a pair of eyes, fired, but was too late, the snow leopard already upon him, teeth sunk deep in the man's neck, already crunching bone, the man's eyes bulging in the flashlight's beam.

Mah heard the burst and came running out of the cave he was in, saw a blur of crimson on white, the big cat disappearing over the snow into the mist surrounding the rocky outcrop.

Mah was shaking. "Comrade Li!" he called, his throat parchment dry. "Li ... Comrade Li!"

The wind howled afresh and filled Mah with foreboding

as he approached the cave. He hesitated at the entrance. What if its mate was still in there?

"Li!" he called again, his voice echoing shakily in the bend of the tunnel. He could smell excrement. Gripping the Makarov, he reminded himself he was an officer and went forward, stopped, and almost ran but stood his ground, forcing himself to look down in the light of the flashlight on the floor at the blood-soaked body of Li, the man's eyes bulging out of their sockets, frozen in fear.

Mah picked up the flashlight and, reminding himself again that he was an officer and picking up the AK-47, holstered his Makarov and made his way forward around the bend. He found nothing but the dried bones of small animals.

As he started out of the cave, a fury of panic and hatred filled him, panic that before he got out the snow leopard would return to reclaim his trespassed territory, and fury at the American pilot who, to his mind, was responsible for Li's death and the fear that he, Mah, had undergone—was undergoing. There were only two caves remaining that he thought were deep enough to investigate. He entered the first one full of apprehension that he might come face-to-face with another wild animal.

When Julia heard the faint tear of a machine-gun burst it sounded further away than it really was. Who were the Chinese—she presumed it must be Chinese—shooting? Was it the old man who had helped her? Had he come back, or was it someone else? Had another pilot been downed? Unlikely, she thought, but why were they shooting? Whatever the reason, it prompted her to try to be especially alert, difficult with the skull-pounding headache that still had her in its grip. She moved the Nuwick candle further toward the entrance so as to see the first bend in the S-shaped tunnel that led to where she was.

The wall on one side, her right, was shiny with water seeping from the top of the cave; the other side, on her left, was drier but, as she was left-handed or, as her male colleagues would call it, a southpaw, it would be the wetter side of the cave she'd have to use to lean on to get a better shot if anyone came in. Perhaps they weren't searching the caves at all. Then what was a machine gun doing out in this godforsaken place?

For several minutes she heard nothing but the wailing of the wind. But there was a definite footfall at the entrance of the cave about twenty feet from the S-bend. She blew out the candle, bracing herself against the wet wall of the cave, waiting. There was a pause and then a beam of light cutting the misty air, a glimmer of it playing about the bend, and she could hear someone breathing. Was it the old man returning after having heard the machine gun?—if they *had* heard it in the nomad camp, in which case it might be another member of a Chinese patrol. But—her head was throbbing like a pulse gone mad—the Chinese wouldn't have had time to—

In the corona of faint light behind the center of the flashlight she saw the outline of Mah's uniform, a faint red star, and fired four times, killing him with the first shot.

The noise reverberating in the cave sounded to her like cannon when in fact the cave muffled the sound. Still it was heard, albeit faintly, in the nomad camp.

There was a furious debate going on in the camp between the Chinese patrol that had just followed the tracks back to camp and the Chinese soldiers who had been left there originally by Mah. They were arguing about whether the patrol that had been out with Mah should backtrack and investigate the shots. It was decided that two of them should go back to the rocky outcrop. As they left, the old man asked if he could be of assistance.

* * *

When the three got to the rocky outcrop and saw the blood marks on the rock, traced them back to the cave and found Li, they didn't need to be told that Li had been attacked by an animal—a snow leopard, the old man said—and one of the two soldiers was suddenly sick to his stomach and they went out.

The old man, in an awkward pantomime of hands and grunts, asked them if they wanted to look for the major, too. They both stared at him as if he were mad and quickly followed their own footprints back to the camp. The others, on hearing the story, needed no enticement to head back to base immediately.

Julia Reid was shaking. She could hear more footsteps, but these were heavy, more distinct, as if they wanted to be heard.

"America!" a voice said. She was sure it was the old nomad, but the headache was distorting her senses.

"Chin-eze dead!"

The relief that passed through her was like a warm shower on a bitterly cold day. Her headache instantly became less intense, and when she saw the old man, his large frame bending over Mah's body, stripping it of the Makarov, ammunition pouches, and Chinese money, she could have kissed him.

Her hands still shaking, she relit the candle. She heard a rustle behind her and turned. In the soft flickering light she saw an extraordinary sight: the old man, apparently not so old, was standing, his pants down, his erection casting a huge shadow on the wall as he smiled down at her.

"My God!" she heard herself say. "No!"

The old man looked crestfallen. "No?" He shook his

head, his scarf down about his throat, his smile toothless. "No?" he repeated.

"No *way*," she said.

He shrugged nonchalantly and, with some difficulty, put it away. He offered her his hand instead. She hesitated for a moment, then took it, and he led her out of the cave, helped her on the yak, and began the trek back to the encampment. He pointed to a cave. "Chin-eze dead!"

She couldn't have cared less. For two days she'd felt as if she'd been on another planet. All she wanted was for the headache to subside—which it did as they went lower toward the encampment. On the way back she was astonished to see the old man putting in the earpiece of what must have been a Walkman in his pack. At one point he turned about with a huge grin. "Chin-eze dead! Many Chin-eze!" Though she didn't realize it then, he was listening to the BBC Tibetan-language world service reporting the end of the war, and she didn't know that within the week she would be taken to Lhasa by truck and would be free.

CHAPTER THIRTY-THREE

IN TIANANMEN SQUARE it was early morning, the sun rising above the marble-sculpted Heroes of the Revolution.

It was eerily silent, students and workers kept back by barricades along the Avenue of Eternal Peace. For once not

even bicycle bells could be heard, and the silence transcended all, the hush broken only by the sound of General
Cheng's footsteps as he emerged, as instructed by Freeman,
from the Forbidden City, the very monarchist refuge that
the Party had always so decried. Passing through the arch-
way across the algae-polluted moat under the shrapnel-
slashed portrait of Chairman Mao on Tiananmen Gate, he
continued to walk across the vast square, alone, toward
Freeman.

In a propaganda stroke worthy of Mao, though he detested the policies of Mao, Freeman had arranged, via the
captured all-China TV and radio headquarters, for all of
China to see him now: General Douglas Freeman personally raising the flag, not that of the U.N. or the United
States but of the goddess of democracy, above Tiananmen.

Tens of millions of Chinese were watching the scene,
glued to their TVs, and they understood immediately. To
underscore the point, Freeman then did what he would later
refer to as a "Doug MacArthur." When the two men saluted, Cheng bowed, all of it recorded meticulously by in-
ternational linkup TV with CNN, Cheng presenting his
sword to Freeman. Freeman, not using an interpreter, asked
simply, if a little awkwardly, in Chinese, *"Nin shi wei
renmin fuwu ne, huan shi wei gongchandong fuwu?"*—Are
you willing to serve the people instead of the Communist
party?

Cheng was stunned. At this point he had expected to be
shot, or at least humiliated. There was a long silence—all
over China and the world. "Upon your honor?" Freeman
added in Chinese. All over China, chopsticks froze above
rice bowls, the tension palpable, as millions awaited
Cheng's answer.

Cheng nodded. "I will serve the people."

Freeman returned the sword to the general.

The silence was broken then by a sound like soft rain that soon became like that of a rushing train. It was the people, over a million of them, students and workers and children flooding out upon the enormous square, unstoppable in their joy. And those who had waited so long for the goddess of democracy to be resurrected from the flames of the Tiananmen massacre of 1989 knew no end to their joy. It was deafeningly noisy, awe-inspiring, and frightening.

Cheng and Freeman ascended the steps in front of the Forbidden City to stand on the podium above Mao's portrait, and they looked south over the square that was now a seething sea of people. Years before, in those few moments on the night of June 3–4, 1989, when the students and workers thought they had won against the tyranny of the Communist party, when the People's Liberation Army had become the army of the party instead of of the people, Beethoven's "Ode to Joy" had burst forth from the loudspeakers only to be silenced moments later by the machine guns of the Thirty-eighth Army. But now "Ode to Joy" boomed once more, together with the thunderous roaring of the crowd. It was Freeman's finest hour.

Freeman's stunningly chivalrous treatment of Cheng made it clear that the United States had no territorial aspiration in China, and this raised America's prestige enormously overnight. All those Chinese spiritually and financially imprisoned by the stop-again, start-again inflexibility of dogmatic Chinese Communist ideology were swarming to the new leaders of China, who included Admiral Lin Kuang, who had also been surrounded by rapturous crowds on his triumphal march from Xiamen to Hangzhou, where he fulfilled his pledge and burned Mao's villa to the ground.

CHAPTER THIRTY-FOUR

EXHAUSTED, FREEMAN WAS returning home in triumph, but en route he received an urgent message in which the president of the United States, offering him his congratulations, asked the general to forego the usual celebratory victory march down Fifth Avenue and the Avenue of the Americas and to cancel any homecoming leave for Second Army. Instead he was to go to the White House—to the president—*"Immediately!"* Another crisis was brewing.

Along with the many inconveniences for others that the president's leave cancellation caused, it meant that it would be awhile before Robert Brentwood would see his Rosemary and his son, whom Rosemary adored. Despite his premature arrival, Robert Brentwood, Jr., was now out of danger and thriving. The leave cancellation also meant that Aussie Lewis and Alexsandra Malof's honeymoon would have to be cut short. Aussie was most depressed, however, by the fact that he had lost all bets taken at the beginning of the campaign. Not a single SAS/D trooper had fallen into the Zhongnanhai lakes or into the moat about the Forbidden City.

The war
that once seemed impossible
is raging everywhere.

Don't miss a single battle of World War III.

**THE WORLD WAR III TITLES CAN BE YOURS
AT A SPECIAL REDUCED RATE.**

For a limited time only,
if you purchase two World War III titles,
you pay only $9.99,

if you purchase three World War III titles,
you pay only $12.99,

and the entire World War III library,
a $36.00 value, **can be yours for only $26.00!!!**

Act now and let the battle rage on.